SPARK

Books in the World of Raphtova

The Reawakening Trilogy
Spark

Ashes

Ablaze

Tales of the Inn
The Curse of the Stoneskin (coming soon)

Operation Brooch (coming soon)

The Wanderer (coming soon)

Leane Winger

✧

SPARK

Book One of the Reawakening Trilogy

This is a work of fiction. The characters, places, and events recorded in this work are the product of the author's imagination or are used fictitiously. Any resemblance to actual persons, living or dead, is purely coincidental.

1. Edition, 2022
Copyright © 2022 by Leane and Jesse Winger
All rights reserved.

ISBN 978-1-7777664-4-3

Published by Leane Winger, Mackenzie BC, Canada
leane.n.winger@gmail.com
leanewinger.com

Cover design by Aiden Walker

For Sam, Ange, Seth, and Jesse

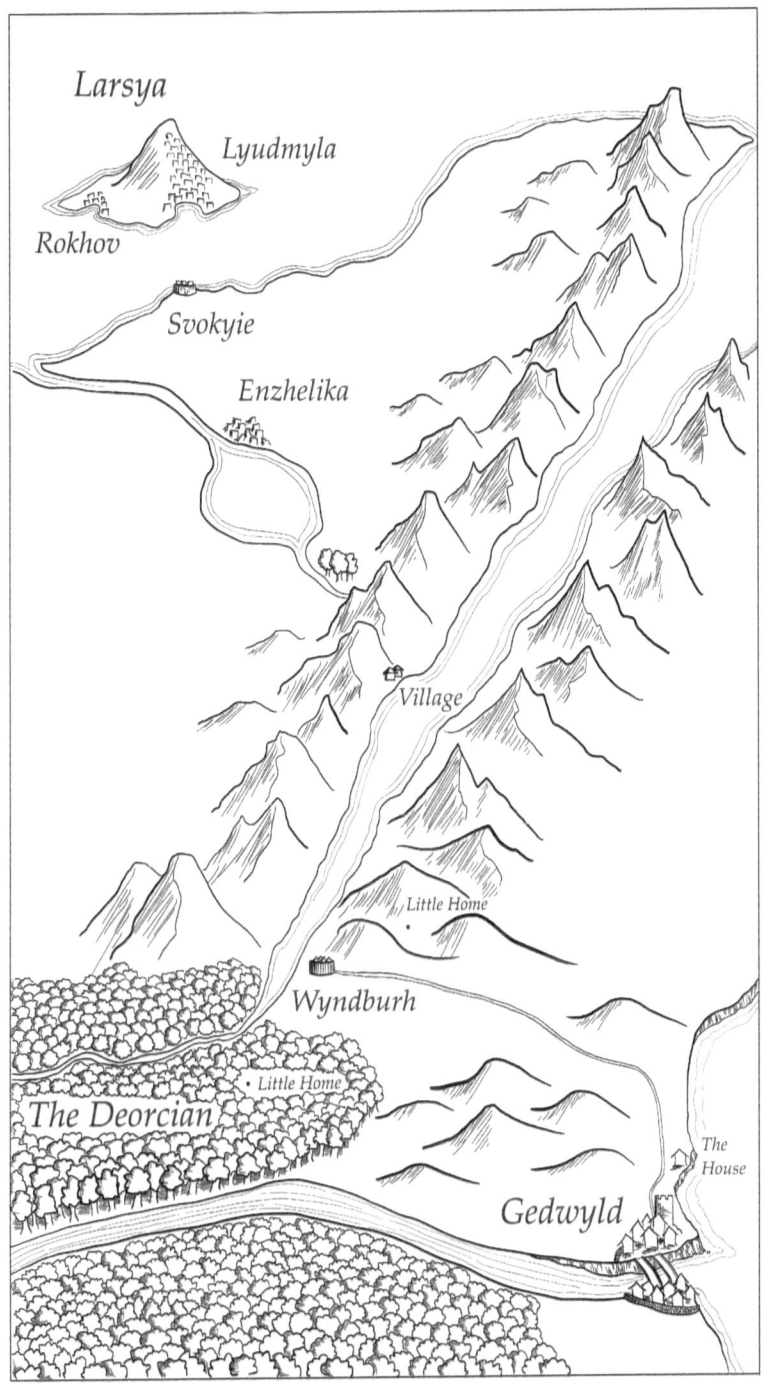

Chapter One

"A human is coming!"

Thea tumbled down the hallway, rebounded off the doorframe, and dropped to the ground at Roland's side, quivering with excitement.

Roland sat perfectly still, staring at the model ship in his hands.

"Roland ..."

Why'd he have to be in vidlas right now when there was so much going on? Of course, it was expected that Elves of their age would start to slow down and take their place in society, but it was becoming all too clear that Roland was aging faster than she was, despite being two circles younger. His rough red granite skin was already quite smooth, compared to Thea's amber diamond skin. And he was becoming far too happy to just sit and stare at—

"Something's coming?" Roland looked up, his emerald eyes twinkling.

"A human is coming!" The words tumbled out of Thea again. "A real human is coming here today!"

"A human?" His eyes widened in surprise. "How do you know?"

"Someone in the Temple heard a message from Enkeli—a real vision! A human is coming today on a ship from the Dark Lands. His name is Davis and he is a great musician. Enkeli wants him to perform in our theatre."

"I thought all the humans died in the Great War."

"I guess not, because there's one coming today!"

"You're sure?"

"Grusha heard it at Nikita's and *they* heard it from one of the priestesses, so it has to be true! Are you going to come?"

"Of course I'll come." Roland glanced down at his work. "We have some time though, right? The transport from Svokiye won't arrive for another three measures."

"What if he hires a private boat?"

"And sails against the tide?"

Thea sighed. "I guess there isn't a *huge* rush. What are you working on?"

"Studying for the big race." Roland held up the model ship.

"Is that a model of the Eagle?"

"No. It's the Raven, from Rokhov. She's our biggest competition. Not that I'd ever admit that to her crew." Roland grinned.

"But you're going to win the race, right?"

"Of course we are. It doesn't hurt to have some tricks up your sleeve, though. Know your enemy, right?" As he turned the model over, his eyes got the distant expression that showed he was using his elf-sight again. Every Elf developed a special kind of sight as they matured into adulthood. Roland had deep sight, allowing him to see inside or through things if he sat and stared long enough. That was always the key—if you sat and stared long enough. Thea hadn't even figured out what kind of elf-sight she had.

She gave a little sigh and put her chin in her hands.

Roland gave her a keen glance. "You don't have to act

so exasperated, you know. I wasn't going to be in vidlas for long."

"That's what you always say, and the next thing you know it's been half a day!"

"Hah, you always interrupt me before it's been that long."

"Of course I do. If I didn't you'd be at it for days on end, just like everyone else."

"It doesn't seem so long, you know, when you have your elf-sight. It's so interesting, it's like no time passes at all." He ran his hand through his brown, mosslike hair.

Thea nodded. "Yeah, I guess. So are you coming down to the docks with me? I don't want to miss the ship coming in."

"Okay." Roland set the model down. "I'll come."

Thea grinned and grabbed Roland's hand. "Come on!"

They ran along the corridor, down the stairs, through the parlour, and out onto the street.

There, the sights and sounds of the city flooded their senses. Brightly coloured banners fluttered overhead, strung between pure white stone arches. The murmur of crowds drifted by on the cool breeze, with the smell of salt and the cry of the gulls.

Children scampered underfoot, tumbling over each other with their rough, boulder-like skin. Mature Elves strolled past at a more dignified pace, their stony skin as smooth and polished as their manners.

Thea and Roland ducked past them as they raced down the street, turning onto one of the steep alleyways that intersected the large mountainside city.

Without a second thought, Thea tucked into a roll

and tumbled down at top speed. Her stone-like skin was tough enough to withstand many bumps and bruises, and rough play was encouraged amongst the younger Elves—it helped smooth out their rough skin.

Thea reached the bottom of the alley, scrambled to her feet, and kept running. She laughed with delight when she saw that Roland was keeping up without any trouble. He wasn't getting too old and boring yet!

They cut through the back of a large textile market, down another alley, and into the harbour district.

News travelled fast in the Elvish capital city of Lyudmyla. The streets around the docks were packed with others who had heard the news and were eager to catch a glimpse of the human when he arrived. A thousand variations of stone-like skin gleamed throughout the milling throng. Light glimmered in a multitude of gemstone eyes.

"I *told* you we should have come sooner!" Thea glared at Roland as they struggled to make headway through the jostling crowds.

Roland looked around. "Just a moment."

"What?"

"Wait here. I'll be right back." Roland disappeared into an alley.

Thea did her best to hold her place in the milling throng. Shopkeepers called their wares. Buskers performed, taking full advantage of the crowd. The savoury smells of street food drifted on the sea breeze. With the hum of excitement all around her, it almost felt like a festival day.

"Come on!" Roland beckoned her towards the alley.

Thea shoved and elbowed her way towards him. The alleyway was deserted.

Leaving the crowds behind, Thea followed Roland down the narrow passageway, over a fence, and down the alley on the other side. Turning a corner, they found the next street to be just as crowded as the last one had been. Dodging their way through the crowds, they crossed the street to the alleyway on the other side. It was a dead end.

Roland gestured to a fire escape ladder suspended above their heads.

"Are you sure—" Thea began.

"Do you want a good view or not?" Roland grinned. "Here, I'll boost you up."

Stepping onto Roland's interlocked hands, Thea was just able to reach the bottom rung of the ladder. She pulled herself up and clambered to the top, stepping up onto the roof of the building. An expanse of rooftops and chimneys stretched out before her like an unfamiliar world.

Roland stepped beside Thea and gave her a sidelong glance. "What, haven't you been up here before?"

Thea shook her head. "I never would have thought—" Movement on the horizon caught her eye. "Is that the transport?"

Roland frowned. "It's early."

"Come on!" Thea started to run, but was soon stopped short by the rambling rooftop maze. Roland led her around chimneys, across narrow planks spanning the gaps between buildings, and skirting the occasional rooftop garden.

"I come up here with the team every now and then," Roland explained. "It's a great spot for fitness training." He thought for a moment and grinned. "And for getting to the docks without being noticed."

Soon they made it to the row of buildings that bordered the harbour. Roland got down on his knees and peered over the edge to the gangways below. Thea knelt beside him to look. Two stories below them, the streets were even more crowded than before.

Roland gestured to a second story balcony a short distance away. "Want a front row seat?"

"Yes, but—"

"Come on, then!" Roland gestured for her to follow. Thea caught up as he crouched on the roof directly above the balcony. It was tastefully decorated, with bronze latticework chairs, an etched glass table, and a flowering vine trailing up the wall.

With a careful leap, Roland vaulted down and held up a hand for Thea.

Thea rolled her eyes and jumped down after him.

"*Excuse* me?"

Thea turned to see a stern-faced Elf emerge from the doorway behind her. The smooth surface of her quartz-like skin showed her to be older than Thea, though not as old as Thea's parents. Her hair was mossy and thick, like every Elf's was, but hers was decorated with small strings of pearls.

Thea gave a nod of respect. "Hello. I'm sorry for our unexpected presence, we were just looking for a place to watch the human's arrival. Have you heard?"

The Elf snorted. "That is all *anyone* is talking about, believe me, but I am afraid that this is a *private* balcony. How did you get up here?"

"Never mind." Roland stepped beside Thea and took her arm. "We can find another place to watch, can't we, *Thea*?"

Thea gave Roland a sidelong glance as he ushered

her towards the edge of the balcony.

"Thea Kirisensk?"

Thea glanced back. "Yes, that's my name."

The expression on the Elf's face shifted. "You are Afonya and Taisiya's child! Of course! I was at a function with your mother once: the Society Gala at the Palace Gardens. Tell me, how is she doing?"

"She is doing well, thank you."

A fond smile spread across the Elf's face. "I remember she was wearing a beautiful green dress with pearls. Such a high society lady! I heard she married up from Second House, though I never would have guessed it by watching her. So high class! That was my very first Gala, you know, though I may say we are well off for being Second House. You should see the nice sitting room we have downstairs. My husband married up from Third House, and he put on airs for I don't know how long. Not that I begrudged him that, of course." She turned back towards the door. "Ilya! Ilya! We have guests! Bring out some refreshments!"

Gesturing Thea and Roland towards the chairs, their hostess smiled amiably. "What good fortune this is such a beautiful day! Thea, I must say you look a lot like your uncle. Diamond skin too, although his is 'pure' diamond, as they say, but you have the same copper tint to your hair. I absolutely adore it! You will have a seat, won't you? Good. My there are a lot of people about today! I don't know if I've ever seen so many down at the harbour. Except when there is an event, of course. Ilya! Oh, there you are."

A sandstone-skinned Elf with a friendly face emerged from the door, carrying a serving tray and a large pitcher. He set them on the table and nodded greetings to Thea and Roland.

"This is Thea Kirisensk," the first Elf beamed as she made her introductions. "She just dropped by to watch the transport come in. This is my husband Ilya, and I'm Kseniya. Do make yourself comfortable. I'll just go grab a few things and be right back. Ilya will keep you company, won't you, dear? Good. Well, I'll be right back, then. Help yourself to the things Ilya brought out, and if there is anything I can get for you, do let me know and I would be happy to oblige. Right. The glasses. I will only be a moment."

Thea glanced at Roland as Kseniya disappeared through the doorway. He eyed the view of the harbour in a casual way, but the tension in his shoulders showed his discomfort. Thea turned to Ilya. "Thank you for your hospitality."

Ilya smiled. "It's no trouble. Um, do you come to the harbour often?"

Thea nodded. "I do sometimes, but Roland comes almost every day. He sails on the Eagle."

Ilya looked at Roland. "The Eagle, eh? So you're First House too."

Roland nodded.

"I hear you're favoured to win the race coming up."

Roland shrugged. "We'll see."

Ilya smiled amiably, but didn't seem to find anything else to say. Thea turned her attention to the refreshments on the table. The serving tray held an assortment of crackers, cheeses, and fruits. The pitcher held some sort of sweet-smelling beverage. Small drops of condensation glistened on its sides.

Kseniya soon returned with some glasses and small plates. With a stream of endless chatter, she urged them to partake, and continued the one-sided conversation as they did so.

The sound of a clanging bell drifted by on the ocean breeze—the signal that a large ship was entering the harbour. Thea tried not to be impolite, but she couldn't help straining her eyes to see the transport appear from behind the lighthouse that marked the entrance of the harbour. It was coming. It was really coming!

"A whole measure early," Roland muttered. "That never happens."

As the transport grew closer, Thea could see members of the crew at work on the deck, preparing for their arrival. The Osprey, or the "transport" as it was often called, was the only vessel to make regular trips between the Elvish island of Larsya and the Dark Lands. Thea had never been to the Dark Lands—very few Elves she knew had—but a small community of Elves lived there, in the fortress-town of Svokiye. The transport ferried resources back and forth, and the occasional passenger, though those were rare and had certainly never been a human.

Thea had heard about humans. They fought alongside the Elves in the Great War. Not that Thea knew much about the Great War. It had happened over a thousand circles ago—long before she was born. Of course, there were many Elves who had been alive at that time, but they were all old and slow now. Thea hadn't ever spoken to any of them. Apparently there were other races that used to live out there, across the sea, but most of them had died in the war. As far as anyone knew, Svokiye was the last fortress of civilization on a continent ravaged by dragons and infested with goblins and other monsters.

But now a human was coming.

The murmur of the crowds grew in anticipation as the Osprey's crew eased her up to the dock and threw across the heaving lines. Thea leaned over the edge of the balcony. Where was the human?

There was a stir on the deck of the Osprey and a cluster of people emerged from the captain's quarters. Thea recognized the captain and several senior members of the crew that she'd met at Roland's house.

There—who was that? Another figure was just visible behind the first mate.

The captain stepped up to the top of the gangplank, his voice ringing out above the crowds. "Well! What a fine reception! I haven't docked to a crowd like this since my racing days!"

There were cheers from the crowd.

"I suppose you've all heard I have a special cargo today. I never knew hazelnuts were so popular!"

Laughter rang around the crowded dockyard.

"Well, where is he?" someone yelled.

The captain feigned surprise. "Who? I don't suppose you could mean this ragamuffin I picked up in Svokiye!" He stepped aside, and Thea caught her first real view of the human. He was shorter than the average Elf, but otherwise seemed quite similar in form and figure. His dark, smooth hair was swept back from a face that bore a keen, eager expression, and his sandy brown skin appeared strangely soft as he waved his greetings.

The crowd enjoyed the captain's joke immensely. Cheers and laughter echoed across the harbour.

"I hear there's a big to-do up at the Theatre today," the captain roared over the noise, "so off you go! Make way for the human—don't trample him now!"

The crowds parted to make way for the human as he stepped down the gangplank. A messenger from the Royal House stepped forward to meet him, and after a couple of quiet words they set off down the street.

The crowd closed in around them, making it almost impossible to see, but Thea caught an occasional glimpse of the human—his strange, smooth hair, so unlike the mossy hair of the Elves, a beaming smile turned upwards to take in all the sights and the crowds jostling him on every side.

A lute hung over his back, but he didn't appear to be carrying much else. His clothes were plain and serviceable and certainly a different fashion than what was typical amongst the Elves, but they seemed to suit him well. Following the messenger from the Royal House, he made his way down the busy street, and the crowd surged after him.

"So!" the captain bellowed. "What's an Elf got to do to get some help around here!" The transport's crew sprang into action and started unloading their cargo as the docks returned to their usual busy clatter.

Thea looked around eagerly, but there was no way down from the balcony without going through the house or climbing back onto the roof. She turned to their hosts. "Thank you for letting us stay and watch."

"It was no trouble at all," Kseniya smiled. "It's a nice little balcony for watching the harbour, if I do say so myself. What an interesting fellow that human was. He looked so soft and squishy. And no fashion sense at all! I wonder why so many people were interested in seeing him. The novelty, I suppose. You don't see a human every day! I wonder how long he will be staying."

"I'm not sure," Thea ventured, "but we were hoping

to go up to the Theatre, so we should probably—"

"Oh yes, that's where everyone is heading. It should be quite interesting, don't you think? I would go myself if it wasn't such a long walk."

Thea nodded. "It was very nice to meet you."

"And likewise, my dear! Do say hello to your mother for me. Kseniya Dmiltaysk—do you think you'll remember the name? She might not remember me, but it was at the Society Gala at the Palace Gardens, and I was wearing a cute little hat with red flowers. She might remember that. I was sitting near the back by the windows."

"I will be sure to tell her."

"And if you ever have a chance to mention our names to your uncle, we'd be ever so grateful. It never hurt anyone having friends in high places!" She gave a little laugh. "High places, and high on the mountain too! That's a favourite little joke of mine. Isn't the view up there divine? I must say that Lyudmyla is the most beautiful city on all Larsya! It's certainly prettier than dirty little Rokhov, and most of the other towns are so small they can hardly count."

Thea gave an apologetic smile. "I really think we should be—"

"You should be going. Of course. I'm sure there will be quite the rush to get seats at the Theatre today. But look at this tray! You barely ate anything!"

"I don't think—"

"I know. We'll send you along with some odds and ends that you can enjoy at the Theatre."

"Thank you, but we really don't—"

Kseniya turned and gestured them through the door. "Oh, it will only take a moment. You just enjoy a word or two with Ilya while I pop into the kitchen."

Thea looked at Roland in consternation, but she couldn't see any way around it. They had to wait to be polite.

As Kseniya disappeared into the kitchen, Roland shifted uncomfortably. "It's a nice house," he ventured. "Very ... decorated."

"Kseniya's done a lot with it," Ilya replied. "She likes that sort of thing."

Silence descended again.

"Should be good weather for the race," Ilya offered.

Roland nodded. "Should be."

Outside, the sounds of the crowd faded away. Thea glanced towards the door.

"Are you going to watch the race?" Roland asked when the silence had stretched on far too long.

"I think I'll be working. I used to watch, though."

Thea fidgeted. She'd heard so many stories about humans. Now was her chance to see one for herself, but he was getting further and further away!

Kseniya finally reappeared, bearing a neatly wrapped parcel. Her farewell pleasantries were painfully long, but Thea managed to keep a cheerful face until she and Roland stepped out the front door and heard it close behind them.

Then they ran up the street as fast as their legs could carry them.

"Why did you let her keep talking?" Roland demanded as they rounded the first corner.

"I was trying to be polite!" Thea gasped. The well-worn road rose higher up the mountainside city with every turn. "They *were* very nice."

Roland stopped to catch his breath. "Nice?"

"To let us use their balcony."

Roland gave her a strange look. "She only let us stay once she found out who you were. Being related to the most important people in First House will do that for you."

"What? Just because my uncle is Chancellor doesn't mean I'm anyone special."

Roland snorted. "Try being a nobody and see how nice everyone is to you then." He shook his head. "*Dirty Rokhov.*"

They started running again, and made it past the aqueducts before stopping again to catch their breath.

Thea leaned against a wall, panting heavily. "Almost there!"

Roland collapsed on a roadside bench with a groan. "I'm going to feel that tomorrow."

Thea stretched her aching legs. "Been a while since you ran the full height of Lyudmyla?"

Roland made a face.

"Come on, we can rest once we're at the Theatre." Thea pushed herself up. Roland didn't move. "Come on!"

"I don't—" Roland looked down. "You know my family doesn't have a box at the Theatre. I don't think I'll be able to get in."

Thea frowned. "You can sit in my family's box. You always have."

A strange look passed Roland's face. "I didn't want to presume ..."

"Of course you can sit with us! Now come on, I don't want to miss it." Turning, Thea hurried on. Thankfully, Roland followed her this time. They crested the last steep stretch of road at an easy jog, rounded the corner, and stepped into the courtyard of the Theatre.

It was a beautiful building. Not as impressive as Enkeli's Temple, of course, but easily among the five most ornate buildings in the city. Its large, domed roof gleamed with gold. Stone carvings adorned its smooth, marble walls. The gilded front doors stretched nearly two stories high and were set with precious stones of all colours.

Outside the doors, a throng of Elves had gathered, pushing and jostling. An official stood outside, encouraging the crowd through in an orderly manner. From the number of people waiting it was clear that Roland was right. If they didn't have a box there was no way they would have made it in.

Bypassing the crowds, Thea and Roland circled to a second set of doors nearby—equally as ornate, though not as large. An attendant opened the door for them and escorted them up to the balcony where the private boxes were.

Often when Thea decided to go to the Theatre, she and Roland were the only ones in her family's box. Today she was surprised to find her uncle and both of her parents already seated and waiting for the performance to begin. They greeted Thea and Roland with polite nods before turning their attention back to their own conversation.

Thea looked around. It was rare to see the Theatre this full. Every box was lined with faces. Even the Queen Regent was present, seated with a crowd of nobles in the royal box.

The seats far below looked equally packed. Polite murmuring filled the air, along with the muted rustle of velvet and silk. A different audience than the raucous crowds at the docks, but just as curious.

A herald stepped onto the stage, draped in robes of gold and purple. Across the Theatre, a hushed silence descended.

"Lords and ladies! People of Lyudmyla! We have today a most distinguished visitor. The Great Enkeli has sent to us from across the sea a human, a musician of highest excellence, servant of the Ancient Wisdom, sworn in the service of Allulien, and he has come to perform in our Theatre today. Lords and ladies, Queen Regent, I present to you our illustrious guest ... Davis!"

The human stepped onto the stage. Smiling, he spread his arms wide in greeting. He wore the same simple travelling clothes that Thea had seen earlier, and the lute still hung over his back. Lifting his hands, he looked towards the domed ceiling high above him and began to speak.

The words were strange. Thea frowned. Did the human not know Elvish? Her heart sank. It would still be interesting to listen to him, of course, but she had been hoping to at least understand what he was saying. She hadn't stopped to consider that humans might have a different language.

A small gasp spread through the audience, starting with those seated closest to the stage, spreading outwards like a ripple. The wave grew closer and engulfed Thea with a warm, tingling feeling. Her ears rang, and suddenly she understood the words that were being spoken.

"—And I praise you, O Ancient Wisdom, for opening the ears of all those who are here, that they may hear your song that I will sing today. May your glory and power be known throughout all Raphtova, even as it is here today."

Thea glanced at Roland. His eyes were wide with surprise. All around her, mouths were open in astonishment. In the temple box, the Priests of Enkeli stared at the human with expressions of shock and incredulity. That was magic—real magic.

Davis smiled and bowed, ever so slightly. "Hello everyone, I'm Davis."

Chapter Two

Gently, Davis held the lute in his arms and plucked the strings. The notes echoed softly around the Theatre as everyone held their breath to listen.

"Today Allulien has sent me to you, to sing for you a song—a song that is sung in the very throne room of the Ancient Wisdom. This is but a humble rendition of that glorious song, but perhaps it will speak to your hearts, as it has spoken to mine."

Davis plucked his lute and began to sing. He sang about the Ancient Wisdom, the creator of Raphtova and all that was good. He sang about the Ancient Wisdom's kindness and love for all created things. He sang about a world that was wounded and bleeding and longed for its creator's healing touch.

Thea listened, enraptured, as the music cascaded around the Theatre like a flowing waterfall, sometimes delicate and gentle, sometimes as full and majestic as a great choir. If Thea concentrated, she could still hear the words of the strange human language, but the magic of the singer carried its meaning into her mind so gently that soon she forgot anything else.

The singer's face was gentle and his eyes sparkled with joy. It was clear that he loved to perform, and even more that he loved the one that he sang about. Thea wondered about that. She had heard about the Ancient Wisdom all her life, but not as someone that she herself could know or care about.

There was something strange about this human. Thea stared. Within his chest, a glowing light appeared. No, it hadn't appeared, it had been there all along, but the veil over her sight had been lifted and she could see his spirit within him. It shone with life and joy, a spirit more beautiful than she could ever describe. It took her breath away, and she understood why he sang with such joy and love—it poured out from his spirit within him, as irresistibly as his music sprang from the lute within his hands.

Time faded and ceased to exist.

Then he was gone from her sight, but still the image of his spirit lingered in her mind.

"Thea!"

Someone shook her. Thea blinked and looked to see Roland laughing at her.

"Gosh, you were in there deep. You didn't even clap when the performance was over!"

Thea looked around. Davis was gone—as were most of the Elves in the Theatre. A few attendants were sweeping up and one or two clusters of Elves chatted in the aisleways as they sauntered towards the doors. Thea's heart sank. "It's over? But it was so short!"

Roland laughed. "Short? He was playing for five measures at least! The day is almost over!"

Thea frowned. "But—" She caught Roland's expression.

"You found your elf-sight, didn't you?"

Thea nodded.

Roland grinned. "Come on, let's go."

They made their way down the stairs and out into the Theatre Courtyard. Overhead, the planet Micai dominated much of the sky, its golden rings already beginning to eclipse Allumen, bringing night to Raphtova.

"So what did you see?" Roland asked.

"It was like I could see right inside him—right into his spirit! It was so beautiful and vibrant and full of life. I know you always said using your sight was so interesting, but now I really understand. I could have watched him all day!"

Roland looked at her again with that strange expression she couldn't place. "Spirit sight. I think that will suit you very well, Thea. I guess I don't have to say 'I told you so.'" He winked. "Can I walk you home?"

"Sure."

A group of astronomers was gathering in the Theatre Courtyard, as they did every night. The eclipse of Allumen was a beloved sight, and an excellent opportunity for study, especially for those Elves whose sight allowed them to observe the vast spectrum of light waves.

Thea watched an elderly Elf settle himself onto a bench and gaze upwards with an eager expression. It made sense now, that impulse to look longer, to see more. If she stared at him long enough, she would see his spirit too.

Something was wrong. Thea felt it in her own spirit, even before her mind understood what she was seeing. That stunted, dead, shrivelled thing ... that couldn't be his spirit ... could it? It wasn't possible! Thea stared, watching for some sign of life, a glimmer of light, something. How could someone be alive, but their spirit inside them be so dead?

What about that Elf over there—pouring over the

charts of the night sky spread out before her on the pavement? No. Her spirit was just as dead and misshapen as the other one had been.

Thea stared around her, a feeling like panic rising in her chest. Those lovers sitting up on the wall enjoying the view together—their hollow spirits flickered with a dull, sickly glow. That shopkeeper—his spirit was callused and dark. That palace guard—her spirit was stunted, just like all the others had been. All the others except Davis.

What had happened to her people? Thea stared at spirit after spirit without seeing even one glimmer of life. Why was Davis so different?

With a wrench, Thea pulled her mind back to the present moment. It was morning. Elves bustled up and down the street before her, going about their daily business.

How had so much time passed so quickly? Her legs ached strangely and her shoulders itched. During the night her hair had grown down the back of her neck and halfway along her shoulders. Elves' hair grew during vidlas, of course, but that had been much faster than she expected.

Rubbing her eyes, Thea tried to orient herself. It was morning, and she needed to find Davis. He would be able to tell her what was wrong with her people, she was sure of it. But where would he be? One of the nobles probably hosted him for the night. It was still early—he might still be there.

Running up the street, she soon passed the arch-lined terraces of the Royal District.

"Your name, Miss?"

Startled, Thea looked up at the stern face of the

palace guard who was questioning her. "Thea Kirisensk."

"Looking for your father? The First House cabinet is meeting in the green room at the Palace today."

"Thank you." Thea swallowed. "Do you know if Davis is there?"

"Never heard of him. Get along with you now."

Thea turned and trotted back down the street. Who would know where Davis was staying? Roland might have heard, and if he hadn't he would know who to ask.

Passing into the Wealthy Merchants' District, Thea let herself into Roland's house. His parents weren't home, but they seldom were. She ran up the stairs, down the corridor, and barrelled into Roland's room.

He was there, staring darkly at the wall.

Thea didn't wait to be polite. "Roland! Roland, do you know where Davis is?"

Roland didn't look up. "He's gone."

Thea's heart sank. "What? No! He can't be gone, I need to talk to him. Maybe he's still at the docks?"

Turning, Roland looked her squarely in the eyes. "Thea. It's been a whole cycle since Davis was here. He left a long time ago."

Thea gasped. Thirty days? How was that possible?

Roland gave a wry smile. "Welcome to elf-sight, Thea. And you complained that I'd be in vidlas for a whole day."

Thea shook her head. It wasn't possible. "You don't understand. I need to speak to Davis right away! His spirit was alive and beautiful, but everywhere else I look I see spirits that are dead or dying. I don't understand what's wrong!" As she stared at Roland, silently pleading that there had been some sort of mistake, she felt her spirit sight slowly tingling into wakefulness. With an inner wrench, she closed herself off from it. If she saw the same dead spirit inside Roland she wouldn't be able to bear it. It was better not to know. She forced herself to look at his face instead. It had a strange, tired expression.

Thea blinked. If it had been a whole cycle … "Roland, did I miss your race?"

Roland nodded and looked away. "Yes, you did."

Thea's stomach felt hollow. "I'm so sorry."

Roland shrugged. "It doesn't matter."

"But I wanted to be there! Did you win?"

"No. The Raven beat us. It was a close one, though."

Thea glared reproachfully. "You could have woken me up."

"I guess so. You just looked like you didn't want to be disturbed."

"That never stopped me from disturbing you before." Her spirit sight tingled at the back of her mind again, pestering for her attention. She shook herself. "I need to find out what's going on. If Davis is gone, what can I do? Did he say where he was going? Maybe I can write to him?"

Roland shrugged. "I don't know. He performed one day and left the next. The priests up at the Temple might know something. It was one of them that heard he was coming, wasn't it?"

"Enkeli's Temple! Good idea!" Thea turned to go, but caught a glimpse of Roland from the corner of her eye. She stopped. "Were you wanting something?"

Roland shook his head. "You go on. You won't be settled until you figure out this problem of yours."

Thea grinned her thanks and raced out the door.

In its place at the top of the mountain, Enkeli's Temple rose high above the rest of the city. Thea ran up the street, past the Theatre and the Royal District to the place where the Palace and Enkeli's Temple stood.

Thea hesitated as she approached the wall surrounding the temple complex. She'd never had much reason to go to Enkeli's Temple before. Its marble walls were tall and imposing, covered with elaborate carvings of the Tilaryn, the winged servants of the Ancient Wisdom. Above the gates were portrayed the four Generals—the greatest and most powerful of the Tilaryn. Thea's tutor had told her about them when she was a child: Allulien, greatest of the four, depicted with a beautiful harp. Micai, second in power, shown with a spear and a shield. Raphea, the third, holding a long flowing bandage, and Enkeli, the keeper of knowledge, holding a scroll.

As Thea passed through the gates, the noise of the city faded into the distance, and she stepped out into a beautiful garden. Nodding flowers lined the broad pathways, birds sang in the trees, and a marble fountain glittered in the light. To the left was the Hall of Messengers, a simple building covered in trailing ivy. To the right rose the Hall of the Keepers, where those who dedicated their lives in the service of Enkeli lived. A distant, melodic chanting drifted through the air.

In front of Thea, the Halls of Knowledge dominated the skyline.

Thea stepped through the large, oak doors and into a room larger than any she had seen before. Ornate shelves towered over her, filled with books and scrolls of every description. Curving staircases led to even higher shelves, and far above it all soared the massive domed ceiling, echoing every breath and step. Everywhere she looked, colourful murals and intricate carvings gleamed in the light of tall, gilded windows.

Between the shelves, Elves sat at large, ornately carved desks, poring over dusty tomes and ancient scrolls, their pens scratching busily. It was said that the entire history of Raphtova was contained within the Halls of Knowledge, recorded and preserved by the Keepers of Knowledge.

Hardly daring to breathe, Thea stepped forward. No one seemed to notice her presence, intent as they were on their tasks.

Thea watched them closely. Maybe they would be different. Maybe these Elves who lived and worked in the heart of the Elvish world would have spirits that were different somehow from all the others she had witnessed.

No. The sad realization crept over her as her spirit sight took in all there was to see. These Elves were no different.

Distant voices drifted through the vast silence.

Passing by the endless shelves, Thea followed the voices to an open door. Cautiously, she stepped out into a small antechamber. Two Elves who had been relaxing by a table looked up at her in surprise.

One of them rose from his seat and came to greet her. His stony skin still showed hints of roughness. "Hello, Miss. Welcome to the Halls of Knowledge. What knowledge do you seek?"

"I want to find out more about Davis."

"Davis ..." The Elf frowned.

"Davis the human, who came from the Dark Lands and performed in the Theatre, about a cycle ago."

Slow recognition crept across the Elf's face. "Oh, Davis."

"I want to know why he's so different."

The Elf gave her a strange look. "Well, uh, Miss, you see, the Halls of Knowledge are vast, with wisdom beyond reckoning, but, ah, it is unusual for them to contain much information about one specific person. Unless that person was one of the great figures in the history of Raphtova, of course. So I can't say that there would be much specific information on this one human that you've mentioned, but from the vast wealth of knowledge contained within these walls, careful research and study would indicate that there is one specific factor that would inform the difference of this Davis from all the residents of Lyudmyla, if seen through a genetic and hereditary lens. That is to say—" He glanced at the older Elf who sat with her feet stretched up on the table. "He is different because he's a human." He gave Thea a solemn nod. "That would be why he is different."

Thea gave him an exasperated glare. "I *know* he's human. But his spirit is alive, and everywhere else I look I see spirits that are dead. Is that a human thing? Do all humans have spirits that are vibrant and alive?"

The older Elf set her feet on the floor and leaned forward. "No, child. A vibrant spirit comes from serving the Ancient Wisdom. There are no substitutions for a dedicated life of service, and no shortcuts. There is nothing so very special about humans. They are people, like everyone else. They just happen to be a different kind of people." She leaned back in her chair. "It sounds to me like you have spirit sight. I am guessing you discovered it very recently? Those I know who have spirit sight have told me it can be very ... disorienting. But be encouraged, with practice you will learn to use it with greater discernment."

"But why was Davis's spirit alive when I've only seen Elves with spirits that are dead? Is it because he serves Allulien? Allulien *is* the greatest of the Generals."

The Elf standing beside Thea appeared to be affronted. "Excuse me! I suppose it is true that Allulien is chief of the four, but there can be no doubt that Enkeli holds the position of most importance. Keeping all of the wisdom and knowledge found in the Halls of Knowledge is the highest calling there can be."

The older Elf nodded sagely.

Thea frowned. "That still doesn't answer why—"

The older Elf raised her hand. "In time you will learn that there is more to spirit sight than degrees of brightness. It is a gift indeed to be able to read the subtleties and beauties that reside within every spirit. What is your name, child?"

"Thea Kirisensk."

The Elf gave a knowing nod. "I will send a message down to your parents. I am sure I could find you a tutor experienced in spirit sight to guide you into greater understanding. Such enthusiasm should not be left unchanneled." She nodded at the other Elf, as if to indicate that the audience was over.

The younger Elf bowed slightly and motioned his hand towards the door. "Is there anything else we can help you with?"

Thea sighed and looked at the ornate floor tiles beneath her feet. "Do you know *anything* else about Davis?"

The older Elf lifted a cluster of grapes from a bowl on

the table. "Well, he certainly wasn't the best musician I've ever heard."

The younger Elf chuckled. "Very true. I know many other musicians who are more accomplished, and no wonder! How long has he lived on Raphtova? Thirty or forty circles of Allumen? We have *children* who have been practicing longer than him! And such a waste, using magic in that flamboyant, extravagant way. Magic is precious and should only be used when absolutely necessary."

The other Elf nodded. "Very irresponsible."

"And he travelled all that way just to sing a song about how the Ancient Wisdom made the world? We are the Keepers of Knowledge. We *know* that already!"

"But Enkeli sent him." Thea spoke in a quiet voice. "There must have been a reason. Don't you know what it is?"

The Elves exchanged a glance.

"No," the younger Elf admitted, "Enkeli did not say why."

"Why didn't you ask?"

The Elf stared at her in surprise. "You don't *ask* Enkeli something like that! Enkeli speaks when there is something that needs to be heard. That is Enkeli's choice, not ours."

"But no one had heard from Enkeli in a very long time. Not until the news that Davis was coming. It must have been important."

The older Elf rose slowly to her feet. "I can see that the question perplexes you, child. If you want to ask Enkeli yourself, I would be glad to show you the proper ritual. Not that you will actually receive a response—few ever do—but you seem to have an interest in the way of the Keepers of Knowledge, and I won't be one to discourage that." She gave the younger Elf a firm glance. "Back to your studies, now. I will show Thea to the meditation chamber."

With some misgiving, Thea followed the older Elf out of the Halls of Knowledge, through the gardens, to the Hall of the Keepers. They passed through a large foyer, where several Elves sat and talked or gazed through the windows. A grand staircase led upstairs to the bedrooms—the Elf explained—and a door to the right led out to the kitchens.

The Elf opened the left-hand door, and Thea stepped through into a large, glass-domed room. Tall, broad-leafed plants reached up towards the sky, and a small fountain filled the air with the gentle sound of water. Several small benches were placed throughout the room, and the Elf gestured Thea towards one.

"This is the meditation chamber," she explained. "Those who wish to hear a new word from Enkeli come here to sit and listen. First you must speak the name of Enkeli five times, then bow yourself to the ground five times, for five is the holy number of the Ancient Wisdom. Ask your question—you only need to do that once—then sit and listen. You may repeat the ritual as many times as you wish."

Thea thought for a moment. "And if I wanted to ask Allulien a question, would I do the same thing, but speak Allulien's name?"

The Elf glanced at her sharply. "Why do you ask? You are an Elf. Elves serve Enkeli, not Allulien."

"But you said Enkeli does not answer. Maybe Allulien will."

"You will learn one day that not every question needs

answering. Our role is to ask and wait. I will leave you here and return to my work in the Halls of Knowledge. If you have any other questions about the service of Enkeli, you can find me there."

Thea watched the Elf go. She felt a little strange about trying the ritual, but it couldn't do any harm, could it? Maybe Enkeli would really speak to her. She knelt on the hard paving stones. "Enkeli. Enkeli. Enkeli. Enkeli. Enkeli." She couldn't help glancing around self-consciously, but there didn't appear to be anyone else in the room. Bowing down, she touched her head to the ground five times, then stood up. "I want to know why you sent Davis to us." Her voice sounded loud in the silence.

After a few moments had passed, Thea sat down on the bench to wait. Daylight streamed through the leafy branches overhead, etching a delicate pattern across the flagstones at her feet. A sleepy bumblebee hummed its way along a row of foxgloves.

How long should she wait? It wasn't like she had anything else to do, or anyone else she could think of to ask about Davis, but the time crawled by so slowly.

A measure later Thea decided to try the ritual again. Still there was no reply. What was Enkeli's problem anyway? Here was a whole temple of Elves who had dedicated their lives in service, but Enkeli never had the decency to listen to them or answer any of their questions! What good was there in following Enkeli when it was all just so much boring ritual and copying things in scrolls?

Thea glanced around again, but she was still alone. It didn't surprise her. If no one ever heard from Enkeli, why bother with the meditation chamber?

She stood up. "Allulien. Allulien. Allulien. Allulien. Allulien." She bowed to the ground again, five times. She couldn't help but feel more urgent this time. "Will *you* speak to me? Why is everyone here so dead?"

Once again there was silence. Thea stormed out of the meditation chamber.

The Elves in the foyer looked up in surprise. Thea marched over to one of them. "About a cycle ago someone here got a message from Enkeli. Do you know who that was?"

The Elf blinked at her. "Of course. That was Khariton."

"Where is Khariton? Can I speak with him?"

"He mostly stays in his room, but I can show you to him."

"Thank you."

The Elf led Thea up the stairs and into the living quarters. High windows sent beams of light down the long, door-lined corridors.

The Elf stopped in front of a door just like all the others and knocked twice. Without waiting for a reply, he opened the door and stepped inside. It was a simple room. A narrow bed lined one wall, and a desk and chair were nestled up against the other. At the end of the room, a large window overlooked the Temple Gardens. In front of the window sat an Elf.

Thea's guide gestured her forward. "Good day, Khariton. There is a guest here who wishes to speak with you." With a bow, he turned and left.

The Elf at the window sat motionless, taking no notice of Thea's presence. He was old—very old. His obsidian skin was the smoothest Thea had ever seen. His mossy hair stretched down his neck and shoulders to cover his entire back. Proper etiquette dictated that she should stand and wait. His attention had been requested, and it would be rude to speak again until he left vidlas and indicated that he was prepared to speak with her.

Thea paced the small room. With someone that old it could be days before the message registered in his mind that someone was waiting to see him, and even longer before he finished whatever it was that he was contemplating. She didn't have that long!

Unable to take the silence any longer, she marched right up behind him. "Well, did Enkeli speak to you or not?"

The Elf didn't move.

"They said you heard from Enkeli, that you were the one that got the message that Davis was coming, but you didn't find out why. Well I want to know why, but they told me the ritual to follow and it didn't work!"

Slowly, Khariton turned his head to look at Thea and his eyes flashed. "Of course not. You don't speak to your General with rituals."

"I knew it! I knew it!" Thea clenched her hands and paced around the room. "So how do you talk to a General? How do you do it?"

Khariton sank back into the window seat and slowly tilted his head. "Why do you want to know?"

"Because I want to ask Enkeli a question."

"Then ask."

Thea blinked. "That's it? But they say no one has heard from Enkeli in ... I don't know how long. Until you did. If it's so easy to ask, why doesn't anyone hear anything?"

Khariton shrugged. "We forget to listen."

Thea stared at Khariton, wondering, but no. His spirit was dead too. Even though somehow he had heard Enkeli's voice. It couldn't be that—

Wait. There in his spirit ... a little flicker. Something was alive in there! Thea jumped in excitement. "You! You're different! You're not really dead!"

Khariton snorted. "I should hope not. Just because I'm old doesn't mean I'm as good as dead."

"No. You don't understand. You actually heard Enkeli's voice! There is something that is still alive, deep inside of you. You're different than everyone else!"

"Different?" Khariton eyed Thea darkly, then turned to look out the window. "No. I'm no different than anyone else. Supposed to check in every morning, then I look up and it's five cycles later. None of us really follow Enkeli anymore. We pretend to, but it isn't real. Not anymore."

"You're supposed to do what every morning?"

Khariton glanced at Thea. "Any Elf sworn in Enkeli's service is supposed to check in every morning. To get the orders for the day. But we get older and we slow down. The days pass by and we forget to remember."

Thea clenched her hands. "I'm never going to slow down!"

Khariton stared at her with a look that was half-amused and half-sad. "We're Elves. That's the way Elves are. We get lost in our heads and we can't serve our General anymore."

Thea glared. "Just because that's the way things are doesn't mean that everyone is okay with it."

Khariton held her gaze for a long time. Finally he gave a little smirk. "I like your spunk, uh, what did you say your name was?"

"Thea. So how does somebody start serving a General?"

"Simple. You tell the General you want to sign up, and they tell you what to do."

"That's all?"

"What else did you expect?"

Thea wasn't sure what to say. The way Khariton explained it was so simple. "And that works for *any* of the Generals?"

Khariton gave her an amused glance. "You fixing to serve a General are you? Which one you got your sights on?"

"You mean I can serve whichever General I want?"

"What kind of question is that? Of course you can. Back in my day, Elves served whichever General they wanted to—and that suited what they were good at, of course. It's true that Elves tend towards taking service under Enkeli, you see Enkeli is *our* General, but that doesn't mean you have to."

"*Our* General?"

"When the Ancient Wisdom created the very first Elves, Enkeli was the General assigned to guide us and teach us about the world. Every race had their own General. To take care of them."

Thea thought about that for a moment. "But there are five races in Raphtova, or at least that's what I learned, but there are only four Generals. Which race didn't get one?"

"There used to be five Generals." Khariton gave her a long glance. "You know the one we call the Deceiver? He was a General once, and the greatest of the Generals, they say, but he turned against the Ancient Wisdom. Some call him the Fallen General."

Stories from her history lessons floated back through Thea's mind. "That was when the Great War started, wasn't it?"

Khariton's eyes darkened. "That was the Deceiver's doing. He wanted Raphtova and set out to take it—killing any who refused him, or twisting their minds to fight for him. All that destruction and death was because of him."

Something in his voice made Thea pause. "Were you ... alive then?"

"Yes. I was a drill sergeant in the army."

Thea gaped. That meant Khariton was more than a thousand circles old! "You fought in the Great War? What was it like?"

"Living death." Khariton stared out the window, as if his eyes saw something Thea couldn't see. "We fought, and died. Elves died. More every day. We had to kill—" He stopped, every muscle as tense as a bowstring. Slowly, he turned and regarded Thea with a dispassionate gaze. "We did our part. When our King sounded the retreat we returned to our island. We haven't left it since."

Thea's mouth felt dry. "The war was over?"

"No. We could not pay the cost anymore."

"What happened to everyone else? The other people in the war?"

"We never heard."

"But don't you care?"

"Why should I care? No news comes from the Dark Lands. I am old and slow. It makes no difference to me what happened to them."

Thea glared. "Well I think that's a stupid way of thinking. Davis came from the Dark Lands, and when I looked at him I saw a spirit that was vibrant and alive. When I look at my own people I see spirits that are dead and rotting. Maybe it would have been better to die in the war than sit around here, dying just the same."

Khariton's eyes blazed. "You know nothing about the world."

"I know I don't, but I am going to do everything I can to find out."

Thea turned and stormed out of the room.

Out of the Hall of the Keepers. Out of the Temple gate. The streets blurred by as Thea left the upper reaches of the city and returned to her family's home in the heart of the First House District. Two stately trees bordered the walkway leading up to the front door. Thea let herself in and slipped past the servants who were busily tidying up the parlour.

Her parents weren't home. They hardly ever were. Her father was busy with his work in the leadership of First House, and her mother kept a full social calendar. Today, Thea didn't care. She raced up the broad staircase and straight into her room, slamming the door behind her.

"Allulien!" Thea yelled at the ceiling. "I am going to serve you!"

A bright, yellow light flooded the room. Thea froze, her back tingling with a strange warmth. The light reflected blindingly off the walls, casting Thea's shadow dark across the floor in front of her.

"You called?" The voice behind her was warm and large, filling the room as if it would burst at the seams.

Hardly daring to breathe, Thea turned around.

Chapter Three

Thea stared up at the shimmering being standing before her. It was Elf-like in appearance, but translucent, as if made of swirling air or water. Within the figure shone a light as bright as Allumen in the sky.

Thea fell to her knees and shielded her eyes. "You ... you came."

"Of course I came." The voice pounded through Thea's head like a drum. "You wanted something?"

Thea swallowed. "I want to serve you."

Allulien seemed to consider this for a moment. "You want to serve me? I am afraid that I do not accept any into my own service, but perhaps what you really wish is to serve the Deity."

The Deity? Something stirred in Thea's mind. Lessons from her old tutor, lost beneath other interests and concerns.

"The one you know as the Ancient Wisdom is named among the Tilaryn as the Deity. If that is the one you wish to serve, I would gladly be your General, and under me you would take your orders. Do you wish to do so?"

"Yes! Yes I do!" Thea looked up at Allulien's face. The expression was stern, but also kind.

Allulien smiled. "You have an eager heart, young one, but I want to be sure that you know: the service of the Deity is a lifelong promise. You are an Elf, and immortal life runs within your veins. A lifelong service is long indeed."

Thea stared at the shimmering figure before her. "I have seen a spirit vibrant and full of life, and I have seen spirits dead and broken. I know which kind of life I want to live."

Allulien smiled. "Then, Thea Kirisensk, I accept you into the service of the Deity. Your responsibilities are simple, though not easy. Every morning you must listen for whatever instructions I may have for you, and you are to obey. There may not be new instructions for you every morning, and you will not always see me as you do now, but you will know when you hear my voice."

Allulien reached out a hand and placed it on Thea's head. A tingling warmth rushed through her whole body and she looked up at Allulien with shining eyes. It was real! She was in the service of the Deity, and she felt like she could sing, or dance, or shout from the rooftops.

Allulien gave her a knowing look. "It is still acceptable to call the Deity by the name given by your people. The Deity is ancient beyond time and wiser than any other, so the Ancient Wisdom is a very good name." Allulien smiled. "Now, are you ready for your first task?"

Thea jumped up. "Yes!"

"You are to leave Lyudmyla and follow after Davis. He has gone to the city of Gedwyld, several days south-east of here. There is much that you do not yet understand, and you will learn it sooner in what you call the 'Dark Lands' than you would here. Today, put your affairs in order and prepare for travel. Tomorrow, you will depart."

Thea's mouth hung open. Leave Lyudmyla and

follow Davis? She had been longing to do that very thing and hadn't realized it until that moment!

"How—how will I know what to do, and where to go?"

"As you go, the way will become clear to you."

Thea nodded and bowed her head. When she looked up again, Allulien was gone.

Thea blinked and stared around her old, familiar room: her bed, messy and unmade, the wardrobe left half open, the old storage trunk, the daylight streaming through the large bay windows. It all looked so ordinary, but within her heart she could feel the warm glow given by Allulien. She was a servant of the Deity, and she was going to go learn from Davis!

Thea laughed in delight.

Pulling her wardrobe open, she rifled through her clothes. What would someone wear on a journey like this? Nothing fancy, or it was sure to be ruined. She picked out some clothes that were comfortable and sturdy and laid them on her bed.

What about when she got to Gedwyld? She wouldn't want to wear travelling clothes all the time! Thea returned to the wardrobe and chose some things to wear when she was studying under Davis.

What else would she need? Food, camping supplies, probably some better shoes if she was going to be walking so far. Thea grabbed her handbag from its spot by the door. Time to do some shopping.

First, she stopped by a leatherworking store and bought a backpack. Next, she went down the mountain to the market district and bought some dried fruit and meat. What other kinds of things did people eat when travelling? Long journeys weren't very common on

Larsya. You could travel the whole length of the island in a couple of days.

After wandering around the booths for a while, Thea bought some nuts, flatbread, and a small pot for cooking on a campfire. The shopkeeper gave her a strange look, but Thea hardly noticed.

Next, she made her way down to the harbour. Carts rattled down the streets. Workers shouted as they tossed bales of goods from one pallet to another.

On a broad lane near the docks stood the Harbour Office. Thea stepped inside and took a moment to let her eyes adjust to the dim light. Crates and barrels lined the walls. Large wooden beams spanned the ceiling, stained dark with age. In the center of the room, an Elf sat at a large desk, his pen busily scratching in a large ledger book.

Thea stepped forward. "Excuse me."

The Elf at the desk looked up in surprise. "Can I help you?"

"Yes, is this the place to make arrangements for the transport?"

The Elf nodded. "Interested in making a shipment, are you? What's your merchant number?"

"Oh, I don't want to make a shipment. I want to ride on the transport tomorrow, as a passenger."

The Elf peered at her closely. "A passenger? What is your business in Svokiye?"

Thea hesitated. "I am looking for someone."

The Elf frowned. "Writing a letter would be more cost-effective, you know."

"It really is important that I go myself."

The Elf's eyes took in the pack Thea had slung over her shoulder. "I suppose I'll send the bill up to your parents' house?"

"No, I'll pay myself. How much is it?" Thea reached into her handbag.

The Elf waved a hand absently. "Pay when you board. The fare is two silver, give or take, depending on the captain's mood. Departs one measure after staph, sharp. Is there anything else I can do for you?"

"Um ... I think that's all. Thank you."

Thea stepped out into the street. What else was she missing? Something to carry water in! Thea hurried back to the market district.

By the time Thea bought a water flask—and several other things she realized that she needed—the planet Micai was large in the sky and nearing Allumen for its nightly eclipse.

Wearily, she climbed the last steep road up to her home, made her way to her room, and sat down on the bed.

What else did she need to do? Getting up, she put her purchases on the chest along with the money for her passage, ready for the next morning, and hung her handbag back beside the door. She wasn't going to need it anymore.

The hair on her shoulders was gone. It must have rubbed off while she'd been busy. Thea stifled a yawn.

What was that little box on the table beside her bed? Thea opened it and found an assortment of pastries and other small delicacies. It was the box of refreshments that Kseniya had given to her and Roland when they watched Davis arrive on the transport. She'd forgotten all about it. Roland must have been carrying it and brought it over sometime when she wasn't home.

Roland! She had been so excited that she'd forgotten

to tell him what was happening. What would he think of her leaving for the Dark Lands? Hopefully he would understand. He had to understand! It was too late to go talk to him tonight—the sky was already growing dark. She would have to go see him in the morning.

Thea threw herself onto her bed and closed her eyes.

Daylight seeped into Thea's senses and she woke up in an instant. It was morning! Thea jumped out of bed. Today was the day she would leave to find Davis!

First, she had to check in. Quickly pulling on her travelling clothes, Thea glanced out the window. In the early morning light she could just see the high domed roof of the Halls of Knowledge. She wasn't the only one who should be checking in.

A short time later, Thea barrelled into Khariton's room. "Wake up!"

Khariton sat staring out his window, just as he was when Thea first met him. He didn't seem to notice the intrusion.

Thea marched up to him and shook him by the shoulders. "Wake up! It's time to check in."

Khariton broke out of Thea's grasp with a speed that stung her hands. He wheeled to face her, eyes blazing. "You!"

Thea glared back at him. "Yes, me. It's morning. Time to check in."

His jaw clenched. "You're lucky I can't make you polish the courtyard with your bare hands."

"Maybe *you* should polish the courtyard," Thea snapped. "You were supposed to check in every day and you didn't!"

Khariton's eyes darkened. "I am not that person

anymore. The younger Khariton ... was different, but I—I am no servant of Enkeli."

"That's right, you're not." Thea gave him a sharp look. "You're a servant of the Deity, and a promise to serve the Deity lasts your whole life. Are you still alive or not?"

"Sometimes I have my doubts."

Thea glared. "It wasn't a trick question. It is time to check in and you are going to check in. Or are you going to willingly disobey the command of your General?"

Khariton stared at her. A deep, inner struggle traced its way across his face. Finally his eyes fell to the floor and his shoulders sagged. "I will obey." He turned and sank to his knees in front of the window.

Thea knelt beside him. Taking a long breath, she tried to settle her racing mind. How exactly did one "check in"? She gave Khariton a surreptitious glance. He knelt with head bowed, an expression of pain lingering on his face.

Thea's gaze returned to the floor in front of her. If there was something specific she was supposed to do, Allulien would have told her.

She closed her eyes and waited to see what would happen.

After what seemed like a very long time, she heard Allulien's voice. Not audibly, from outside of her, but a soft voice within her heart, whispering, "It is time." Of course, she knew what Allulien wanted her to do today. Today she would leave Lyudmyla.

Thea looked at Khariton kneeling beside her. The flame within his spirit was larger now, pulsing like a heartbeat. When he looked up, there was a strange expression in his eyes.

"Did Enkeli speak to you?"

"Yes."

Thea smiled and looked out at the garden. It was beautiful, glistening in the early morning light. No wonder Khariton enjoyed watching it so much. Were there gardens like that in the Dark Lands? Probably not. She felt the enormity of what she was about to do settle like a heavy weight over her shoulders. She glanced at Khariton. "I am leaving today."

"I know. Enkeli told me."

Thea picked at a piece of lint stuck to the hem of her travelling clothes. "I've never left Lyudmyla before. I don't really know what I'm doing."

"Yes you do." Khariton fixed his keen eyes on her. "You are following orders."

Thea smiled. "Yes, I am."

Khariton rose to his feet. "You'd better go now."

Thea nodded and got up to go. At the door she paused and looked back. "Thank you."

Khariton saluted, and in that clipped movement Thea caught a brief glimpse of the young drill sergeant from so long ago. With a grin she turned and strode out the door.

The first thing she needed to do was find Roland. She took the shortcut to his house, but it was quiet and empty. Thea sighed. Okay, Roland often trained with the rest of the Eagle's crew during workday. Maybe he was down at the harbour.

Thea ran down the mountain, through the narrow, winding streets and found her way to the dock where the racing boats were moored. The Eagle was there, but there was no sign of Roland.

The racing headquarters was nearby. Tentatively,

Thea poked her head through the door. An Elf sat at the desk.

"Excuse me," Thea ventured, "do you know if the Eagle's crew is training right now?"

The Elf shuffled through some papers on her desk. "Yes, I believe so. Fitness training this workday."

"Do you know where they are? I need to speak to Roland."

The Elf tapped thoughtfully with her finger. "I can't say that I heard. Fitness schedules don't usually specify location. They could be anywhere. Say, you're Thea, aren't you?"

"Sorry, got to go." Thea hurried down the street, fear hammering in her chest. What if she couldn't find Roland before the transport sailed? She had to obey her General's orders, but she didn't want to leave without saying goodbye!

What could she do? If she went home and got her bag she could keep looking until the moment she had to get on the transport.

Thea nodded, turning back towards the upper reaches of the city. She would write a letter for Roland, too, just in case.

Thea raced up the steep mountain streets without a pause to catch her breath. As she turned between the two large trees in front of her family's home she staggered, her heart pounding loudly in her ears.

Pulling open the front door, Thea ran towards the stairs, then paused. Her parents were in the parlour. She hadn't thought of saying goodbye to them.

Thea's mother looked up. With a shriek, she ran to Thea, holding her in a tight embrace. Then she grabbed Thea's shoulders and shook her. "How dare you give your father and me such a fright!"

Thea's mouth hung open. "What—"

"It is all nonsense," Thea's father said in a stern voice. "I am sure it is only an idle tale, as I told the Harbourmaster myself. No one from First House would ever have reason to leave Larsya, so clearly there has been some sort of mistake."

Thea's mother shook her again. "You unruly child! Your mischief keeps me awake at night, longing for the day when you finally slow down and take your place in society, but behaviour like *this* will bring disgrace on our House!"

Thea's father rested a hand on his wife's arm. "Calm down, my dear. I am sure this is all a misunderstanding."

Thea eased her shoulders out of her mother's grasp. "I'm not sure what your current understanding is, so I can't say if there has been a misunderstanding, but I *am* leaving. I was going to tell you just now."

Thea's mother shrieked.

Her father looked shocked. "What is this about, Thea?"

"I have entered the service of the Deity—the Ancient Wisdom—and my General has commanded me to leave Lyudmyla today."

Thea's mother clung to her husband. "It is just like the priestess from the Temple said! She needs proper training or she will do something foolish!"

Thea's father shook his head. "I heard that the religious life interests you, Thea, and I suppose that is respectable enough for a high-ranking person in First House, but you must remember that you are second in line for Chancellor once your uncle and I become too old. The people of Lyudmyla are willing to accept some mischief from young people, as a matter of course, but we'd better let this all blow over before any questions are raised."

Thea looked from her father to her mother. "But I *am* going. Allulien has commanded that I go to the Dark Lands, and I must obey."

Thea's father frowned. "That is quite enough, Thea. If you will not listen to us, I will send for the Chancellor to make a ruling in this situation. You will wait here until he does so."

"How long will that take? I need to leave on the transport today."

"You will not be going anywhere today. Your uncle will come when his duties at the Palace allow him to do so, and this will all be settled in due time. Now go to your room and wait."

Thea allowed herself to be ushered to her room. She had to go there anyway, to get her bag. Her bag—

The door clicked shut behind her.

Her bag was gone.

Quickly, she searched the old storage chest, just in case, but it was empty except for some blankets. Closing the chest, she searched her wardrobe, but her pack was not there. It was gone. She ran to the closest window and looked down. The courtyard pavement far below would make for a very uncomfortable landing. She was trapped.

Thea paced her room. She had to obey Allulien's orders, but how? Her parents wouldn't let her out until her uncle had come, and there was little hope of that happening before the transport sailed. Her room on the upper floor made sneaking away difficult, if not impossible, and even if she managed it, she had nothing to take with her and no money to pay for the transport. What was she going to do?

She paced until exhaustion dragged at her limbs. With nothing else to do, she collapsed on her bed and fell into a fitful sleep.

A muffled thud jerked Thea awake. Sitting up, she stared around the room. Nothing had changed. Had her uncle come? She ran to the door and listened.

Someone was talking, but their voice was muffled and far away. It didn't sound like her uncle.

Disappointed, Thea paced over to the window. The harsh brightness of Allumen high in the sky meant that it was almost staph, the time in the middle of the day when most of the inhabitants of Lyudmyla would rest and shelter from the heat. After staph the transport would be sailing, and she was supposed to be on it. If she couldn't obey her General, what was she going to do?

Look in the chest.

Thea blinked in surprise at the thought. Why should she look in the chest? It was ridiculous, but somehow the thought felt important.

Shaking herself, Thea walked over to the old storage chest and opened it. Lying on top of the blankets was a strung recurve bow. What was it doing in her chest? It hadn't been there before! But it was a beautiful one. Its red polished wood was carved with a delicate design of leaves and vines, inlaid with gold. She had never seen anything like it.

Gingerly, Thea touched the bow. It was real. Beside it lay a quiver filled with arrows. Carefully, Thea lifted them out of the chest. A piece of parchment fluttered to the ground. Thea picked it up. There were words on it, written in a scrawling, messy hand:

This is Raybow. I fought with it in the War. Hasn't been touched since then but she's as good as new. Enkeli wants me to give it to you. Watch for my signal, then get your ass out there and follow your General's orders. Khariton Oryzny

Thea's hands started to shake. Yes, she was going to obey. She was going to obey and nothing was going to stop her!

She stared around her room. What kind of signal did Khariton mean? And how would she get out of her room when the signal came? She looked down at the chest. A long coil of rope lay beside the place where Raybow had been.

"Thank you, Khariton," Thea whispered. Snatching up the rope, she laid Khariton's gifts on her bed. She had a way to escape, but what else could she bring? All of the travelling supplies she had gathered were gone and she didn't have the time or money to buy more.

Her eyes rested on the small box on the table beside her bed. The refreshments from Kseniya! It wasn't exactly travelling food, but at least it was food.

What could she carry it in? Her handbag. It still hung by the door. Thea grabbed it off its hook and dumped its jumbled contents onto the table. The box of refreshments barely fit into the small bag, but she managed to squeeze it in.

A bright light flashed outside her window.

Peering outside, Thea stared at the beacon of light

flaring up from the dome of the Halls of Knowledge. Was that Khariton's signal? The whole city was going to see that! But maybe that was the point. Everyone would run and stare and pay no attention to one Elf slipping off towards the harbour. Thea grinned.

Quickly, she uncoiled the rope and looped it around a bedpost, carefully dropping the ends out the closest window. She could hear a hubbub in the distant streets as more and more people saw the strange flaring light.

Thea slipped the quiver's baldric over her shoulder. Thankfully the handbag had a long strap; she slung it over her other shoulder and climbed onto the windowsill. The ground seemed a long way down. Carefully, she held Raybow under one arm, grabbed the rope tightly in both hands, and lowered herself over the side.

When her feet touched the ground, Thea pulled the rope down and bundled it up. Raybow had a small hook by its grip that clipped onto the baldric so the bow could hang down her back. It took a moment of fiddling, but she managed to make it secure.

Picking up the rope, Thea hurried around the corner of the house and almost bumped into Roland.

"Roland!" Thea gasped. "Thank goodness!"

Grabbing his hand, Thea pulled him along as she dodged around the corner and into a narrow alleyway. It was deserted. She turned to Roland. "I need to leave Lyudmyla."

He nodded. "I heard something about that."

"Allulien appeared to me, Roland, and told me to go to the Dark Lands. I need to go today."

Roland stared at her for a moment, then nodded. "Okay. Come on."

Thea hurried after him. "Do you think we can make it to the harbour without anyone seeing us?"

"The harbour?" Roland turned to face her. "Every single person down there has been told to look out for you. There is no way you are getting on the transport without someone noticing. We're going to Rokhov. I know someone there who might be able to help."

"Who?"

"Svetka. The captain of the Raven."

Thea hurried after Roland. "You're going to ask the captain of the *Raven* for help?"

"She's good at what she does, and she doesn't mind breaking a few rules." He stopped to peer around a corner. "So exactly how much trouble are you in?"

"My parents told me I can't go and shut me in my room until my uncle could come."

Roland stared. "Your parents called the Chancellor?"

"He's just my uncle."

"He is the most powerful person in First House, Thea. If he says you can't go ..."

"I'll be gone before he can make a ruling on it."

Roland looked at her for a moment. "So we want to avoid those palace guards standing just around the corner?"

Thea swallowed. "Probably."

Roland gestured her away from the corner and they went back along the street, turning onto a different alleyway.

"Here, give me that." Roland took the rope from Thea and coiled it properly. He looked up at the fire escape ladder hanging above them. "Ready for some climbing?"

Thea grinned.

Chapter Four

On the rooftops the light of Allumen seemed even more intense. Thea shaded her eyes and stared out across the sea. The distant Dark Lands looked like a smudge on the horizon.

"What is *that?*" Roland stared at the beacon of light flaring up from the dome of the Halls of Knowledge.

"Khariton's signal. I think he's running it as a sort of distraction so I can get away."

Roland frowned. "Who's Khariton?"

"He's someone who fought in the Great War. He lives up at the Temple now. He's the one who gave me Raybow." Thea gestured to the bow hanging down her back.

"It's beautiful."

Thea nodded. "He's done a lot to help me. I think Enkeli told him to."

As they watched, the light over the Temple flickered and went out.

Roland glanced at Thea. "I guess it's time to go."

The houses high in the First House District were not packed together as tightly as the buildings surrounding the harbour. It took some backtracking to find a route where they could scramble from house to house. Soon the sounds and smells of the upper market drifted up to them on a lazy breeze.

Thea wasn't used to being out during staph. The heat

from Allumen made her feel tired and lightheaded.

Dong. The tolling of a low bell broke through the muffled noise. Thea froze. "The alarm! Roland, are they really looking for me?"

"It might be about something else," Roland didn't seem convinced, "but if not, we still have a little while before the runners can take the news to the guards. Come on."

Crouching out of sight of the streets far below, they scrambled as quickly as they could along the uneven rooftops. Thea's head pounded as she struggled to keep up.

Two houses later, a shout rang out behind them. Roland grabbed her arm and pulled her behind a squat chimney where they huddled, breathing hard.

The tramp of several feet approached.

"Hey Nika!" a voice called from just out of sight. "You're last to the mark. Twenty pushups."

A chorus of laughter and one groan echoed across the rooftops. Roland's eyes widened.

"Next mark is the end of the upper market. Go!"

Roland stood up, just as several Elves in white tracksuits ran past their hiding place.

"Hey! Hold up!" one of the Elves called to the others. Thea recognized him as the captain of Roland's sailing team. With a grin he strode towards them. "Roland! There you are! You're lucky Coach didn't notice you were missing when he sent us off for a run."

The team gathered around Thea and Roland, elbowing and jostling each other.

Roland shrugged. "Sorry for skipping out, but I need to help Thea. I'm going to have to miss the rest of training for today."

The captain looked surprised. "Miss training? Come on, Roland, I know you're better than that."

Roland stepped closer and spoke in a low voice. "Look. Thea and I have some urgent business in Rokhov and we want to stay under the radar for a while. I'll catch you as soon as I can."

"Oh, of *course*, urgent business with *Thea*." The captain gave a cocky grin and tapped the side of his nose knowingly. A couple of the Elves chuckled. "I *suppose* I can cover your ass when Coach asks where you've got to."

Loud, urgent voices drifted up from the street below.

Roland glanced at Thea then turned back to the captain. "You don't mind a bit of fun, do you? There might be some folks out looking for us. It would give us a head start if you could keep their attention for a while, say if you ran the rooftops down to the harbour, making some noise, but not showing who you are."

The captain stretched. "Well, I don't know. What do you think, team?"

Grins and shrugs showed that the team thought it sounded like good fun.

"Deal, Roland," the captain shook his hand. "But it will be an extra round of pushups from you tomorrow for the trouble." He gave a cocky grin and waved the team away.

Roland pulled Thea behind the chimney as the team disappeared over the next rooftop. There was a shout from further down the street.

When everything was quiet again, Roland and Thea crept to the side of the building and Roland swung himself down onto a ladder. He looked up at Thea. "That might be enough rooftops for now."

After a long, winding course through back alleys, they made it to the outer reaches of Lyudmyla. Relaxing their pace, they returned to the main road leading towards Rokhov. Few people travelled during staph, and those they passed didn't even glance in their direction.

"You were looking for me?" Roland asked after they had been walking for a while.

Thea nodded. "I wanted to tell you that I was leaving, and why I was leaving. It all happened so fast, I didn't have a chance to tell you before. I decided to serve the Deity, and Allulien appeared to me and told me to go follow Davis and learn from him."

Roland looked thoughtful. "It's because of your spirit sight, isn't it?"

Thea nodded. "I learned that it is only serving the Deity—the Ancient Wisdom—that can make someone's spirit bright and alive. It seems like most people here have forgotten what it really means to serve the Deity, and that's why everyone's spirit is so dead and broken."

They walked for a while in silence.

"So what is my spirit like?" Roland glanced at Thea out of the corner of his eye.

Thea looked down at the worn, cobbled road. "I didn't look at it. I was scared that it might be dead like everyone else's, and I couldn't bear seeing that." She looked up at Roland, an idea growing in her mind. "Roland, will you do something for me? I told you about Khariton. He serves the Deity but he is so old that he forgets to check in with Enkeli like he's supposed to. Could you go wake him up every morning—first thing—and remind him to check in? He understands a lot about serving the Deity, even if he has to be reminded that he knows it. Ask him. He will teach you and maybe ... maybe you can serve the Deity too."

Roland's expression was hard to understand, but he nodded. "I will wake him up every morning for you."

When Rokhov came into view, Thea and Roland left the road once again. Unlike Lyudmyla, Rokhov had gates and walls, and Thea didn't want anyone knowing where she'd gone.

After sneaking through a corn field, Roland led Thea across a dirt lane and around a dishevelled farmhouse to a low shed tucked up against the wall. Roland boosted Thea onto the roof and scrambled up after her. From the roof it was an easy climb over the wall.

"How did you know how to get in?" Thea asked as she dropped to the ground inside.

"I've done quite a bit of scouting around here. The team uses this route when we come to prank the Ravens."

Thea stared. "You *prank* the *Ravens*?"

"And they prank us back. Don't worry, we're even."

Cautiously, Thea followed Roland through the narrow, dusty streets. She couldn't help but notice that everything in Rohkov seemed dirtier and shabbier than she was used to seeing in Lyudmyla. The houses were narrower and packed tightly together.

"Why aren't we using the rooftops here?" Thea asked.

Roland made a face. "We found out the hard way that the city guards in Rokhov patrol the rooftops as well as the streets, and they're far more likely to be suspicious of anyone they find up there. It's easier to blend into the crowd on the street."

The harbour in Rokhov was smaller than

Lyudmyla's. Thea stared at its rough wooden wharves and much-mended sails.

Rows of narrow, shanty-like buildings surrounded the docks. Roland approached a door that looked as if it hadn't been painted in far too long.

"Lucky for us, Svetka lives alone, so we shouldn't have to deal with anyone else." He opened the door and stepped inside.

Thea followed, and found the inside of the hovel to be a small, comfortable apartment. A narrow bed lined one wall, and a collection of sea glass lined the counter of what appeared to be a very small kitchen.

"Svetka—" Roland called, and turned. A sword appeared at his throat.

"Roland, damn you," a voice growled from the shadows behind the door and an Elf stepped out into the light. She glared at Roland for a moment, then reluctantly lowered her sword. "Where's the rest of your bloody team?"

"Back in Lyudmyla being model citizens."

The Elf seemed to consider this with some skepticism. Slowly her gaze took in Thea from where she was standing behind Roland. "Who's your friend?"

"This is Thea," Roland gestured with a grin. "Thea, this is Svetka."

"Pleased to meet you," Thea replied, out of habit more than truth. Svetka had a wild, hardened look about her, as if she'd do more than merely point a sword at your throat.

"So, Roland," Svetka examined her sword casually before sheathing it in one smooth motion. "Come to grovel after the race?"

"Not at all." Roland leaned casually against the door.

"But that was a nice trick, shortening your keel to cut over the Chebokan Shoals."

Svetka gave him a sharp look. "Why are you here?"

Roland glanced at Thea, then took a long, slow breath. "We need your help."

Svetka raised an eyebrow and seemed to study him for a moment. "Trouble?"

"Sort of. Thea has received General's orders to go to the Dark Lands, but some high ups aren't too pleased at a young noble from First House running off without their permission. She needs to make the crossing today."

Svetka sat down on the small chair in the corner and leaned back, giving Roland an incredulous look. "Sounds like trouble."

Roland watched her for a moment. "You going to take her?"

Svetka crossed her arms. "What's in it for me?"

"Just that you'd be doing the right thing."

Svetka glared.

"And that you'd be sticking it up the ass of everybody who is anybody in Lyudmyla."

A hint of a smile flickered across Svetka's face, but her eyes remained serious. "I don't get myself mixed up in Lyudmyla politics."

Roland looked at her with an innocent expression. "Politics? I never said anything about politics. You'd just be doing a favour for a friend."

Svetka raised an eyebrow. "And what would your captain say?"

"My captain doesn't need to know anything."

Svetka's face finally broke into a smile. She shook her head. "You're alright, Roland, even if you are First

House. One ride to the Dark Lands, for the knowledge that no one wants me doing it." She strode across the room and pulled twice on a bit of rope that was hanging unobtrusively from a corner of the small window. "The crew will have the Raven ready in two shakes of a rat's tail. You coming, Roland?"

"No. The team is expecting me back and I shouldn't keep them waiting." Roland looked at Thea, and she saw that unexplainable expression in his eyes again.

Svetka seemed to notice it too. She gave Roland an incredulous look. "Well, you know what I think about the rest of your team, and if they don't like it they can take a long walk off a short pier."

Roland shook his head. "I have a commitment to be there, and I've already pushed my luck. There are lots of people in First House who would like a spot on the team."

Svetka shrugged. "Well, I'm going down to the Raven to see how she's doing. You two make sure you have a proper goodbye before you come down." Grabbing a small bag off the bed, she stalked out the door.

Thea looked at Roland. For the first time since Allulien's appearance, she felt a sickening sense of misgiving. It was really happening. When she stepped onto the Raven she would be leaving behind everything and everyone she knew. She had been so excited about going she hadn't really thought about everything she would be leaving behind. "Roland—" her throat tightened. What could she say to him?

Roland looked down at something in his hand. "This is for you." Gingerly, he held it out—a silver brooch, shaped like a flower.

It glimmered as Thea took it and held it up to the

light. "It's beautiful. Thank you."

Roland gave a little smile. "I thought you'd like it." He hesitated, then looked at her with an earnest expression. "Thea, I know you have to go. I'm not going to try to stop you or tell you not to go, but could you ... could you promise me that you will come back someday?"

Thea looked up into Roland's troubled eyes. He was afraid. They had always been close friends, more like family than their own families had been, and now he didn't know if he would ever see her again.

Thea's heart sank. Would she ever come back? She'd seen how dead her people were, and her family was going to be furious with her for leaving. It would be hard to come back, but she wasn't ready to say that kind of goodbye.

She held the brooch tight. "I promise."

Svetka's voice echoed through the door. "You could always go with her, Roland you dumbass!"

Roland looked at Thea in consternation. "You know I can't do that."

Thea nodded. "I know." Roland couldn't let his team down.

Slowly they walked out the door and down to where the Raven rested by the docks. Several members of the crew moved around the deck, preparing for their departure.

"Tide's turning," Svetka called, "time to go."

Roland nodded.

"Goodbye," Thea whispered and gave Roland a hug.

Roland smiled. "Here. This is yours." He handed Thea the rope he had been carrying and helped her step onto the Raven's deck. He glanced at Svetka. "Safe sailing."

Svetka made a face. "Watch yourself, Eagle Boy."

Roland tossed the mooring line onto the deck and waved as the Raven slipped away from the dock.

Thea watched as Roland's figure grew smaller and was swallowed up by the ramshackle buildings. Overhead, the Raven's black sails creaked in the brisk wind that propelled them forward. Thea noticed Svetka watching her.

"So where are you headed?" Svetka asked, stowing the mooring line out of sight.

"I'm going to Gedwyld."

"Never heard of it."

"I was told it is several days south-east of here. If you can drop me off in Svokiye, I would very much appreciate it. I will walk from there."

"*Near* Svokiye, not *in* Svokiye. I know a spot where you can jump ship easily enough."

"Thank you."

Thea leaned over the rail and watched as Rokhov disappeared from view. The great mountain Larsya, after which the Island was named, loomed large against the sky. Already she could see the outskirts of Lyudmyla.

The brisk wind was a refreshing change from the oppressive heat of staph. Soon Micai, the planet around which Raphtova orbited, would appear over the horizon and begin its climb towards Allumen.

Had her parents realized she was gone? Hopefully Roland would talk to them and help them understand why she had to leave.

Thea turned her attention to the Raven and her crew. She had always considered herself a loyal supporter of the Eagle, but she couldn't help but admit that the Raven was a beautiful ship. Everything was spotless and in its place, and her crew treated her with a respect she wasn't used to seeing from the crew of the Eagle.

Thea remembered the look in Roland's eyes when he talked about the Raven. Could it be that he sometimes wished he wasn't First House?

They rounded the great promontory, and the full expanse of Lyudmyla spread out before them, from the gleaming dome of the Halls of Knowledge near the peak, down to the comfortable villas that bordered the seaside.

The clanging of a bell rang out across the water.

"The transport is sailing." The first mate spoke under his breath to Svetka, but it sounded more like a question.

Svetka's eyes were fixed on the mouth of the harbour. Moments later, a small white boat shot into view. "I thought as much," she muttered between clenched teeth. Turning to Thea, she gave a sardonic smile. "Looks like we're going to have company."

Thea frowned. "I don't understand. Roland's team was training today, not sailing."

Svetka stood tall, holding onto the rigging with one hand. "Steady as she goes!" she called to her crew, then glared at Thea. "Who knew you were coming to us?"

"Nobody."

"Really." Svetka's voice dripped with sarcasm. "No one knew you were going to Rokhov."

"Just Roland's team."

"Well there's your answer."

"But they were helping us get away!"

"Maybe they *were*, for as long as the fancy struck

them. Airheads. The lot of them." She glanced at Thea. "Well, your Roland has a decent head on his shoulders. Or I thought he did."

"But they didn't know we were coming to *you*."

"It doesn't take much to put two and two together, even if you have to count on your fingers. Besides, there was probably someone on lookout at the harbour. You weren't exactly hiding away below deck."

The Eagle approached on an interception course and ran up the signal flag that meant they wanted to talk.

"Should we take in some sail?" the first mate asked.

Svetka watched the Eagle with narrowing eyes. "They aren't sailing the way they usually do. Get closer, but not too close."

As the Eagle drew closer, the first mate came and stood beside Svetka. "Is that old Long Arms?"

Svetka swore under her breath, then yelled, "Hard to port!"

Thea clung to the rail as the Raven cut through the ocean swells, flinging spray through the air. She watched in terror as the Raven shot directly in front of the Eagle, forcing the Eagle to tack sharply. Shouts and curses tore past on the wind as they barely missed a collision.

Thea stared at the unfamiliar faces on the Eagle's deck as the ships parted ways. "That's not the Eagle's crew!"

Svetka glared at the ship falling quickly to stern. "They've crewed her with the coaches and trainers. I'll be damned if I let *them* catch us."

"I don't understand. Why are they here?"

"It seems that somebody really doesn't want you going to the Dark Lands. Someone with enough clout to call on the fastest ship in the city to do their dirty work for them." Svetka smiled grimly. "Eagle or no Eagle, we'll get you where you're going."

"They've changed course!" the first mate yelled over the wind. "They're heading for Svokiye!"

Svetka's eyes glittered. "They want to race, do they?" She nodded to the first mate, and the crew of the Raven sprang into action. Svetka winked at Thea. "You might want to hold on."

Thea clung to the rail as the Raven surged through the dashing spray. She had never been on one of the ships during a race. All around her the members of the crew took their stations, grim determination glinting in every eye.

Thea looked up at Svetka. "You beat the Eagle in the race, didn't you?"

Svetka grinned wildly into the blowing spray. "Against the Eagle's team we did. Now we're going to beat the coaches."

Thea watched breathlessly as the expanse of sea and sky rushed past. The dark shadow in the distance grew to become a low bank of forested hills that spread across the horizon. The Raven kept its distance from the Eagle, but as land drew nearer they crossed paths once again. The Eagle was ahead, but only just.

Svetka strode over to Thea's side. "We're going to sail for the harbour, then change course at the last moment so the Eagle can't follow us. When we're in the next bay, jump out and swim for shore. If you're lucky you can make it to cover before anyone comes to see what we're doing. You can swim?"

Thea frowned. "I can swim, but what about my bow? And my food? Won't they be ruined?"

"Here." Svetka picked up a bundle of dark cloth and tossed it to Thea. "Wrap them in this oilskin. It'll be better than nothing."

Thea knelt down and did her best to spread out the oilskin cloak on the pitching deck. Unclipping Raybow from the baldric, she laid it in the center of the cloak, along with the quiver and her handbag.

A sudden lurch made her grab her things to stop them from rolling away. She glanced up in time to see the Eagle pass directly in front of them, narrowly missing a collision. Quickly, she pulled her bundle together.

Svetka watched her work. "You got a compass in that bag of yours?"

"No. I had one, but it was taken away."

The Raven heeled sharply again.

The first mate swore. "Are they *trying* to hit us?"

Svetka glared across the ocean spray at the Eagle. "They're trying to force us away from Svokiye. Ready about! Two can play at that game."

Thea clung to the rail and her oilskin-wrapped bundle as the Raven swept through the waves, spray flying in the wind. The distant shore quickly grew closer.

"Here!" Svetka called, and Thea just managed to grab a small object tumbling through the air. It was a compass.

"It's an extra. I won't miss it."

"Thank you." Thea slipped it into the bundle with the rest of her things.

"Anything else you're missing?"

Thea thought for a moment. "I don't have a flint."

Svetka glared. "You're planning to travel for days

through the Dark Lands and you don't even have a flint? Next you'll be telling me you don't have a knife."

Thea blinked. "Uh …"

Svetka swore. "You don't have a *knife*?" She pulled the knife off her belt, sheath and all, and stormed over to Thea. "You're taking this. There's a flint attached on the side here. See?"

"But—but that's your knife. I can't just take it."

Svetka rolled her eyes. "I'll send the bill to Roland, alright? Just take the damn knife."

"Harbour ahead!" the first mate called.

Svetka shoved the knife into Thea's hand and turned away.

The wooden palisade of Svokiye was in clear view now, and closer with every breath.

The Eagle drew alongside as the Raven raced towards the breakwater and the entrance of the harbour. One of them would have to slow down soon, or risk a collision. Heads appeared over the palisade, pointing and shouting.

"Steady … steady …" Svetka yelled. The breakwater drew closer at an alarming speed. "Now!"

With a shower of spray, the Raven tacked away from the harbour, shot between the rocks, and out into the smooth waters of the bay, out of sight of the wooden palisade.

Thea stared as the rugged coastline rushed by, bordered by gnarled, stunted trees. The Dark Lands.

"Your ride's over," Svetka called. "Time to jump!"

Shakily, Thea stood up and clutched her oilskin bundle. "Thanks for everything, Svetka."

Svetka scowled. "Jump, dammit!"

Thea jumped.

Chapter Five

Dark, frigid water closed over Thea's head. Kicking vigorously, she struggled back to the surface and gasped for breath, the water stinging her eyes. Shouts echoed in the distance.

Lifting her precious bundle out of the water as best as she could, Thea started swimming for shore. Waves broke over her head and tugged at the oilcloth, threatening to wrench it from her hands.

Finally her feet touched the ground. Staggering through the surf, she stared around the rocky, windswept beach. It was too exposed. She had to find somewhere to hide.

Tucking her bundle beneath her arm, she clambered up the rugged crags into the shadow of the trees. They grew in a wild, untamed mass, their roots clinging to the bare rock. Thea pushed her way through, crawling into the thickest of the underbrush where she sank to the ground, coughing and shivering.

Wind whistled in the wizened branches overhead, mingling with the distant roar of waves crashing on the shore below. Thea shifted, trying to see the Raven through the tangle of roots and branches, but her limbs gave out beneath her and she sank to the ground again.

Slowly, her pounding heart subsided. She was in the Dark Lands, where she was supposed to be. And Svetka would be proud, because in the end the Raven had pulled ahead of the Eagle.

Were those voices on the wind? Thea froze, hardly daring to move or breathe. Cautiously, she scanned the tangle of branches surrounding her. No one could find her here, could they? The voices—if they had been voices—died away and were lost in the murmur of the wind.

Through a gap in the branches overhead, Thea watched Micai rise higher and higher into the sky. It was said that Micai was named after one of the Generals—the Protector. Thea shivered. She could really use some protection now. Silently, she closed her eyes and whispered a prayer.

Exhaustion swept over her like a wave.

When she opened her eyes again, Micai's expanse filled the night sky, glowing with a soft blue-green light. Its golden rings shimmered through the branches overhead.

Cautiously, Thea moved. Her back ached and her head pounded.

What was that? Thea turned and froze. Someone was sitting beside her in the thicket!

The person smiled. "Did you have a good sleep?"

Thea's mouth hung open. There was something unnatural about the voice, and as she stared she realized that the person was translucent and glowing slightly. And the face ... she had seen that face before, in the great mural above the gate of the Temple.

"You ... you're Micai."

Micai smiled. "Sure am. Well you're up now, so I should get moving. Lots going on tonight."

Thea just stared. She *had* asked for protection, but she hadn't expected Micai to literally come and protect her.

Micai took a swig from a large mug Thea hadn't noticed before, then gave her a nod. "See you around."

Micai disappeared, leaving only the wizened trees gleaming softly in the light of the great planet that filled the sky.

After a long time, Thea wrenched her eyes away from the place where Micai had been and slowly crawled out of the thicket. Finding a bare patch of ground, she unrolled the oilskin. Everything inside seemed to be alright, though a little damp.

Draping the oilskin over her shoulders, Thea pinned on Roland's brooch and slung Raybow over her back. Pulling the compass out of her bag, she held it up to Micai's faint light and found her bearings.

Her mouth was dry and her throat ached. Hopefully there was water somewhere to the south-east.

Progress was slow as she pushed her way through the wizened coastal trees. Twigs and branches caught at her clothes and hair, and she had to keep changing course to avoid unpassable thickets.

Finally she stumbled out onto a narrow dirt track. It ran east to west, but it would be easier to walk on than the trackless forest. She'd travel east now, then go south once it was morning.

Soon the path came to a place where it crossed a small gorge. From the shadows beneath the bridge, the murmur of running water filled the air. Scrambling down the rocky incline, Thea stepped ankle-deep in the rushing stream. Crouching, she drank deeply.

Was that a noise? Thea froze. It sounded like footsteps. Someone was coming along the path!

Thea crouched in the deeper darkness beneath the

bridge. The footsteps drew closer, then stopped.

"You know that Elf there's a search warrant on?" A voice spoke from above Thea's head.

"Aye?" a second voice replied.

"Good thing we haven't seen her."

"Oh, aye."

"'Cause if we saw her we'd need to report it to those toffs up at Larsya."

"True, that."

"I'm sure she's far to the south by now, what with there being regular patrols on the coastal trail."

"Aye. Certainly."

Thea heard a low chuckle, then the footsteps moved on and faded into the distance.

Thea's heart pounded in her ears as she crept out of her hiding place. She had to go south as soon as possible. She didn't want to risk running into any other patrols.

Before her, the trickling water gleamed in Micai's soft light. The stream came from the south. Maybe she could follow it.

Clambering up the side of the little cascade, Thea made her way along the creekbed. The rocky gorge, swept out by rain and snowmelt, was wider than the lazy stream that occupied it now, and there was space for Thea to walk comfortably alongside it. The light from Micai helped her not to stumble too badly on the uneven stones, and soon the path was far behind her.

As the first rays of Allumen's light emerged from its nightly eclipse, Thea scrambled up the bank and found a little hollow in the forest where she could sleep. Gently she laid Raybow, the quiver, and her bag along a fallen log, bundled the cloak up as a makeshift pillow, and fell asleep.

When she woke, workday had all but passed and staph was approaching. Ravenously hungry, she opened the small box from Kseniya. The pastries inside were very old and stale, but Thea hardly noticed as she wolfed them down.

After getting a drink at the creek, she slowly climbed back up to her campsite. The sweets weren't sitting well in her stomach. She felt sick, and as she looked in the small box that held her food, she felt even worse. Two cookies and a rather squashed piece of cake were all that stood between her and becoming very hungry.

Memory nagged at the back of her mind. There was something she was forgetting. To check in! Of course! Kneeling by the mossy log, Thea waited in silence.

A warm, overwhelming presence swept over her. She looked up.

Allulien stood before her, eyes twinking. "Welcome to the Dark Lands, Thea. You completed your first task very well."

Thea swallowed. "I don't think I could have done it without Roland and Svetka. And Khariton."

Allulien smiled. "I did not ask you to complete your task alone. Often what seems impossible becomes possible with timely aid."

Thea nodded. "You'll make sure they don't get in too much trouble, won't you?"

Allulien appeared thoughtful. "The obedient often find themselves 'in trouble' with those who have turned their back on the Deity's ways. But you do not need to worry. No harm will come to them. And now your task for today is to continue in the instructions you have been given: travel south-east towards Gedwyld, and as you need further instruction, you will receive it."

Thea nodded. "I will. But—" her worry burst out, unbidden, "—I don't have any food. How will I eat?"

Allulien glanced at the small box sitting on the log nearby. "You have food."

"But not very much. What will I do when it's gone?"

"Then you will learn about the provision of the Deity."

Thea opened her mouth to protest, but Allulien was gone. She glanced around the small forest clearing. The air was growing warm, and insects buzzed lazily. She would travel, and obey, and just have to trust that it would all work out somehow.

Without a water flask, she was uneasy about straying too far from the creek, but it seemed to come from a south-easterly direction, so for now she could follow it without too much trouble. The air was cooler in the ravine, too, which made travelling during staph much more bearable.

Not long after staph, Thea reached a place where a rockfall had dammed up the stream. Beyond, the water nearly reached the walls of the ravine, stretching in a long still pool.

"You ever skipped rocks before?"

Thea blinked, and Micai was standing in front of her, just a little further along the pool.

To her surprise, Thea found herself stooping down to pick up a flat little stone and skimmed it across the surface of the water. It hopped twice, then sank to the bottom.

Micai nodded in approval. "Watch this." Micai picked up a stone and skimmed it along the water. It bounced on and on until it was out of sight.

Thea was impressed, but also bewildered. What was Micai doing here, and why were they skipping rocks?

Micai grinned. "It's a nice day, isn't it? I don't often get some time off. Not that this is time off, mind you, but a casual protection job is a nice change. I figured you wouldn't mind the company either."

Thea gaped. "I—I don't mind. I just hadn't expected to be keeping company with one of the Generals."

Micai flipped a stone in the air. "It's true, we don't often bother with being visible. Saves time avoiding the whole 'do not be afraid, I'm not planning to smite you today' thing."

Thea followed Micai along the shore of the pool. "Um ... what do you *normally* do?"

"Well, I'm the Protector. I protect, and I give orders to those under my command. High stakes situations, divine judgement, stuff like that."

"That sounds interesting."

"I guess so, but it is nice to have a quieter day for a change."

Thea was silent as they walked past the pond and along the stream beyond. What could she say to Micai? She was just a normal Elf, and a young one at that. She'd never even seen a Tilaryn until two days ago, and now she was casually walking with one of the most powerful Tilaryn in all of Raphtova. He ... or was it she ... didn't seem to think it was strange at all.

"Excuse me," Thea ventured, "I hope this isn't a strange question, but are you a he or a she?"

Micai didn't seem to mind. "Tilaryn don't come in male or female. We're just Tilaryn. Procreation isn't a part of our job."

Thea supposed that made sense. She'd never heard of a baby Tilaryn before.

"I guess you could use 'they' if you need a pronoun. Seems a bit more personable than 'it'." Micai gave her a wink.

Thea couldn't help but smile. She knew that she should be careful to show Micai proper deference and respect, but somehow she felt her discomfort melt away, as if she was talking with an old friend.

"Can I ask another question?"

"Try me," Micai grinned.

"The Fallen General is a Tilaryn, right?"

Micai gave her a keen glance. "A Fallen Tilaryn, yes."

"It's just that I always heard the Fallen General called a he, not a they."

Micai examined a stone, then threw it into the stream with a *plonk*. "When the Fallen One rebelled, he rejected a part of who he was. He thought that would make him stronger, but it didn't." Micai stared thoughtfully at the rippling water for a moment. "Separation brings weakness, not strength. That's a good one to remember for later." Micai grinned and continued to walk along the riverbank. "That's one of the best parts of serving the Deity. We get to work together."

Thea's stomach ached and she realized that she was desperately hungry. Getting out her small box of food she looked at Micai. "Would you like a cookie?"

Micai looked at her in surprise. "You have cookies?"

Thea nodded. "Two. Want one?" She held it out.

Micai grinned and took the cookie. "Thanks. You know, I can't think of the last time I had a cookie."

They sat on a couple of boulders and watched the

stream chattering down a small cascade.

Micai's mug appeared again out of nowhere. They took a long swig and held it out to Thea. "Want some?"

Thea didn't dare ask what it was, but took the mug. It was heavy and cold, with beads of condensation dripping down the sides. She took a careful sip and found that the liquid inside was some sort of beer, but better than any beer she had tasted before.

Micai grinned. "Good, isn't it?"

Thea nodded. In comfortable silence, she sat beside Micai, eating her stale cookie and drinking beer. Somehow, it was the best meal she'd ever had.

They were just starting to walk again when Micai cocked an ear, as if listening to something that Thea couldn't hear.

"Allulien needs me for something. Got to go."

Thea felt strangely disappointed. "Oh. Okay."

There was a small breath of wind and Micai disappeared.

Thea stared at the place where Micai had been standing. Around her, untouched wilderness stretched out in every direction. She was alone, but somehow not as alone as she had been before Micai had come.

Thea walked until the light began to fade from the sky, then found another camping spot for the night. After pushing some rocks into a small ring, she collected a few sticks and fallen branches that she could use for firewood. Getting out Svetka's knife and flint, she tried striking a spark. It fizzled and went out.

She tried again. And again.

Finally the leaves caught fire, but the sticks she had found were too large and the tiny flame went out.

Finding some smaller twigs, Thea tried again. This

time she was able to keep the flame alive, and slowly it grew. She fed the small fire with stick after stick, until she realized that everything she'd collected had been used up. Quickly she scrambled to collect more, but before she could return to the fire, it burned out.

Determined not to give up, Thea set out to find more fuel. Searching further afield this time, Thea found an old, rotting stump with a small berry bush growing out of the top. She went closer to investigate. It was a huckleberry bush, and the berries looked ripe. Quickly, Thea ran back to her campsite, grabbed Kseniya's box, and filled it with the small berries.

After she had successfully gotten the fire started, Thea sat beside it and enjoyed her supper of cake and berries. Thankfulness welled up in her heart. She had enough for her meal after all.

Thea woke the next morning with a song running through her mind. She sang it aloud as she went to the stream to wash her face and have a drink.

For days so bright, filled with delight,
We give our thanks and praise.
Each little flower shows your power,
The mystery of your ways.

It was a simple children's song that one of her family's servants had taught her when she was very young. She'd never really thought about the words before, but somehow they seemed to suit her mood that morning.

Returning to her campsite, Thea knelt to check in. Soon she felt the warm brightness that heralded Allulien's presence.

"I liked the song you were singing, Thea."

Thea smiled up at Allulien. "I like it too. It's been a long time since I felt like singing."

Allulien's eyes twinkled. "Hopefully you will find many more reasons to sing as you go."

Thea nodded. "Do you have any instructions for me today?"

"Yes, but first I have a question: when you looked at Davis, what did you see?"

"I saw a spirit that was bright and alive." Thea was silent for a moment, then asked tentatively, "What do you see when you look at him?"

"I see someone with a heart fully given to the Deity—the most beautiful thing there is." Allulien gave a small smile. "Thea, today you will leave the stream you have been following, which would lead you too far to the east. Instead, you will journey directly south."

Uncertainty welled up from the pit of Thea's stomach. "But I don't have any way to carry water with me. How will I drink when I get thirsty?"

Allulien looked at her with a glint of sternness in their expression. "Maybe as you travel today you should keep singing that little song you sang this morning. You could write a second verse for it."

An image of Davis rose in Thea's mind. He wouldn't have been worrying about food and water.

"You will learn as he did," Allulien spoke as if reading her thoughts. "One of the most important lessons is to accept each day as it is given. Worry only makes the road harder."

Allulien disappeared, leaving Thea with her thoughts. After cleaning up her campsite, she took one more drink from the stream and set her face towards the south.

It was a nice day for walking. Allumen shone brightly overhead and a cool breeze rustled through the trees. As she walked she thought about the song she had been singing. Slowly, she found words for another verse:

Day after day you guide my way,
I'll follow where you lead.
East, south, or west, your way is best,
You'll give me what I need.

It wasn't quite right, but Thea sang it again and again, changing the words and the rhymes as she tried to find something she liked better.

Staph was approaching when Thea heard a familiar laugh and Micai stepped out from a grove of trees.

With a smile of delight, Thea hurried to greet them.

Micai nodded at her cheerfully. "Mind some company for a bit?"

"That would be wonderful! I was hoping I'd see you again."

"Well that's good. People aren't always glad when I show up." Micai winked. "You're heading south today, aren't you?"

"Yes, did Allulien tell you? I was worried about not following the stream anymore."

"There's no need to worry about that," Micai reassured her. "There's a really nice spot I know of, just up ahead a bit."

Sure enough, after walking another measure or two, Thea heard a rush of water ahead. Climbing down a gentle slope, they found a small waterfall cascading into a little pool, surrounded by large, shady trees.

Wading into the water, Thea drank deeply, then found a place where she could sit and enjoy the beauty of the scene before her.

Micai looked up at the sky. "It's staph now. Aren't you going to sleep?"

Thea frowned. "I don't know. Allulien told me to travel south today. Doesn't that mean I should keep going?"

Micai laughed. "Allulien wants you to travel south, not kill yourself. Sleep is important. If you don't sleep properly you won't make it very far."

"I guess so."

"Trust me on it. If you needed to push hard because you had to make it there by a certain time, Allulien would tell you that. But you're just travelling. No rush. So you can sleep."

Thea had to admit that she felt very tired. Finding a comfortable spot not far from the waterfall, Thea lay down. She fell asleep as soon as her head touched the ground.

When Thea woke, Micai was sitting nearby. Staph was past, and she had slept through part of restday as well. She sat up and looked at Micai reproachfully. "Why didn't you wake me up?"

Micai shrugged. "You needed the sleep. There's no rush, you know. Workday is for working, and your work right now is walking. Restday is for other things—like finding food and ... you know ... maybe resting?"

Thea frowned. "I won't get very far if I only walk during workday."

"But—" Micai gestured with their large tankard, "you will be able to continue for many more days if you take proper care of yourself."

Thea blinked and reminded herself that this was Micai that she was talking to. Arguing probably wasn't a good idea. "Okay," she conceded, "so now what do I do?"

"I thought we'd start out with some foraging. You're getting a bit hungry, aren't you?"

Thea nodded. All at once her stomach reminded her, urgently, that she hadn't eaten anything all day.

"Alright." Micai stood up. "There are lots of good pickings to be had around here, if you know where to look. See this here? It's wild carrot. The roots are pretty good eating, I've heard. And if we just head this way over to the clearing, I saw some berry bushes earlier ..."

Soon Thea was able to satisfy her hunger, and she and Micai harvested enough berries, roots, and leaves for an evening meal. There were still a few measures left in the day, and Micai suggested that she practice shooting Raybow.

Thea felt embarrassed. "I'm not very good at shooting," she admitted. "I've only been up to the archery range in Lyudmyla a few times."

"Well, practicing sounds like a good idea, then," Micai replied with a cheerful grin.

Thea didn't do as poorly as she thought she would, although Micai's instruction and encouragement certainly helped. After she finally managed to hit the target that Micai had set, she collected her arrows and sat down for a rest. Micai sat beside her, tankard of beer in hand. Overhead, the planet Micai had risen high in the sky and was approaching Allumen for its nightly eclipse.

Thea stared at it thoughtfully. "It's named after you, isn't it?"

Micai nodded and looked up into the sky. "The great protector. Shielding the world from the heat of

Allumen."

Thea looked at the Tilaryn sitting beside her. "You shield the world, don't you? At least, that's what I learned as a child. You fight against evil and protect us."

Micai nodded and looked thoughtfully down into the large tankard.

Thea's gaze returned to the great planet overhead. "Why did we lose the Great War? If you were protecting us, I would've thought we would have won."

Micai looked at her for a moment. "The war isn't over, you know. We're still fighting against the Fallen One. It's just you Elves that think it's over, because you left."

"But ..." Thea struggled to grasp the enormity of the statement, "but the Elves left the war a thousand circles ago! And it's still happening? Why didn't you stop the Elves from leaving?"

Micai shrugged. "That's how the Deity made the world. All the people of Raphtova can choose whether they want to obey the Deity or not, and we aren't allowed to force them. When the Elves decided to retreat to their island and leave the rest of Raphtova to its fate, that was their choice to make."

Thea felt sick. "Didn't that make the Deity angry?"

"I know it made Allulien angry." Micai looked up at the sky with a strange expression. "Have you ever considered why it is that the great protector planet shields the world from the heat of Allumen?"

"I guess it would get too hot." Thea looked at Micai. "And the water would dry up and things would start to die."

Micai's gaze did not flicker. "It is mercy—to shield the world from too much glory. To postpone judgment in hope of repentance."

Thea looked up at the sky. "Allumen is named after Allulien, isn't it?"

"Yes. The keeper of the glory of the Deity."

"And Raphtova is named after Raphea, the Healer."

"Yes. The one who bears the pain of every person living on this moon."

In the sky, the other three moons of Micai were visible, moving toward their conjunction that marked the beginning of a new cycle. "Enk, Kel, and Eli." Thea spoke their names out loud. "Named after Enkeli."

Micai smiled. "Yes. Rushing across the sky, doing the Deity's will."

Thea thought about the stuffy, dead ritual of Enkeli's Temple. She couldn't picture the Keepers of Knowledge rushing anywhere. Well, maybe some of the names of the celestial bodies were more literal than others.

They watched in silence as the massive planet overhead eclipsed Allumen, and green-blue darkness fell across the land.

Micai stood up. "It's time for you to eat your evening meal and go to sleep. You have another day of travel tomorrow."

Thea nodded, and Micai disappeared.

Lost in thought, Thea wandered back to her campsite beside the waterfall. Without making a fire, she ate her fill of the food that she and Micai had foraged, then wrapped herself in her cloak and fell asleep.

Gradually, Thea's life fell into a sort of rhythm. She woke up every morning and checked in. On most days, Allulien appeared and gave her the directions for her day's travel. Every day she walked until staph, when she would find somewhere to rest. After staph she spent time foraging and practiced shooting Raybow. Despite her best efforts, she hadn't succeeded in hunting yet, but every day she found some berries or wild greens that she recognized—just enough to not go hungry, but never any extra.

Almost every day, Micai appeared and walked with her for a while. Sometimes it was just for a measure or two, but sometimes they stayed almost all day, helping her with her foraging and archery practice. They talked a lot, and Thea was grateful for the company.

Once, Micai shot a couple of rabbits and showed her how to skin and cook them. They shared the evening meal that day, passing the tankard of beer back and forth as they sat by the fire.

Another night, Thea woke to the howling of wolves. Alarmed, she started to get up, but then she saw Micai sitting by her small fire, a spear held loosely in their hand.

Micai noticed her gaze. "Don't worry. I'm here."

Thea smiled and lay down again.

The next day as she was walking with Micai, she asked something that had been puzzling her for a while. "Why have you been spending so much time with me? I mean, I enjoy it, but don't you have other, more important things to do? You said that the war is still going on."

Micai looked thoughtful. "It's true that there is a lot going on. There always is. But I don't do all the protecting by myself, you know. That's why there's a whole company of Tilaryn under my command, as well as the humans and others who have decided to enlist. It takes the whole team, and we could always use more hands. But you know what they say about delegation—pass along the boring jobs, not the ones you want to do."

Thea grinned.

The days were getting warmer. Thea was glad when it was staph and they could take shelter from the heat. She woke from her sleep to find that Micai had shot a couple of rabbits and was preparing them beside a lively campfire.

Thoughtfully, Thea spread out the oilskin and sat on it. It had a small image of a raven stitched on the shoulder. Unpinning Roland's brooch, she turned it over in her hands. "I wonder how he's doing." She looked up at Micai. "You know a lot, don't you? Do you know if Roland is doing alright?"

Micai looked up from the fire. "Roland? Oh, I'm sure he's doing quite well."

Thea thought she caught a twinkle in Micai's eyes. "Do you know that for sure?" When Micai didn't respond she looked back down at the brooch. "Sometimes I wonder if I should've asked him to come with me."

"There's not much point worrying over what could have been," Micai mused, poking at the meat with Thea's knife. "If it was very important, Allulien would have told you to take him."

Thea frowned. "Is it always obvious what the Deity wants you to do? I feel like it should be, but then I think about the way that the Elves left the war and I wonder if they knew that was wrong. It's hard to imagine that someone would disobey the Deity on purpose."

"Is it really that hard to imagine?" Micai gave her a curious look. "Raphtova is full of people who disobey the Deity. They lie and cheat and steal. They hoard food and wealth while others die from not having food or shelter. There are some—and not a few—who willingly serve the Fallen One, killing innocent people, spreading lies about the Deity's goodness and power, and trying to bring all of Raphtova under the shadow of evil, once and for all."

"And you let them do that? Aren't you supposed to be the one who brings judgment and protects the world from evil?"

Micai's eyes flashed. "Do not wish for judgment! How do you think your own people will fare when judgment comes, when they have turned away from the service of the Deity, worshipping books and scrolls rather than the Giver of Wisdom? Judgment knows no partiality. When it comes, it comes upon everyone in its path, and first of all on those who call for it. You cannot call for judgment and escape from that judgment yourself." Micai looked down at the tankard they so often carried and spoke in a low voice. "Don't ask for judgement. Ask for mercy. Because one day the only mercy available will be judgment."

Silence hung over the small clearing.

"I'm sorry, I didn't ..." Thea stammered, but the words died in her throat.

Micai stared into the fire, a haggard expression in their eyes. "I had to banish a full third of my own kin, never to return home again. Many of them died by my hand. I longed to show mercy, but the time for judgment had come." Micai sighed. "Perhaps within that judgment was its own kind of mercy." Micai's heavy gaze turned to Thea. "One day you will be required to carry out the judgment of the Deity. Then you will understand."

Thea sat in silence for a long time.

"What I don't understand," she said finally, "is what happens to the people who can't obey the Deity. Khariton told me that when Elves get old we can't serve the Deity anymore, because we get too slow and forget to check in. But that doesn't make sense. Why would the Deity make us unable to obey? That wouldn't be our fault then, would it?"

Micai gave her a sidelong glance. "I don't think I am the right one to answer that question. Maybe tomorrow you will have a chance to ask someone else."

They ate their meal, and the rest of the day passed in silence, each lost in their own thoughts. When evening came, Thea wrapped herself in her cloak and lay down, but Micai continued to sit and stare at the embers of the fire, bathed in the blue-green glow of the planet that filled the sky.

The next day the land that Thea passed through was rocky and rough. She scrambled across boulder fields and waded through tiny streams that poured in cataracts over the rocks.

Not all of the rocks underfoot were steady. Thea lost her balance several times, and once when the rock beneath her feet shifted unexpectedly, she stumbled and fell, scraping her arm against the sharp, jagged rocks.

Struggling back to her feet, Thea looked at the long, jagged cut and the blood dripping down her arm. She didn't have any bandages. What should she do? After washing it in a stream the bleeding stopped, but her arm throbbed quite badly. With a sigh she carried on walking. That was the one thing she knew she needed to do. Eventually her arm would stop hurting.

Workday stretched by, but Micai still hadn't come. What if they didn't come at all?

Thea stumbled on. Passing a large boulder, she saw someone waiting at the side of the narrow deer path. It was a Tilaryn, but not Allulien or Micai. This Tilaryn wore robes as white as light and had a face with a stern, thoughtful expression. Thea recognized the face from the murals in Enkeli's Temple. This was Raphea, the Healer.

The realization was followed closely by another: whoever had created those murals in the Temple had depicted the Generals with such accuracy that she could recognize them by their appearance. She couldn't imagine any Elves knowing the Generals that well.

Raphea watched her as she approached. "Greetings, Thea. I believe that you had a question for me. I would be glad to walk with you for a while."

"Thank you." Thea looked at Raphea with incredulous awe. It still seemed strange to her that such powerful beings would be interested in talking with her.

They walked in silence for a while. The scrape on Thea's arm throbbed, but she tried to ignore it. Somehow Raphea's presence demanded silent respect more than Micai's did.

Finally Raphea spoke. "You want to understand why the Elves are the way that they are, and you worry that it seems impossible for an Elf to live in lifelong obedience to the Deity."

Thea nodded.

"The answer is that for every strength there is a weakness. The Elves have been given many good and useful abilities, and your endless lifespan allows you to achieve great learning and skill in those abilities you possess. The danger of such a long lifespan, however, is that if you are not careful, time begins to blur and lose its meaning. The secrets of elf-sight become more interesting than the living people beside you, and certainly more interesting than the lives of those far away across the sea."

Raphea stopped and looked into the distance. "Every race of Raphtova has its own strengths and weaknesses. If they use their strengths to help others and heal the hurts of the world, then they are following the will of the Deity. If they use their strengths only for their own benefit, or through their weaknesses add to the hurt and brokenness in the world, then they have turned away from the will of the Deity."

"But if the Elves were created to slow down, how can they be blamed for that?"

"Elves do not slow. In fact their minds and bodies increase in speed as they age, which is what allows them to use their elf-sight with such depth and precision. The danger in this gift is seen when an Elf refuses the discipline to slow their mind to the speed of the world around them. Lost within their minds, they lock themselves out of the world they were created to inhabit, neglecting the service of the Deity and the care of the people of Raphtova. In this, the Elves have no one to blame but themselves."

The pronouncement of guilt landed heavily in Thea's spirit. "So the Elves have failed."

"Not all of them." Raphea turned a keen glance on Thea.

Thea felt very self-conscious beneath that glance.

"But I am only one Elf! What difference can that make? I can't change my people or make up for everything they have lost. I couldn't even get Khariton to listen to me!"

"Khariton does not listen to anyone, so you are hardly unique in that respect." Raphea's eyes flickered with an expression that might have been amusement, if such a stern face could ever seem amused. Thea felt absolutely bewildered.

"Who can ever tell the difference that one person can make?" Raphea spoke with a thoughtful expression. "Nothing is impossible. Even so, you are not the only Elf in the service of the Deity. There are others. Some of them are asleep and some are awake, but you are certainly not the only one. Does that answer your question?"

"I ... I think so."

Raphea looked down at Thea. "You are hurt," they said in a matter of fact voice.

Thea glanced at the cut on her arm. She had forgotten about it, but now the wound began to throb again.

Raphea reached out a hand and touched it. Thea watched the red line on her arm fade and disappear without a trace. The throbbing pain was gone. She looked up at Raphea and saw a flicker of pain pass through their eyes. On their arm a bloody cut appeared, just the same as Thea's had been. Then it faded and disappeared.

"That is what it means to heal the hurts of the world," Raphea said in a solemn voice.

We could not pay the cost anymore.

Khariton's words echoed in Thea's mind. Her people had decided that caring for Raphtova was not worth the pain, and they had withdrawn into themselves. No wonder their spirits were dead.

Raphea walked on and Thea followed, a new question burning in her mind.

"If Elves weren't made to slow down, how can it be avoided? I've never known anyone who didn't become slow—or as you said, too fast and lost in their mind."

"The Deity has not asked an impossible thing of your people, Thea. Your own bodies were made to tell the passing of time. Have you ever wondered how it is that an Elf can be in vidlas for a hundred circles or more, yet not die from starvation? It is true that to sit like a stone does not take much nutrition, but it does take some. The mosslike hair of the Elves receives energy from the light of Allumen, even as the plants do, and if you are properly attuned to it you can recognize the coming and going of Allumen's light, even when in deepest thought."

Thea's eyes widened. That was why an Elf's hair grew to cover more of their bodies, the longer they were in vidlas! It made so much sense. And of course, Elvish homes were made with massive windows, especially in the places where older Elves lived.

"So Elves can learn to know when it's time to check in? All by themselves?"

"Yes, they can."

Thea gave a wry smile. She couldn't wait to tell Khariton about that! He would grumble to no end. She ran her hand absentmindedly through her hair. "You said elf-sight is a gift, but it can take days or even cycles for an Elf to really study something. How can we use our gift properly if we're not allowed to?"

"Study is not the problem, but a lack of care for

anything but your own interest. A skilled Elf may take two or three days to locate a tumour in a hospital patient, but that is not a selfish thing to do. In fact it would be within the will of the Deity for them to do so. And for those who are required to check in every morning, a leave of absence may be granted for a time, in order to complete the Deity's objectives."

Relief flooded over Thea. It all made so much sense. The only thing she couldn't understand was how the Elves had missed the truth for so long.

"There is always a way to obey the Deity," Raphea spoke as if in response to her thoughts. "Sometimes you just need to ask what it is."

They walked for a while in silence before Raphea spoke again.

"It is also important for you to understand that you do not have to disappear into the state that you call vidlas to be able to use your elf-sight. With sufficient training, you can access your gift while walking and talking in the normal, slow world. This skill will be very useful for you in the days to come. I suggest that you practice it."

Thea nodded.

"I must leave you now." Raphea turned to her with a keen expression. "I am needed elsewhere. Continue to be diligent, and you will do well."

"Thank you," Thea replied, and Raphea disappeared. Once again Thea was alone, but she had a lot to think about.

The next day, Micai joined her again. Thea greeted them with joy, and they spent most of the day together.

The next few days were much more normal, at least

what Thea had come to see as normal. Micai came and went, and Allulien appeared every morning to guide her on her way.

There was one question lingering in Thea's mind, though, and one day she worked up the courage to ask Micai about it.

"Why did the Elves leave the war?" Thea glanced at Micai, but they were not looking in her direction. "You were there, weren't you? Do you know why they left?"

Micai was silent for a moment. "They left because it was war." Micai stared into the distance, as if seeing something that Thea couldn't. "Have you ever had to tell a child that their mother or their father is never coming home? Or have you stood beside a parent as they weep over their children who will never return? Have you heard the screams of those whose bodies have been torn apart, begging for death because the pain is too great?" Micai's eyes were dark. "You hear of your people's disobedience and it disgusts you. Would you cast judgment upon them?"

As Micai spoke, images flashed before Thea's eyes: swords and shields stained with blood. Monsters and horrible creatures tearing flesh with razorlike fangs and claws. Tilaryn swinging mighty swords, felling countless numbers with each stroke. Elves, humans, and other creatures running, cowering, crawling, fighting—against each other, against the monsters, against their own people.

She felt it—the visceral fear, the anguish, the screams and cries. People were dying. Death was so utterly foreign to her—Elves didn't die! But she saw them die now, saw the despair in the eyes of those who struggled on. And for one dreadful moment, she caught a glimpse of a dark and terrible Tilaryn, from whom all of the destruction and death came forth.

The vision faded and Thea found that she was on her knees. Tears streamed down her face.

Micai was kneeling beside her. They looked at her with eyes more gentle than any Thea had ever seen. "Yes, they disobeyed, and disobedience is always wrong. But perhaps you can offer them compassion. And mercy." Micai looked into the distance. "I shielded you from the worst of it. No one should have to see what they saw."

Thea felt numb. "And this war ... it's still going on?"

"The Fallen One's hold on this land runs deep, and many choose to serve him rather than face his wrath. The resistance is small, but valiant. Davis, the human you met, is a part of it. They fight on, in quiet, secret ways, but one day the war will rage loud again. We are doing all we can to be ready."

"Can't the Deity just win, and defeat the Fallen One for good?"

She saw the look in Micai's eyes and knew the answer.

"It's mercy, isn't it?"

Micai nodded. "Yes. Mercy."

The next morning Thea awoke to find Allulien waiting for her. Thea scrambled to her feet in surprise. Had she slept in? No, Allumen had only just left its nightly eclipse, and an early mist hung in the air.

"It is time, Thea." Allulien spoke in a voice that shook the ground. "There is someone I would like you to meet."

As Allulien spoke, the mists closed in around them

and began to glow with a bright yellow light.

The mists dissolved, and Thea was no longer standing in a forest. All around her was a large, open space, filled with Tilaryn, stronger and more terrifying than anything she had seen before. Every Tilaryn shone with a bright inner light as they moved about their business, unconcerned with Thea's presence. Overhead, even more Tilaryn passed by, flying with large, powerful wings.

There was a loud screech and a large, golden-feathered Griffin swooped overhead, beat its glistening wings, and soared out of sight.

In front of Thea, a path opened. She walked forward through the glittering hosts until her eyes were completely dazzled by the brightness. As she walked, she realized that the Tilaryn around her were singing—a song so heartbreakingly joyful that it made her want to laugh and cry and dance and sing all at the same time.

Then the Tilaryn hosts before her drew aside and she saw a throne, large and magnificent, and on the throne sat a being so beautiful and bright that Thea could hardly bear to look. Her knees buckled beneath her and she fell to the ground.

"Thea Kirisensk." The One on the Throne spoke her name.

Thea looked up. The One on the Throne was looking at her with an expression of love and deep gladness like she had never seen before.

"Rise."

Thea felt herself lifted as if by unseen hands, and set on her feet once again.

Silence fell, and Thea felt horribly self-conscious. What was she supposed to do? Glancing around, she saw that beside the throne was a great Tilaryn, more powerful and terrible than any Thea had seen thus far. As Thea looked, her mouth fell open. It was Allulien, but Allulien unlike she had ever seen them before, shining as strong and bright as Allumen in the sky.

Next to Allulien stood Micai, terrible and powerful, a sword of pure light unsheathed in their hand. There was no doubt now that Micai held the power to strike down a host of Tilaryn with a single word. Power and strength radiated from them, a power that had been veiled before, but was now fully displayed. Thea could hardly believe that such a being would ever have sat with her by a fire and shared a mug of beer, and yet she knew beyond a doubt that it was true.

Beyond Micai stood Raphea, stern and magnificent, bearing on their body countless scars that shone like fire. Beyond, there was another great Tilaryn, but the One on the Throne spoke again, and Thea forgot about everything else.

"Thea Kirisensk. Many days ago you entered my service, and have been found faithful in doing so. Your name has been put forward by my Generals to take a position in the war against the Fallen One. Do you accept this charge?"

Thea's mind raced as she stared at the glory before her. How long had it been since any Elf stood here? Her people had failed in their service to the Deity, but now Thea knew that she could choose nothing else. She must give her life, or die within as surely as the countless dead spirits she had seen on the streets of Lyudmyla. There would be at least one Elf who would be faithful.

"I will," Thea replied, and the universe went dark.

Chapter Six

When Thea awoke, she was lying in a small clearing in the forest. Her cloak was spread over her like a blanket, and nearby a small campfire crackled cheerfully.

She sat up and looked around. Apart from herself, the clearing was empty. The light of Allumen in the sky showed that it was early morning. Was it the next day, or had no time passed at all? Thea was surprised to find that she felt neither hungry nor thirsty.

Kneeling by the small fire, she checked in for the day. Allulien did not appear, but Thea felt, rather than heard, a quiet voice in her heart say *continue south-east*.

Thea walked until staph, but Micai did not come to walk with her. Finding a shady resting place near a river, she took refuge from the heat of the day and slept.

When she awoke, she set about foraging for her supper. She searched the area, but couldn't find any berries or other plants that she recognized as edible.

Striking out further from her campsite, Thea continued to search, but her efforts proved unsuccessful. Restday passed, and she searched further and further afield, but she couldn't find anything to eat.

The light in the sky was fading, and Thea had turned to walk back to her campsite, when she caught a small movement out of the corner of her eye. It was a partridge. Slowly, she unclipped Raybow from her baldric and fitted an arrow to the string. The partridge stood, motionless. Thea pulled back the bowstring and shot.

She expected a flurry of feathers as the bird flew away. Instead, there was silence. Surprised, she crept closer, and there lay the partridge, with the arrow through its chest. She had hit it! Gingerly, she picked it up. It was dead.

A strange hollow feeling ached in her chest as she stared at the dead bird in her hands. Kneeling there in the shadowy clearing, Thea whispered, "Thank you, Deity, for this bird that died so I can eat."

Bringing the partridge back to her camp, Thea set it on the ground and looked at it critically. Now what? She would have to pull the feathers off, wouldn't she? That turned out to be much more difficult than she expected, but finally the bird was plucked. At least, plucked well enough. Thea frowned. She had the distinct impression that there were certain parts on the inside of the bird that shouldn't still be inside when she cooked it. With some misgiving, Thea pulled out her knife and got to work.

It was well after dark when the partridge was finally cooking over the fire. Thankfully it was a clear night, and Thea could see well enough to make her way down to the nearby river to wash herself and her clothes.

Her meal was very late that night, but Thea smiled as she ate by her little fire. She couldn't wait to tell Micai about her first successful hunt—

A shiver ran down her spine. It was hard to think about Micai in the same way, after what she had seen in the Throne Room. For the first time since she left home, she felt a longing for normal, Elvish friends, who didn't have the power to smite you with a single glance.

How long had it been since she left? She looked up at the moons in the sky and mentally calculated. It was twenty-six days since she crossed the sea on the Raven and her journey had begun. Almost a whole cycle. How were Roland and Svetka doing now?

Putting the leftovers of her meal in her food box, Thea curled up to sleep. It wasn't very often that she had food left over at the end of the day. She smiled as she closed her eyes. It was nice not to wonder where her breakfast would come from tomorrow.

A strange sound startled Thea into wakefulness. It was morning, and something was scuffling around her campsite. She sat up and was blinded by a sudden flurry of black wings. The creatures—they seemed to be the wrong shape for birds—disappeared into the foliage above Thea's head. She blinked and looked down. Fragments of her food box were strewn all around her campsite, and her bag was gone.

Thea scrambled to her feet. Had the creatures carried it off? No—there it was behind a tree, with the hind end of a black, fox-sized creature sticking out of it, but instead of a tail it had ... feathers? Hearing her approach, the creature wriggled its way backwards out the bag and turned to look at her. Its head looked like a fox, but it had a beak instead of a snout, and it stared at her with small, beady eyes. Svetka's compass was clamped firmly in its beak.

"Hey! Drop that!" Thea shouted and waved her arms.

The creature unfolded its black wings and flew up into the treetops, taking the compass with it.

"Hey!" Thea yelled, "give that back!"

There was a flurry of rustling and cawing in the branches overhead, then silence.

Thea craned her neck to spot the strange creatures. She had never heard of anything like them—and they'd stolen her compass!

Partridge bones crunched under her feet, scattered amongst the fragments of her food box. Once again she didn't know where she would find her food for the day.

With a sigh, Thea picked up her empty bag. Thankfully Raybow was alright, and she kept her knife on her belt.

Leaving her campsite behind, Thea found a clean patch of ground and knelt for her daily check in.

Allulien was silent.

Thea waited, but as the silence stretched on and on, she reluctantly rose to her feet. It was time to continue with her day. The river nearby came more or less from the south-east, so she would follow it. At least she wouldn't have to worry about finding water.

Workday was almost past, and Thea was starting to look for her next campsite, when she noticed something strange: a pillar of stone rising out of the river bank.

Moving closer, Thea ran her hand along its smooth surface. It was almost as tall as she was. Looking across the river, she could just see another pillar, almost exactly like the first. They looked as if they had been made long ago, and embedded firmly in the ground. But why? She hadn't seen any sign of civilization since she left the coastal path so long ago. Was she finally getting close to Gedwyld?

Thea continued along the riverbank. What was that

there? A crumbling stone wall, almost entirely covered in ivy. Fascinated, she followed the wall away from the river until it disappeared in the forest. There she found another wall, in better repair than the first. She followed it to the foot of a small hill.

Was that something on top of the hill? Thea scrambled up and found another pillar, larger than the ones by the river. The light of Allumen gleamed off a large lake, not far to the south. At the foot of the hill she could see a stone house, crumbled with age. Beyond it were more houses. And more houses. All of the plain between the hill and the lake was filled with the ruins of a great city—crumbling walls, half-fallen arches, roads cracked and buried in ancient rubble.

Silence hung in the air, broken only by the hissing of the wind.

What was this place? It was clearly uninhabited. Even the birdsong and scurrying of small creatures had faded away. The only movement was the gentle motion of trailing vines and dead grasses blowing in the wind.

Carefully, Thea walked down the hill and into the ruined city.

The ruins were larger than they appeared from above. The broken arches soared above her head. The doorways that were still standing were large enough for her to step through, and she explored several of the houses with interest, but the passage of time had obscured all signs of the kind of people who had once lived there.

All through staph and into restday, Thea wandered the ancient streets, almost in a trance. How long had it been since someone else had walked there? The ancient cobblestones were worn and smooth. Through age, or because of constant use so long ago? Her footsteps echoed among the half-standing walls and dark hollows where partial roofs were still intact. It felt like walking into the past.

Finally she approached the shore of the lake and found the buildings there to be larger and even more interesting than the others had been. Carvings and colourful mosaics, worn by the elements, could still be seen on the crumbling walls. Rows of stone seating indicated some kind of ancient theatre, now open to the sky. Stone fountains stood dry in the midst of tumbled down courtyards, and staircases wound up into nothingness.

On the front of a large, flat stone, Thea found engravings that looked like letters. Brushing the lichen away, she knelt on the dusty ground and tried to read it.

Enzhelika. The word sounded familiar. Where had she heard it before?

Enzhelika, named in honour of Enkeli.

Why, that had been the name of the Elvish capital city before the name was changed to Lyudmyla. Or at least, that had been her understanding of the history. Was it possible that the capital city used to be somewhere else entirely? Had this city once been the capital of the Elves?

She stood up and looked around. If this city had once been full of Elves, what had happened to them? Had the city been destroyed in the Great War? It did not look like a city that had seen war. It looked as if it had been deserted, then worn down by the passage of time.

In her heart she knew the truth that she had never been told: the Elves had abandoned it, long ago, when they left for the safety of their island, never to return.

Thea stared around at the ancient city, still magnificent even in its ruin. The pain of what was lost ached in her heart with an unbearable sadness. The Elves used to live in the Dark Lands. How many other cities were there, abandoned or ruined by war, forgotten by those who were forced to leave them behind?

A sound of movement caught Thea's ear. Startled, she looked around. Were those footsteps? How was that possible?

Around the corner of the ancient building, walked an Elf.

Thea stared. The Elf was female and completely naked. Not that that was entirely unusual—among the Elves, clothes were more of a fashion accessory than a necessity—but what was an Elf doing here, in this ruined city?

Thea's mouth hung open. "Who are you?"

The Elf gave her a suspicious glance. "I was about to ask you the same question."

Thea swallowed. "I'm Thea. Are you one of the Elves who used to live here? Is this still your home?"

The Elf glared. Her eyes were blood red and very strange. Thea had known several Elves with ruby eyes and a couple with garnet eyes, but this Elf's eyes didn't look like gemstones at all. "This is not my home," the Elf said with some distaste. "I am merely passing through."

"Are you from Svokye?" Thea asked with sudden misgiving. She had assumed that all danger of pursuit had passed long ago.

The Elf snorted. "I am not *from* anywhere. The land is my home and I sleep where I wish."

"You don't have a home? Was it destroyed in the Great War?"

"War?" The Elf looked deeply suspicious. "What do you mean?"

Thea felt a sudden misgiving. "The war between the Fallen One and the servants of the Deity. There is a war going on, isn't there?"

"I do not know about a war," the Elf said in an icy voice.

Thea couldn't shake the feeling that there was something very strange about this Elf, not to mention her presence in a place where Elves hadn't lived for a thousand circles or more. "You said you are passing through. Where are you going?"

"That does not matter. I am the guardian of these lands and I go where I wish."

"You're the guardian of these lands? Do you know the way to Gedwyld?"

"Gedwyld?" The Elf looked surprised. "That place is far from here. Why do you seek it?"

"I am looking for Davis, and I heard he was going there."

The Elf gave her a keen look. "Davis the Bard? I am familiar with that human."

"You are?" Thea's eyes lit up. "Isn't he wonderful? My General is sending me to learn from him."

The Elf did not appear to share her enthusiasm. "That is a long journey just to study beneath a bard. I know several others who live closer."

Thea gasped in delight. "There are others like Davis? I hoped there was! There is no one like him on Larsya."

"Larsya?"

"It's the Island of the Elves. Don't you know? Or have

you never been there?"

The Elf shrugged. "I had never seen an Elf before this day. I know of them, as one of the five peoples of Raphtova, but most of my interactions are with the humans, when I can't avoid them."

"But ... you *are* an Elf."

The Elf just stared at her with those strange red eyes. They were not Elf eyes.

Thea swallowed. "What are you?"

The not-Elf shook her head, as if Thea's lack of understanding was a nuisance that she often had to put up with. Turning, she walked away.

"Wait!" Thea hurried after her. "You said you know where Gedwyld is. Are you going that way? Or can you point me in the right direction? I had a compass, but these black crow foxes took it and now I'm not sure how to find my way ..."

The stranger stopped and looked at her with an amused expression. "You never met a crox before?"

"We don't have any on Larsya, and I've never really travelled before."

The stranger looked aghast. "You've never travelled before and you're going all the way to Gedwyld?"

Thea's heart twinged with misgiving. "How far is it?"

The stranger looked her up and down. "On two legs like that, it would probably take you two cycles or more."

Thea did her best to conceal her dismay. Another sixty days at least? How was she going to make it that far?

The stranger cocked her head. "You're just a pup, aren't you?

Thea straightened her shoulders. "I may be young,

but I am a servant of the Deity. Allulien has promised to guide me to my destination."

The stranger didn't seem to be impressed. "I will show you the way. Follow."

She walked at a very fast pace. By the time they reached the edge of the ancient city, Thea was hot and out of breath. The stranger turned to her in a businesslike manner.

"You see this lake? Follow along the shore until you reach a large river that feeds it on the far side. Follow the river to its source in the mountains. On the far side of those mountains there is a deep inlet from the sea. At the root of the inlet is a small town and from there you can find a road to Gedwyld." Turning, she walked away.

"Wait!" Thea called, but the stranger stepped into the forest and disappeared.

Thea tried to follow, but there was no sign of the Elf. The Elf who wasn't an Elf.

Bewildered, Thea returned to the lake. Night was approaching, but she didn't relish the thought of sleeping so close to the ruined city.

Trying to push her hunger from her mind, Thea followed the shore of the lake until the light had faded from the sky. Nearly collapsing from weariness, she curled up amongst the roots of a gnarled oak tree and fell asleep.

Thea woke the next morning with one thought impressed upon her mind: she was hungry. But first she had to check in. Thea knelt and waited.

There was nothing but silence.

Worry rose in Thea's mind. If Allulien didn't speak to her, how would she know what to do?

Continue south-east. That was the last that she'd heard from her General. From what she could see, following the strange Elf's instructions would take her roughly south-east. Apparently that was the way to Gedwyld, and to Gedwyld she had to go.

Thea sighed and got to her feet. She would follow the strange Elf's instructions, at least until Allulien told her what else to do.

It was nice travelling along the shore of the lake. A lively breeze chased ripples across the surface of the water and rustled the branches overhead. She did her best to ignore her hunger as she walked along.

Occasionally she passed another stone wall, overgrown and crumbling with age. Behind one of these she caught sight of what appeared to be fruit trees—wild and unkept. Climbing over the wall, Thea went to investigate. It seemed to be the remains of an orchard, long abandoned. Small green fruits were barely visible beneath the dense foliage. There were apples, small and hard, and plums and pears. None of them were ripe yet, but the plums and pears were matured enough to at least be partially edible. Gratefully, Thea satisfied her hunger and picked enough to fill her small bag.

As staph approached, Thea reached the edge of the forest. Beyond, low hills covered in scrubland and heather stretched as far as she could see. She stopped and rested there, tucked under the edge of the forest. As evening approached, she heard the howling of wolves in the distance.

For the next span of days, Thea walked along the shore of the lake. The hottest time of the Great Heat had come. The air was still and oppressively warm without the shade of trees overhead. She tried wading along the shallows at the shore of the lake for a while. That provided some relief from the heat, but it made her progress much slower than she wanted it to be. There was also something about the black murky depths beyond her sight that made her nervous. She didn't wade through the lake again.

Ever since Thea's experience in the presence of the Deity, Micai had not come to walk with her. It lingered in her mind, like something that wasn't quite right. Micai used to join her almost every day. Why not anymore?

As Thea walked on and on, a dull weariness settled over her spirit. She bitterly missed Micai's company. Anything would have been a welcome change from the dull monotony of walking by herself, day after day, with the endless scrublands on one side and the endless lake on the other. The only company she ever had was a group of crox, which followed her for a while, only venturing near when they saw that she had something to eat.

Food was harder to find now. Some days she was unable to forage or hunt anything and had to go to sleep hungry. Sometimes she woke at night to the sound of wolves in the distance or some kind of large creature scuffling nearby, and she longed for Micai's reassuring presence.

One night she woke to see animal eyes staring at her, glinting red in the firelight. Whatever kind of creature it was was lost to the darkness, but it was large. She shifted slightly, and a low growl rumbled through the shadows. Wolves howled in the distance and Thea shivered. After a long time, the eyes faded into the darkness, but Thea had a hard time falling back asleep.

The next day as she walked she caught a flash of movement out of the corner of her eye. She turned, but couldn't see anything.

A little while later, another movement caught her eye. Nothing seemed to be there, but a chill crept down her spine. It felt like something was watching her.

A few steps later, a branch rustled in the distance. Thea's heart began to race. Was something following her? Whatever it was, it didn't show itself. Glancing over her shoulder, she forced herself to carry on.

Something tugged at her clothes. Blackberry canes. Gingerly, she tried to untangle herself.

A few berries still showed among the brown, curling leaves. They were small and dry, but she hadn't found anything to eat all day. Quickly, she set about picking and eating all that she could reach.

A movement caught her gaze.

Out of the shadows beneath the trees, a grey wolf emerged, stalking closer on silent paws.

Thea stared. Another wolf slunk out of the shadows at her side. A third bared its teeth and crouched as if to spring.

Thea stepped back, berry canes snagging at her clothes.

A low, rumbling growl rose from the wolves as they advanced towards her.

Thea snatched Raybow off her baldric. With shaking hands, she tried to put an arrow to the string.

A tawny blur shot out from the undergrowth, passed in front of Thea, and launched itself directly at the largest of the wolves. The wolf and its attacker tumbled over each other, righted themselves, and wheeled to face their opponent.

The wolf and the cougar watched each other with flattened ears and fur bristling. The cougar crouched low to the ground and hissed. The alpha wolf bared its teeth and growled. The other two wolves crouched, waiting for an opportunity to strike.

The cougar made a swipe with its claws, barely missing the wolf's snout. The wolf snarled, and the cougar hissed menacingly.

They stared at each other for a long moment, then the wolf backed down. Eyeing the cougar distrustfully, the wolves turned and slunk into the shadows.

The cougar lashed its tail and paced for a while longer, watching its enemies depart. Then it turned towards Thea and stared at her with blood-red eyes.

Thea had seen those eyes before.

As Thea watched, the cougar changed and morphed before her eyes into the figure of a female Elf who stood, glaring at her.

Thea watched in amazement. She had heard about shapeshifting spirits that lived in the forest. They were one of the five races of Raphtova. "You're a Dryad!"

The Dryad looked at her with an unimpressed stare. "You are very fortunate that you are not dead right now."

"Thank you for chasing them away." Thea swallowed. "I'm sorry. I never met a Dryad before."

"You never *realized* you met a Dryad before. We seldom announce our presence."

Thea frowned. That might be true, but she suspected that there were no Dryads on Larsya. The news would have gotten around eventually, and everyone would have been talking about it.

"I have been following you for several days now." The Dryad scanned the surrounding trees with a keen gaze. "These lands are not safe and I doubted your ability to fend for yourself. It appears that I was right."

"My General is looking after me," Thea replied, somewhat defensively. She wondered, though, what would have happened if the Dryad had not been watching her. "Maybe my General was protecting me through your presence."

The Dryad snorted. "No one told me to stand guard but myself. As much as I sometimes wish to, I cannot leave the helpless and stupid to their fate. Dryads are the guardians and I cannot renounce my nature." The Dryad gave Thea a cold stare. "I will take you as far as the road."

Thea looked at the Dryad in surprise. "You will? I mean, that is very kind of you, but if you don't want to—"

"Do I have a choice? You will go to your death if you attempt the journey on your own, and if I must follow you I may as well show you the shortest route and be through with the task sooner."

Thea blinked. "You are very kind."

"I am not kind." Hard steel glinted behind the Dryad's eyes. She turned and walked away. "Come."

Thea hurried after her. "If I am to travel with you, could I have your name, please?"

The Dryad didn't look back. "Some call me 'Death on the Night Wind'. That would do."

Death on the Night Wind? Thea frowned. "Do people ever shorten it to something?"

The Dryad turned to look at her. "People do not usually call me anything." She seemed to think for a moment. "If you prefer short names you could call me as the wolves do," she pulled back her lips and bared her teeth, "Arl."

"Arl?" Thea tried to say it the way the Dryad had. It sounded more like an animal snarl than a name.

The Dryad nodded and resumed walking. Thea hurried after her.

She followed Arl until the light of Allumen began to fade.

Arl turned to her abruptly. "You will sleep here tonight." Transforming into an owl, Arl flew up to a branch on a straggly tree and stared at her.

Uneasily, Thea wrapped herself in her cloak and lay down. In the sky overhead, the three moons moved towards their conjunction. It was the start of a new cycle. She couldn't help but think of the last time she watched the conjunction, sitting and sharing beer with Micai. She missed Micai's friendly smile and reassuring presence.

Overhead, Arl stared at the shadowy world with unblinking eyes, silhouetted against the light of the blue-green planet. It was a long time before Thea fell asleep.

Chapter Seven

When Thea woke the next morning, Arl was nowhere to be seen. After looking around for a moment or two, Thea knelt to check in.

Once again, Allulien was silent.

A feeling of movement in the air made Thea look up.

Arl stood behind her with an impatient gleam in her eyes. "It is time to proceed. Follow me."

Thea grabbed her things and followed. It had been so long since Allulien had said anything at all.

Arl walked at a fast pace that Thea found hard to keep up. Soon she was lagging behind, and Arl had to come back and find her. This happened again and again until finally Arl turned to her with unconcealed frustration.

"I will change forms into something that walks at the pace you seem to prefer. I will not be able to speak your language, but if you speak my name I will change back into Elf form so that we can converse."

Without waiting for a reply, Arl shifted into a shorter creature, with a humanlike upper body and legs like a goat. Thea knew it must be the shape of a Faun, though she had only heard about them in stories.

Arl continued walking and Thea followed, but it was much easier to keep up now.

Thea watched Arl's Faun-shape with interest. There were five races of people in Raphtova, she knew.

Humans and Elves were two of them. Now she had met a Dryad and seen what a Faun looked like. The only other race was the Minathrils, or Half-Dragons. She wondered if Arl could turn into one of those as well.

Thea had to admit to herself that Arl didn't seem like the kind of person who served the Deity. She was so harsh and uncaring. But then, she was going out of her way to protect Thea, so who could say for sure?

Slowly, Thea allowed her spirit sight to take over her senses. She knew what to expect, though that did not make it any easier to see. There was no light of the Deity in Arl's spirit.

A sharp voice jolted her to her senses. Arl the Faun was glaring at her. Whatever she had said was probably the equivalent of "keep up you idiot" in the Faun language. Thea sighed and kept walking.

Arl wasn't interested in conversation, so Thea had a lot of time to think. Raphea had told her it was possible to use her elf-sight without entering vidlas. How hard would that be? As she walked behind Arl, Thea tried to maintain her spirit sight without slacking her pace. It was difficult, but as the day dragged by she had a lot of time to practice.

The longer she looked at Arl's spirit, the more fascinating it became. It was not light, but somehow it contained the very life of the plants and creatures of Raphtova, as if it was in some way linked with the world itself. Thea watched in fascination, until she noticed Arl glaring at her again.

They continued to walk along the lakeshore, now approaching what had once been the far side of the lake.

Without warning, Arl transformed into an eagle and took off into the sky. Thea watched her go, wondering about the sudden change. It must be very useful to be able to change forms—to be able to walk or run or fly or swim as the need arose. She shielded her eyes to watch the speck that was Arl circling high in the air. What was she looking for?

The slap of waves on the shore caught Thea's attention. That was strange. There wasn't any wind.

Out in the center of the lake—almost beyond Thea's sight—the distant waters were churning and bubbling as if stirred by some powerful, unseen force.

Her spirit sight tingled, then she saw it—a large tentacled creature, almost transparent, glowing with a sickly darkness. A tingling certainty crept down Thea's spine. Whatever it was, it was watching her.

Arl dove down from her great height, turning into Elf form moments before landing on the ground. "We should leave now," she said in an even voice. "From here we can cut across land to the river without following the lake any further." She turned and strode away into the scrubland. Thea followed.

Once the lake was far behind them, Thea quickened her pace to walk alongside Arl. "What was that ... that thing in the lake?"

Arl frowned. "What do you mean?"

"There was some kind of tentacled monster in the lake. I saw it churning up the water."

"I saw no monster, but the churning of the water was not natural. I have seen such a phenomenon on that lake before, but never to that extent. It did not bode well for us."

Thea nodded. "Whatever it was, it was watching us."

They walked in silence for a while, then Arl spoke. "How could you see something that eagle eyes could not see?"

"I—" Thea thought for a moment. "I think it must have been some kind of spirit. I can see things that aren't visible."

Arl watched her for a while with her penetrating gaze. "That must be very useful," she conceded reluctantly.

After taking a short rest during staph, they continued to walk for the rest of the day. Thea did not protest. She was glad to put as much distance between herself and the lake as possible.

That evening Arl went hunting as a falcon, bringing a small rabbit back to the place where Thea was settling down for the night. When asked if she wanted Thea to prepare it for her, Arl explained that she ate as the animals did, and left to hunt her own meal. Thea made a small fire and prepared and cooked the rabbit for herself.

That night as Thea lay down to sleep, she saw once again the form of an owl, watching from the twisted branches overhead.

Early the next day they reached the river and began following it upstream. As they walked, Thea ventured to express a thought that was growing in her mind. "Arl, I noticed that you've been staying up to watch at night. I was thinking, if we're going to be following this river for the rest of the day, you could turn into a small creature and ride in my bag for a while. Then you could sleep."

The Dryad seemed to consider this for a moment, then gave a decisive nod. "Wake me if anything happens."

Before Thea could blink, Arl had shrunk down into

the form of a squirrel—the biggest, fattest squirrel Thea had ever seen. Opening her handbag, Thea set it on the ground and Arl climbed inside. Gingerly, Thea lifted the bag and hung it over her shoulder.

"Are you comfortable enough?"

"*Tsk!*" the squirrel scolded from inside the bag.

"Okay. I'll let you sleep."

In silence, Thea walked along the riverbank. Before long, the river left the rocky scrubland behind, and Thea found herself walking through a forest once again. The shade was a welcome relief.

Rustling and muffled caws filtered through the leaves overhead. Instinctively, Thea tightened her grip on her bag.

Some time later, Thea rounded a tree and found herself face to face with a large bear. Startled, the bear huffed and stood up on its hind legs.

Thea took a step back. "Uh … Arl, there's a bear."

Arl exploded from the bag, growing rapidly into the largest bear that Thea had ever seen. Thea stumbled back and got out of the way as Arl huffed at the bear, fur bristling.

The bear appeared to be completely baffled by the sudden appearance of this strange bear. It landed on its rump, dropped to all fours, and lumbered off through the trees.

Arl waited until the bear was well out of sight, then shifted into Elf form again. She looked at Thea. "Perhaps I will walk with you for a while, to ensure that he does not return unexpectedly."

As they walked, Thea was pleased to see that Arl remained in Elf form. That meant they could talk.

"Arl, I couldn't help noticing that sometimes you

turn into a female creature and sometimes into a male creature. Is there one that you actually are?"

"No. Dryads can take any form they wish. The true Dryad within is our seed. The flesh is just a clothing that we change as we wish."

"So what should I call you?"

"You call me Arl. That is acceptable."

"I mean do I use he or she when I am talking about you?"

"It does not matter to me. Most call me by whatever form I am in at the time because they know no different."

Thea thought for a while. "The Tilaryn aren't males or females. Micai said I could call them 'they'. Would that work for you?"

Arl glared. "I really do not care what you call me."

They walked in silence for a while.

"So if you aren't male or female, do Dryads have children?"

"No. The Mother Seed created the number of Dryads that there are to be in Raphtova, and that number remains. When a Dryad dies, their lifeseed is planted in the ground, awaiting the day it will grow into another Dryad."

The Mother Seed—was that the Dryads' name for the Deity? Thea glanced at Arl. "So in a way you are like the Elves and live forever, but instead of not dying you live over and over again."

"No. We do not live forever. Every time the lifeseed grows, a new Dryad begins. My seed has existed since the birth of Raphtova, but I only know the circles that Arl has walked upon it."

Thea wondered how old Arl was, and how long

Dryads usually lived. "Is it strange to know that you will die someday?"

Arl looked at her for a moment. "I was going to say that everything dies eventually, but I suppose that is not true. Is it strange to you that you will not die? That is simply the way you were made. Death is a part of life that very few avoid, and in these lands it often comes sooner than it should."

Thea and Arl followed the river higher and higher into the mountains. Many days passed. Gradually the land became harsher. Strong winds blew, with little to protect them from its buffeting. Almost every day Arl had to drive off a stalking wildcat or a pack of coyotes.

Thea saw other things, too. Glimpses of strange shapes creeping through the night. Dark spiritual presences that Arl could not see.

One night Arl left their camp and returned a while later, covered in blood.

"Goblins," they said in response to Thea's glance. "One got away." Arl's gaze communicated more than their words: if one goblin got away, they would be seeing more goblins very soon.

The next day Arl seemed more impatient than usual as they waited for Thea to finish her daily check in. When Thea finally finished and looked up, they spoke. "Today we will cross the pass to the other side of the mountains. Be quiet and follow close behind me."

The deer path they followed up the side of the mountain was steep and narrow. At their side, jagged cliffs stretched down into rock-filled chasms below.

Arl was on high alert, pausing frequently to smell the wind or listen to a sound in the distance. No goblins appeared, but nothing else appeared either. The mountain pass was strangely devoid of wild creatures, large or small.

After following the narrow path for several measures, Arl rounded a shoulder of rock and stopped short. Beyond, a rockfall from the heights above had completely blocked their way. Arl looked at Thea darkly but did not say anything, merely gesturing for her to turn around and return the way they had come.

After retracing their path, Arl led Thea along another route, up and over the shoulder of the mountain. Switchback after switchback, Thea plodded on, as Arl paced ahead of her, now an Elf checking for footing on an unstable bit of path, now an eagle taking to the sky to survey the surrounding area.

The higher they climbed, the more agitated Arl became. Slowly the great planet rose through the sky, heralding the approach of night, but still the mountain loomed over them and the path led higher.

Allumen was passing behind the rings of Micai when Arl returned to walk beside Thea.

"I know that you are tired," Arl said in an unsympathetic voice. "Soon we will reach the highest point on our path. Troll Gulley. I have heard that it is safe enough to traverse in daylight," they glanced at the darkening sky, "but if the goblins have informed the trolls of our presence, the crossing will not go well. If you could grow a pair of wings and fly with me, now would be a good time to do so." They gave Thea a sidelong glance. "Since you cannot, we will have to risk the trolls."

"Will the trolls attack us?"

"If they do, you will run and make it through the pass

as quickly as you can. I will deal with the trolls." Arl gave Thea a disapproving look. "I don't suppose you can run very fast."

"Not as fast as you." Thea thought for a moment. "If you turned into a creature that was large and fast, perhaps you could carry me? Then we could both get through quickly."

Arl stared at Thea for a long moment. "I believe our extremity is great enough to warrant it, but you will not request me to do so again." Arl's form began to grow, shifting into the shape of a giant elk.

Heart pounding, Thea scrambled onto a nearby boulder, then gingerly pulled herself up onto the elk's back. Not trusting the clip on her baldric to hold, she unclipped Raybow and tucked it under her arm. Leaning down, she stretched her arms around the muscular neck in front of her.

With a sudden leap, Arl began to run. Thea clung with all her strength as the world rushed past in a blur of fading light.

After a while, she felt Arl's pace slow and they came to a stop. In front of them, the light from Micai illuminated a narrow gorge. Arl's ears twisted this way and that, every nerve tensed for a sudden dash.

Thea wondered if she could hold on by Arl's antlers, but it was too late—Arl sprang forward, galloping at full speed towards the narrow gorge.

The darkness closed in as Arl entered the pass. Hoofbeats echoed across the walls of rock stretching far above them.

A crash shook the darkness. Thea looked up. Stonelike figures moved along the top of the ravine, silhouetted in blue-green light. Trolls!

A rumble of grinding stone echoed from the heights above as an enormous boulder tumbled down into the ravine. It struck the ground in front of Arl with a sickening crash.

Thea pressed her face against Arl's back and clung desperately as Arl leapt through the cloud of debris and continued galloping down the ravine.

Harsh cries and shouts echoed from above, followed by a rattle of smaller stones.

Something struck Arl's back, just behind Thea. Arl stumbled, their neck shaking free of Thea's grasp. Scrambling, Thea clung to Arl's back. Raybow was slipping. She couldn't hold on.

That moment the world opened on either side of them again as Arl shot out the other side of the ravine. They bounded two steps down the mountainside, then stopped so abruptly that Thea slid to the ground, landing in an uncomfortable heap. In an instant, Arl spun around and charged back towards the ravine.

Thea lay in the dark, trembling and clinging to Raybow. The pounding of Arl's hooves stopped abruptly, and the scream of a cougar pierced the night air. Shouts and cries echoed across the mountain. Thea closed her eyes, trying to forget the images of war and blood and death that played across her mind.

Some time later Arl returned, still in cougar form and streaked with blood. Thea stood and silently followed Arl down the side of the mountain. Later, they stopped to rest in a small hollow where a rivulet trickled its way down the mountainside. Arl sat by the stream and started to lick and groom their bloodied fur. Thea had a drink, then collapsed into a dreamless sleep.

The next two days were spent descending the mountains. They made slower progress than usual—Thea was unbelievably sore, and Arl had several cuts and bruises.

Thea sighed with relief when they finally made it down to the long inlet on the other side of the mountains. It was a grey day, overcast and muggy, with a threat of rain. Thea stepped down onto the rocky shore, trying to catch the fitful breeze that ruffled the turbid waters. The smell of salt in the air reminded her of home, but it was different. This was not the open sea.

Across the fjord, another mountain range rose, as tall and forbidding as the one they had just traversed. Fortunately, their path did not lead that way.

They travelled south along the shore, away from the distant sea. Evening was approaching when Arl gestured for Thea to walk alongside them.

"We will need to travel inland for the rest of this day. There is a human village ahead."

Thea's heart leapt. "Are we going to stay there tonight?"

Arl glared. "No. We are going to avoid it altogether."

Thea's heart sank. It had been so long since she had seen a house or slept on a bed. "Why? There isn't a problem with humans, is there?"

"Humans can be just as dangerous as goblins if you're not careful. I avoid them whenever possible."

Thea frowned. Davis hadn't seemed very dangerous to her. "I'd like to see the humans. I've only ever seen one before."

"Trust me, there isn't much to see."

"But it won't take us out of our way if we just pass through."

Arl scowled. "If you wish to see the humans I will not stop you, but I am going around. Don't keep me waiting on the other side."

Arl turned into a bobcat and slunk off into the undergrowth.

Eagerly, Thea strode along the shoreline. Soon she approached a cluster of strange, squat buildings, made of rough stones and roofed with wooden shingles. Tendrils of smoke drifted out holes in the rooftops, then sank to fill the air with a murky haze. Someone stood in front of one of these structures, chopping wood. Someone else passed by, their shoulders bowed beneath the weight of a yoke and two large buckets. Another human threw seeds to a few chickens in what might have been some sort of garden.

Thea watched with interest. The humans reminded her of Davis—they had the same soft-looking skin—but they went about their work with lowered eyes and stooped shoulders, very different from Davis's poise and confidence. Within, their spirits were dark with weariness and fear.

Slowly, Thea became aware of hushed whispers and murmuring voices. Glancing around, she realized that a small crowd of humans had gathered around her, eyeing her with suspicion.

Thea smiled at them. "Hello."

Startled, the humans stepped back. A large, burly man who seemed to be a leader among the group stepped forward and spoke in a language Thea didn't know. She'd forgotten that humans spoke a different language, but from the man's body language she guessed that he was asking who she was.

"I am Thea," she replied, gesturing to herself. "I am

just passing through."

The humans exchanged glances of curiosity and confusion. Another one spoke, as if asking her a question.

"I'm sorry, I don't speak the human language," Thea replied. A vague feeling of concern started to grow in the back of her mind. The humans were clearly curious about her, but something about their manner was threatening as well.

"I am going to continue on my way now." Thea gestured, knowing that they couldn't understand her.

The humans seemed to be discussing something, while keeping their eyes on the strange intruder. Thea took a step to move away from them, but two of the humans stepped in front of her to block her path.

The large, burly man jabbed a finger at her chest. Wait—was he pointing at the brooch? The man's fingers closed around it and he gave a great tug. It came loose in his hand.

They couldn't take Roland's brooch! Thea threw herself at the man and wrenched it from his grasp. All around her, the humans gave sounds of alarm and drew back. Fear and anger glinted in their eyes. The woodcutter raised his axe.

Alarmed, Thea stepped back. Something hard hit her arm. She wheeled around to look. Someone had thrown a rock!

"Arl!" Thea turned to face as many of the humans as she could. "Help?"

The human with the axe rushed at her. Thea jumped out of the way just as something whizzed behind her.

Pain exploded.

Thea woke up in darkness, her head pounding. Slowly she pieced back together the events of the day. Why had the humans attacked her? She hadn't done anything wrong!

Somewhere in the distance, thunder rumbled. Thea tried to move and groaned in pain.

Where was she? Gingerly, Thea lifted her head and looked around. She was inside some kind of building. Glimmers of blue-green light filtered through cracks in the walls and gaps in the ceiling. The air smelled strongly of straw and animal feces. The dust filled her lungs. She coughed violently.

Wincing with pain, she shifted into a sitting position and waited for the pounding in her head to pass.

She was holding something tightly. The brooch from Roland, of course. Slowly she opened her clenched fist. It throbbed where the corners of the brooch had cut into her skin.

She held the brooch gently in her open hand, tears stinging her eyes. She missed Roland. She missed her own people. Longing for her own bed and her own home flooded over her. The silver flower gleamed gently in the blue-green light.

In the rafters overhead, something moved. Startled, Thea looked up to see a shadowy raven staring at her with blood-red eyes.

"*Damn you,*" the raven croaked, then ruffled its feathers and flew away through a gap in the roof.

Unsteadily, Thea got to her feet and peered through the dusty darkness. There—those faint lines of light might indicate a door. Unconsciously, her hand strayed to the place where her handbag usually hung in its place over her shoulder. It wasn't there. Thea felt around her body. The baldric was gone too, and—Thea froze. Where was Raybow? She fumbled around in the darkness, panic rising. Raybow was gone! She stumbled towards the door and tried to open it. It was locked.

"Hey!" she shouted. "Let me out!"

Someone from the other side of the door responded in a loud, sullen voice that she could not understand.

Thea rattled the door again, but it wouldn't budge. Was there another way out? Thea stumbled her way around the barn, feeling in the darkness, but there were no other doors or windows.

Where had Arl gone? Surely there was something they could do to get her out. Thea returned to the door. "Let ... me ... out!" she called, as if speaking slowly and clearly would help the human understand her.

All she received in return was a low grumble in the same unknown language.

Thea leaned her head against the door. She should never have chosen to pass through the human village. If only she could talk to them like ... her eyes widened. Like Davis had talked to the Elves. That was magic—she could still remember the feeling that had washed over her in the Theatre. It reminded her of the warm glow placed inside her by Allulien.

Fragments of lessons—long forgotten—rose in Thea's mind. Each General granted access to three domains of magic. Her tutor had taught her about them. There was something about understanding ... something about protecting ... she couldn't remember.

Davis was able to communicate with the Elves, though, and he served beneath Allulien. Thea knew she was no Davis, but in theory she could do the same thing.

Her heart pounding in her ears, Thea knelt in front

of the door. "Deity, please let this human understand what I am saying, like we were able to understand Davis at the Theatre." For one brief moment, she felt the surge of tingling power.

Standing up, Thea put her mouth to a crack in the door. "Excuse me."

She heard an intake of breath, but the human outside didn't say anything.

"I don't mean you or your people any harm. Please let me go."

"You can talk?" The voice outside was thick with suspicion. "What are you?"

"I'm an Elf and I'm travelling to Gedwyld. I was just passing through."

"An Elf? Elves are from children's stories. What are you really? A strange kind of troll?"

"I really am an Elf," Thea insisted. "The creator of the world made five races and the Elves are one of them. We've lived to the far north for hundreds of circles, which is why you've never met us, but Davis the human is a friend of mine, do you know him?"

"Davis the Bard? Wandering around, telling tall tales? I've heard he's a decent sort of person. If you're a friend of his, you might not be too bad."

"Could you let me out? I was locked up for no reason, and all my things were taken away."

The human made an indistinct sound. "Eh, I don't know. The foreman would be angry if I let you go against orders." He seemed to think for a moment. "I'll tell you what. I'll go and get the foreman and you can talk to him yourself. Alright?"

"Thank you. I would appreciate that."

Thea listened as footsteps receded into the distance,

ending in a sickening thud.

Moments later there was the scrape of the bolt being pulled aside and the door was flung open. Arl thrust Raybow and the handbag into Thea's arms and stormed off into the night.

Her rope had been crammed inside the bag. Slinging its strap over her shoulder, Thea hurried to follow. She caught up with Arl beyond the borders of the small village. "What did you do to the human?"

Arl snorted. "No worse than they did to you. He should wake up. Sometime."

"But he hadn't done anything wrong. He said it was the foreman who had me locked up."

Arl glanced at Thea long enough to cock an eyebrow. "You can speak Common?"

"No, not at all, but the Deity's magic let me talk to him."

Arl stopped. "You can do magic?"

Thea suddenly felt self-conscious. "Yes, I can. Because I serve the Deity."

Arl snorted. "That would have been useful to know."

"The magic doesn't let me do whatever I want. It has to be something from the three domains of my General."

"Which are ...?"

Thea fidgeted with the bag at her side. "I don't remember."

After a brief, incredulous stare, Arl strode on into the night.

Thea followed. Would the humans chase after them once they noticed she was gone? They had seemed quite frightened of her. Hopefully they would decide to leave well enough alone.

In the near-darkness of night, Thea watched Arl walking in front of her. They could have gone on and left her trapped in the barn, but they didn't. "Thank you for helping me. And getting Raybow and my bag."

Arl shrugged and continued walking.

A new idea rose in Thea's mind. "You can change into any form, right? If you take a human form could you teach me the human language? It would be nice to be able to speak to them without having to use magic."

Arl gave her a sidelong glance. "You want to speak to humans again after that reception?"

"I'm going to Gedwyld to study under Davis, remember? I'm going to be doing lots of talking to humans."

Arl seemed to consider this. "I will teach you Common. That is the language humans use for trade between their towns and cities. Without a knowledge of Common, travel in populated areas can become very ... difficult."

Thea nodded. "I think I'm starting to understand that."

After walking in silence for a while, Arl turned to Thea again. "I apologize for my curiosity, but if you are studying to be a bard, why do you not sing or play an instrument? That seems very strange to me."

Thea felt her face get hot. "I ... I guess I forgot to."

Allulien had liked it when she sang, but it had been so long since she felt like singing. It had been so long since she heard Allulien's voice at all. Was she even listening anymore, or had she begun to believe that there was nothing left to hear?

Ashamed, Thea vowed that she would never let that happen again.

Chapter Eight

Over the next several days, Thea and Arl travelled along the shore of the inlet. It was easy walking, comparatively, but the air seemed close and muggy. They passed the occasional village or lone fishing hut but were always careful to give them a wide berth.

Thea made a point of singing as she walked, which seemed to both annoy and amuse Arl. She sang songs about the Deity—simple little songs she was taught as a child. Sometimes she made up new words for them. It was not uncommon for Arl to transform into a bird and fly off to do some scouting while Thea sang, but Thea decided not to feel offended.

There was still no sign or word from Allulien or any other Tilaryn. Thea tried not to feel discouraged, but she sorely missed their presence, especially Micai's friendly company. As she walked, she thought about the things they had taught her, and for the first time, she expressed to Arl her desire to only travel during workday. To her surprise, Arl did not resent this, but instead used restday to start teaching Thea to speak Common.

Thea threw herself into her new task, spending every spare moment to learn all that she could. The days flew by, and soon she was able to hold a basic conversation—hopefully enough to communicate with any humans that might happen upon them.

One day as Thea stared across the narrowing inlet, she saw something that looked like a wooden palisade on the far side of the water.

Arl noticed her curious glance. "That is Wyndburh, where the road begins."

"The road?" Excitement rose in Thea's heart. The road would lead her to Gedwyld! She looked back and forth along the long inlet. "How do we get there?"

Arl gave her a sidelong glance. "Some take a boat, but given your previous reception from humans, I doubt the wisdom of that course. I usually fly across, but since you have yet to sprout wings we will need to take the long way around." Arl turned and continued to walk along the shore.

Thea hurried to follow. "How long will that take?"

"Four days. Possibly longer. The Deorcian does not offer easy passage to those who walk on two legs."

"What's the Deorcian?"

Arl pointed ahead. To the south, Thea could see trees. In the distance, wooded mountains pierced the sky. Was Arl talking about the mountains? Thea hoped they didn't have to walk that far, but Arl didn't seem interested in offering further comment.

The shores of the inlet were forested now. Thea found this pleasant at first, but soon the undergrowth became so thick that it was hard to find their way forward. The tangle of trees grew right to the water's edge and stretched up the sides of the mountains, which left them no choice but to struggle through the thickets. Branches pulled at Thea's clothes and caught in her hair.

They made very little progress as the day dragged on. Usually Arl would speak with Thea as they walked, so she could practice her Common, but today they walked in silence. Staph came and went, but Arl did not offer to stop and rest.

Thea was nearly collapsing from weariness when Arl finally gestured that they were to stop for the night. Arl did not leave to hunt, but instead built a rough shelter of tree branches and told Thea to eat from the extra food that had been gathered and stored in her bag over the previous days.

The next day they followed the shore deeper into the forest. The trees were larger now. The heavy canopy of branches overhead cloaked the forest floor in shadow, with only an occasional ray of Allumen's light piercing down through the gloom.

Thea followed Arl in silence as they wound their way through the trees. The forest was uncannily quiet. There was no sound of birds in the branches overhead or any scurrying of small woodland creatures. The only movement was the gentle rippling of the wide river they now travelled along, flowing down through the forest towards the sea. The far shore was close enough that the branches of the trees touched overhead, but still Arl continued along the shore, deeper into the forest.

Finally Thea ventured to ask, "Aren't we going to cross the river?"

Arl sent a dark glance in her direction. "And how would we do that?"

"Well, it's not that wide anymore. Couldn't we swim?"

"The current here is strong. We will continue until we find a safe crossing place." Arl glanced around the darkening forest. Their pursed lips discouraged any further comment.

Evening was falling when they finally encountered a large fallen log that spanned the width of the river. Arl approached it cautiously, sniffing the air and listening intently. Finally they turned to Thea. "We will cross."

As quietly as she could, Thea scrambled up onto the log and stared across the expanse of the river. The water was dark and deep. From her high vantage point, she could see that although it showed barely a ripple, the river swept beneath the log with a strength that could carry away something much larger than herself.

With a rush of feathers, a raven swooped over her shoulder and perched on a branch above the river, glaring at her with blood-red eyes. Arl was ready in case she fell.

Stretching out her arms, Thea carefully set one foot in front of the other and tried to keep her eyes on the far bank of the river. Arl's glare was unnerving.

Below, the river rushed on, dark and silent.

Step by step the far shore grew closer, then she passed high above the river's muddy banks and beyond to the tangle of bushes bordering the river.

Somewhere in the distance something rustled and cracked.

A solid bolt of darkness hit Thea's side, tumbling her off the log into the undergrowth below. As she tried to catch herself, she felt feathers turn to skin and a hand clamped over her mouth.

"Quiet." Arl hissed. "Goblin."

Thea blinked, dazed by the impact.

Arl crouched over her, every muscle tensed, watching the trees around them with narrowing eyes. "There is never just one goblin."

Arl faded into the shadows and Thea was alone.

Doing her best not to disturb the undergrowth that shielded her, she sat up and tried to look around.

Through a gap in the branches, a movement caught her eye. A small, dark figure was creeping through the forest. It moved its head back and forth, as if trying to discern where a noise had come from. Thea froze and held her breath, but the creature did not seem to see her.

Thea stared in horrified fascination as the goblin crept past. It had a small bow in its hands and a quiver of black arrows at its belt. Crouched as the goblin was, it was hard to get a really good look at it, but Thea could see that its face was creased in a look of intense concentration. Light shone in the goblin's spirit.

A tawny blur streaked out of the undergrowth.

"Arl! No!" Thea lurched to her feet.

The goblin turned and loosed its arrow, striking the cougar on the shoulder. Arl hissed and crouched to spring.

Thea ran forward. "Stop! Don't hurt them!"

The goblin paused, hand halfway towards grabbing another arrow.

There was no doubt, now that Thea had a chance for a better look. The goblin's spirit was bright and alive, filled with the light of the Deity. She gestured urgently at Arl. "You are not going to hurt this creature!"

Arl glared at Thea and lashed their tail.

The goblin looked from Arl to Thea with an expression of confused suspicion.

A crash shook the forest behind them. Thea turned, her eyes widening as a giant creature emerged from the trees, its body a deeper darkness in the shadow of nightfall. With a growl, it lifted itself on its hind legs, towering above their heads. Its dark, leathery hide stretched from its clawed forearms to its sides in a strange, winglike shape. Beady eyes glared at them from a reptile-like face and it snarled, showing a row of sharp, razor-like teeth.

In an instant, the goblin had an arrow to the string. The black arrow hit the creature's chest and disintegrated, barely making a mark.

Arl sprang, teeth bared to sink into the monster's leathery hide. With a large clawed hand, the monster swatted them away. Drops of blood streaked Arl's chest and they tumbled into the undergrowth with a crash.

The goblin shot again then ducked for cover, shouting something in a language Thea couldn't understand.

The monster lunged forward, and darkness seemed to flow from it, staining the night an even deeper black. Thea scrambled to get out of the way.

With an eagle cry, Arl swooped down at its face, talons extended. The monster's arm clawed the air and Arl swerved away, just out of reach.

With shaking hands Thea grabbed Raybow off her back and put an arrow to the string.

The monster shot its head forward, snapping at Thea with teeth as long as her arm. She stumbled back, dropped Raybow, and fell—her foot caught by a tree root protruding from the ground.

With a shout, the goblin appeared from behind a tree and shot another arrow. The monster swivelled its head towards its assailant, and Thea threw herself out of the monster's reach.

As she cowered behind a tree, there was another crash, followed by an eagle scream. Peering out from her hiding place, she saw the monster swatting at its head. Raybow lay forgotten at its feet.

Tensing her body for a sudden dash, Thea waited until the goblin appeared for another shot, then ran as fast as she could, seized Raybow, and turned to run.

Something hit her side and sent her tumbling, but this time she clung to Raybow with all her strength. She scrambled to her feet, grabbed an arrow from her quiver, turned, and shot. The arrow blazed with white light as it streaked through the air and struck the monster with a blinding flash. The monster screamed in pain. Thea gasped. She had never seen Raybow do something like that before.

Another black arrow struck the monster as Arl launched out of the treetops with a cougar's scream, teeth and claws digging deep into the monster's head.

The monster staggered and fell. With a snarl, Arl sank their teeth into its neck.

The monster trembled, then lay still. Silence descended over the forest once again.

The goblin stepped out into the clearing, another black arrow nocked. They circled the monster cautiously, then shot the arrow into the base of its skull. The monster didn't move.

With a satisfied nod, the goblin turned to face Thea. "Thank you for your help," they said in simple Common. "It was very … unexpected."

Now that Thea could get a closer look at the goblin, she saw that it was indeed small—only half Thea's height, with a thin face and large eyes. Its clothing was black, wrapped tight with strips of leather, and it had a chaotic mass of dark hair that had been pulled back from its face with a leather cord. Its hand did not stray far from its quiver of arrows.

Arl hissed at it.

Quickly whispering a prayer for understanding, Thea spoke with a confidence she didn't quite feel. "I am Thea and this is Arl. You do not need to fear us. We are friends."

Arl shifted into Elf form, staggered, and glared at Thea. "*Friends*?"

Thea didn't move her gaze from the goblin's face. "Any servant of the Deity is my friend."

"It shot me!"

"And you were attacking it! I can see what a person is like inside, and this goblin is not an evil creature."

"But I know goblins." Arl glared at it with narrowing eyes. "I have killed many goblins, and I *will* kill more."

"Stop it, Arl!" Thea hissed urgently. Arl was speaking in Elvish, but the intent of their words did not need a translator.

The goblin drew itself up to its full height, which wasn't much, and spoke carefully. "I have killed shape-changers before. If you hurt my people, I will kill you."

"We are not here to hurt your people," Thea said quickly, before Arl could respond. "We are passing through on our way to Gedwyld."

"I see." The goblin eyed Arl. "I never met someone who does not want to hurt us, but you killed the dark thing, so I will let you go."

"What was it?" Thea looked at the motionless form at their feet. It wasn't radiating darkness anymore.

"A dark thing," the goblin replied.

"Were you hunting it?"

"Hunt or be hunted. It had already killed two of our

children." A look of pain gleamed in the goblin's eyes.

"I—I'm sorry," Thea stammered, unsure of what to say.

"Sorry?" The goblin looked at Thea with confused suspicion. "Anything would kill a Little."

"A Little?" Thea asked, unsure of what the goblin had meant.

"That's us. The Littles. Anyone would kill the Littles."

"The Littles? What's a Little? I thought you were a goblin."

The creature shrugged. "Other people call us goblins, but our name for our own kind is the Littles. Because we're little."

It was true. The creature standing in front of Thea was little. If she hadn't known better she might have guessed it was a smaller sort of human. Not that she'd seen many humans. Maybe they would look different compared side by side.

The Little looked beyond Thea towards Arl. "Your companion is injured. If you will accept our help, my people will care for their wounds as a payment for killing the dark thing. You are a two day's journey from any settlement other than ours."

Thea looked at Arl who had withdrawn from the conversation and was attempting to clean an ugly looking wound in their shoulder. Blood dripped from several deep slices across their chest. Thea hurried over. "Arl, are you alright?"

Arl looked at Thea icily. "No."

"I mean—are you going to be alright? We need to get those bandaged. I don't have any bandages or anything ..." She stared at Arl in concern.

Arl glared. "I've never used bandages before."

"But Arl, if we go with the Little, their people will help you."

"The *what*?" Arl staggered. Their face spasmed with pain.

The Little appeared by Thea's elbow. "My people can care for your injuries. If you threaten anyone, I will kill you."

Arl snarled at the Little.

"Please, Arl," Thea pleaded, "you are really hurt. This person said they can help you."

"My name is Elora," the Little supplied.

Thea's heart sank. Cold hatred glinted in Arl's eyes, clouded as they were with pain. What could she say that would get through to them?

"Arl, you killed the dark thing and Elora wants to thank you by caring for your injuries."

A strange look flickered across Arl's face. "The *dark thing?* That was an athexe! They're deadly. I'd never down one by myself. It was that bow of yours. Why didn't you tell me it could do that?"

"I didn't know it could. I never shot a monster before. But it is a bow from the Great War—I mean when the Elves used to fight against the Evil One. I guess it was made to fight evil things."

"I was also made to fight evil things." Arl's eyes settled on the Little's face and started to narrow again.

"Elora was fighting it too," Thea interposed quickly. "It had killed two children and her people will be very thankful that it is dead."

"More dark things will come soon," Elora interjected. "That fight made too much noise."

Arl gave a furtive glance over their shoulder. Small patches of Micai's distant light glimmered through gaps in the canopy overhead, giving only a hint of visibility to the otherwise pitch black of the forest. "How close is this settlement?"

"Not far," Elora replied. "Follow me."

Elora set off through the trees and Thea followed close behind. She tried to move as silently as their stealthy guide, but it was hard to see in the deep darkness beneath the trees. Thea cringed every time she stepped on a branch or brushed noisily against an unseen shrub or tree.

She could feel, rather than hear, Arl's presence close behind her. Arl wasn't happy about going with Elora, but what could they do? They couldn't spend the night in the forest when another athexe might appear, and someone really should look at Arl's injuries. Besides, Thea wanted to know how it was that a goblin—or rather a Little—had the light of the Deity in them.

They had been walking for quite some time, when Elora disappeared. Thea felt Arl tense beside her and laid a warning hand on their arm.

"This way." Elora appeared again beside them and gestured to the undergrowth. Amongst the scrubby branches, Thea could see a low, dark hole that she would have supposed to be an animal burrow.

Cautiously, Thea followed Elora into the tunnel, crawling on her hands and knees to fit through the small entranceway. It was very dark. Thea felt along the rocky wall with her hand, stretching her other hand before her to avoid running into their guide.

After rounding a corner, there appeared to be some sort of light ahead. Not daylight or firelight, but a strange green light that silhouetted Elora walking along the passage before her. The tunnel had grown somewhat wider and taller—plenty large for a Little, but Thea still had to duck to avoid hitting her head on the uneven ceiling.

The light came from a small lantern affixed to the tunnel wall, but instead of a candle or flame it held a cluster of glowing fungi.

"Kais." Elora spoke in a low voice, and another Little stepped out of the shadows in front of them. They spoke together in low, urgent voices, then the other Little hurried away into the darkness.

"Off to get the welcoming committee I suppose," Arl grumbled in Thea's ear.

Elora turned to look at them. "Kais will warn the others of your arrival, so they will not be too alarmed. It is not much farther now."

Thea glanced at Arl. It might have been the strange light of the fungus, but their face looked very pale and tight.

They passed a small antechamber, presumably where the other Little had been waiting, then rounded another corner. The passageway was lined with fungus lanterns now, and the walls and ceiling were smooth.

"What are they?" Thea ventured to ask Elora.

Elora glanced at her. "Lights. You don't have any?"

"Not like that. Our lanterns usually use candles or oil."

"We used to have lights like that, but they burn out and then you need more candles or oil. These lights do not burn out and all we have to do is water them." Elora thought for a moment. "And they make the tunnels smell better."

The passage turned a corner, then ended at a large, wooden door. It was open, and Elora led them through it into the large room beyond. The walls of the room were lined with the same strange lanterns. On one side was a large stone fireplace, where a lively blaze cast a warm, comforting glow. The other side of the room was spanned by a narrow counter, stacked with cups and dishes of all shapes and sizes. An oversized basin was surrounded by an assortment of pipes and levers.

The center of the room held several tables lined with simple wooden benches. Thea was pleased to find that the room was tall enough that she could stand upright again, but only just.

Around the room were several other doors, and through one of these another Little appeared, with a strange wrinkled face and arms full of bottles and bundles.

"This is Sami, my grandmother," Elora explained, hurrying forward to relieve her of her burden.

Elora and her grandmother exchanged a few words, then Elora turned to Arl. "She has agreed to treat your injuries. I have explained to her that you are a shape-changer, but I suggest that you do not change shapes while you are here. Shape-changers are not loved by the Littles."

"The feeling is mutual," Arl muttered under their breath.

Elora ushered them towards the fire. "My grandmother does not speak much of the Big language, but I will stay and translate for you."

Thea watched as Sami bustled around the fireplace, laying out rolls of bandages and bunches of herbs. Crossing the room, she filled a large bowl with steaming water from the pipes above the basin, and set it beside a pile of clean white towels.

As she worked, Sami chattered away in her own language, somehow managing to make her understanding clear enough through inflection and gestures: "pass that here", "hold still", "this should only hurt a little", *"I said hold still"*.

Satisfied that Arl was in good hands, Thea turned her attention back to the room they were in. The Little they had met in the passageway had returned and was speaking with Elora. Noticing Thea's glance, Elora gestured for her to join them. "This is Kais. He is my ... I don't know the word in the Big language. We are promised to each other."

"Promised to be married?"

"Yes." Elora glanced at Kais and smiled.

Kais was a bit taller than Elora, with sandy-brown hair and a friendly face. He smiled at Elora then looked up at Thea. "Thank you for helping Elora kill the dark thing. You and your friend are very welcome here."

"I am glad that we could help. Thank you for welcoming us." Thea glanced over to where the elderly Little was scolding Arl with a motherly tone that seemed to communicate "why don't you take care of yourself properly".

Elora followed Thea's gaze. "We never show others the way into our tunnels, but with a wound like that you would not last long in the Trees. I couldn't leave you there."

The light in Elora's spirit glowed brighter as she spoke. Thea could see the same light shine inside Kais as well. Over by the fire, Sami sparkled as bright as a diamond.

Other Littles passed through the common room, carrying baskets and other burdens. They glanced curiously at the newcomers and gathered in small clusters to whisper and peer over their bundles. Their clothes were simple, but sturdy and well-made, dyed in a variety of woodland colours.

They didn't all have spirits as bright as those Thea saw in Elora, Kais, and Sami. There were some whose spirits were dim or a mottled mixture of light and dark. Some had hardly any light inside them at all, but they still seemed to get along with each other, jostling and nudging each other as they stared at the strange visitors.

"Forgive me," Kais spoke, "but you are the strangest Big that I have ever seen."

"Big?" Thea asked, pulling her attention back to her companions. "I'm sorry, I don't understand."

"That is our name for people who are not a Little," Elora explained.

"Oh. Do you mean humans? I'm not a human, I'm an Elf."

Elora shrugged. "If you are big then we call you a Big. It makes no difference. To us, Bigs are all the same. They try to hurt us and we try to stay away from them."

"I was always taught that there are five races," Thea mused, "Humans, Elves, Fauns, Minathrils, and Dryads—the shape-changers, you know. But if there are only five races, where do the Littles fit in?"

Elora's eyes flashed. "Why do we need to fit in? We exist, isn't that enough?"

Kais put a gentle hand on Elora's shoulder. "We seem to get overlooked a lot. Probably because the Bigs are bigger than us. But someday we'll find our place, won't we, Elora?"

One short, slender Little caught Thea's eye. He stood

apart from the others and stared at Thea with dark eyes. Thea had seen many curious or wary expressions from the congregating Littles, but there was hatred in those eyes.

"Zaki!" Elora had noticed the young Little and gestured for him to join them.

Without any acknowledgement of the invitation, the Little turned and left the room. Elora and Kais exchanged a glance.

"I will show you to your room," Elora said, turning to Thea. "We do not often have guests, but recent deaths in our community have left an empty room. You and the quiet one may sleep there tonight."

The room was small but pleasant, with two sturdy—though rather short—beds and a table with two chairs. There was no fireplace, but Thea was surprised to feel a gust of warm air.

Elora pointed to a small metal grate that covered a hole in the wall. "We have air tunnels in the walls. They bring warm air from the fire and fresh air from outside. Then it is never too hot or cold."

Thea examined the grate with fascination. She'd never heard of something like that. Elvish houses usually had a fireplace in every room—at least they did in Lyudmyla, in the houses she was familiar with. Now that she thought about it, what was it like for the people in Rokhov, or in Svokyie? Did the poorer Elves have the same comforts that she had experienced all her life?

When Thea returned to the common area, the tables had been set with wooden bowls and spoons. Littles were bustling about the room in preparation for what appeared to be a large communal meal. Thea was shown to a seat and Arl came to sit beside her.

"How does your shoulder feel?" Thea asked, looking at the large bandage wrapped around their shoulder.

Arl glared at her and did not reply.

Soon a company of about thirty Littles had congregated in the room, chattering excitedly as they gathered around the tables. Elora and Kais joined Thea and Arl at their table, but the rest of the Littles found other places to sit, keeping a cautious distance between themselves and the large strangers.

It was a simple meal of soup and bread, but to Thea it was delicious. Elora and Kais were happy to talk with her and answer whatever questions she had, but all through the meal Arl watched the room with dark, glowering eyes and didn't say a word.

After they were alone in their room, Arl lay down with their face towards the wall. Thea puttered around the room for a while, cleaning out her bag and checking Raybow's remaining arrows. Finally she sat down on the bed and polished Roland's brooch with a bit of cloth. "Does your shoulder hurt?" she ventured.

Arl didn't reply.

"Elora and Kais seem like really nice people, don't they?"

Icy silence filled the room.

Thea decided to try one more time. "How far do you think we are from Wyndburh now?"

A low growl filled the silence. Thea sighed and put the brooch down on the table. A small lantern hung above the door, filling the room with its strange green light. A closer examination showed it to have an adjustable lampshade. Dimming the light to near-darkness, Thea lay down on the empty bed and fell asleep.

Chapter Nine

The next day Arl was hot and feverish. Sami bustled in and out of their room with poultices and bowls of hot water, while Thea lingered nearby and tried to help as best as she could. Finally Sami shooed her away, and Thea returned to the large common room, unsure of where else to go.

Kais looked up from where he sat by the fire. "You seem worried. Is something wrong?"

"It's Arl." She joined Kais by the fire. "They aren't doing well at all."

"Sami will do everything she can." Kais gave a reassuring smile. "She is a good healer. I think she has cared for all of us at one time or another."

Thea ventured a smile of her own. "It is very kind of her to help so much."

"If there is someone to care for, Sami will always be there."

Across the room, several Littles were using the basin and pipes to wash the dishes. Thea had seen similar pipes in the bath rooms, where hot water from the fire was channelled into washing basins and bathtubs.

"Have you always lived here?"

"Yes, Littles have lived here for generations." Kais' eyes roamed the room with a familiar, contented expression. "This was always one of the biggest homes in the area."

A very comfortable home, too, Thea considered. It was so unlike the large, brightly lit homes of the Elves, but it was cozy and warm. Everywhere she looked, handcrafted wood gleamed in the gentle green light of the lanterns.

"Where did the Littles come from?"

"We live here. In the Trees."

"No, I mean ..." Thea struggled to find the right words with her limited vocabulary, "... who made you? I never heard of the Littles until I met Elora."

"The Great Big Big made us."

Thea blinked. "The Great Big Big?"

Kais nodded. "The Great Big Big made everything in the world. The trees, the birds, the Littles. Not the dark things."

Thea gasped with understanding. "The Deity! Of course! The Deity made all the peoples of Raphtova."

Kais nodded. "I heard that name used before, but we prefer our name. The Maker isn't just a Big. The Maker is the *Great Big* Big. Bigger than all the other Bigs."

Thea smiled. There was something so delightfully simple about the names that the Littles gave to things. They made sense. Now that she thought about it, of course the Deity must have made the Littles, and yet ... the Halls of Knowledge said that there were only five races. If that was true, where did the Littles *really* come from?

Soon the room was bustling with Littles preparing for their next meal. Kais hurried off to help, and Thea was left alone with her thoughts.

The next day Arl was well enough to get up. After Thea's regular morning check in, the two of them spent much of the day in the common room, for the most part left to themselves. A small party of Littles bustled around the room, sweeping the floor and wiping down the tables. Thea recognized one of the Littles as the youth that Elora had called Zaki. He kept eyeing them from across the room, but didn't seem interested in getting any closer.

Arl watched the fire with a sullen expression. Once or twice, Thea tried to start a conversation, but Arl had little to say, and silence soon fell again.

Raised voices across the room drew Thea's attention. It seemed that one of the older Littles had told Zaki to do something and he was protesting. The older Little pushed a broom into his hands and gestured him away.

With a sullen expression, Zaki stalked across the room and began to sweep the hearth. He was careful not to look at either of the strangers close at hand, but finished his job quickly and returned to the far side of the room.

A short while later, one of the older Littles called him back, pointing out the bits of ash and fragments of wood he had left behind in his hurry.

With a scowl, Zaki grabbed the broom and started again, sweeping with rough, vigorous swipes. As he turned, the handle of the broom swung out behind him and struck Arl's bandaged shoulder.

Arl yelped in pain. "Damn you, goblin!"

With a clatter, the broom dropped to the floor as Zaki wheeled to face Arl, a knife drawn in his hand.

Thea froze and a shocked silence fell across the room. Arl and the Little stared at each other with blazing eyes.

Arl's muscles were tensed, ready to spring.

Zaki spoke through gritted teeth, strange words that Thea didn't know.

Panic rose in Thea's heart. What was going on? *Oh Deity, let me understand what he is saying!*

With a surge of magic, the words tumbled into place in Thea's mind as the Little continued his tirade: "Goblin filth. That's all we are. The Big Bad hates us and the Bigs hate us. Well, just because everyone hates us doesn't mean we can't hate them back. I'm not afraid of you, shape-changer. I'll kill you!"

The door opened and Elora and Kais stepped into the room. Thea could feel their intake of breath as they saw what was happening.

"Zaki!" Elora exclaimed. "Put that knife down. Now!"

Zaki pointed his knife towards Elora, across the room full of aghast Littles, and back towards Arl with determined precision. "I'm going to kill it. You can't stop me!"

"Zaki." Kais' voice was gentle, but insistent. "Zaki, look at me."

Zaki's maddened eyes flickered, then moved reluctantly to Kais' face. Kais held out his arms and stepped towards him with an expression of compassion and reassurance.

Zaki's face crumpled and he started to cry.

Quickly, Kais crossed the room and held the trembling boy in his arms.

With a deft movement, Elora removed the knife from Zaki's unresisting hand and set it high on the mantelpiece above the fire. She looked at Thea with tired eyes. "His parents are both dead. His father was killed by a dark thing, and his mother was shot by a Big, only two cycles ago. Kais and I have tried to take him in, but we are no substitute for what he has lost." She looked at Zaki, held close in Kais' arms. His shoulders heaved with wrenching sobs. Elora spoke softly. "All of my family was killed, except for my grandmother and myself, but that was long ago now. The wound in my heart is not so raw anymore."

As if in response to her name, Elora's grandmother entered the room. Without a moment's pause, she bustled over to the silent group by the fire, making soothing clucking noises.

Her presence seemed to provide some relief to the silent Littles, who began to breathe once again. She said a few gentle words to Zaki, which Thea could almost certainly understand as some form of "come on dear and have a nice cup of tea".

Elora spoke to her grandmother in a low voice, then turned to Thea. "I think that your friend has had enough excitement for today. My grandmother will bring them back to their room and make sure they are comfortable."

Thea glanced at Arl who stood unmoving, as if utterly dumbfounded by something. "Arl," she said quietly, "I think you should lie down again. You're still not well."

Expressionless, Arl allowed Sami to lead them away. Thea watched them go until the door was shut behind them. When she looked around again, Zaki and Kais had also gone. She looked at Elora. "Is there anything I can do to help?"

Elora sighed. "No. It was just not a good time to have Bigs in our home. Not a good time for Zaki, anyways."

Thea glanced around the room at the Littles who were once again going about their business. Her heart nearly broke to think about the way that they were killed and hunted without even a second thought. *Everyone hates us.* What kind of a life was that?

She looked at Elora again. "Zaki said something about a 'Big Bad'. Who is that?"

Elora sat down and stared into the fire. "The Big Bad is the one who was supposed to take care of the Littles and teach us about the world. But he didn't. He hated us and left us alone."

Every race had their own General, to care for them. Khariton's words came back into Thea's mind. "And this Big Bad rebelled against the Deity—or rather, against the Great Big Big, didn't he? Was it the Big Bad that made the monsters and the dark things?"

"Yes. That is why we call him the Big Bad. He does bad things and he hurts us. Some Littles choose to serve the Big Bad. They hope that he will help them if they show that they are useful, but that never works. In his mind we are worthless. He does not care if we live or die."

Thea listened in fascination. So the Littles *were* one of the five races after all. The Fallen General was supposed to be their guardian, but instead he rebelled against the Deity and abandoned the Littles. But if the Littles were one of the five, which of the other races was not? Or were the Halls of Knowledge wrong?

Thea leaned forward. "And you choose to serve the Great Big Big instead. I saw the light inside you right away. That's why I told Arl not to—" She faltered. Would she have let Arl kill the creature if she hadn't seen the Deity's light?

Elora looked at her with a strange expression. "If only we could all see what lies inside. That would make life so much easier, don't you think?"

Thea nodded and looked away. What would have happened if she hadn't been learning to use her spirit sight while in the waking world? Raphea had told her it would be important, but she never would have guessed that it could have meant the life of this fiercely compassionate creature sitting beside her. Even if there had been no light in Elora's spirit, wouldn't it have been better to show mercy?

The next day Thea and Arl stayed in their room. Thea didn't want to risk another altercation with Zaki, and Arl showed no interest in moving from the bed on which they sat.

They were still sitting in silence when there was a knock on the door and Elora entered.

"Grandmother has told me that the silent one's shoulder is beginning to mend. Tomorrow you may continue with your journey."

"Thank you," Thea replied, assuming that Arl wouldn't say something so polite.

Elora glanced at Arl, gave Thea a quizzical look, then turned and shut the door behind her.

Early the next morning, Sami showed Thea how to change the dressing on Arl's shoulder. Arl stood motionless as Thea tied and re-tied the bandage until Sami expressed approval of her work and gestured at a pile of bandages, indicating that Thea was to take them with her.

Thea had just finished putting them in her small bag when Elora arrived with her own bag slung over her shoulder. "If Grandmother has finished, we will be going."

"Yes, I believe so," Thea replied, glancing at Sami. "Thank you for helping my friend."

Sami smiled and nodded cheerfully, pressing a small, cloth-wrapped package into Thea's hands.

After saying goodbye to Kais, Thea and Arl followed Elora through the twisting maze of tunnels.

"We will take a different tunnel than the one we entered through," Elora explained over her shoulder. "This one will lead you much closer to the end of the Trees, where there is less danger of dark things and other monsters."

As they stepped through a wooden door and into a long, fungi-illuminated tunnel, Elora looked at her guests with a bemused expression. "The way may seem long for those who are too tall to stand. If the silent one wishes to change shape into something shorter, that would be acceptable."

When Arl did not change shapes, Elora shrugged and led the way down the passage.

As they walked, Thea ventured a question that had been growing on her mind. "Why do you live here, in these tunnels beneath the Trees?"

Elora gave Thea a brief glance. "This is Home. Why would we live anywhere else?"

"Because there are monsters in the forest, and the Bigs who see you try to kill you. Wouldn't it be safer for your people to live somewhere else?"

"And where would we go?" Elora's voice sounded angry. "Everywhere you go there are Bigs or there are monsters. Here we are as safe as we can be, under the ground where no one can find us."

Thea shook her head in silence. Surely there must be

somewhere, but she wasn't the one whose life was in danger. The Littles had lived there for a long time, and they had managed to keep going. Somehow.

The tunnel was long and very straight. Thea appreciated the light given by the regular lanterns on the wall, but soon her neck and shoulders were aching from constantly being hunched over.

Still they walked on, until Thea was certain that they must have walked for most of the day. Finally Elora halted by a small alcove in the side of the passage and another Little emerged. Elora spoke to them briefly in their own language, then gestured for Thea and Arl to continue following.

The passage began to curve and became much smaller, but in the absence of the small green lights, daylight glimmered ahead of them.

Finally they rounded one last corner and crawled through a small opening, out into the forest.

As Thea stretched her aching neck, Elora turned to speak to them.

"We keep a guard at each of our tunnels. It gives us a warning of any unwelcome visitors." She glanced at Arl. "Do not try to return without an invitation."

"I understand," Thea said quickly. "Thank you again for your hospitality."

Elora nodded and disappeared into the undergrowth.

Thea looked around. Daylight filtered down through the canopy of leaves overhead. A large forked tree arched above the place where Thea knew the tunnel opening must be, but it was so well concealed that she couldn't see it at all. She glanced at Arl. The Dryad had barely spoken to her the entire time they were with the Littles. Now they stepped forward through the trees without even a glance in her direction. Thea hurried to follow.

They walked in silence. The trees didn't grow together as thickly as they had in other areas of the forest, and Thea was pleased to see signs of normal woodland creatures. They must have made it out of the Deorcian at last.

Thea and Arl walked for the rest of the day, only stopping once to drink from a stream and eat the biscuits that Sami had sent in the small package.

As evening approached, they reached the end of the trees and looked down a long, gentle slope towards a small town, surrounded by a wooden palisade. Tendrils of chimney smoke drifted up into the darkening sky. Beyond, tilled fields stretched in every direction, scattered with small wooden huts.

Beside Thea, Arl's form shifted from a female Elf to a male human. "Welcome to Wyndburh. From here you will find a road that will lead you to Gedwyld." Arl gestured into the distance, where Thea could just make out a thin, dark line that may have been a road.

Thea looked at Arl. "You said you were only going to take me as far as the road, didn't you?"

"I will go no further than Wyndburh. The lands to the east are not familiar to me."

Thea's heart sank. She didn't want to leave Arl now, while they were still recovering from their injury. What if something happened to them?

Arl strode down the hill and Thea hurried to keep up. To her surprise, Arl walked directly towards the distant palisade.

"Wait—we are going into the town?" Memories of angry, suspicious faces rose in Thea's mind.

"I want a drink," Arl replied without expression. "Keep your hood up and don't talk to anybody. If you get yourself in trouble I'm not saving you this time."

Chapter Ten

Night had fully fallen by the time they reached the town. Arl strode up to the large wooden gate and gave a firm knock.

A gruff voice called out from the other side, "Whaddyawant?"

"Tavern," Arl replied in a voice just as gruff.

There was the scrape and thud of bars being pulled aside, and the gate opened with a flood of harsh yellow light. A human who matched Arl in size and build peered out at them and grunted. "Red Eyes. I told you to stop comin' in after dark. I got a job t'do."

Arl strode through the gate as if they owned it, barely giving the human a second glance. Thea hurried to follow.

"Oi! Who're you?" the human demanded, barring her way.

"They're with me," Arl growled. "None of your business."

"All right. All right." The human stepped back and let Thea walk past. "To the tavern with ye."

Thea looked at Arl in amazement. How well did they know the people here? Arl strolled through the town with a broad-chested swagger that seemed to communicate that they knew what they were doing, and everyone else could mind their own business.

After several questioning glances her direction, Thea

began to mimic Arl's way of walking and was surprised to find that the curious glances stopped. If she acted like she belonged, no one seemed to give her a second glance.

Arl led Thea towards a large, dirty-looking building and pushed the door open. Inside, Thea was met with a smoky haze and a cacophony of noise. It was a large room and appeared to be some kind of eating house with many tables, several of which had groups of humans sitting around them. To the side was a long counter, behind which a tall man seemed to be using a rag to push around smudges of grease from one side of the counter to the other.

Arl paced over to the counter and waited for the man to acknowledge their presence.

"Ah, hello again," the bartender said, looking up from his task. "A beer, then?"

Arl nodded. Taking the mug of beer that was handed across the counter, they stalked off and sat in a shadowy corner of the tavern, slouching in their chair.

Thea followed Arl, feeling quite self-conscious. She was certain that getting a drink would cost money, and she didn't have any. But as far as she knew, Arl didn't have any money either.

A large stone fireplace dominated one side of the room, casting stark shadows and filling the room with a smoky haze. Several indistinct figures sat or dozed in front of the fire, while many more were gathered around several of the large wooden tables. They were all humans, as far as Thea could tell, but they were a varied bunch. Some were slender and some were large. Many of them wore simple, drab-coloured clothing, but a few were more finely dressed. Some were not wearing much at all. There were men and women, some chatting and laughing, some sitting in silence. Their skin gleamed in all sorts of shades, with varying amounts of creases and wrinkles.

The humans varied in size too. One woman was so tall she had to stoop not to hit her head on the wooden beams that crossed the low ceiling. Over by the fire a short, bearded figure was draining the contents of a large tankard. Was that a small human or a large Little? Thea couldn't tell, although the lack of any other Littles in the room suggested that it was probably a human.

The door of the tavern opened, sending the lantern flames dancing as a gust of night air flowed through the smoky haze. A tall figure skipped through the door. Her stone-like skin glimmered green in the firelight.

Thea stared. Was that an Elf? What was an Elf doing in Wyndburh? The newcomer waved a friendly greeting to everyone in the tavern, then vaulted herself up to sit on the counter, chatting cheerfully with the bartender.

Thea watched the Elf closely. There was something that didn't seem right about her. For one thing, her hair wasn't thick and short like Elf hair. Instead, it was long and thin, more like the hair of some of the humans she had seen. But unlike the humans, her hair was a brilliant white, fading at its tips into a bright, unnatural green that almost matched the colour of her skin.

Thea nudged Arl. "Look over there. That person looks like an Elf, but there's something wrong about her. Is she a Dryad?"

Arl's eyes followed Thea's gesture towards the figure that was laughing uproariously at something the bartender had said.

Arl glared. "That is not a Dryad."

Thea stood up and glanced furtively around the room. Arl had said not to talk to anyone, but she needed to know more about this person. Quietly, she moved towards the strange Elf who seemed to have captured the attention of everyone sitting around her. She wore simple travelling clothes, brightly coloured, with a wilted chain of daisies draped around her neck. From the smooth surface of her skin, Thea would have guessed that she was quite old, but this stranger acted nothing like a mature Elf.

She waved a greeting as Thea approached. "Hello! Come and join the fun! I love meeting new people! I'm Sylica, what's your name?"

"Um, I'm Thea," Thea replied, glancing nervously around, but everyone seemed remarkably at ease, despite this strange, loud Elf sitting in front of them.

"Isn't this fun?" Sylica grinned. "There are so many nice people here. Harold and I are best friends already." She waved cheerfully at the bartender, who blushed.

"Here," he stammered, putting two mugs on the counter. "For you and your new friend. Why don't you go find yourself a table? I've got my work to tend to."

Sylica nodded cheerfully. "Okay! Come on, Thea, let's go sit by the fire. Isn't this a neat old place? It makes me think of the taverns back home, only so much bigger!"

A group of people sitting by the fire moved out of the way so that Sylica and Thea could have a place to sit. Sylica thrust one of the mugs into Thea's hands. "Here, this is for you! Isn't Harold so nice? I like coming here every day, just to see all my friends. Hello!" She waved enthusiastically at an elderly-looking woman across the room who waved back with a confused, though pleased, expression.

"Where are you from?" Sylica asked, turning back to Thea with hardly time for a breath. "I haven't seen you around here before."

"I ... just arrived," Thea managed to stammer. "I come from Lyudmyla. Have you—"

"What a nice sounding place. Lyudmyla. Even the name sounds special. I'd like to visit it someday. Aren't there so many interesting places in the world?"

Thea nodded distractedly. Something about the stranger's presence made it hard to focus. "I'm sorry, but what are you?"

Sylica grinned. "Why, don't you know? I'm a Little, of course."

Thea stared. "A what?"

"A Little. You know." Sylica smiled as if that clearly explained everything.

"I'm sorry," Thea stammered, "but you're not ... you're not *little*. You're as big as I am, or bigger."

"Well, I grew a lot," Sylica admitted, as if sharing some sort of secret. "My mom said I must have really loved my vegetables."

"But you ... *look* like an Elf. Sort of."

"What's an Elf?"

Thea stared at the Elf sitting beside her. "*I'm* an Elf. And you look like one too. See? We have the same kind of skin." Thea held her arm up beside Sylica's.

Sylica looked at them with a puzzled expression. "Mine is green and yours is kind of yellow."

"But they both look like stone," Thea explained, "and your eyes look a lot like mine. It's just your hair that's wrong."

Sylica twirled her hair around her fingers. "I like my hair. Isn't it pretty? The white part is just like my dad's.

He used to say that I gave him his white hair, but I always thought that should have been the other way around, since it's usually the parents that give things to their children, but he's very smart so I'm sure he knew what he was talking about."

"Where—where are you from?" Thea asked, trying to get a word in edgewise.

"Oh, I come from Home, of course."

"Home?"

"That's where I live," Sylica smiled. "It's off that way, you know." She waved a hand towards the far corner of the room.

Thea stared at Sylica in bewilderment. She didn't look like a Little at all, but she kind of talked like one. "Are there a lot of Littles where you come from?"

"Oh yes, lots and lots. Some of my best friends are there, like Mom and Dad and Uncle Bob. He's so much fun, you have to meet him someday."

"Are they as tall as you are?"

"Oh no. They're all quite short. I don't think they ate enough vegetables when they were younger. Like the Big Book says: What you put in your mouth only makes you bigger if it doesn't go out your bottom."

Thea stared at Sylica in bewilderment, but before she could say anything, Sylica turned towards the small bearded figure hunched over in a chair, just beyond the circle of firelight.

"It's a Little!" she shouted, jumping up and running towards him. "I haven't seen another Little in so long! Hello!"

The bearded figure startled, shook itself, and scrambled to get out of Sylica's enthusiastic embrace.

"Look at you!" Sylica beamed. "I think we must be

related!"

"No no—" the small man staggered drunkenly. "Not polite—calling names. Height discrimination."

"Sylica!" Thea managed to get between them and turned towards the offended man. "I'm sorry. There are actually a kind of small people called the Littles. They are very nice people. Sylica wasn't trying to insult you."

To Thea's consternation, a small crowd had gathered around them, excited to be witnessing a long lost reunion. The bearded man turned and glared at them. "Nothing to see here. Go on, now."

As the crowd dispersed, the man sank back into his chair and lifted his tankard. It was empty. The man set it down again with a growl.

"I'll get you some more!" Sylica offered, seizing the tankard and skipping off towards the bar.

The man frowned and slouched deeper into his chair until Thea could hardly see any face between his dark, bushy eyebrows and large, unkept beard. Beneath his grubby leather tunic, chain mail gleamed.

"I really am sorry for bothering you," Thea apologized again. "Sylica seems to be an interesting sort of person, but I think she means well. What's your name? I'm Thea."

"Ulfgar. Blade for hire." He straightened a little and broadened his shoulders, as if trying to make himself appear larger.

Thea could feel Arl's glare from across the room, but no one had seemed inclined to attack her or lock her up yet. Maybe she could risk a bit more conversation. "Pleased to meet you, Ulfgar. Are you from here?"

"No. Just passing through." He reached for his tankard but it wasn't there. He frowned.

"Where are you from?"

Ulfgar waved a dismissive hand. "Don't remember."

"Have you been in Wyndburh for long?"

"A while." Ulfgar shrugged. "Finding work where I can."

Sylica returned with three mugs of ale, which she handed out with a smile. "Isn't this so much fun? I love making new friends! Maybe next we can go join the party outside too. There's a whole crowd out there with torches and everything! Like the Big Book says: Lots of hands makes the fun funner!"

Thea gave Sylica a sharp look. She sounded cheerful enough, but the thought of a crowd with torches made her nervous. "Excuse me," she said and exited the conversation as quickly as she could.

Crossing to the door, Thea peered outside. There was a crowd carrying torches, but to Thea's relief they didn't appear to be congregating around the tavern. Pulling her hood to cover her face again, Thea slipped out of the door and walked confidently towards the crowd, trying to act as if she belonged there and knew what she was doing.

Soon she was jostling among the band of humans who were murmuring to each other and milling about the street. Thea sidled up to a middle-aged woman and asked in her very best Common, "What's the plan?"

"Root 'em out and kill 'em. Down to the very last one!"

A murmur of agreement rose from those nearby.

"Oh. Yes." Thea's throat felt dry. "And who was that again?"

"Those goblins. They've raided our farms for the last time!"

"Yeah!" Another voice chimed in. "Death to the goblins!"

Fear rose in Thea's heart. This was the kind of thing Elora had talked about. But surely they were safe in their tunnels. No one knew where they were. "Don't you think we should talk to them instead? Maybe there's been a misunderstanding."

"Talk to them?" The woman turned a suspicious eye towards Thea. "What are you on about?"

An elderly man shoved Thea's shoulder. "Goblins don't talk, they kill!"

Shouts of agreement rang around the street.

"But ... what if they're not really goblins at all? What if they're tiny people who—"

"Get out of here," grumbled a large, burly human with two swords strapped across their back. "Who are you, anyway?"

"Me?" Thea stuttered. "Oh, I ..." she stumbled backwards and ducked behind another cluster of humans. What was going on? Why were the humans going to kill the Littles?

She circled around to a lanky young man who was handing out torches. "Are we going into the forest?" she asked, as gruffly as she could.

"Goodness. No." The man seemed startled. "There's monsters in there."

"Of course." Desperate, Thea tried again. "So we're going ..."

"To deal with that hole up north. The one causing all the trouble."

"Right ... and where is it exactly?"

"Hey, what's your deal?" The man eyed her suspiciously. "You're a stranger here, aren't you?"

Thea tried to slip into the crowd again.

"Hey!" the man called from behind her. "Who was that?"

Ducking into the shadow of a wall, Thea pulled her cloak tight and tried to act as if she belonged there. As soon as the man's back was turned, she slipped back through the tavern door. She couldn't let the mob kill a whole community of Littles! But what could she do? If she tried to stop them, she was sure to get locked up again, or worse.

There were fewer people in the tavern now. Thea paced the room. She felt like she had a responsibility to Elora and her community. Even if these were different Littles, they were still Littles! They didn't deserve to be hunted and killed like this.

But it was late, and in the morning she was to take the road towards Gedwyld. That was what Allulien had told her to do, and she hadn't been told any different. She had to obey, but surely Allulien would want her to help the Littles, not leave them to their fate. It had been so long since she'd heard Allulien's voice.

Collapsing on her knees beside a bench, Thea held her face in her hands. "Allulien," she whispered, "Allulien please tell me what to do. I want to help the Littles, but you told me to go to Gedwyld. I don't want to disobey, but I can't bear to think of those poor creatures being killed like that."

The noises of the tavern faded around her as she waited, hoping desperately for an answer.

It would be within the will of the Deity for you to do so.

Thea looked up. Was that her own thought, or had someone spoken to her? No, everyone around her seemed unconcerned with her presence. Had that been Allulien's voice? It sounded more like Raphea. Of course, Raphea had told her about the importance of doing what she could to help others and heal the hurts of the world. As long as she was doing that, she had permission to delay her journey.

She jumped up and looked around the room. What could she do? She could hardly expect Arl to help her, but Sylica seemed to be familiar with the idea of Littles. Maybe she would help. Thea hurried over to the fireside where Sylica was still cheerfully talking at Ulfgar.

"—So then I told him I was going to make a boat and sail across the sea, and he said that was a *great* idea so I knew that it must be a great idea, because Uncle Bob always knows when something is a great idea, so I—oh hi, Thea, want a candy? I forgot to give you one earlier, so here's two." Sylica reached into her bag and dropped two small paper-wrapped sweets into Thea's hand.

"Sylica, you like Littles, don't you?" Thea said quickly. "There's some Littles nearby who need our help."

Sylica's face lit up. "There's Littles that live here? I have to go meet them!"

"Shh—not so loud!" Thea glanced around anxiously, but no one was paying attention to them. "The people here don't like the Littles. They want to kill them."

"Why would they do that?" Sylica protested. "They haven't tried to kill me, and I'm a Little. Everyone has been so nice and friendly!"

"But they don't know that the Littles are the Littles. They call them goblins and they're going tonight to try to kill them."

"Damn it." Ulfgar heaved himself out of his chair.

"Are they going already? I'm not drunk enough for this." He downed the contents of his tankard and looked around as if he was missing something.

"What are you talking about?" Thea demanded.

"Goblin hunters," Ulfgar muttered. "There's a bunch of them going tonight and they told me to come along."

"No!" Thea gasped. "You can't do that! The Littles are people. If you kill them it will be murder!"

Ulfgar grabbed a battered helmet off the floor and shoved it over his unruly hair. "What else am I supposed to do?" he grumbled. "There's nothing to do here but drink and I'm bound to drop out of reality at this rate." He grabbed Thea's mug—mostly untouched—and downed its contents too.

"Wait—" Thea grabbed Ulfgar's arm. "If you were going to go with them, do you know where they are going? Do you know where the Littles live?"

"The what's?"

"The goblins."

"Oh. Sure. I know where they are."

"You do?" Thea almost danced for joy. "That's wonderful! Can you take us there?"

"Can I what?" Ulfgar grabbed Sylica's mug, but it was empty.

"Take us to the goblins before the mob gets there."

Ulfgar frowned. "Why would I do that?"

"It would give you something to do other than drinking," Thea offered.

"Blade for hire," Ulfgar's words slurred slightly. "Pay me, I fight."

"I don't have any money," Thea admitted. She glanced at Sylica. "I don't suppose you—"

"Come on, Ulfgar, it will be fun!" Sylica grinned,

slapping him on the back. "And another round of drinks on the house!"

"Are *they* paying you?" Thea demanded, gesturing to the murmur of voices that could be heard drifting through the door.

Ulfgar muttered something unintelligible.

"If they're not paying you, why not go with us instead?" Thea cried, guessing the source of his reluctance. "Please, Ulfgar! It's the right thing to do, I promise!"

Ulfgar felt around beneath his chair and produced two axes, which he shoved through his belt.

"This is so exciting!" Sylica danced a little jig. "Three adventurers setting out against the odds!"

Thea thought she saw something gleam in the depths of Ulfgar's spirit. "You *are* going to help us?"

Ulfgar mumbled something into his beard, which Thea decided to accept as a confirmation.

"Let's go right away!" Sylica cried.

"Wait—" Thea's heart sank. "How are we going to get past the mob without them seeing us? If we wait until they've gone we will be too late!"

"I know!" Sylica grinned. "I'll tell them to let us go first!"

"No!" Thea grabbed Sylica's arm. "Don't you dare go out there! They'll try to stop us." Thea glanced around the room. How could they get past the mob? She hurried over to Arl. "Arl, you know this town. How can we get out without anyone seeing us?"

Arl glanced at Thea with emotionless eyes. "You can't."

"But we have to!" Thea insisted. "There's a mob out there with weapons and torches and they're going to go kill the Littles. We have to warn them!"

A strange expression crept across Arl's face.

"Please, Arl," Thea begged. "Can't you think of something? Can you help us get out of the town without them seeing us?"

Arl sighed and stood up. "Follow me."

Ignoring Sylica's offer of candy, Arl stalked towards a door on the far side of the room. Thea and Sylica hurried to follow. Ulfgar slung a large bag over his back and staggered after them.

They followed Arl up a flight of steps and through a bedroom where Arl opened a window and proceeded to climb outside onto the roof of a low shed close by.

"We're climbing on a *roof?*" Sylica squealed. "How fun! I've never—"

"Shh," Thea hissed.

One by one they climbed onto the roof and followed after Arl, from one roof to the next, until they were standing above the high wooden palisade that surrounded the town. Thea could see the flickering lights and hear the murmuring of the mob in the streets far below.

Arl knelt beside a low, squat chimney and gestured at Thea's bag. "Rope."

Quickly, Thea pulled the rope from her bag and handed it to Arl. Arl wrapped it several times around the chimney and dropped the long end down over the palisade. Holding the wrapped end tight, Arl nodded for Thea to climb down the rope.

Making sure that Raybow was secure, Thea grabbed the rope with both hands and lowered herself over the palisade. When her feet touched the ground she let go and stepped away from the rope, glancing anxiously around her, but the fields beyond the palisade were dark and silent.

Sylica slid down next, and Ulfgar followed with a clatter of loose weaponry. With a soft thud Arl landed beside them and handed Thea the rope.

"Thank you, Arl," Thea whispered.

Arl stared at her for a moment, then transformed into an eagle and flew off into the night sky.

"Wow!" Sylica stared as Arl disappeared into the distance. "I always wanted to fly!"

Thea shoved the rope into her bag. "Which way do we go, Ulfgar?"

Ulfgar frowned for a moment, then gestured vaguely to the north.

Together, they crept away from the palisade and set off through the silent fields. Ulfgar led the way, plodding at a steady even pace. Sylica dashed back and forth like a puppy, excited to be going for a walk.

By the light of Micai, Thea could see a range of hills stretching before them, and soon they were hiking up the slopes of the closest one.

They were about halfway up when Thea glanced back into the dark valley below. She could just see Wyndburh, a darker shadow among the dark fields. Streaming out from it was a row of tiny, flickering light.

"They're coming!" Thea gasped. "We need to hurry!"

They stumbled on through the shadowy night. Thea tried to urge Ulfgar faster, but he only seemed to have one pace of travel.

The rough path they were following curved around the side of the hill and wound its way down into the valley beyond. A pack of crox startled at their approach, flying up into the planet-lit night with a sudden burst of noise.

Ulfgar stopped and peered around at the hills surrounding them.

"Are we almost there?" Thea asked, glancing over her shoulder in the fear that she would see a stream of torches pouring over the ridge behind them.

"Oh. Well." Ulfgar peered around the scrubby bushes and long grasses that covered the hillside. "We should be there pretty soon. Not much farther now, I'd say."

Thea gave Ulfgar a suspicious glance. "You *do* know where they are, right?"

"I know where they are," Ulfgar grumbled, "I just don't know *exactly* where they are."

"You don't know?" Thea cried. "How are we going to find them?"

"Past the stream, they said." He gestured into the shadows further down the valley. "Just start looking, I guess."

"But we don't have time for looking! We need to find them right now!"

"Look!" Sylica grinned. "A beech tree! Littles love beech trees!"

Thea gave Sylica an exasperated glance. "Those are the Littles that you know, Sylica. We don't know what these Littles like."

Sylica nodded confidently. "Let's go look. They like to have a big tree over their doors so they can find them from far away. Our homes are like that too."

Thea exchanged a glance with Ulfgar, but he didn't have anything better to offer, so they followed Sylica towards the shadowy tree in the distance.

As they approached it, they found it to be growing out of the hillside, surrounded by a tangled mat of gorse bushes and grass. There was no tunnel entrance to be seen.

Sylica stood with her hands on her hips, her forehead scrunched up into a frown. "I thought it would be there."

Thea remembered the large tree above Elora's hidden tunnel. "Maybe it is." Crouching down, she began searching through the long grasses that surrounded the tree.

Pushing a scrubby bush aside, she caught a glimpse of a darker shade among the shadows. Reaching out her hand, she found it to be a small hole, no larger than the entrance to an animal den. "I found it."

"What?" Sylica protested. "Littles don't live in holes like that! Their homes have windows and doors and gardens out the front!"

"Not here they don't," Thea muttered. Ducking low to the ground, she crawled through the hole. As she expected, the hole widened almost immediately, although she still had to crouch almost double to walk through it.

"Well that doesn't make sense." Sylica crawled along behind her, even as she protested. "But I've never been in an animal home before! I wonder what we'll find!"

Thea gestured for Sylica to be quiet and crept forward as silently as she could. In darkness, she followed the weaving passage until she rounded a corner and saw a small lantern mounted on the wall. Beyond it, a wooden door blocked the passage.

"Look at that!" Sylica's whisper echoed eerily. "I didn't know animals used doors!"

Thea glanced back. Beyond Sylica's hunched figure, Ulfgar strode comfortably, his head just brushing the ceiling.

Taking a deep breath, Thea turned back to the door and gave it a solid knock. The thump sounded dull and hollow in the cramped passage. There was no reply.

Thea tried knocking again. "Hello," she called. "We are here to help you. Please let us in."

There was no sound in response, besides the beating of her own heart.

She tried again. "There are humans coming to kill you. You need to get away from here. Right now!" Grabbing the handle, she tried to open the door, but it wouldn't move.

"Trouble with the door?" Ulfgar grumbled. "Let me through. I'll try."

Thea and Sylica pressed themselves to one side of the tunnel as Ulfgar squeezed past. He looked the door up and down for a moment, took a step back, then charged towards it, his axe glinting in the fungal light.

With a splintering crash, the door broke in half and sank back on twisted hinges.

"Ulfgar!" Thea gasped.

"That's how you deal with a door," Ulfgar muttered and stepped through it into the room beyond.

Chapter Eleven

Thea hurried after Ulfgar, stepping into a room much like the common room in Elora's community, but this room was smaller and had fewer tables. Glowing green lights lined the walls, and on the far side of the room a cluster of Littles were huddled together, staring fearfully at the intruders.

Thea held up her empty hands in a reassuring gesture. "We're here to help you. Don't be afraid."

Sylica squealed in delight and rushed at the terrified Littles, who scrambled to get away. Her voice rose above the chaos, chattering excitedly in a language that Thea couldn't understand. The Littles stopped and stared at her with bewildered expressions, as if they could hardly believe their ears.

Hesitantly, one of the older Littles spoke, and Sylica responded with enthusiasm, waving her arms in the air and accidentally knocking down one of the lanterns.

"Sylica," Thea hissed, hurrying over to her side. "What are they saying? What are *you* saying? I didn't know you could speak their language!"

"This is Faris," Sylica replied, gesturing to a Little with thin white hair and a stubby beard, "and this is his home. I understand him well enough—different dialects you know—but I can't figure out if we are related."

"Did you tell them the humans are coming?"

"Oh. Right." Sylica frowned. "No I didn't."

"Sylica!"

Sylica turned to the Littles and spoke quickly. The Littles looked at each other and shifted nervously.

"Please tell them to come with us," Thea said hurriedly. "They aren't safe here."

Sylica spoke again, and the Littles began talking among themselves. Some of them looked fearful. Some looked angry. Others gestured at the intruders and at the broken door.

"What are they saying?" Thea asked, but Sylica was caught up in the conversation and didn't respond.

An argument seemed to be arising among the Littles. They didn't have time to argue—the humans were already on their way!

Magic burst out of Thea, filling the room like an invisible wave. "Listen to me!"

The Littles fell silent and stared at her in surprise.

"I know you have concerns, but you need to leave. Now."

"Where will we go?" one of the Littles demanded.

"I don't know," Thea admitted, "but we can figure that out later. Right now we need to get you out of here!"

"This is our home!" another Little replied. "We can fight them off!"

"With a broken door?" another Little muttered.

"Listen," Thea insisted. "There are many Bigs coming, right now, and they want to kill you."

"Then we'll kill them back!" one of the Littles grumbled. "They can't take our home from us!"

Once again a hubbub rose as the Littles began to bicker and argue.

"I told you we shouldn't have taken that food!"

"It's your fault, Hana! If you hadn't—"

"What was I supposed to do? We were starving!"

"Bar the door and don't let them in!"

"They're Bigs. You can't trust them."

"Yeah, we can't trust them." Suspicious eyes glared at Thea and her friends.

Thea waved her arms for attention. "Listen to me!"

The Littles fell silent once again.

"Please come with us." Thea looked from face to face, willing them to listen. "I know the Bigs have hurt you and that you don't trust us, but I *know* that you are not goblins. I don't want you to die, and I promise that I will find you a new home."

In the silence, a bell chimed a note, clear and high.

"Someone entered our tunnel." The Little called Faris spoke in a low voice.

The bell rang again. And again.

"Many people are entering our tunnel." His voice was grim as he turned to speak to the other Littles. "To stay and fight would not be smart. We must go."

Spurred into action, the Littles grabbed their makeshift weapons. Scattering around the room, some grabbed bags and bundles that had been lying on the benches. Some pulled the lanterns off the walls.

"Come on!" Thea urged them as she felt the effects of her magic fade.

Faris gestured for everyone to follow him down another passageway. Thea hurried after them, Raybow in her hand. She didn't want to shoot a human, but she could hold them off for a little while if she had to.

The passage wound on and on, the only sounds the scuffling of many tiny feet and an occasional excited squeal from Sylica. Thea kept glancing back over her shoulder, but no torches appeared.

Finally they emerged from the tunnel into a narrow valley. Micai filled the sky above them.

"Where are we?" Thea whispered, but no one replied.

Faris led them on, up through the valley until they crested a ridge and looked down on the fields surrounding Wyndburh.

Faris stared up at Thea and said in very rough Common, "Now what?"

Thea looked down at the Littles. Their clothes were rougher and more threadbare than the Littles she had met before. Their faces were hardened and their hands were calloused, but they looked up at her with large, expectant eyes. Even Sylica and Ulfgar seemed to be waiting for what she would say. This was all her idea, but now she had no idea what to do.

Deity, please help us, Thea whispered, her eyes scanning the distance for anything—any idea of where to go or what to do. She didn't know these lands. Elora said that nowhere was safe for the Littles, so who did she think she was, promising to find them a new home? Never mind a new home, what about a place to hide right now?

Elora. Thea stared at the darker shadows in the distance that marked the place where the Deorcian began. There were monsters there, but Elora had said they were safe in their tunnels. Would they take these Littles in and give them a new home? Even if it was temporary, it would be a place to get out of the way and evade the humans before searching for a new home.

Thea turned to Faris and pointed at the distant shadows. "We are going to the Trees."

A murmur rose among the Littles as her words

passed from mouth to mouth.

"Trust me," she said, in the simplest Common she could muster. "The Bigs won't follow us there." She didn't know that for sure, but she could only hope. Right now she'd rather face the monsters than the mob she knew was at their tail.

Following Thea's lead, the company of Littles hurried down the hillside towards the valley below. Some of the Littles seemed quite elderly. A few were only children. They hurried as best they could, but they weren't following a path, and the hillside was rough and at times quite steep. The Littles had a hard time keeping up to Thea's pace. Soon they were lagging behind.

As they reached the border of the fields, Allumen emerged from Micai's eclipse and bright daylight flooded across the land. Thea's heart smote her. She was supposed to be checking in, but here she was, trying to hurry the Littles across the open fields in what was now full daylight. How she could use some help from Allulien now!

A shout arose in the distance and Thea turned to see dark figures emerge from over the ridge.

Thea turned back to the Littles. "Run!"

Faris scooped up one of the small children in his arms and ran. Sylica darted over to one of the older Littles who walked with a cane and slung his arm over her shoulder, half lifting, half dragging him along. Sheathing his axe, Ulfgar heaved a child up under each of his muscular arms and started pounding his way across the field.

Thea ran ahead, practically vibrating with impatience. They weren't going fast enough! The humans were going to catch up! Glancing over her shoulder, she could see them barrelling down the hill towards them, gaining ground far too quickly.

A shout from the direction of Wyndburh caught Thea's attention. They had been seen. A party of humans waving spears and pitchforks emerged from the town and rushed towards them, charging as if to cut them off from the front.

The Littles continued to run as the two groups of humans drew closer and closer.

"You got any other ideas?" Ulfgar shouted. A spear sailed over their heads. He gently dropped the children he had been carrying and whipped his axes out of his belt, flourishing one in each hand.

"Wait!" Thea yelled. "Wait! Stop running!"

Ulfgar, Sylica, and the Littles stopped and stared at her in shock.

"Just walk," Thea explained, her mind racing. "Walk like you belong here and you're just passing through. Don't look at the humans, just walk past them."

With wide eyes, the Littles turned and started to walk towards the distant forest. Glancing over her shoulder, Thea saw the humans looking at them with bewildered glances. They had also stopped running and now moved towards the Littles cautiously, muttering to each other as if they suspected some kind of trap but couldn't figure out what it was.

The Littles walked on, beyond the intercepting party from the town. The humans trailed along behind them like a strange, uneasy parade, beyond the town and its fields, up the slopes beyond, right up to the edge of the forest.

As the Littles passed the first trees, the humans fell further and further behind, seemingly reluctant to follow their strange prey into the land of the monsters.

Perhaps they were thinking "good riddance". Maybe they decided that their job was done, but not a single human followed the Littles into the Deorcian, and soon they were completely out of sight.

Thea breathed a sigh of relief. The Littles were safe from the humans. Now she had to find the entrance to Elora's home. She peered this way and that as they walked deeper into the forest, but nothing seemed familiar.

The Littles walked silently, staring around them at the darkening trees.

Thea began to feel uneasy. It shouldn't be nearly evening yet, but the woods grew darker and more silent the further that they went. Had she missed the way entirely?

A distant howl broke the silence.

Thea's heart sank. Oh no. Not wolves.

The Littles looked at each other nervously as they continued to follow Thea. Ulfgar eyed the surrounding forest intently, an axe gripped in each of his hands. Thea's heart began to race. If only she could find the tunnel entrance!

A shadow appeared. Thea's spirit sight saw it before her eyes did. A low figure crept towards them through the darkness beneath the trees. It looked like a wolf, but darkness flowed from it, staining the woods around it with an even deeper blackness. Another wolf appeared. And another.

Thea grabbed Raybow off her back and put an arrow to the string. "Stay behind Ulfgar!" she hissed to the Littles as she took aim at the largest of the wolves. Two more wolves appeared in the corner of her vision, circling around the small clearing where the Littles were clustered.

Thea shot. The arrow blazed white as it sped through the shadows. The wolf snarled and dodged out of the way, unharmed.

With shaking hands, Thea nocked another arrow. Ulfgar stepped beside her, brandishing his axes.

An eagle's cry pierced the silence as a bolt of darkness fell from the sky, directly towards the alpha wolf. The moment before it struck, the figure expanded and became an enormous bear, landing on top of the wolf with a sickening thud. The bear's eyes blazed red in the darkness.

"Arl!" Thea yelled, waving her arms in the air. "I know that bear!"

With a snarl, the wolves attacked. Two launched themselves at Arl, and together they tumbled through the trees, a mass of claws and teeth and fur. Another wolf rushed at Ulfgar, who strode to meet it, axes cleaving the air.

Someone screamed.

A wolf was among the scattering Littles, something pinned beneath its bloody claws.

Thea shot. The blazing arrow struck its mark with an explosion of light and the wolf sank to the ground.

Snarls and shouts filled the air. Thea wheeled and was about to shoot again when a large, forked tree caught her eye. Was that the entrance? Ducking away from the fight, Thea ran to it and searched madly through the undergrowth. Yes, there was a hole, right where she thought it would be.

Thea turned back to see Ulfgar hack an ugly wound in the shoulder of one of the wolves. The Littles were pelting the tumbling mass of bear and wolves with a barrage of sticks and stones.

"Sylica! Faris!" Thea yelled. "Over here!"

Arl roared as another wolf fell, lifeless. The final two wolves fled into the shadows and disappeared.

Faris and Sylica were kneeling over the injured Little. Thea hurried to join them. Blood was everywhere.

"We're almost there," Thea urged them. "Come on, we need to go!"

Arl stepped out of the trees in the Elf form that Thea was most familiar with. Their nose was bloodied, and it looked like the wound on their shoulder had been opened up again.

"Arl!" Thea hurried over to them, gesturing to the alarmed Littles that the new intruder was safe. "I am so glad to see you!"

Arl glared at her. "I thought you knew better than to return to the Deorcian."

"But we had to find the Littles a home." Thea looked around the cluster of frightened Littles. "The humans were going to kill them."

"So you brought them to the Deorcian?"

"I'm bringing them to Elora."

"Elora told you not to come back."

Thea pushed through the worry that rose to choke her. "She will understand. I know she will." She set her face towards the concealed entrance. "I will go talk with whoever's on guard. Wait here with the Littles."

Getting down on her knees, Thea crawled through the tunnel until it widened and she could stand again. How far had it been before the first lantern? She felt her way along the wall until she saw a glimmer of light ahead.

"Hello!" she called. "It's Thea. I'm a friend. I need to talk to you." Thea crept forward, round the corner, and found herself face to face with Kais.

"Kais!" Thea gasped. "I'm so glad to see you!"

Kais stared at her. "What is going on? We did not expect to see you again."

"The humans were going to kill the Littles. I had to help them, but I didn't know where to go. Can we shelter here? The wolves were attacking us."

Kais took a moment to absorb her story, then nodded. "Of course we'll take them in. Are they outside?"

Thea nodded and hurried back along the tunnel. When she emerged with Kais, the forest seemed darker than it was before.

"Faris!" Thea called.

Faris hurried over. His shirt had been ripped, and he held a long strip of cloth in his hands. "What is it?" He stopped short when he saw Kais.

"Uncle Faris?" Kais rushed forward and embraced him. Putting his hands on the elderly Little's shoulders, Kais spoke quickly in the language of the Littles.

With a gesture, Faris led Kais to the injured Little.

A clamour rose from the Littles as they approached. Thea ran over to Arl who was eyeing the forest with a suspicious glare. "We need to get everyone inside. Can you do something to help carry the injured one?"

"I will be rear guard," Arl said in a stiff tone. "That is all."

Turning away, Thea hurried to where Faris and Kais were kneeling over the injured Little. The rough bandage wrapped around her wounds was already soaked through with blood.

"Can we get them inside?" Thea asked, kneeling beside them.

"Lead the others in." Kais gestured Thea away.

Thea stood up. "Come with me," she called to the Littles. "There is a safe place close by."

Cautiously, the Littles followed Thea towards the tree, but when they saw the hole they followed her inside willingly enough. She led them as far as the antechamber, then told them to wait there and hurried back to see how Kais and Faris were doing.

They had managed to make a rough stretcher out of branches and their shirts, and with Ulfgar's help they were lifting the injured Little onto it. Thea stepped beside Sylica who was watching them with wide eyes.

"Come inside, Sylica," Thea urged her. "The Littles there need you. Maybe give them some candy."

Cheered by this suggestion, Sylica clambered through the hole and disappeared from view.

Working together, Ulfgar, Faris, and Kais managed to navigate the stretcher through the narrow hole. Thea followed close behind them, then realized that Arl wasn't following. Crawling back out of the hole, she caught a flash of red eyes through the shadow of the trees.

Thea hurried over. "Arl, aren't you coming?"

"I was told not to return."

"Elora meant don't come back to hurt them. You're not hurting them now, you're helping them!"

Arl looked away.

"Please, Arl. You're hurt, and they have no reason to be anything but thankful for what you've done."

Arl did not respond.

Thea stomped around to look Arl square in the face. "Since when did you take orders from a goblin, anyways?"

A strange, almost amused expression flashed through Arl's eyes as they seemed to consider this.

"So you'll come?"

Arl sighed. "I will come."

Back in the tunnel, Thea and Arl soon caught up to the Littles as they made the long trek towards the living quarters. From what Thea could gather, Kais and Faris had gone on ahead as quickly as possible with the stretcher, leaving Sylica and the rest to plod along at their own pace.

It was a long walk, and it felt even longer now. Two long days of travel and a sleepless night with all of its danger and worry had worn away Thea's strength until she had nothing left. Step after step, she forced herself to carry on.

In the darkness ahead, Sylica's footsteps echoed as she tramped up and down the long procession of Littles, offering candies and encouraging words.

Just one more step. Just one more step.

A new sort of murmur ahead.

There—a wooden door, and light glinting beyond.

Ducking through the door, Thea stopped, face to face with Elora.

Elora stared at her, motionless, eyes moving from Thea to Arl standing beside her. After a long moment, she spoke. "Come." She turned and walked away.

Thea followed, through corridors that seemed much longer than they had before, until she stepped through the door into the room that she and Arl had slept in only two nights ago.

Elora shut the door behind her and turned to face them with cold, emotionless eyes.

"Why?"

Chapter Twelve

"Why did you do this?"

Thea stared at Elora. Exhaustion swept over her body like a wave and she staggered. Her head was pounding. She couldn't think clearly. "They were going to die," she mumbled, struggling to remember the basic Common she had learned. "I couldn't let them die."

"Do you understand what you've done?" Elora's eyes flashed.

"I know what she has done." Arl shifted into human form, speaking in a cold, forceful voice. "She risked her life to help your people. At least you could be grateful."

Elora spoke sharply, but the words drifted beyond Thea's ability to comprehend. The room swam in her vision and her legs collapsed.

Strong arms picked her up and set her on a bed that was far too short. She felt like she should protest something, but she wasn't sure what.

When she woke, she was alone. No, she wasn't alone. Arl was lying on the other bed, watching her. Gingerly, Thea sat up. Her head didn't pound as much anymore.

"When you are awake, Elora wishes to speak with us," Arl said in a dry voice. "We seem to be in some kind of trouble."

Waves of concern and relief washed over Thea as her mind reassembled the events of the previous day.

Hunger gnawed at her stomach. "Do you think there might be something we can eat?"

"I suppose we can ask." Arl stood up and walked to the door. "Are you coming?"

They made their way to the common room in silence. There they found Elora and Kais waiting for them, along with what seemed to be the remains of breakfast, long cold, but to Thea it looked like a feast.

After Thea and Arl had eaten, they joined Elora and Kais by the fire. Elora looked tired, but Kais paced back and forth with a nervous sort of energy.

Thea waited in silence for what they would say.

"We made it in time to save Dana," Kais said at last. "Sami is nursing her as we speak, and it looks like she might make it. It was a very close call."

"I am glad to hear it," Thea said in a quiet voice. She was watching Elora closely.

Elora returned her glance. Leaning forward, she sighed. "I was not truthful with you when you were here. I did not have to be. You were guests and not entitled to know our situation. But maybe I should have said more." Her gaze slowly took in the comfortable room surrounding them. "We are not safe here. The Trees have never been safe, but now there are more monsters all the time. They hunt us whenever we leave our holes, always searching for how to find us. We know that we cannot stay here, but we have nowhere else to go." She looked at Thea with tired eyes. "And now you bring us more mouths to feed, leading the monsters right to our tunnels. We will not turn our own people away, but what can we do?"

Of course. Thea's heart sank. She should have known that bringing the Littles to Elora would make things harder, not better. But what choice did she have? If there really was nowhere for the Littles to be safe ...

But was there? Sylica had said that where she came from the Littles lived in homes with large doors and windows and gardens. That must be a land that was safe. She glanced around the room. "Where's Sylica?"

"The strange one?" Elora gave her a curious look. "I believe she was trying to help Grandmother."

As Kais ran to get Sylica, Thea stared into the fire, her mind racing. It seemed too good to be true, but if Sylica was right, perhaps that was the answer they were looking for.

Soon Sylica came through the door and approached them with a cheerful bounce. "Sami said to tell you that the worst is over now and Dana should be on the mend soon. Isn't that great?"

Thea looked at her intently. "Sylica, when you talk about your home, you speak of a place where Littles can live in safety. Is that true?"

"Oh yes." Sylica nodded enthusiastically. "It is such a good place with farms and rivers and forests that are a lot safer than this one, and the Bigs there never try to kill the Littles."

"Would you be able to lead us there, if we wanted to go? And would more Littles be welcomed there?"

"Of course!" Sylica beamed. "We love making new friends, and there are lots of spots for new homes. We should go right now! Then you can meet all my friends!"

Thea glanced at Elora. "What do you think?"

Elora watched Sylica with a cautious expression. "Where is this place?"

"It is past the road and the water, uh ... east!" She gestured to the far side of the room. A glance between

Elora and Kais indicated that the direction she had pointed was definitely not east.

"How far away is it?"

"Oh, very far. I had to travel a long, long time to get here."

Elora shifted uneasily. "We could never travel that far with this many people. What if the journey is too hard for the old or the injured?"

Thea leaned forward. "I can go with Sylica and learn the way. Then I will know if the journey is safe and exactly how far it is."

Elora looked at Thea with a strange, guarded expression. "Why would you do that?"

"I promised Faris and his people a new home, and I have to keep my promise."

Elora gave a decisive nod. "I will go with you. Maybe this land can be a home for my people too. Kais will guard our people while we are gone."

Kais put his hand in Elora's. "Just hold the dark things off a little longer, right?"

He spoke lightly, but Elora seemed to sense his unspoken worry. She gave him a reassuring smile. "We will travel quick and be back soon."

"Yes," Thea agreed, "we want to find you a home as soon as we can. Will you let Arl stay here while I'm gone? I think Sami should look at their shoulder again."

"I am not staying here," Arl interjected in an emotionless voice.

"But Arl—"

"If you are searching for this land of the Littles, you will need someone to protect you."

"But you said you weren't going beyond Wyndburh."

"Dryads are protectors. If I have to keep checking on

you to make sure you aren't in some kind of trouble, I might as well just come."

Thea smiled. "Thank you, Arl. We would be glad to have you with us."

"I will be there to protect *you*," Arl said icily. "The others travel at their own risk."

"How soon will you go?" Kais asked.

This was debated for some time, but it was finally settled that the expedition would depart in two days' time. That would give time for the travellers to be rested and fully prepared for their journey.

There was much excitement amongst the rest of the Littles when they heard about the upcoming departure. Faris thanked Thea with tears in his eyes, and promised that he would do all that he could to aid her in her quest. Sami bustled about, preparing food for the journey. Elora and Kais spent much of their time alone together, making preparations of their own.

On the morning of their departure, Thea woke earlier than usual and knelt to check in. As the all too familiar silence stretched on and on, a deep feeling of isolation rose to choke her.

"Allulien," she whispered, "I haven't heard anything from you for such a long time. I've tried not to mind, and I've tried to do what you said, but it's so hard. You used to talk to me every day, and Micai and Raphea would come and walk with me, but now there's nothing. Why did you leave me alone? How am I supposed to know what to do if you don't tell me? I just want to know if I'm doing the right thing."

Beyond the door, Thea could hear muffled sounds as others woke and prepared for departure.

"We should go."

Thea looked up at Arl. "I know." She sighed and got slowly to her feet. Grabbing Raybow and her bag from beside the bed, Thea and Arl made their way to the common room where they found Ulfgar sorting through his plethora of axes and knives. A large pack lay on the table beside him.

Thea looked at him in surprise. "Ulfgar! Are you coming too?"

"What of it?" He stuck his hand in the bag that was longer than his arm and started rummaging around.

"I thought you would go back to Wyndburh."

"Wyndburh?" Ulfgar grumbled. "What have I got for me there? I'm sure they'd be so happy to see me now." He shook his head. "Do you know how many places I can never show my face again?"

Thea watched him for a moment. "We don't have any money to pay you."

Ulfgar shrugged. "Maybe I'll find work on the road. No work for me here, it seems." He looked around the cluster of Littles who were gathering to see the party off. "Do any of you have some beer on you? I'm not drunk enough for this."

Elora entered the room with a large bag slung over her back, just as Sylica skipped into the room through another door. Sami had filled a bag for her with food and blankets and medical supplies.

"Are we ready to go?" Elora asked, glancing around the room.

"I think so," Thea replied. "But where's Kais? I thought he'd be here to say goodbye."

"We'll meet him in the tunnel." Elora picked up her bow and clipped her quiver of black arrows to her belt.

"Follow me."

With a wave to the assembled Littles, Thea followed Elora into the tunnel. It was the same passage that she and Arl had entered through when they first met Elora. Thea watched her dark, lithe figure creeping along in front of her. Arl's catlike tread padded close behind.

"Isn't this fun?" Sylica's whisper echoed down the narrow passage, and beyond, Thea could hear the tramp of Ulfgar's boots.

Kais was waiting for them in the antechamber. "The area has been quiet all night," he said to Elora in a low voice. "Nothing knows that you are coming."

"Good. Keep everyone inside today."

Kais nodded. "Be careful."

Elora gave him a reassuring smile, then turned and continued down the tunnel. Thea followed. Kais gave her a friendly nod as she passed by.

After crawling through the smallest part of the tunnel, Thea emerged into the forest beyond. Early morning light glimmered in the branches high above, but no beam passed through the leaves into the gloom of the forest floor below.

Elora gestured the direction that they were to travel.

Without a sound, Arl shifted into the form of a cougar and slunk into the shadows. Elora followed just as silently, an arrow nocked on the string of her bow.

Thea hurried to follow, painfully aware of every branch that rustled as she brushed past. Ulfgar sounded like he wasn't even trying to walk quietly, and Sylica hummed softly to herself. Thea gestured for them to be quiet. In the unnatural silence of the forest, every small sound seemed amplified.

Cautiously, they crept through the trees. Thea tried

to focus on her own movement and being as silent as possible, but it was hard not to worry about what was to come. How far was it to Sylica's home, and what would they find there? What would Allulien think about what she was doing?

All through the long workday they continued through the trees. Thea was starting to feel tired, but she knew that neither Arl nor Elora would want to stop as long as they were still in the Deorcian.

Her spirit sight tingled. Barely visible through the trees ahead, she could see Elora's light shimmering in the gloom. Glancing over her shoulder, she saw Sylica shining like a beacon. Beyond, Ulfgar's spirit was dull and lifeless. Above her, darkness flowed through the trees. Thea stared. Slowly, her eyes took in figures hunched in the branches above their heads. Dark, vulture-like figures with glowing eyes. They were watching them.

"Elora?" Thea hissed.

The figures plunged toward them.

"Look out!" Thea threw herself to the ground. Sharp talons grazed her shoulder as the stench of rotting flesh filled her nose. Shouts and chilling screeches exploded through the silence.

Thea scrambled back to her feet. One of the birds had knocked Sylica to her back and was trying to tear her face with its beak—each swipe barely missing its wildly flailing target. Another bird landed on Ulfgar's shoulders, sinking its talons through his chain mail shirt. Feathers flew as Ulfgar waved an axe in each hand, trying to dislodge his assailant. Three more birds circled him warily, waiting for a moment to strike.

A black arrow flashed through the air and Thea

ducked instinctively. There was an explosion of feathers and another nauseating stench of rottenness as a bird just above Thea's head flew back into the branches above.

Thea snatched Raybow off her back, but before she could put an arrow to the string, another giant bird dove towards her and she threw herself to the ground.

A tawny blur streaked overhead, striking the bird and tumbling with it into the undergrowth. The smell of putrid flesh made Thea retch.

Another black arrow flew as Thea struggled to her feet and lifted Raybow.

Something swooped towards her and she shot. The arrow blazed with light as it struck the bird, which crashed to the ground in an explosion of feathers and stench.

Thea looked up. The branches above them were dark with birds.

"Run!" Elora yelled. "There's too many!"

With a gruff roar, Ulfgar shook the giant bird off his shoulders and landed a killing blow on the bird pinning Sylica to the ground. Thea shot once more, then turned to follow.

Sharp pain exploded through her shoulder. Stumbling, she waved Raybow wildly, hoping to strike something. With a snarl Arl leapt over her head, tackling her attacker to the ground.

Thea staggered to her feet and ran. Something dark flashed overhead. A bird swooped down, seized Elora in its talons, and lifted her into the air.

"Elora!" Thea yelled. Something struck Thea's head and she tumbled to the ground.

A roar shook the forest. Thea pushed herself to her

knees. Where was Elora?

Overhead, the bird beat its massive wings, sending waves of stench through the trees. Elora struggled and kicked, dangling in midair.

Grabbing an arrow, Thea shot. She missed.

With a screech, the bird threw Elora upward and caught her in its beak, landing on a thick branch overhead.

With a yell, Ulfgar jumped out of the branches, striking the bird in the neck with his axe. The bird jerked to face him, Elora still dangling from its beak. With a wild, reckless gleam in his eyes, Ulfgar grabbed Elora and jumped.

With a screech, an eagle shot over Thea's head and swooped beneath them. With a tumbling crash, Ulfgar, Elora, and the eagle hit the ground in an untidy heap. The ground beneath them shook, then collapsed in a shower of dirt and fallen leaves, dropping them into blackness below.

"Arl! Elora!" Thea yelled, running towards the gaping hole. Something dark swooped over her head and she threw herself to the ground. As soon as the shadow had passed she staggered to her feet. All around her the birds were closing in.

"Come on!" Sylica grabbed her hand and jumped into the hole.

Jerked off her feet, Thea fell, tumbling in a cascade of debris. With a thud, she landed in darkness. The rumble of falling dirt and stone faded into silence.

Shakily, Thea got to her feet. "Is everyone okay?"

A dim green light appeared as Elora pulled a fungus lantern from her pack. She held it up and peered into the gloom.

Ulfgar stretched and grinned at the bedraggled-looking eagle. "Thanks for the catch."

Arl shifted back into human form and glared at him. "*Never* do that again."

"Come on." Elora gestured to the group. "I think I know where we are." She set off down what appeared to be a long corridor, crumbling and filled with debris.

Dim light filtered down from the shaft through which they had fallen, and Thea thought she could hear the screeching of the birds, cheated of their prey.

"What were they?"

"Dark birds," Elora replied.

"Musharoc," Arl replied at the same moment. They glared at each other.

Without another word, Elora turned and stalked down the passageway. One by one, the others followed. It was hard to see, with only the one small light leading the way. Thea stumbled over the bumpy, uneven floor.

"This is like a Little's tunnel, but very dirty," Sylica commented, looking around the corridor with interest.

"That's exactly what it is," Elora replied grimly.

"Is it still lived in, do you think?" Thea asked.

"No. There used to be many Homes in the Trees. Ours is the only one left."

They walked in silence through passageways that showed signs of once being inhabited, stepping through broken doorways and passing lanterns with dead, lightless fungi inside them.

"Why are they gone?" Thea whispered.

"Dead." Elora said simply. "Many were killed. Some tried to leave and find a new home. We never heard from them again."

They stepped out into what had once been a common

room. There were tables—broken and rotting. An old, crumbling fireplace dominated what had once been a stone wall.

Ulfgar dropped his pack on the ground. "Food time, isn't it?"

Thea glanced around the group. They had been travelling for most of the day and everyone looked tired. "I think that's a good idea, Ulfgar. We can eat and sleep and make it the rest of the way out of the Deorcian tomorrow."

Elora frowned. "These rooms aren't stable. We shouldn't sleep here."

"Will it be safer than sleeping up in the trees?"

Elora didn't offer a response.

Soon Thea and Ulfgar had food set out for the rest of the group. They ate in silence. Even Sylica seemed subdued, glancing around the abandoned room with an expression of troubled concern.

After supper, Thea encouraged everyone to lie down and get some rest. Sylica obliged at once, curling up beside what would have once been the fireplace.

Elora picked up her bow. "I will keep watch."

"*I* will keep watch," Arl countered with flashing eyes.

Thea sighed. "Can you at least take turns?"

When neither Arl nor Elora appeared to be backing down, Thea wrapped herself in her cloak and lay down on the hard dirt floor.

Ulfgar's snore echoed through the silence.

Thea stared at the ceiling, illuminated with strange, unflickering shadows from the lantern's dull green light. What had it been like for the Littles who lived here—picked off one by one by the monsters of the Deorcian, or hunted by humans who thought they were nothing more than another kind of monster themselves? There had to be a better life for the Littles somewhere. The Deity wouldn't have made them for a life like this.

A distant rumble shook the floor beneath her feet. Sitting up, she saw Elora and Arl exchange a glance. Silently, Elora drew an arrow from her quiver.

Arl crouched with one ear to the ground. "Something is coming."

Slowly, Thea became aware of the stench of decaying flesh.

Elora's eyes glinted with a hard light. "The dark birds. They never give up on their prey."

"They found another way in?" Thea glanced around in alarm. She could hear a scrabbling, clattering sound in the distance. It was growing louder.

Quickly, she shook Ulfgar and Sylica awake. Gathering their things together, they followed Elora down one of the passageways, away from the approaching noise.

They hurried as silently as they could, past the dark openings of other corridors and rooms. The stench of death seemed to follow them.

The passage wound on and on, until they rounded a corner and found that the tunnel in front of them had been completely filled with rocks and dirt and mouldering leaves.

Hurrying back, they tried another corridor, but it was also completely barred by debris.

The stench was growing stronger now. Thea listened in alarm as the scuffling sounds grew louder.

Elora turned to hurry back down the corridor.

"Wait." Arl eyed the collapsed passage in front of

them. Shifting into the form of a badger, they sniffed the air for a moment, then burrowed into the mess of debris. Chunks of dirt and leaves and rotting wood flew back into the tunnel.

Elora stared at the darkness of the passageway behind them. "Do we have time?" she asked in a low voice.

"If Arl thinks we can get out, we have a pretty good chance," Thea whispered. The sound of their pursuers was louder now, echoing down the tunnel towards them.

Elora gave her a dark look. "Get your bow."

Elora positioned herself at the rear of the group, arrow trained on the spot where the tunnel curved beyond their sight.

Unclipping Raybow from her baldric, Thea stood beside her and put an arrow to the string.

The stench grew worse and worse. Thea fought the urge to retch or collapse beneath its overwhelming presence.

The sound of scrabbling claws and rasping breath filled her ears.

Something appeared around the corner and Elora shot. Thea shot a moment later, and in the flash of light from Raybow she saw the deformed figure of the musharoc collapse on the tunnel floor. Somehow it seemed larger and even more terrifying than before.

As soon as it collapsed, another musharoc clambered over it, making it a little closer before Thea and Elora's arrows dropped it to the ground.

"Arl?" Thea called. "Are you through yet?" Another musharoc crawled over the dead, and then another. There was no room for their wings to outstretch, but they seemed to use them like another set of legs, shuffling towards their prey with terrifying speed.

Thea shot and shot, but every time a musharoc fell, another appeared in its place. Reaching for another arrow, she found that her quiver was empty.

"Elora ..." Thea looked up in alarm at the advancing monsters, realizing in a flash that the Little had also stopped shooting.

Elora drew the knife she wore at her belt. "Get back!"

"Elora, wait!" Thea struggled to draw her own knife. The musharoc was almost on top of them.

Sylica shouted.

Thea stumbled back. The ground beneath her feet was moving. It surged up into a wall of dirt, cutting off the musharocs from their prey.

Thea stared in shock.

"Come on!" Sylica cried in a cheerful voice.

Beyond Sylica, a narrow tunnel stretched up through the debris. Ulfgar pushed his axes this way and that, widening the passage.

The wall of dirt began to shake. Thea turned and dove through the tunnel, following close behind Ulfgar. Dirt was in her hair, in her face.

Behind her, Sylica continued to chatter cheerfully. "I always thought it would be so interesting to be a burrowing kind of creature. Burrows are so snug and cosy and—"

Thea emerged from the ground in a shower of dirt. Scrambling, she got out of the way. Sylica emerged behind her. Then Elora.

Where was Arl? Behind a pile of dirt, Thea caught a glimpse of movement that grew in size to a large bear. As everyone scattered, Arl shoved the pile of dirt over the hole and stomped on it firmly.

Thea glanced around. They were still surrounded by trees, but beyond them she could see open skies and rolling hills. She gasped. "Are we almost out?"

"Come on!" Elora gestured, and everyone ran. Out, beyond the trees, into the green-blue light of Micai.

They ran until the Deorcian was a smudge on the horizon behind them. Then, as Allumen appeared and cast its light across the land, they found a sheltered hollow. Collapsing on the ground, Thea fell asleep.

Chapter Thirteen

When Thea woke, it was staph. Allumen's heat beat down on their little campsite mercilessly. Getting up to look for a drink, she found that the hollow they had slept in had once contained a spring of water, but now it was completely dry. Arl had flown around the area, looking for water, but the closest stream was a three-measure walk away. By the time they reached it and had washed and bandaged their wounds, the day was all but gone. It was decided that they would stay there by the river for the night and resume their travel at first light the next morning. Arl went hunting, and Elora taught Thea how to make arrows for her bow. Ulfgar seemed caught up with the contents of a small flask he produced from his bag. Soon he was snoring noisily.

A mist hung over the land the next morning as they packed their bags and prepared to depart. Thea had woken up early to complete her check in, and she joined the group just as Arl returned from scouting the area.

Shifting back into human form, Arl turned to Sylica. "Where do we go now?"

Sylica blinked in surprise. "You're asking me?"

"We're travelling to your home."

"Oh, right." Sylica nodded enthusiastically. "We need to go east."

"Are you *sure* we need to go east?" Elora asked pointedly.

"Oh yes. I came along the big road that goes to Wyndburh and it comes from the east."

"There is a road that comes from the east," Elora conceded. "If you're sure that is the way you came, then that is the way we will go. But not by the road."

"I won't argue you there," Arl muttered.

Thea looked from Arl to Elora. "Wouldn't it be faster to travel on the road? We told Kais we wouldn't take long."

"Roads have their own kind of delays," Arl replied in a grim voice.

Ulfgar slung his pack over his shoulders. "Are we going or what?"

They set off in a generally eastward direction. The land was rocky, with scrub-covered hills sprawling in every direction. Arl flew ahead to scout the way, but even so they had to backtrack several times when they found themselves blocked by impassible bluffs or valleys filled with briers. They only had three water skins between them, so they were constrained to follow streams and rivers whenever they could. Days passed, but Thea had to wonder just how far east they had actually managed to get.

Finally, they stumbled upon a track that headed roughly west to east. Thea sighed with relief. The hills had been growing larger and rockier, and their passage had become more difficult with every passing day. The track appeared to have once been a road, and although it was mostly overgrown with weeds and trailing brambles, it was still much easier to follow than scrambling over the rocky hills.

The road wound up the side of a large hill. From the top, Thea stared at the view spread out before her. Rocky hills stretched as far as she could see in every direction, though to the east they seemed to get taller. On the tops of several of them she could see what looked like ruined buildings of some sort. Perhaps just piles of stones.

They followed the road down into the next valley, where a lazy stream meandered its way around the foot of the hill. There the road crossed the stream on an old stone bridge and continued to wind its way up the hill on the far side.

Allumen beat down overhead as they approached the old bridge. Beneath its stony arch, dark shadows brooded and began to grow. Thea froze as a squat, rock-like figure appeared, climbing out of the shadows towards them.

A troll! Instinctively, Thea took a step closer to Arl as the troll growled and turned to face them.

Arl crouched and snarled. Elora's hand went to her bow.

The troll stood on the bridge, glowering at them. Its skin was stony and rough, with thick limbs that made it look more like a walking rock than a living creature. Thea could see its darkness staining the air around the bridge.

Arl tensed to spring, but Ulfgar pushed them aside and strode towards the troll.

The troll bared its teeth and growled. Ulfgar growled back.

"Should we help him?" Thea gasped, but Arl was watching Ulfgar's advance with an expression of amused interest.

As Ulfgar stepped onto the bridge, the troll lunged forward to meet him, swinging its stone-like fists.

Ulfgar dodged the blow, ducking low, and wrapped his arms around the troll's thick waist.

The troll roared and tried to free itself from Ulfgar's grip, but Ulfgar held on. Muscles bulging, Ulfgar lifted the troll into the air and heaved it off the side of the bridge. The troll disappeared with a splash.

Brushing off his hands, Ulfgar turned back to face Thea and the others. He shrugged. "Trolls blunt my axes."

With an amused smile, Arl strode down to join Ulfgar on the bridge. Cautiously, everyone else followed.

Elora's bow was still in her hands as she eyed the bridge suspiciously. "There is never just one troll," she muttered under her breath.

Thea wasn't sure. The darkness beneath the bridge wasn't as dark as it had been before.

They crossed the bridge without incident, and followed the old road as it began to wind its way up the next hill.

A strange sound echoed across the valley. Thea glanced back in alarm.

The troll had reappeared, standing in the middle of the river with water dripping off its shoulders. A horn was in its hand, which it blew with a loud braying sound.

Elora's arrow flew, striking the troll in the arm.

That same instant, Arl transformed into an eagle and dove towards the troll, but before Arl could reach it, the troll disappeared beneath the water with a splash.

At the side of the road, a large rock began to grow

and uncurl, taking the form of another troll. It growled. On the other side of the road, another troll appeared.

Ulfgar unsheathed an axe with each hand and looked at them with a resigned expression. "But I'm open to blunting my axes if they insist."

A boulder tumbled down the slope of the hill towards them. Thea dodged out of the way and turned to see even more stony figures higher up the hill.

Arl wheeled and dove towards them.

With a roar, the trolls at the side of the road charged. A black arrow struck one's shoulder and ricocheted off into the heather. Ulfgar swung his axes, striking the other with the clang of steel on rock.

Grabbing Raybow, Thea shot. Her arrow flashed with light as it hit the closest troll. It stumbled back and fell to the ground.

"Keep moving!" Elora urged them. "There's just going to be more!"

Another troll emerged from the boulders. All around them, shadowy darkness crept closer.

"Come on!" Thea shouted, gesturing for the others to follow.

Ducking a troll's swinging fist, Sylica trotted after Thea. The clang of Ulfgar's axes rang across the mountainside.

Thea rounded a boulder and found herself face to face with the largest troll she had seen. A black arrow whizzed past her shoulder and struck the troll in the eye. It sank to the ground.

Behind Thea, Elora kicked another troll in the stomach and sent it rolling down the steep hillside.

More trolls emerged from the rocky slope. Ulfgar was completely surrounded now. He held his axes at arm's length, spinning them in a wide circle that just managed to keep the trolls back.

Another troll swung its club-like fists at Sylica, then sank to the ground with two black arrows lodged in the crease of its shoulder. Elora dodged behind a boulder again.

A rock whizzed past Thea's head. Far up the slopes of the hill, Arl screeched and dodged as the trolls at the top of the ridge hurtled head-sized rocks into the air.

Why were there so many trolls?

She could use magic to understand people. Could she use magic to understand questions?

Her gaze landed on the stone ruins that crowned the hilltop. Understanding filled her mind with a jolt of magic: They were walking straight into troll territory. Those ruins were their home.

"Arl!" Thea waved her arms.

Arl tipped into a dive and swept towards her. The trolls scattered at the eagle's approach.

"Come on!" Elora gestured for everyone to keep moving up the hill.

"Wait!" Thea cried. "We can't go up there, that's where the trolls live!"

"How do you know?"

"Because of magic."

"What?" Elora stared at her.

"Haven't you seen her do magic yet?" Arl asked with an amused expression, then leaped out of the way as a troll emerged from the shadows beneath a boulder. More trolls appeared across the rocky slope.

"We need to go around." Thea gestured everyone away from the overgrown road they had been following.

"How far does the troll's territory go?" Elora asked.

Thea took a step back as the trolls closed in. "I don't know!"

"This way!" Arl called, then shifted into the form of a large bear. Bursting past the startled trolls, Arl ran south, and everyone hurried to follow. Around the side of the hill they ran, until the trolls were left far behind.

"Do you think they're gone now?" Sylica asked as they stopped to catch their breath.

"Are you kidding?" Elora shook her head. "Look at all those rocks out there. Any one of them could be a troll."

That moment, a troll emerged from the boulders beside them, charging at Ulfgar with a growl.

"Seriously?" Ulfgar protested. Dodging the blow, he shouldered the troll in the stomach, knocking it onto its back.

Two more trolls appeared.

Arl took off into the air and everyone else started running again. They reached the overgrown road where it descended the far side of the hill and kept on running. It was easier running on the road, but Thea's legs ached as she forced herself on, step after step, through the valley and up the next hill, higher and higher.

Finally her legs collapsed beneath her and she sank to the ground. Wearily, Thea glanced around and saw that they had made it to the top. There weren't any ruins on this hill. She sighed with relief.

Ulfgar rested his hands on his knees, breathing heavily. Sylica sank onto her back, limbs splayed out in every direction. Elora crouched nearby, her bow in her hand. Her eyes didn't stop sweeping the area. Arl circled the hilltop once, then landed beside her.

Slowly, Thea became aware of the tendrils of darkness, creeping up from the ground around them.

She stared, concern slowly pushing its way through the haze of exhaustion.

Something grabbed her leg.

Before Thea could react, her legs were pulled out from under her and she fell to the ground. Shouts and cries filled her ears.

Thea struggled and kicked, but whatever had hold of her legs wouldn't let go. Twisting around, she tried to pull herself free, but the pain in her legs made it hard to think. She struck at the troll with her hands, but the harder she struggled, the harder the grip on her legs became. Grabbing Raybow, she struck the troll on the head. The bow glanced off its stony hide, but the troll loosened its grasp just enough for Thea to wriggle free. She scrambled to her feet and backed away from her attacker.

Beside her, Elora was pinned to the ground with a troll on top of her. She twisted and writhed, desperately trying to reach the bow that had been knocked out of her grasp.

Thea grabbed a rock and threw it at the troll's head. Startled, the troll staggered back. Elora seized her bow and kicked the troll in the face.

Three trolls were on top of Arl, who fought in bear-shape. Another troll had grabbed the shaft of one of Ulfgar's axes, and they tugged it back and forth, growling at each other.

Sylica grabbed the frying pan that was hanging off the outside of Ulfgar's pack, pulled it loose, and hit the troll firmly on the back of the head. It crumpled to the ground, its hands still locked around Ulfgar's axe.

"*My* axe," Ulfgar grumbled, snatching it back.

A vice-like grip grabbed Thea from behind, pinning

her arms to her sides. Struggling, she felt herself lifted off the ground, then hurtled through the air. She hit the ground with a thud. She was rolling, tumbling, falling—and struck something feathery and warm.

She clung to Arl as the world stopped spinning around her and saw with dismay that she was only one step away from a sheer cliff.

"Thank you, Arl," she whispered.

The eagle glared at her, then grabbed the back of her clothes in their talons and flapped laboriously back towards the hilltop.

They rose higher and higher until Arl released her and she found herself freefalling—directly on top of a troll.

She landed with a thump that shook every bone in her body, rolled, and landed in a heap. Shakily, she got to her feet.

The last of the trolls had scattered. Arl landed beside Thea with a smug expression.

"What did you do that for?" Thea demanded.

The eagle just cocked its head and preened its feathers.

"Just look at these things," Ulfgar grumbled, holding his axes this way and that in the light. "All bent out of shape. It will cost more than a copper to get these fixed."

Elora rubbed a shoulder gingerly. "Is that the lot of them, then?"

Arl transformed back into human form. "I doubt it."

"Damn," Elora grumbled. "I need to make more arrows." She searched the hilltop, but very few of her arrows were undamaged.

Overhead, Micai was well on its way towards

Allumen's nightly eclipse.

"It's going to be dark soon." Thea gave Arl a sidelong glance. "We should find somewhere to sleep."

Arl snorted. "Where the trolls can jump us again?"

"We need to rest. We can't keep running forever."

"They all ran away. Can't we just stay here?" Sylica suggested.

"No. They'll be back soon enough." Elora kicked the ground with disgust and sent a stone tumbling down the hillside.

"Where do we go?" Thea asked.

"I guess I'll scout," Arl grumbled. A spasm of pain crossed their face as they shifted into eagle-form once again and flapped laboriously into the sky.

"Arl—" Thea called, but Arl was gone.

"Well?" Ulfgar slung his pack back over his shoulders. "Might as well keep walking."

As they descended the hill, Thea eyed every single boulder they passed with a look of deep suspicion. She jumped every time she thought she saw or heard something move behind her.

At the foot of the hill they found another small river, but the old road didn't cross it. Instead, it turned north to follow the river's winding course.

They were beyond the largest of the hills now.

A shadow descended and Arl landed beside them.

"Did you find somewhere?" Thea asked.

"Just beyond the river."

The water was shallow and murky, barely reaching the banks of what had once been a much larger river. The Great Heat was taking its toll, and there was still more than a cycle left before Micai's orbit would lead Raphtova further away from Allumen's heat.

After refilling their waterskins, they stumbled on to the place that Arl had found—a sheltered alcove tucked into the next hillside. Before anyone sat down, they eyed it cautiously.

Thea let her spirit sight fully take over her senses. There wasn't any darkness nearby.

"Hey!"

Someone shook Thea's arm. She returned to the present moment with a gasp.

Elora stared up at her with a frown of concern. "You alright?"

Thea blinked, taken aback. "Yes, I'm fine."

"You sure?"

Thea nodded. "I was just—" Of course. Elora would never have seen an Elf using their sight before. "That was just vidlas. I was using my elf-sight to see if there are any trolls here."

Elora seemed to consider this.

With a frown, Ulfgar swung the blunt end of his axe, smashing the top of a boulder. Fragments of rock tumbled on the dusty ground. He grunted. "My way's easier."

"There aren't any trolls here," Thea assured him. "I couldn't see any darkness from them at all."

Ulfgar stared at her for a moment, then proceeded to smack his axe against every suspicious-looking rock in the area.

The rest of the group began to set up camp. Arl left to go hunting and returned with a small deer, which Elora cleaned and skinned.

Thea and Sylica meticulously cleared the area of any brush that could catch fire and made a small ring of stones in the middle of it. It was dangerously hot and dry to be making a fire, but none of them—besides Arl—relished the thought of raw meat, and the rest of their food was gone.

That night they took turns sleeping, standing watch, and cooking strips of meat on their small fire.

Wolves howled in the distance.

The next day they continued walking east. Arl circled slowly overhead, and everyone else walked in silence—except for Sylica, who seemed to be the only one unaffected by the previous day's events.

"... And then I thought, what if we have meat strips wrapped *around candy* and you know what? It was the most delicious thing I had ever tasted! Except maybe that time when I got to have chocolate cake and blueberry pie at the *same time* which was absolutely *amazing*. But I always think everything tastes better with candy, don't you think?"

Elora sent her a withering glare. "Can't you *ever* be quiet?"

Sylica gave her a knowing nod. "My Uncle Bob asks me that exact same question, but it seems like such a silly one because I always sleep at night time, and when I'm sleeping I don't talk. Unless I talk in my sleep. Do I talk in my sleep? I never asked anyone before!"

"Can't say that I've heard you," Elora muttered, then jumped. "What was that? Oh, it's you, Ulfgar."

Ulfgar strode along behind them, turning his head from side to side as he walked. His axe struck every suspicious-looking rock with a loud *clang*.

As staph approached, the heat of the day became unbearable. They huddled together beneath the thin patch of scrub brush that was all the shelter they could find.

Finally their thirst drove them to keep walking.

"Look," Elora gestured as they rounded the next hill. "There's a cloud on the horizon."

Sure enough, a low cloud hung in the distance, almost like a distant range of mountains.

"I've been watching that for a while now," Arl responded in a dry voice.

Elora shot them a glare.

"Do you think it will rain?" Thea asked.

Arl shrugged, and they continued trudging on.

Thunder rumbled in the distance. Slowly, dark clouds rolled towards them and stretched to fill the sky.

Thea found herself holding her breath. If only it would rain …

A crack of lightning illuminated a nearby hilltop.

"Have you noticed that there hasn't been any more trolls lately?" Sylica asked cheerily.

"Can't say that I noticed," Ulfgar muttered under his breath.

"*I'm* noticing that we should try to find a sheltered spot," Elora retorted, scanning the area with a keen eye.

A gust of wind blew dust into the air as thunder rolled above them.

Thea glanced around. Where could they find shelter? Beyond the next hilltop, a darker shadow stretched up through the billowing clouds. "What's that?"

Arl took off into the sky, beating their wings rapidly to make headway against the wind. They returned like a streak of lighting, transforming before their feet hit the ground. "Fire! Get back!"

"Fire?" Thea protested. The column of smoke was thicker and darker now. "But it's going to rain!"

"It hasn't rained yet," Arl glared. "Come on, I'm not going to get caught here."

Glancing anxiously at the column of smoke, Thea and the others hurried back the way they had come. Surely it would start raining, wouldn't it?

Red flames flickered along the side of the distant hill. It was distant, but not distant enough.

They hurried on, stumbling over rocks and tangles of brush. Smoke billowed towards them, filling the air.

"What ... will ... we do," Thea gasped, "if it doesn't rain?"

"Shut up and run!"

They were already running. Behind them, the fire blazed higher.

Thea's lungs burned. Her legs felt like they were going to collapse.

Arl soared into the air, barely visible in a sky darkened with smoke.

"Come on, rain! Rain!" Thea whispered, glancing back over her shoulder.

The flames were close—racing down the slopes towards them.

"The river!" Arl landed among them, gesturing urgently. "Go! Go!"

Feet pounding, they raced down the hill. A wave of heat engulfed them. The roar of the flames filled their ears.

Water splashed beneath Thea's feet. Hurtling herself forwards, she landed in the water with a splash.

Gasping for breath, she struggled to the surface and staggered across to the far bank where Arl crouched in the shallows.

The fire roared towards the river, reflecting red in

the tepid water.

Overhead, thunder rumbled, and rain began to fall. It rained harder and harder, pummelling the dusty ground, blowing in sheets across the hissing flames. Slowly the fire flared, smouldered, and faded into ash.

Elora sank to her knees, raindrops tracing lines down her soot-stained face.

Beside Thea, Sylica did a little dance, laughing and clapping her hands.

Ulfgar rolled onto his back and groaned.

They watched as the beating rain soaked the fire-scorched land, turning it into a soggy mess. The river at their feet rushed to fill its banks with muddy, soot-filled water.

Utterly exhausted, Thea stared glumly at the overgrown road by which they sat. They were back in troll territory, and they had lost all of the progress they had made that day.

"Now what?" Elora asked.

Thea glanced at Arl who was hunched motionless by the river. "I guess we find somewhere to sleep."

Elora nodded and got slowly to her feet. "I'll scout this time."

She returned a short while later and led the others to a small rock outcropping that gave no more than an illusion of shelter from the deluge.

Shivering, Thea wrapped herself in her cloak and lay down, staring at the sheets of rain driven past by the wind.

One by one the others joined her, huddling together against the cold and the wind. The last light of day faded from the sky.

Chapter Fourteen

Thea woke up the next morning, cold and sore. On one side, Ulfgar snored noisily. On the other side, Sylica was curled up into a ball that seemed much smaller than Thea would expect from her size when standing.

Gingerly, she extracted herself from between them and looked around. The sky was still overcast, but the rain had stopped and the wind had fallen to a gentle breeze. Elora sat a short distance away, staring out into the distance. Arl was nowhere in sight.

Clumsily, Thea tried to wring some of the water out of her sodden clothing, then knelt to check in. Exhaustion dragged at her mind. Again and again, she realized she was lost in her thoughts and had to pull her mind back to the task of listening. It had never been so hard when Allulien and Micai would come and speak to her. She missed their presence and companionship. Not that she didn't appreciate the companions that she was travelling with, she reminded herself, but it had always seemed that Allulien and Micai had been there to help her. Now she felt the responsibility of her task, and she was nowhere closer to finding a home for the Littles than she'd been the day before.

Getting to her feet, Thea joined Elora on the small bluff where she sat. From her vantage point, Thea could see the blackened hills where yesterday's fire had raged.

"We probably don't want to travel those hills now,"

she mused, glancing at Elora.

"We don't?" Elora continued to stare into the distance.

"Well ... wouldn't everything be covered with soot and ash? I don't think it would be very nice to walk through."

"Probably not."

"And won't the fire have chased away all the animals? It would be harder to find food."

"Maybe."

"But we still need to travel east."

"Yes, we do."

"Maybe we should take the road instead."

Elora gave her a sharp glance.

Thea sighed. "Why don't you want to take the road?"

"Bigs travel on the road. I'm a goblin. Remember?"

"But you're not a goblin. You're a Little. Why can't people just learn to accept you?"

"Good question." Elora stared into the distance with a tired expression.

Thea sat in silence until she noticed that the others in their campsite were stirring.

Sylica bounded up to greet Thea with a cheerful "good morning" as she approached. Ulfgar was looking at his empty flask with an expression of dismal resignation.

Arl returned, shifting into human form to land beside Thea. Their eyes flashed with a grim light. "Night mares. A whole herd of them."

"Whats?" Sylica demanded, overhearing Arl's report.

"Fire horses. They're attracted to wildfires. I counted at least six in the hills east of here."

"Are they a problem?" Thea asked.

Arl glared. "Flaming death horses?"

"Oh."

"What's going on?" Elora asked.

"Night mares," Arl reiterated with a sigh. "East of here."

"What's the point of all that?" Ulfgar muttered, trying to shake a final drop or two out of his flask.

"It means we shouldn't go through those hills," Thea said slowly, "but we still need to go east."

"So we're taking the road, then?" Sylica asked.

"The road is dangerous." Arl folded their arms. "We should not go that way."

"These hills haven't exactly been safe either," Thea protested. "Unless we want to face the night mares, we will have to go around—to the north or the south. Do you know what's south of here, Arl?"

"The hills to the south get larger and rockier. I have seen that from the air. Eventually we would reach a great river. Gedwyld is at the mouth of that river."

Gedwyld. For a moment, Thea's heart leapt, but no. She had to find a home for the Littles first. Then she would go to Gedwyld and learn from Davis.

Thea shook her head. "Bigger hills, and a human city in our way. I don't think south is an option."

Arl nodded. "I would agree."

"That means we will travel north."

Arl frowned. "I would not agree."

"Are there other options?" Thea looked from face to face. Arl and Elora shifted uncomfortably. "If you can't give me another option, then we should take the road."

"And what will I do if we meet travellers on the road?" Elora demanded.

"Keep your hood up and don't talk to anybody."

Arl gave Thea a sharp glance.

"Besides," Thea continued, "we're a pretty large group and most of us aren't goblins. Maybe they will leave us alone."

Sylica's face scrunched up into a confused expression. "But none of us are goblins."

"Exactly." Thea nodded. She looked at Arl.

Arl sighed. "We will take the road."

There was no breakfast to be eaten, so they tightened their belts and set off in a northerly direction, looking for food as they went.

As staph approached, they stopped and took stock of what they had gathered—a rabbit caught by Arl and another Elora had shot, a few handfuls of small, shrivelled blackberries, and some nettles.

All the sticks and brush they could find were wet, but they finally managed to start a fire and cooked up a stew in the pan that Ulfgar carried.

After eating and cleaning up, they pressed on towards the road.

Thea promised herself that this would be the last day of walking so long. Once they were on the road they would stop and rest during restday, like Micai had taught her to.

As they walked, the clouds scattered overhead and Allumen's light beat down on them once again, filling the air with a muggy haze.

Rounding a hill, they saw a broad valley stretched out below them. A lazy river wound its way along the valley floor, beside a wide, dusty road.

The air in the valley was hot and still. They found a shallow place to ford the river and waded across. The road turned out to be no more than a reddish dirt track, beaten flat and wide from frequent travel. The heat-baked, almost bricklike dirt radiated the warmth of the day. There were no other travellers in sight.

They walked in silence, for the most part. The warm, still air wrapped Thea's mind in a cosy, sleepy feeling. Swallows swooped overhead, and cicadas buzzed in the long grass. Sylica sang softly to herself.

Thea wondered again if they should stop and rest for the rest of the day, but it was so easy to walk just a little further. Every step was a step closer to their goal.

After a while, the road entered a small forest. The shade was a pleasant relief from the heat. Allumen's light shone down through the leaves like a stained-glass mosaic overhead.

As they rounded a bend in the road, Thea saw a couple of carts up ahead, pulled off to the side of the road with a large campfire crackling cheerily beside them.

Silently, Elora pulled her hood over her face and slowed her pace to walk alongside Thea. Neither Ulfgar nor Sylica seemed apprehensive, however, and continued to stride confidently along the road.

As they passed by, two armoured figures stepped out from behind the carts. "Hello there!" one of them called with a firm but friendly expression. "What's your business?"

"Blade for hire," Ulfgar replied, strolling towards them. "My axes in exchange for food and drink. Mostly drink."

The broad-shouldered woman who had spoken laughed and slapped Ulfgar on the back. "Sounds like our kind of people! Eh, Dreogan?"

The man frowned and eyed Elora suspiciously.

"What's your deal? You can't be blades for hire, you have a child with you."

Thea stepped in front of Elora. "We are not blades for hire. Ulfgar is, but the rest of us are travellers." Glancing around, she noticed that Arl had disappeared.

"Travellers?" The man smiled. "That's alright, then. Where are you headed? Gedwyld?"

"Yes," Thea replied, figuring that was true enough. She *was* going to Gedwyld, as soon as she was finished helping the Littles. "Is it far yet?"

The man nodded. "Five more days of good travel. The road new to you?"

"It's my first time, though not the first for all of my companions." She glanced at Sylica.

"You know about the bandit trouble, then?"

Thea frowned. "Bandits?"

"Tell you what." The woman gestured towards the side of the road. "Come join our campfire for the night and we can swap news more comfortably. There's safety to be had in numbers, that's for sure."

Thea hesitated, but Ulfgar and Sylica seemed eager enough, so she followed the humans over to the campfire where a large pot was simmering and a delicious smell drifted through the air. Wherever Arl had disappeared to, they would be fine on their own for a while.

Pulling up boxes and crates, they all sat down around the fire.

"So what's your business in Gedwyld?" Dreogan asked, his feet stretched up on a pile of firewood.

"I am looking for a bard called Davis," Thea explained, deciding that her business with the Littles was not information she was free to share. "I am going to study beneath him."

"A bard, eh? Travelin' and singin' songs and the like? Sounds like a good life to me." Dreogan smiled. "Arisan here has a fine voice, don't you?" He elbowed the broad-shouldered woman who scowled at him.

"Enough of that. You know I don't sing until I have at least three beers in me. Speaking of which—" she heaved herself onto her feet "—you all look thirsty. We've got plenty of drink to spare."

Mugs were procured, filled, and passed around. Elora accepted the mug handed to her and drained it in one swig.

"Would you look at that!" The woman laughed. "Even their young'un can throw it back!"

After her three mugs of beer, Arisan was persuaded to sing them a song. After that, Ulfgar sang a drinking song he'd learned on his travels.

"Come on then," Dreogan urged them, "the stew's hot. Might as well eat."

The stew was delicious, and everyone—besides Elora—talked cheerfully while they ate. Every now and then, Thea glanced at the surrounding trees and wondered where Arl had disappeared to. Hopefully they wouldn't mind being left out.

By the time they had finished eating, night had fallen. Dreogan and Arisan retired to their wagons, allowing Thea and the others to sleep by the fire.

As Thea drifted off to sleep, she wondered why Arl and Elora had been so uneasy about other travellers on the road. This certainly seemed a lot nicer than wandering the trackless hills by themselves.

When Thea woke it was still night. Someone was

shaking her. Startled, she opened her eyes to see Arl leaning over her.

"Quiet," Arl hissed. "We're leaving. Now."

"But—" Thea began, but there was a creak from beyond the coals of the fire and Arl disappeared. A raccoon slunk away into the shadows.

What was going on? Thea's mind was fuzzy with sleep. Slowly her eyes closed again.

A gentle tug jerked her awake. What was that? Someone was pulling on her bag. Startled, Thea struggled to sit up and found Arisan kneeling over her, a knife in her hand.

"Quiet," the woman hissed. "We don't want any accidents now, do we? Hand it over."

"What?" Thea struggled to wrap her mind around what was going on. "Hand what over?"

"Your bag."

"But there's nothing in it. Just a rope."

Arisan snorted and jerked the bag open. When she saw that there was really nothing in it besides the rope, she turned on Thea. "Where do you keep your money?"

"I don't have any money."

"What? Of course you do. Who's carrying it?"

Arisan eyed the shadowy figures that lay around the fire. To Thea's alarm, Dreogan knelt over Ulfgar's recumbent figure, removing his weapons.

Getting off Thea, Arisan strode over to Elora and held her knife to her throat. "*Now* you'll tell us where your money is."

Thea stared at her, aghast. "You can't just take our things!"

"Consider it payment. For our hospitality." Arisan glared. "Now hand it over."

"I told you, I don't have any money."

"Then give me that." She pointed at Raybow. "Now."

Panic rising, Thea gestured at the others. "Maybe—maybe Ulfgar or Sylica have money. I don't know."

Arisan's eyes narrowed. "Dreogan. Any money on the short one?"

"No," Dreogan grumbled. "Some nice axes, though."

"Try the tall one. I'm staying right here." Her knife gleamed in the dim light of the fire.

Dreogan knelt over Sylica. "Ho now, what's this?" There was the small sound of a cord being cut, and Dreogan lifted a small leather pouch into the light. Opening it, he reached inside and frowned. "Candy?"

Walking over to the fire, he eyed the handful of candies with a suspicious eye, then dropped them on the ground and reached back into the bag, pulling out another handful of candy. Pulling the drawstring open, he tipped the bag over and candy spilled onto the ground.

"What's that?" Arisan asked.

"Candy."

"Candy? What else is in there?"

"I'm trying to see." He shook the bag and more candy fell out. More fell out, and the pile grew at his feet until it was much larger than the size of the bag.

"What the blazes?" Dreogan cried, shaking the bag as more and more candy continued to fall. "What is this?"

Startled by his cry, Sylica sat up. Ulfgar staggered to his feet. Elora's eyes opened—she froze as she saw the knife held above her neck.

"Where's my bloody axes?" Ulfgar roared.

"Stay where you are or the child dies!" Arisan yelled.

Dreogan continued to stare at the growing pile of candy in bewildered shock. "It's still coming out!"

"*What's* still coming out?" Arisan demanded. "What are you doing?"

"Try one! They're really yummy!" Sylica offered cheerily.

"Leave the sweets and find their money!" Arisan raged.

"*Look* at this!" Dreogan cried. "Just look!"

A brief look of confusion crossed Arisan's face and she glanced at the candy.

With lightning speed, Elora struck the knife away, darted to her feet, and kicked Arisan in the gut.

As Arisan crumpled to the ground, a cougar sprang from the undergrowth, tackling the bewildered Dreogan to the ground. Candy scattered every direction.

With a roar, Ulfgar grabbed his axes and joined in the fray.

Thea leapt to her feet. "Don't kill them!"

"What?" Elora paused, her knife at Arisan's throat.

"Don't kill them. We will take what is ours and we will leave. They will not stop us."

"They won't, will they?" Elora muttered.

"They won't give us any trouble, because they know what will happen if they do," Thea replied in an even voice.

Grumbling, Ulfgar sheathed his axes. Arl slunk back into the shadows.

Arisan put her hands on her head. Dreogan lay on the ground, groaning.

"Hey," Sylica peered around the campsite. "Where is my pack, anyways?"

After some searching, Thea and Sylica found the

missing packs in one of the wagons. The scattered candies crunched underfoot as they reassembled their gear and prepared to leave.

At Elora's insistence, Thea allowed her to tie the bandits back to back by their wrists.

"I'm sure they'll get themselves free eventually," Elora muttered, "but at least they won't be tempted to follow us."

Sylica retrieved her candy bag, and after a quick glance around the campsite to make sure nothing had been forgotten, Thea and her friends continued down the road.

As the road emerged from the forest, the first light of day glimmered in the sky. They stumbled on, eager to put as much distance as they could between themselves and the bandits' campsite.

They didn't talk about their narrow escape. Thea knew that if she did, Arl and Elora would have said, "I told you so." But there was something that Thea did want to know.

"What exactly is that bag?" Thea asked Sylica, one moment when it was possible to have a private conversation.

"It's a bag of candy," Sylica grinned. "Want one?"

"Where did you get it?"

"My Uncle Bob gave it to me."

"Where did *he* get it?"

"He made it."

"Did he make many ... unusual things?"

"He made lots of *useful* things, like a bell that rang every time I was coming to visit him!"

"That doesn't seem very unusual."

"It rang all by itself."

Thea frowned. She'd heard of people being able to do magic through the Deity's power, but she'd never heard of someone making magical *things*. "I think I would like to meet your Uncle Bob when we get to your home."

"Oh. He's dead. Mom said it was an accident in his workshop. But he made this candy bag for me. Isn't that nice?"

There was something different about the tone of Sylica's voice. Thea looked at her closely. "Is it strange? To know someone who has died?"

"Oh, I don't know." Sylica spoke with her usual, bouncy manner, but Thea thought she caught a strange, strangled sound at the back of her voice. "Everyone dies eventually, you know."

"*Not* everyone dies eventually," Thea replied. "Elves never die, unless they're killed or have a horrible accident. We don't die from getting old."

Sylica blinked in surprise. "Wow, really? I never met someone who was going to live forever before."

"But ... *you're* an Elf."

Sylica shook her head. "I'm a Little, remember? I told you that."

"But—" Thea protested.

"Mom told me that the Great Big Big takes care of the people who die," Sylica said firmly. "That's what the Big Book says."

"The Big Book?"

"The book about the Great Big Big, of course. Haven't you read it?"

"Not by that name," Thea replied, shaking her head. *The Scrolls of the Ancient Wisdom.* How different they sounded when a Little—or rather, someone who talked like a Little—was talking about them.

"Do you serve the Great Big Big?" Thea asked.

"Of course I do," Sylica grinned. "Doesn't everybody?"

"No, not everybody. Like those bandits we met. They wouldn't have tried to steal from us if they were serving the Great Big Big."

Sylica seemed to think about this for a moment. "Maybe they just don't know about the Great Big Big yet."

"Maybe." She gave Sylica a sidelong glance. "Do you serve under a General?"

"A what?"

"Um ..." How could she explain the Generals? "The leaders of the Tilaryn. You know, they're very powerful and do things for the Great Big Big."

"Oh." Sylica nodded sagely. "The Big Bigs."

The Big Bigs? Thea shook her head. Sometimes she wasn't sure if the Littles' way of talking made things simpler or more confusing. "Do you serve under one of them?"

"Why would I serve under a Big Big when I can just serve the Great Big Big?" Sylica seemed puzzled.

"Well, my General gives me my orders," Thea explained, "and the power to do magic."

"Oh right, I saw you do magic before!" Sylica grinned.

"Can you do magic?"

"Oh, no." Sylica shook her head. "But I like seeing people do magic. Like watching Uncle Bob work—that's one of my favourite things to do! Besides eating, of course. And dancing! I can dance while I walk. Look!"

Sylica skipped down the road, spinning and leaping. Thea was left alone with her thoughts.

As staph approached, they gathered in a shady spot beside the river for a rest.

"I was thinking," Thea said, watching the river drift by, "that we really shouldn't be walking all day. If we'd stopped and rested properly yesterday, we wouldn't have been caught by those bandits so easily."

Elora frowned. "I thought you wanted to travel as quickly as possible."

"I know. But a friend of mine taught me that workday is for working, and restday is for resting. We've been pushing ourselves too hard, and we're tired. If we don't slow down, I don't think we'll make it all the way."

"All the way?" Ulfgar protested. "How much farther are we going?"

"I don't know," Thea admitted. "Sylica?"

Sylica scratched her head. "Well ... I know I walked a long time. I don't really remember how far."

Thea shrugged. "I guess I'm saying that if we don't know how long the road is, it's best to be prepared for a long one."

"That does make sense," Elora admitted. "I could use the chance to make a few more arrows."

"And we could take the time to look further away for our food," Arl added, "so we'll eat better."

"I won't complain about eating better," Ulfgar replied, and that seemed to settle it. No more walking during restday.

At Arl's suggestion, they crossed the river and set up their camp in a copse of trees, out of view of the road. They were able to take the time to set up a more comfortable camping area, which was nice, and even erected a leafy bower as an additional protection against heat or rain.

Thea was able to learn more about fletching from Elora, and when Arl returned from hunting, Sylica collected some fresh herbs from the hillside to flavour the meat. Ulfgar sharpened his axes, humming a little song to himself as he worked.

The next morning everyone seemed to have more of a spring in their step, and there was less grumbling. Thea smiled with satisfaction. Clearly, Micai was right. It was better to rest during restday.

They walked until staph, then once again looked for a place to set up camp. It was impossible to ford the river—the banks were too steep and the water flowed deeper—but they found a shaded spot not far from the road.

Just as they were settling down to sleep for staph, a company of five wagons trundled into view, pulled by teams of oxen. On the foremost wagon, three armoured figures lounged behind the driver.

The wagons approached their campsite, then creaked to a halt. One of the armoured figures vaulted to the ground, chain mail clinking.

"'Ere now, what are you lot doing?" the guard demanded.

"Resting," Ulfgar replied without opening his eyes.

"You look like a suspicious bunch," the man continued. "Bandits?"

"We're not bandits," Thea replied, getting to her feet. "We're just travellers, resting from the heat of the day."

"Travellers don't stop and rest in these parts," the man objected.

Another guard jumped down from the wagon. "Is it trouble?"

"Loitering with ill intent, I'd say. Call out the guard

and look for an ambush."

"That's not true," Thea protested. "What are you talking about?"

The guards ignored her, and the second guard strode back to the wagon and rang a bell.

Several more guards appeared along the row of wagons. Some of them scattered through the surrounding fields, but some approached Thea and her companions with suspicious glares.

"Now state your *actual* business," the first guard demanded, his arms crossed in front of him.

"We are travelling east," Thea replied, "and that's all there is to tell. This road is free for anyone to use, isn't it?"

"For any normal innocent person, sure," the guard countered, "but what are you? Some kind of troll?"

"No!" Thea protested. How could anyone think she looked like a troll? That was preposterous!

The guard's eyes took in Thea's companions. "Two trolls, a goblin, and a couple of ruffians. Troublemakers, if I ever saw them. Be off, or I'll set the guards on you."

"We haven't done you any harm!" Thea protested. "Leave us alone!"

The guard nodded to the rest of the guards who had gathered around. "Drive them off. This is a nice campsite, we'll stop here for a couple of measures and let the animals rest."

"Wait—we were here first!" Thea protested, but the guards pushed her away.

"Up now. Get along with you," a guard grumbled, kicking Ulfgar in the side.

Ulfgar didn't seem to move, but an axe flicked up from his belt into his hand.

The guard growled and drew her sword.

"No!" Thea cried. "Don't hurt anyone!"

Sylica brushed past Thea and waved her arms cheerfully in the air. "Isn't this great?" she smiled, "a nice big campsite with room for lots of people! And we have candy for lots of people too! See? Here's one for you, and one for you ..."

She bustled off between the guards, handing out candies left and right.

The guards hesitated, as if unsure of what to do with this new development.

Sylica continued chattering away. "Are you guarding these wagons? That is so nice of you! I thought you looked like nice people as soon as I saw you. I just love making new friends! It's like the Big Book says: A new friend a day keeps the doctor away. Unless, of course, your new friend is a doctor, but that is great too!"

The first guard cleared his throat. "We're evicting you, remember?"

"Oh yes, carry on," Sylica agreed cheerily. "It's so nice to see you doing such a good job taking care of those wagons. You know, I got a ride on a wagon just like these when I was coming this way before. Are these the same wagons, do you think?"

"Couldn't say, miss ..." the guard scratched his head.

Sylica gasped. "Marvin, is that you?" She ran to the second wagon and threw her arms around an ox's thick neck. "It *is* Marvin! He's one of my best friends in all the world!"

The well-dressed humans sitting on the wagon looked at each other in bewilderment.

"I think—" the guard tried to scrape together his dignity, "this campsite isn't as good as it seemed to be.

Guards! Carry on, now."

Rambling back to the wagons, the guards swung themselves up. The drivers shouted at the oxen, and slowly the wagons continued down the road.

Sylica stood at the roadside waving a cheerful goodbye. When the last of the wagons had rumbled out of sight, she bounced back to Thea. "That was so nice of them, to let us have our campsite after all!"

"Darn right," Ulfgar grumbled, tipping his helmet over his eyes.

Chapter Fifteen

The wagons didn't return, and no other travellers passed as staph stretched into restday. Arl left to go hunting and the rest set about their usual small tasks.

The warm, hazy sky settled over their campsite like a blanket. Even Sylica seemed sleepier than usual, resting with her chin on her hands as she watched the swallows soar over the fields. No breeze stirred the tall dry grasses.

Slowly, Micai rose higher in the sky. Thea glanced at the far horizon. Arl wasn't usually gone so long.

A chorus of raucous cries rose in the distance. Thea rose to her feet. Peering through the shimmering haze, she tried to find the source of the sound.

Dark shapes filled the distant sky. They were wheeling, dive-bombing a larger creature that circled and dove, as if trying to get away.

Thea froze. Musharocs? No, the shapes were wrong. These looked more like four-legged creatures with wings, surrounding an eagle whose form seemed very familiar.

The distant cacophony erupted into cawing and crow-like screeches. Crox.

Beside Thea, Elora eyed their approach, her hand on her quiver. "Think Arl needs a hand?"

Arl seemed to be carrying something small in their talons—a rabbit, perhaps. The crox screeched and dove, trying to wrench the prey from Arl's grasp.

Arl swerved, but not fast enough to avoid their assailants' sharp beaks. Arl screeched in pain.

In a flash, an arrow was in Elora's hand. Aiming slightly away from the approaching crox, she gave a shrill whistle and shot.

At the twang of the bowstring, the mob of crox scattered in every direction, protesting loudly.

Arl landed beside Thea in a flurry of feathers that was instantly replaced by brown, sweat-covered skin. Grasping the limp rabbit in a bloodied hand, they heaved it at Ulfgar. "Cook it."

Arl turned and limped away.

Thea and Elora joined Arl where they leaned against a gnarled tree trunk. Cuts and welts covered Arl's body.

Seeing Thea's worried expression, Arl made a face. "They're just scratches. I'm fine."

"What happened?" Elora asked.

Arl nodded to the spot where Ulfgar was examining the mutilated rabbit. "That was all I could find. If I'd shifted, those crox would have had it from me in a heartbeat."

Thea glanced at the sky. No crox were in sight, but she could hear the sound of them in the distance. "Why were there so many?"

"They're scavengers. Where there's food to steal, their packs get bigger and bigger."

"What do they scavenge from?"

"Around here? Humans."

Elora's mouth formed a thin, hard line.

The next day as they walked, Thea noticed a narrow track leading away from the road. A short while later, there was another. Peering down it, Thea caught a glimpse of a small log hut, surrounded by a split rail fence.

Later she caught sight of a human on the far side of a field, chopping a pile of logs into firewood.

She glanced at Arl. "Do people live here?"

Arl nodded sullenly.

When staph came, they took care to conceal their campsite more than they usually would. Arl kept watch while the others slept.

Restday was hot and muggy. At Thea's suggestion, they went out in pairs to forage for their evening meal.

"Be careful where you look," Arl said in a grim voice. "Don't take anything from a homestead unless you want angry humans on your tail."

Thea and Elora followed the riverbank towards a distant copse of trees. Thea dug up a few roots that she recognized. Elora found some mushrooms.

It was cool and pleasant in the shade of the trees. Thea eyed the leafy branches overhead. There were beech trees, but she couldn't see any nuts on them.

The ground jerked out from beneath her.

"Watch your step, there!" a voice called from beside her feet.

Stepping back in alarm, Thea looked down. An old man lay on the mossy ground beneath the trees, his arms folded behind his head.

"Oh, I'm sorry," she stammered, "I didn't see you there."

Elora placed a hand on her bow.

"Not to worry," the old man chuckled. "Won't be the first time someone has trod on me, and I'm sure it won't be the last. Coham's the name."

"I'm Thea."

"Pleased to meet you, Thea, and your friend," Coham cracked a large smile that was missing several of its teeth. "I'd shake your hand, but as it happens I am quite comfortable where I am at the moment. Do make yourselves at home." A large, two-handed sword lay on the turf beside him, but the old man didn't show any inclination of picking it up.

"I'm sorry if we don't accept your invitation," Thea replied slowly, "but we've had some trouble with bandits, so we've learned to be cautious of strangers."

"Trouble with bandits, eh?" Coham scratched behind his ear. "What breed were this lot?"

"Um, humans?" Thea offered.

"They invited us into their camp, then tried to mug us in the night," Elora said in a dry voice.

"Oh, the friendly traveller trick. Oldest one in the book." Coham nodded sagely. "Now *my* favourite trick is when one of the bandits rests by the side of the road, all innocent like, and when travellers stop by to chat, the rest of the buggers jump out from behind them."

Alarmed, Thea looked behind her, but there was no one there.

Coham cackled as if enjoying a good joke.

Heart pounding, Thea glared at the old man.

He shook his head, still chucking to himself. "No, no. I'm not expecting any company but my granddaughter Beatrice. She's just gone to get some water, so she'll be back any time. Ah, here she comes now."

Tramping footsteps approached, but it was Ulfgar who emerged from the trees.

"Well, there," Coham observed thoughtfully. "You

are much more bearded than Beatrice."

"Ulfgar, this is Coham," Thea said, feeling as if an introduction was necessary. "He's ... um ..."

"Blade for hire," Coham grinned. "Selling my services to the highest bidder."

"For hire?" Thea stared. "Aren't you a bit ... um ..."

"Still going strong," Coham flexed a thin, sinewy arm. "Can't stop now. The mercenary life doesn't provide much of a retirement plan."

"I see." Thea felt a little bewildered, but Ulfgar stretched himself out on the turf close by and tipped his helmet to shield his eyes from the light.

"And what is your lot in life?" Coham asked, staring up at the shifting leaves. "I can recognize an old campaigner anywhere, but I can't place you two." He shot a keen glance at Thea and Elora.

"We are ... exploring." Thea replied cautiously.

"Ah, adventurers," the old man nodded. "I remember my adventuring days well enough myself. All the ladies loved an adventuring man back then, and—"

"Grandfather!" A woman's voice drifted through the trees and a large woman with thick braids strolled into view. "Are you harassing these poor people with the story of your life?" Her eyes took in the strangers. "Goblin!" She drew a long sword from the scabbard at her waist.

In a flash, Elora had an arrow to her bowstring.

"Excuse me," Ulfgar grumbled, "that's sizeist language, that is."

"No, no." Thea got between Elora and Beatrice and held her arms out wide. "No one is going to do any fighting here."

"Darn right," Coham chuckled. "Bad form, attacking

someone in the middle of hearing your old granddad's life story."

"But that's a goblin!"

"Manners, Beatrice, manners," the old man scolded.

Beatrice and Elora glared at each other.

"Besides," Thea said, "this is not a goblin at all. This is a Little, and her name is Elora. Elora, this is Beatrice, Coham's granddaughter."

"A Little? What's that supposed to mean?" Beatrice protested.

"It means that there are no such things as goblins," Thea replied in an even voice. "They are actually Littles and they are not evil creatures."

"Goblins, Littles, it doesn't matter what you call it, as long as you let me kill it," Beatrice scowled.

"That would be very unwise," Arl said, appearing behind Beatrice. "If you take one step towards the small one, I will kill you."

Coham nodded approvingly. "Excellent form, excellent form."

"What?" Beatrice protested.

The old man chuckled. "Forgot to watch your back, did you my dear?"

Beatrice glared, but her grandfather didn't seem to notice. He gave Arl a friendly nod. "Always nice to meet other travellers on the road."

"Travellers?" Beatrice protested. "Goblins aren't travellers!"

"Well, I don't know," Coham replied thoughtfully. "I never heard of a Little before, but you learn something new every day. Trust me, I've been around for a lot of them. Well ..." Slowly, with limbs creaking and groaning, Coham pushed himself up off the ground. "It is time for Beatrice and I to keep moving. Got to find someone to be our highest bidder, right my dear?"

Beatrice sighed and sheathed her sword. "Right, grandfather."

Coham turned a keen eye on Thea. "Now I feel in my bones that trouble is headed this way. You lot don't stay out in the open tonight, you hear me?"

"Oh." Thea looked at the strange, wizened man. "Thank you."

Nodding his head sagely, Coham heaved his sword up onto his shoulder and tottered off through the trees, followed by Beatrice.

Thea watched them go. "Are there really people like that, who just walk around and look for work, even when they are so old?"

"That's what I do," Ulfgar grumbled. "If you don't have a home you've got to make a living somehow."

"I guess so," Thea conceded. She'd never really thought about what it would mean to not have a home. She had a home she could return to, if she really had to. Not that there would be many at home who would be glad to see her back. She fingered her brooch thoughtfully. "What do you think he meant, that trouble is headed this way?"

"I don't have the slightest idea," Elora shook her head. "Out of his mind."

"Maybe." Ulfgar sat up and straightened his helmet. "But when his type says danger, they know what they're talking about. I reckon we take his advice."

"But how?" Thea demanded. "What kind of shelter can we find?"

Elora sighed. "I guess we start looking."

Thea glanced around the group. "Where's Sylica?"

After searching the entire area, Thea finally found Sylica, lying on her stomach beside a small pond, throwing flowers to the ducks.

Wearily, Thea dropped to the ground beside her. "Sylica, what are you doing?"

"Floating flowers on the water," Sylica explained cheerily. "Don't they look so nice, bobbing up and down beside the ducks?"

Thea shook her head. She wasn't sure what world Sylica lived in, but apparently it was a world where danger didn't exist.

"We were worried about you," Thea added, after the silence stretched on for too long.

"Oh." Sylica seemed to consider that for a moment. "But you found me."

"Yes, but I didn't know I was going to find you. Something might have happened."

A thoughtful frown wrinkled Sylica's nose. "But it always turns out alright in the end. The Great Big Big takes care of us."

"I know." Thea sighed. "Just ... try to stay closer to the rest of us next time. Okay?"

"Okay!" Sylica grinned and put her last flower behind her ear.

After collecting some wild apples growing by the pond, Thea led Sylica back to the others. They had been scouting the area for some kind of sheltered spot to camp in for the night, but hadn't had any success.

"I know what!" Sylica exclaimed when the problem was explained to her. "We can ask one of the farms nearby! Someone is bound to have a barn or something we can sleep in."

The others exchanged unsure glances.

"I don't know," Thea said slowly. "Do you really think someone would offer us a place to stay?" But then ... the Littles had given her and Arl a place to stay, and even helped them. Surely there must be humans out there who were kind-hearted too. "I guess we could try."

Elora raised an eyebrow. "You really think a Big would invite me in?"

"How can they, unless you give them a chance to?"

Elora stared at Thea for a long moment. "I guess you're right. So who is going to go ask?"

Thea glanced around the group. "Well, not me or Sylica. In my experience, humans sometimes respond strangely to Elves. And not you, Elora. Sorry." She thought for a moment. "Arl? You could change into human form and go."

Arl gave her an incredulous glance. "If I'm our best chance, then our chances are *very* low."

"Ulfgar?"

"Hmm?"

Somehow, Thea felt that Ulfgar wasn't the right person to send on any errand, but what other option did they have? "Would you go to a farmhouse and ask them if we can sleep in their barn for the night? And ask nicely? Without threatening them?"

"I guess so," Ulfgar grumbled.

Together, they walked down the road until they found a promising laneway. Pack and axes clanking, Ulfgar trundled around the bend.

Thea waited anxiously, pacing beside the road. Micai was already high in the sky overhead and night would be coming soon.

She didn't have to wait long. Ulfgar trudged back down the laneway.

"Any luck?" Thea asked.

Ulfgar shook his head.

A breath of cool, damp wind made Thea shiver. "I guess we try asking someone else?"

No one objected, so Thea led the way further down the road until they came to the next laneway. Without a word, Ulfgar turned onto it and trudged into the distance.

As they waited, Micai eclipsed Allumen and green-blue darkness fell over the land. Elora pulled her lantern out of her bag. Her other hand fidgeted with the quiver at her side.

They heard Ulfgar's approach before they saw him. He trudged into view with a sullen expression on his face.

"What did they say?" Thea asked.

"No one answered."

"It's getting late." Arl glanced around the shadowy fields.

In the dim light of night, Thea couldn't see as far as she could before. She looked at Arl.

Arl sniffed the air. "Fog."

Thea frowned. She'd really hoped that they could find somewhere to stay, but now it was dark, and it was going to get darker.

"I guess we should find a place to camp."

Arl nodded and slipped off into the night.

"That ditch looks pretty good," Ulfgar mumbled.

"Come on," Thea gestured to the others, "we might as well follow the road while we're looking."

A short while later, Arl returned to the group and led them to a small hollow, sheltered by two tall trees.

As they were setting up their camp, the fog rolled

over them, thick and clammy. Thea could barely see the far side of the hollow.

Arl shifted into owl form and flew off to scout, while Elora built a fire and Thea took stock of the food they had foraged. There were roots, mushrooms, and apples, as well as three small rabbits and some nuts. More than they needed for one meal.

The fire was a welcome relief from the damp cold of the fog. They huddled close around it as they cooked and ate their supper.

When the meal was finished, Sylica wrapped herself in a blanket and lay down by the fire. Elora watered her lantern and put it away in her pack.

Thea sat and watched the swirling fog drift by. It made her think of foggy days back home on Larsya. The fog would mean the ships couldn't sail, and she and Roland would go exploring.

The smell of rotting flesh filled Thea's nostrils. Looking up, she caught Elora's glance.

"Is that—" Thea began, then stopped as the conversation around the fire fell silent.

"The dark birds," Elora breathed.

Ulfgar groaned.

"But how ..." Thea protested. "I thought they only lived in the Deorcian."

Elora jumped up and put an arrow to her bowstring.

Thea scrambled to her feet and stared out through the billowing fog. It was impossible to see, but that smell was unmistakable, and Elora said they never gave up on their prey ...

"Do you think they know we're here?" Thea whispered.

Elora nodded her chin towards the campfire. That

gave away their presence if nothing else did.

"Should we put it out?" Thea whispered. "How many do you think there are?"

"Quiet," Elora hissed.

Thea glanced around the small circle of light. Where was Arl?

With a soft moan, Sylica stretched and rolled over in her sleep.

Thea knelt beside her. "Sylica," she whispered, gently shaking her shoulder. "Sylica, wake up."

Something dark swooped over her head. With a cry, Thea threw herself to the ground and she felt a rush of wind. Something landed beside her.

"Musharocs," Arl hissed. "Twelve. Coming this way."

Heart pounding, Thea got back to her feet. Sylica blinked up at her sleepily.

"Twelve?" Elora's eyes were wide. "We can't fight half that many."

"Not out in the open." Arl's face was grim.

Thea grabbed her bag. Beside her, Ulfgar dumped the remains of supper into his oversized pack and slung it over his shoulders.

As silently as they could, they followed Arl into the shadows. Soon the light of their fire was lost to the fog-laced darkness.

It was impossible to see more than two paces away, but they stumbled on. Thea kept glancing back, expecting to see dark shapes emerge from the deep shadows that seemed to follow them.

Something loomed out of the darkness before them—a tree, gnarled and ancient. Creeping past it, they entered some kind of forest, all but invisible in the gloom.

Another wave of stench washed over Thea's senses. Arl appeared at her side, gesturing for her to move faster.

Thea hurried on, jumping at every crack of a branch underfoot. Cold sweat tingled down her spine. Her heart pounded in her ears.

Suddenly the darkness around her wasn't quite so dark. Glancing back, Thea saw the shadow of the trees, now left behind. Out of the sky, something swooped towards her.

A black arrow sailed overhead. The musharoc screeched, its wings beating the air in an explosion of feathers and stretch.

Thea gasped, fumbling to grab Raybow off her back.

"Go! Go!" Arl hissed, "Don't stop!"

Clutching Raybow, Thea ran, stumbling through the darkness.

An eagle scream cut through the shrieks of the musharocs.

Sylica was beside her. Running. Where were the others?

Thea's foot struck something. With a cry, she fell, knees colliding with the bare, rocky ground.

Someone grabbed her hand. Pulled her up.

Sylica grinned, then ran on, almost pulling Thea off her feet.

The fog swirled around them. It was impossible to see where they were going.

What was that? Something dark loomed out of the fog. Some kind of stone wall.

A deafening shriek split the air above Thea's head as something struck her shoulder. Pain exploded and Thea crumpled to the ground. A choking stench filled her nostrils. She couldn't breathe.

Sylica yelled. The sound seemed muffled and far away.

Something was pulling Raybow. Thea clung to her bow with all her strength, but her right arm wouldn't work.

"Come on!" Sylica yelled. "Let go!"

Staring up at Sylica, Thea released her hold.

Sylica staggered back, lifted Raybow, and swung it over Thea's head.

It struck something with a solid *thud* and the musharoc shrieked. Searing pain shot through Thea's shoulder as her assailant tumbled back, its talons dislodging from her flesh.

Sylica grabbed Thea and pulled her back to her feet, shoving Raybow into her unresisting hands.

"Come on!" Sylica gestured, disappearing into the darkness.

Thea staggered, dark spots swirling in her vision. Gripping Raybow, she took a deep breath and tried to follow. Her hands met the cold stone wall.

Feeling her way along it, Thea tried not to listen to the screams and cries that seemed to fill the darkness behind her.

The wall ended. No, it didn't end. It was an opening—some kind of open gate with stone arching above it. Thea stumbled through. In the shadowy fog, she thought she could see some kind of courtyard, overgrown and empty.

"Elora! Arl! There's some kind of wall!" It wouldn't keep the monsters out, but maybe ... maybe ...

Thea hurried through the darkness towards the large, deeper shadow that loomed ahead of her.

It was a building. A large, stone building, stretching up into the darkness. There were windows, dark and empty, and ancient vines that covered much of the wall.

Could there be ... Yes! A door! Thea hammered on it with all of her might.

"Arl!" she yelled, "Sylica! Elora! Ulfgar! Over here!"

Thea hammered on the door again. Was anyone inside?

Footsteps pounded towards her and a musharoc screeched overhead.

Ulfgar appeared out of the fog, took in the situation, and raised his axe, running at full speed towards the door.

Thea grabbed the handle and turned it. The door opened.

She stepped aside as Ulfgar plunged past, then hurried after him through the open door. Elora shot one last arrow into the darkness, then dodged inside. Arl and Sylica followed.

Thea slammed the door shut and felt around frantically to see if there was a lock.

Arl leaned their back against the door, breathing heavily.

As Thea's eyes adjusted to the darkness, she saw Elora watching out of the closest window. "They haven't come up to the door," she muttered. "Why haven't they come up to the door? They know we're in here."

Quietly, Thea crept over to her. "Could I use your lantern?"

Reluctantly, Elora lowered her pack and pulled out the lantern.

Taking it, Thea looked around the room in which they found themselves. It was a large room and completely empty, except for a large fireplace that dominated one of the walls. The floor was wooden, smooth and polished. Across the room from the door, a large gap in the wall loomed dark, like a window without any glass, and an open door beside it.

Creeping closer to investigate, Thea found another room on the other side, a room with counters and shelves and a large oven. And two more doors.

"Are you exploring?" Sylica whispered in her ear. "Can I come too?"

Thea jumped, then tried to steady herself. "Uh, sure."

"Is this a kitchen?"

Thea looked around the empty room again. "Maybe." It might have been a kitchen once, but she had never seen a kitchen that looked so empty.

Going through another door, they found a smaller room that appeared to have once been a pantry, but the shelves were bare.

In the floor, a large trap door lay open, and stairs descended into darkness below. In the dim light of the lantern, Thea inspected the stairs. They seemed solid enough.

"Let's go!" Sylica grinned. "Like the Big Book says: If you're going down, you might as well go feet first!"

Thea shook her head. "I don't think the Big Book says that."

"Of course it does!" Sylica beamed. "My dad says I have a very special memory. Come on, let's see what's down there."

Thea's shoulder throbbed, but she followed Sylica down the steps. At the bottom they found a dark room filled with casks and barrels.

"A wine cellar!" Sylica squealed excitedly.

"A what cellar?" Ulfgar's voice drifted down from above, and soon his heavy tread was heard coming down the stairs.

Thea looked around in the lantern's strange green light. This was the first room that wasn't empty. In fact, many of the kegs looked like they were still full.

"That's more like it," Ulfgar muttered, tapping on one of the barrels.

"Ulfgar, they're not ours." Thea watched him in concern.

"No one else is using them."

Thea had a closer look at one of the barrels. It bore a small label: 691. The writing was Elvish.

Thea stared at it. What was a barrel of Elvish wine doing here, so far away? And what did it mean, 691? Was that when the barrel was made? That would have been before the Great War!

Somehow, Ulfgar had gotten the barrel open. "Cheers," he said and took a swig. He stopped, looked at the barrel, then took an even longer drink.

Thea's head started to pound. She lifted her hand to rub her forehead, and a spasm of pain shot through her shoulder. Gingerly, she felt it and looked at her hand. It was red with blood.

"I think I should lie down," she mumbled faintly.

"Come on," Sylica grinned, "I'll help you up the stairs!"

Sylica led her back to the great room where Arl paced restlessly in front of the door. Elora sat on the floor, wrapping a bandage around her knee.

"Anyone home?" she asked as Thea and Sylica came and sat beside her.

Thea shook her head, then winced as another spasm

of pain shot through her body.

"The place looks abandoned to me," Sylica replied. "Oh and do you have another bandage? Thea's shoulder needs some help."

"No sign of the dark birds?" Thea asked as Elora bandaged her shoulder.

Elora frowned. "Nothing."

Outside the windows, the fog was brighter than it had been. Was it morning already?

"I wouldn't have considered this place secure, with so many windows and doors," Elora muttered, as if to herself, "but I don't know if we'll find a more sheltered spot."

Thea nodded and lay down gingerly on the floor.

Exhaustion swept over her like a wave.

Chapter Sixteen

When Thea woke, Arl was still pacing beside the door. Elora sat quietly, fletching some arrows. Sylica was asleep on the floor beside her. Daylight seeped through the windows, but from her position on the floor she couldn't see anything through them.

Gingerly, she sat up. "Where's Ulfgar?"

"Passed out in the wine cellar." Elora stared down an arrow to see if the feathers were straight.

"And this place really is abandoned?"

"It seems so. Everything is empty."

Thea's eyes roamed around the room. However long it had been abandoned, it didn't appear to be very old. The dark wooden beams gleamed, and the fireplace looked like it was in perfect condition. It wasn't anything like the ruined places she had seen.

"There's an upstairs," Elora added. "More empty rooms."

Thea got slowly to her feet. "I'll go look at them."

Up a gentle flight of steps, Thea found a wide hallway. Through one door she found what may have been a meeting room, like the great room downstairs, but smaller. Down the hallway she found several smaller rooms, each with a window at the end. The final door led into what appeared to be a small living quarters: a sitting room, and beyond it a small bedroom, each with large bay windows that let in lots of light.

Thea walked over to a window and looked outside. There was nothing to see but whiteness. The fog was brighter in the light of day, but it still obscured everything beyond the walls of their refuge.

Thea walked into the bedroom. The bedframe was still there. Thea ran her hand along its smooth wood. It reminded her of her bed at home.

A gleam of light on the floor caught her eye. Bending down, she saw something small, stuck between the floorboards. Pulling out her knife, she gently pried it out.

It was a silver coin. Thea turned it over in her hand. It looked just like the coins at home.

First the wine label, and now a coin. She had thought she was the first Elf to ever travel this far, but maybe that wasn't the case.

Were there any other signs that Elves had visited before? Thea examined the room closely, but couldn't find anything else.

Thoughtfully, Thea wandered back downstairs. What was this place, anyways? There was something familiar about it, but she couldn't understand why.

Something glimmered on the doorframe. Curious, Thea hurried over to look.

The doorframe was engraved with writing—Elvish writing—and the words glowed with a spiritual light.

Thea stared. She had never seen words glow like that before. The doorframe was written with words of protection, calling on the power of the Deity to keep evil away and protect those within its walls.

"That's why!" she cried.

"What's why?" Elora demanded.

Sylica woke and sat up sleepily.

"These words. Look!" Excitement rose in Thea. "They are magic words, saying that this place is protected by the Deity's power. That's why the musharocs can't come in. This is a safe place, where evil has no power."

Elora stared. "Places like that exist?"

"Of course!" Certainty welled up inside Thea. She turned to Sylica. "Your Uncle Bob could make magical things, so why couldn't someone make a magical door?"

"The dark birds haven't attacked us yet." Elora looked out the window with a suspicious glare. "I wonder where they are?"

Sylica looked at the writing curiously. "What language is that?"

"It's Elvish, of course," Thea replied. "You really don't understand it?"

"Why would I? There's no Elves around here."

Thea ran a hand along the doorframe. There used to be Elves here. The wine and the coin could have been obtained through trade and travel, but this doorframe was carved by an Elf. There was no way around that. And now that she looked around her again, she knew why it seemed familiar. It reminded her of some of the buildings back home. Those dark beams were set like the ones in the Harbour Office. The fireplace was just like one in her uncle's audience chamber. Without even stepping outside, she knew where the stables would be, and the outbuilding for the gardeners. This building was made by Elves.

She walked to the nearest window and looked out. Sure enough, there was another, smaller building, barely visible through the fog. It would be the stables, of course. She could almost picture in her mind how the gardens would have looked. Maybe there was even a fountain, like the courtyard in Enkeli's Temple.

But what was an Elvish building doing here, so far away from Larsya? Had Elves really lived here, so long ago? The humans and Littles and Dryads of these lands had never even seen an Elf.

A deep sadness filled her heart. If the Elves had never fled to their island, how different things would have been! Maybe the races would be working together to fight against evil, instead of hating and hurting each other.

A loud groan echoed from the distant wine cellar.

Hurrying down, Thea found Ulfgar holding his head and looking around with a vaguely confused expression.

"What world is it?" he groaned, as Thea came into his view.

"Are you okay?" Thea asked, kneeling beside him.

"Bugger off," Ulfgar mumbled, pushing her away. "Let me die in peace."

As gently as she could, she helped him to his feet. "Come on, let's go upstairs."

As soon as he emerged into the light, Ulfgar groaned and shoved his helmet down over his eyes. "Why does everything hate me?" he mumbled under his breath, but he allowed Thea to guide him to where the others sat on the floor in the great room.

Elora got him a drink of water, which Ulfgar accepted with great reluctance.

"What now?" she asked, turning to the rest of the group. "The dark birds are out there, but we can't keep hiding forever."

Thea glanced at Ulfgar. "I don't know if we're quite ready to leave yet."

"Let those who are tired or injured rest," Arl said in a firm voice. "The day is already half past. We will continue our travels tomorrow." They glanced at the door.

Elora laid a hand on her bow and eyed Arl intently. "When you go out there, you will tell me first."

Arl glared.

"Are we going to fight the bloody monster things?" Ulfgar staggered to his feet. "Sounds like a plan."

"Arl never said—" Thea protested, but Arl silenced her with a wave.

"Your shoulder is hurt. You stay here."

"What?" Thea scrambled to her feet. "I want to help too!"

"Can you help?" Arl asked. "Can you even hold your bow?"

Thea tried, but she was only able to draw the bowstring back halfway before her shoulder spasmed in pain. She had to admit she would be a liability, rather than a help in the fight. "Does someone else want to use Raybow, then?" she asked, somewhat reluctantly. "It was made to fight creatures like this."

"Sure, I could use it," Sylica replied. "I'm not great at shooting, but it can't do any harm, right?"

"Careful, please," Thea whispered, as Sylica took Raybow and the quiver of arrows.

Thea watched anxiously as Arl and Elora slipped silently through the door. Ulfgar clattered noisily after them.

With a flurry of wings, two musharocs rose above the outer wall, screeching, but they did not come any closer. Elora shot two arrows and one of the monsters fell, shrieking, from the sky.

"We don't even have to approach them." Elora gave a grim smile. "These are the kind of terms I like to fight on."

Arl shifted into cougar form and stalked silently towards the gate. Ulfgar ambled after them, his helmet low over his eyes.

More musharocs rose into the sky and Elora shot again. Another musharoc fell. "And that's two," Elora muttered to herself.

Thea watched from the doorway. The musharocs screeched angrily, but the magic of the building prevented them from getting any closer to their prey.

Arl darted through the gate, followed by Ulfgar, and the sounds of the fight drifted through the billowing mists.

After a while, Ulfgar returned. His nose was bloodied, but otherwise he seemed mildly pleased with himself. "All dead," he reported. Stomping past Thea, Ulfgar pushed his way inside, and she could hear his footsteps going through the kitchen, down the stairs into the wine cellar.

Arl returned a short while later and curled up in the corner of the room, licking blood off their fur. Elora smiled as she sorted through the arrows she had collected from the bodies of the musharocs. Sylica returned Raybow to Thea.

"They're all dead now?" Thea asked.

"Yes." Elora looked up from her work. "Arl made sure."

Arl stretched with a smug half-smile, then curled up to sleep.

"Would it be okay for me to go outside?" Thea asked. "I could do a bit of foraging."

Arl seemed to consider this for a moment, then shifted into human form. "Don't go far."

"I won't," Thea promised.

Arl gave a curt nod, shifted back into cougar form, and curled up to sleep.

With Raybow on her back, Thea wandered outside. Avoiding the gate where the fight had taken place, she walked over to the outbuilding she had guessed was the stable. Sure enough, she found it to be a long, low building with a row of stalls along each side. On the other side of the stable, she followed the inside of the wall, past trailing vines and overgrown gardens.

She found the gardener's hut and peered inside. Stacks of empty pots lined one of the walls, and an old rake leaned against another. Thoughtfully, she wandered along the wall until the large building loomed into view again. If she ignored the disarray of the gardens, she could almost imagine herself to be back in Lyudmyla, at some sort of manor house, maybe along the seashore.

A gull cried in the distance, and a strange longing rose in her heart—a longing for what could have been. What would it have been like, to arrive here and be met by her own people, instead of emptiness? The dark windows could have been full of light, the empty rooms full of laughter and song. That was how it should have been.

Having completed a full circuit of the wall, Thea approached the gate. There were Elvish words engraved along its arch: "Peace to all who enter."

What kind of Elves had lived there, so long ago? Had they died in the Great War? Or had they abandoned it and retreated to their island, fading into oblivion, like

Khariton, and choosing to forget all that they had left behind?

In the sky above her, the fog thinned just enough that she could see Micai, approaching Allumen for its nightly eclipse. The fog was passing. Tomorrow they would continue on their quest to find a home for the Littles. Hopefully they didn't have too much further to go.

The next morning Thea woke up early. Her shoulder was feeling much better, but it still ached when she tried to use it.

Silently, she stood up without waking her sleeping companions. Even Arl was asleep, curled up as a large bear in front of the door. Climbing the stairs, Thea made her way to the private chambers she had discovered the day before. There was something comfortingly familiar about them. If the bed had a mattress, she would have been tempted to sleep there.

Kneeling by the window, Thea bowed her head and waited to see if Allulien would speak. The silence rang in her ears, but she almost thought she felt, rather than heard, one word impressed upon her heart:

Soon.

Thea watched out the window as the light of morning stole across the gardens far below. There was a door in the wall, on this side of the house, and beyond it was the sea.

Thea stared. This was a different sea than the one she knew. The northern sea was grey and rough. This sea was as calm as glass. Allumen's light gleamed on its shimmering blue water.

Thea hurried downstairs to find the others waking.

"Come look!" she urged them. "We've found the sea!"

Sleepily, Sylica and Elora followed Thea through the kitchen, out the back door, through the gardens, and out through the door in the wall, emerging on a bluff high above the sea. An ancient path, wide and smooth, wound down the slope to the shore far below.

Thea gestured at the vast horizon. "It's the sea."

When her companions didn't reply, she added, "I didn't know we were close to the sea."

Sylica scratched her head. "Well we had to get to the sea eventually. That means we're almost there."

"Almost where?"

Sylica grinned. "Almost home!"

"Really?" Thea looked around eagerly. "Which way do we go now?"

Sylica pointed out beyond the far horizon. "That way!"

Thea stared at Sylica. "Your home is across the sea?"

"Yes," Sylica grinned. "That's where I came from!"

"Why didn't you tell us that?" Elora turned on Sylica, eyes blazing. "We can't get across there, it's impossible!"

Sylica seemed taken aback. "But you said you wanted to visit my home."

"And how are we supposed to get across the sea?" Elora demanded.

A dark shape swooped overhead and Arl landed beside them. "What's going on?"

"Sylica's home is across the sea," Thea explained. "We didn't know that, because she never told us."

"How are we supposed to get across there?" Elora glared at Sylica. "How did *you* get across?"

"I made a boat. Uncle Bob helped me. He thought it was a great idea."

"How are we supposed to make a boat?" Elora demanded. "I don't know anything about making boats, and I don't have money to buy one—if anyone would be willing to sell to us. And even if we made it across the sea and found your home, we would still have to find a way to return with all of my people, and all of Faris' people!"

Sylica grinned hopefully. "Well, we could try!"

"No." Thea stared across the glittering sea. "We are not abandoning this land or escaping across the sea." She turned to face the others. "We need to find a home for the Littles *here*."

"Here?" Elora protested. "Where everyone hates us?"

Sylica looked crestfallen. "It's a very nice home. Don't you want to come see it?"

Thea took a deep breath. "Listen. My people used to live here. The Elves made this house. They had homes here, even cities. But the Great War began, and my people ran away across the sea. They abandoned the rest of the world and left you to fight alone. That was wrong. The Elves never should have left." Thea looked down at the Little standing by her side. "Elora, I don't want your people to make the same mistake that my people did."

A heavy tiredness filled Elora's eyes. "If not across the sea, then where?"

Thea glanced at the large stone building behind them. "This place is safe. Do you think …?"

"And be trapped here like we were trapped in our tunnels?" Elora glared. "Once the Bigs found out we were here we'd never be able to leave without them hunting us."

Thea's heart ached. "I know. Let me … let me think

for a while. Maybe I'll think of something."

She turned away and started walking along the rocky bluff. She couldn't let the Littles down. She had promised to find them a new home, and she needed to keep her promise. If she'd only gone to Gedwyld first, maybe Davis would have taught her what to do, but it was too late for that now. What should she do?

"Keep showing mercy."

Startled, Thea turned. Micai sat nearby on a big rock, mug in hand.

"You don't happen to have any cookies, do you?" Micai asked with a grin.

Thea gasped in delight. "You—you're here! It's been so long!"

Micai raised the mug in a salute. "You haven't *seen* me in so long. There's a difference."

"But you're here now, and this fixes everything!" Words rushed out of Thea. "We're trying to find the Littles a home, but we can't go across the sea and I didn't know what to do! Do you know of a place where the Littles can live?" She waited in breathless anticipation.

Micai smiled and gave Thea a thoughtful look. "Don't you want to know why I'm here?" There was something in that glance that reminded Thea of the last time she had seen Micai—in the throne room of the Deity. They were not just a long-missed teacher and friend, they were one of the most powerful beings in all of Raphtova, the bringer of the justice and mercy of the Deity.

Thea lowered her eyes. "Yes. I want to know why you are here."

Micai nodded. "First things first. There will be time for catching up later." The mug disappeared and Micai leaned forward intently. "It is time for you to take your first task in the war against the Fallen One. The Deity needs you."

Fear rose in Thea's heart. "But ... I promised to help the Littles. I can't just leave them now."

Micai stood and gave Thea a sharp look. "You accepted a position in the war. Are you going to follow your orders?"

Thea swallowed. "Yes. I will obey my orders."

There may have been a twinkle in Micai's eyes, but it was quickly swallowed up by the stern expression that made her think of the throne room. "The monsters of the Deorcian are increasing and growing stronger. We've been monitoring it, but over the past few days the increase has been exponential. We need to get the Littles out of the Deorcian. Now."

"They're in danger?" Thea's eyes widened. "What can I do?"

"Your orders from Allulien are to return as quickly as possible and convince the Littles to make their escape. They know and trust you, so you are our best chance of convincing them to do so."

The Deity wanted her to help the Littles after all! Relief and concern flooded Thea's mind. "But ... but how can I tell them to leave when I still don't know where to lead them?"

Micai's face was more serious than Thea had ever seen it. "We only have five days until it will be impossible to get them out. The Littles have barricaded themselves in their tunnels, but their defences will not hold for long. A home can be found later. First get them out."

The magnitude of Micai's words left Thea gasping for

breath. "We only have five days? How is that possible? It took us more than ten days to come this far!"

"Your travel was not direct and you encountered many difficulties on your journey. This time all of our resources will be deployed in clearing the way for you and you will be travelling on the most direct route possible. If you start now, you can make it in time. Just." Micai gave her an appraising look. "And this is not a time for resting. You will be travelling as fast and as far as you can. Do you understand?"

Thea nodded. "I—I need to tell the others. We need to leave right away!"

Stumbling in her haste, Thea ran back to the place where she had left Elora and the others. They were not there.

"Elora!" Thea called. "Elora! Arl! Where are you?"

She ran through the door and almost tripped over Elora who was hurrying towards her.

"Elora!" Thea gasped, "We need to leave right away!"

Elora frowned. "What's going on?"

"I heard from the Deity. Your people are in danger!"

Elora stared at her.

"Come on," Thea called, running past her. "Get everyone together, quick!"

Thea found Arl and Sylica in the great room, but Ulfgar was nowhere to be seen.

"What is going on?" Elora demanded, hurrying to join them.

"I heard from the Deity that the monsters in the Deorcian have become even more dangerous since we left. We have to get the Littles out of there as soon as possible."

"But we still haven't found somewhere for them to

go," Elora protested.

"I know, but there isn't time. We have to get them out first. Then we can find a home for them."

Elora frowned and the others looked at each other doubtfully.

"They've barricaded the tunnels," Thea whispered. "We have to make it there before they can't hold them any longer."

"How do you know this?" Elora asked, but Thea could see the fear rising in her eyes.

"I am a servant of the Deity, and this is what the Deity wants us to do."

"And is it possible?" Elora asked.

Thea nodded. "We will have help."

"What are we waiting for?" Ulfgar grumbled, staggering into the room. He had removed one of the smaller kegs from the wine cellar and strapped it precariously to the top of his pack.

Thea stared at him.

"What?" Ulfgar muttered. "Got a drink for the road."

Elora and Sylica grabbed their packs, and Thea slung Raybow over her back.

Ulfgar barely fit through the door with his extra load, but somehow he managed it, and the others followed close behind.

Thea stepped through the door last. She thought she heard, at the edge of hearing, a faint wailing cry. The wind rustled the long grasses and trailing vines. Gently, she closed the door. "I'll come back someday," she whispered.

The others were already through the gate. Thea hurried to follow them. "We will travel directly west," she explained as she caught up, "and we will walk as fast as we can, as long as we can keep it up all day. We are only going to stop to sleep."

"I thought you said it was better to rest," Arl commented, glancing her direction.

"That's true, but now we have orders to get there as fast as we can."

"Orders?" Arl's voice lowered to a growl. "I don't take orders from anyone."

Thea paused, looking from face to face. "I have to follow orders, because I have sworn to serve the Deity. Elora is coming because the Littles are her people and I know she doesn't want to leave them in danger. There is no need for the rest of you to come, though, if you don't want to."

"Well, what else am I going to do?" Ulfgar grumbled and started trudging down the road.

"Oh, I serve the Great Big Big too," Sylica grinned. "It's always good to do what the Great Big Big says."

Thea looked at Arl. "I'll understand if you don't want to come. You've come so much farther than you ever said you would."

Arl glared at her for a moment. "Damn you," they muttered, then strode off through the trees. "Ulfgar!" they called over their shoulder. "West is this way!"

A gleam of light flickered in Arl's spirit.

Chapter Seventeen

They walked all day, with only a short stop to sleep during staph. By the time night fell, they were stumbling from weariness. Finding a sheltered hollow on the side of a hill, they lay down and slept.

Thea woke as the first gleam of Allumen's light emerged from its eclipse. She lay and watched the light flicker through the rings of Micai. A strange energy surged through her limbs. The fatigue of the previous day was gone.

Thea.

Thea leapt to her feet. Someone was calling her. It wasn't one of her companions—they were still asleep.

Thea.

The voice echoed, soft and insistent. Thea hurried to follow, away from their campsite, further up the hill. She rounded a grassy bluff, and Allulien stood shimmering before her.

Thea sank to her knees, relief surging through every fibre of her being. Allulien had come. At last.

She looked up into her General's face. "What would you have me do?"

"You have already received your orders and are following them." Allulien smiled. "Well done, Thea. The great silence is over."

"The great silence?" Something ached, deep in Thea's

chest.

"There are times when questions are answered and orders are clear. There are other times when you must hold to that which you have already been given, even when no new word comes."

Thea's voice constricted to a whisper. "You didn't come for so long. I didn't understand why."

"You do not always need to understand why, Thea. No one can see the whole picture of what is going on, and sometimes not knowing is the easiest way to hold the course." Allulien's smile was gentle. "But that doesn't mean you can never know why. The Enemy's forces are strong in much of the land that you have been travelling through. If any of us were to show ourselves, we would betray our presence to them as well as to you."

"But you said that you would guide me, then you left me alone."

"You were not alone. You had the guide and protector that was prepared for you."

"You ... you mean Arl? But Arl said they don't follow orders."

"That is true, but we know Arl well. All we had to do was place you in their path, and we knew that they would guard you and show you the way. It had to be their own choice, though, which is why we could not appear to you while you travelled under Arl's protection. Every creature in Raphtova has the choice of whether to serve the Deity or not. If I was to appear and speak with you in front of Arl, that would take away part of their choice."

"But—but Arl is still with me now."

"Arl has chosen to join you in the task you received

from the Deity. They are now a companion and no longer a guide, and at this moment your companions sleep deeply in preparation for another long day of travel. They will not wake until you return to them."

Thea's mind was racing. "You said the silence is over. Does that mean I'll get to see you again, and Micai too?"

Allulien smiled. "Yes you will, but remember that once again you are approaching a stronghold of the Enemy. You will not see us often, because we cannot give the Fallen One a chance to discover our plan. You will not see us, but you will see the evidence of our work. No dangers lie between you and the Deorcian, and we will ensure that it remains so. The Deorcian itself will be an entirely different matter, but we will do all we can to ensure that help can reach you, even there."

Thea nodded. Overhead, the full light of day flooded across the sky. She got to her feet. "Should we be going now?"

"One final thing. You are aware that you have received a measure of the Deity's power, and have done magic within the domain of comprehension, which is good. You also have access to the domains of blessing and charm, and I believe that these may become important to you over the next few days. Do not be afraid to use your magic. It is not something to hoard or save, as some forgetful ones would want you to believe." Allulien's eyes flashed. "As long as you are within the will of the Deity, your magic will return every time you check in." Allulien's gaze settled on the distant campsite. "Last night I blessed your sleep, giving all of you the strength to continue your journey. Tonight, that will be your task."

Allulien disappeared, but it seemed to Thea that Allulien's light still shone across the hillside as she ran back to the campsite to wake the others.

Rounding the corner, she saw a large, flat stone that she hadn't noticed before. It was filled with fruits and nuts.

The others started to wake as Thea approached. She could see in their eyes that, just as Allulien had said, they were well rested and ready for another long day of travel. After eating their breakfast, they set off once again, heading as directly west as the rocky hills allowed.

As the end of the day approached, Arl gestured to a thin wisp of smoke, curling up from beyond the next hill.

Elora grabbed her bow. "I'll scout."

"Wait." Thea held out a cautioning hand. "I was told there wouldn't be any trouble on the way. It must be fine."

Elora glared. "What if it isn't fine?"

"I'll scout," Arl offered. "I'm faster."

"You can fly ahead if you want," Thea replied, "but the rest of us are going to keep going."

As they rounded the next hill, Thea could see a small campfire burning down in the valley. There didn't seem to be anyone beside it.

Arl joined Thea and the others as they approached the campfire.

"There's no one here," Arl reported. "I searched the whole valley, but I couldn't see anyone."

The campsite looked like it had once been occupied, but there was nothing left besides the small fire. Above it, a spit held the carcass of a small deer, which seemed to have been roasting for some time.

Awe and thanksgiving rose in Thea's heart. "I think the Deity has given us our supper."

"What?" Arl protested. "Someone left behind their supper so we could eat it?"

"I don't know. Maybe something happened and they had to leave in a hurry, but however it happened, it has been abandoned and we are hungry."

Ulfgar heaved his heavy pack to the ground. "Drink's up!"

Arl circled the area one more time, but could not find any sign of the people who had made the campfire. Finally, they had to admit that no one was coming back for their meal.

Everyone ate well, and they packed up the leftovers for the following day.

At Arl's insistence, they travelled on a little farther, setting up their own camp a comfortable distance from the abandoned campsite.

As they settled down for the night, Thea thought about Allulien's words. How exactly would she bless everyone's sleep? Allulien said she could, but she didn't know how.

But there was that warm glow she carried in her heart. Gently, she stretched it out to cover their entire campsite. "Please, Deity," she whispered, "let everyone sleeping in this place have a blessed sleep and not feel tired from the long travel."

Deep in her heart, Thea felt the assurance that her prayer had been heard.

Sylica wrapped herself in her blanket and lay down on the ground, looking up at the sky with sleepy eyes. "Aww, that's nice," she mumbled, "you made a little tent for us."

A tent? Thea looked around, but couldn't see what Sylica was talking about.

"The tent." Sylica pointed above their campsite. "It's all gold and sparkly."

"Do you mean the blessing on our campsite?"

Sylica nodded.

"You can see it?"

"Sure." Sylica rolled over and hummed sleepily. "It's just magic."

Thea stared. "You can see magic?" She was able to *feel* magic, certainly, but she had never heard of someone being able to see it.

A faint snore rose from Sylica's sleeping form. Thea shook her head. Was it possible that Sylica's elf-sight was a kind of magic sight? She had never heard of such a thing, but Sylica was a very unusual Elf.

No one else seemed to notice the magical blessing tent. One by one, they lay down and fell asleep.

The next morning Thea checked in, but Allulien did not appear. Remembering Allulien's words, Thea didn't feel disappointed. They must be getting closer to the Deorcian. Sure enough, Arl returned from a quick scout with the news that just over the next ridge they would be entering the land that had been burned by the wildfire. They hadn't seen any sign of night mares, but even so everyone was on high alert as they traversed the blackened hills.

Just before staph, they crossed the river into troll territory. Thea could tell that everyone was on edge. Ulfgar walked with an axe in each hand, eyeing every boulder with suspicion. Elora kept an arrow on the string of her bow, ready to shoot at a moment's notice.

Only Sylica seemed unconcerned, skipping along with an exuberance that nothing could drag down.

Finally they approached the river with the bridge, where they had first encountered a troll. Avoiding the bridge entirely, they waded across the river further downstream.

"I don't understand." Elora stared back across the river. "There were so many trolls before, but not a single one now."

Thea ran her hand along Raybow thoughtfully. "Allulien said the way would be safe. I don't know how, but that was the promise."

Arl frowned and gestured for everyone to keep moving.

The rest of that day they hurried on, and the next day. Occasionally, Thea recognized a landmark from their outward journey, but for the most part the hills all looked the same to her. They continued west, as straight as they could go. It was amazing how much more ground they could cover when they weren't wandering through the trackless hills looking for the best way through, or trying to find water and food. Somehow, the straight way always led them to food or water just when they needed it.

The mood in the group was lifting. They knew that they were getting closer to their goal, somehow making it in less than half the time they had taken to traverse it before. Even Ulfgar seemed to have a spring in his step, despite the heavy load on his back.

When evening was approaching, they crested a particularly rocky ridge and found a narrow valley beyond it. A small stream trickled down from the heights above, and along its banks grew tangles of berry canes, loaded with fruit.

Thea smiled. The Deity really was providing for them, just as Allulien had said. But they only had two days left to get the Littles out, and they hadn't even made it into the Deorcian yet.

The next day they were rounding their second ridge when they saw the Deorcian, stretched out like a shadow before them.

Without a word, they stopped. They had almost reached their goal, but the most dangerous stretch was still before them.

Thea looked at Elora. "You'll be able to find your way home?"

Elora nodded. "I've lived my whole life in the Trees. I know my way home."

"We will follow your lead." Thea glanced from Elora to the rest of the group. "Try to avoid a fight if you can. We're just trying to make it through."

"We want to make it through *and* make it out again," Elora corrected. "If we are followed, we will not be getting out again."

"Then we'll make sure we aren't followed, but that doesn't mean we have to fight. It would be better to not be seen at all."

"I'm not the one that will be seen." Elora shot Ulfgar a keen glance. "Lose the barrel."

"Right." Ulfgar sat down with an impassive expression. "It's lost."

"What's that supposed to mean?" Elora demanded.

Ulfgar leaned back and tipped his helmet over his

eyes. "Where the drink goes, I go."

Thea put a hand on Elora's shoulder. "I think Ulfgar will be extra quiet, even with his barrel. Won't you, Ulfgar?"

Ulfgar tipped his helmet back and looked at her. "What was that?"

"You're coming with us. We're not going to make you leave."

A flicker of confusion crossed Ulfgar's face. "What?"

"We want you to come with us." Thea glanced at Elora, whose face seemed to be calculating their chances of survival with Ulfgar versus their chances without him. "*Right*, Elora?"

"Right." Elora relented. "Let's go. The sooner we're through, the sooner it's done."

Creeping as silently as they could, they approached the closest of the trees. Elora led the way, followed by Thea, then Ulfgar, Sylica, and Arl in the rear.

Thea held her breath as her senses were engulfed by the unnatural silence of the Deorcian. Even in the middle of the day it was dark and shadowy beneath the trees. She found it hard to see the others with the sight of her eyes, but she couldn't risk relying on her spirit sight. It would be disastrous if she slipped into vidlas now, and she knew how easy it was to do, even when she was trying not to.

Elora crept from shadow to shadow. Thea followed, ears straining for any sign that their passage had been detected, but as workday passed, the forest surrounding them remained silent. Thea glanced up, but the branches overhead were dark and still.

Elora froze, barely visible in the shadows ahead. Slowly she turned and gestured for Thea to stop.

As silently as possible, Thea glanced back at Ulfgar and passed on the gesture. Then her eyes scanned the shadows. What had Elora seen?

Slowly, almost silently, a darker form emerged from the shadows. It was large. Its lizard-like face and long, clawed limbs reminded her of the creature that Elora had called a dark thing and Arl had called an athexe. She held her breath as the monster stalked closer and closer.

Before it reached them, the athexe stopped and turned away. Thea watched its shadowy form until her spirit sight no longer felt its darkness.

Elora breathed a silent sigh and gestured that they could keep moving. Carefully, she steered the group away from the direction that the monster had gone, and soon they left it far behind.

A low rumble echoed through the forest. Elora froze, then gestured for Thea to get down.

Another athexe emerged from the shadows. Silently, it stalked past them, stopped, then returned the way it had come.

Elora shook her head. Once again, they had to change their course.

A little while later, Thea's spirit sight tingled into wakefulness. The shadows up ahead exuded a darkness that could be felt.

Hurrying forwards, she laid a hand on Elora's shoulder.

Elora startled, but didn't make a sound.

"Up ahead," Thea whispered in her ear.

Elora frowned and peered through the gloom. Slowly Thea's eyes took in the creature that her spirit sight had already seen. The athexe crouched in the shadows, motionless, looking intently in their direction.

Silently, Elora stepped further back into the undergrowth.

"How are there so many?" Elora muttered under her breath.

Thea peered through the undergrowth at the motionless figure. "At least they haven't attacked."

Elora frowned. "They always attack. I don't understand."

"Maybe they haven't seen us."

Elora gave her a dark glance and slunk back towards the others. After a quick consultation, she set off in a new direction.

Only a little while later, Elora froze again. Glancing back, she gestured to Thea that there were two athexes, one on each side of them.

Thea listened intently. She could hear the giant creatures moving. They were both getting closer.

"Quick!" Elora hissed, gesturing for the others to follow.

As quickly and quietly as they could, they hurried on. No one wanted to be caught between two athexes. One was dangerous enough.

As they passed through an area of even deeper shadow, Elora stopped.

"What—" she breathed.

Directly across their path, a large pile of uprooted trees had been formed into a crude barricade. It stretched around them on both sides, circling them in.

Thea stared.

"Get back! Get back!" Elora hissed, pushing everyone away, back the way they had come.

With a snarl, two athexes emerged from the shadows

behind them, blocking the way out of the cage-like barricade.

"That's impossible!" Elora gasped.

With a flurry of wings, Arl took to the sky.

"They don't know how to make traps!" Elora stammered. "They're not that smart!" She looked around desperately as the monsters stalked towards them. "And they don't work together!"

"I told you things had gotten worse!" Thea snapped. Drawing an arrow, she shot, striking the closest athexe with a blinding flash of light. She felt her shoulder twinge, but at least she could shoot.

Elora's arrow ricocheted off the athexe's leathery hide. It roared.

Sylica stared around the trap with wide eyes. "What do I do?"

"Here." Ulfgar grabbed out his frying pan and shoved it into Sylica's hand. "Hit them with a hard thing."

A rumbling crash echoed from behind them. Thea looked back to see another athexe, climbing over the barricade towards them. "We have to get out of here!"

"And how are we supposed to do that?" Elora demanded, firing arrow after arrow at the advancing athexes. Her arrows made no difference. The athexes stalked closer and closer.

"I could use some help here," Elora gasped.

Help. Remembrance shot through Thea like a flash and she threw her magic at Elora's bow. Elora's arrow ignited mid-flight and plunged into the monster's chest. It roared in pain.

"What?" Elora stared at her bow in shock.

"I blessed it, it's fine!" Thea yelled. Spinning, she shot at the monster that had reached the top of the barricade.

The barricade shuddered and started to tumble inwards.

Arl swooped overhead. "Get out of there!" they yelled, free-falling for a moment, then shifting back in time to plunge their talons into the monster's hide.

With a blood-curdling yell, Ulfgar charged.

"Ulfgar!" Thea yelled.

He plunged forward, ramming head first into an athexe's belly. With a splintering crash, his barrel broke in a deluge of wine. The monster staggered back.

"Charge!" Sylica yelled and ran after him, waving the frying pan.

Thea ran. With a tumbling crash, the barricade collapsed.

"Look out!" she yelled. Something hit her side, throwing her to the ground.

Rolling to her back, the dark form of an athexe filled the sky above her.

Someone yelled and the athexe staggered and fell. A bright light flashed in Thea's vision as a lithe figure stabbed a dagger into the monster's back, jumped, and landed beside her.

It was Roland.

Thea stared. "What—what are you—" she gasped as Roland pulled her to her feet.

The athexe staggered to its feet with a snarl. Thea grabbed Raybow, but before she could shoot, an axe flew through the air, striking the athexe in the face, and it sank to the ground again. Ulfgar appeared at a run. Grabbing the shaft of his axe, he tugged it with all his might.

Another athexe crashed through the trees towards

them. A sudden smell of wine flooded Thea's senses as the monster staggered and spat out a long splinter of wood.

"Hey! What's his name?" Roland gestured at Ulfgar who had just managed to free his axe.

"Ulfgar," Thea hissed, spinning to face the monster.

"Hey Ulf!" Roland yelled, running over to him. "Want a lift?" Without waiting for a reply, he grabbed the short man, and with a spin, flung him towards the athexe.

With a gasp, Thea threw the rest of her magic at Ulfgar. His axes blazed with light and he crashed into the athexe, knocking it flat onto its back. The athexe shuddered and lay still.

Ulfgar staggered to his feet and stared at the axes in his hands, a bewildered smile creeping over his face.

With a crash, another athexe staggered into view and fell to the ground, Arl's talons embedded in its face.

For a moment everything was silent, then Thea felt a shockwave of magic pass through her. Who did that? It seemed to have come from Roland.

Glancing around the small clearing, she hurried back to Roland's side. "What are you doing here?"

Roland grinned and sheathed his knives. "Looking for you. I heard you might need some help."

Thea gasped. "*You're* the help Allulien sent? But how? What—"

"Shh!" Elora hissed. "Come on!" Silently, she slunk into the shadows.

Thea gave Roland one more glance, then turned to follow. Roland's spirit was as bright as a beacon of light in the gloom of the shadows. She had to know more, but it had to wait.

Chapter Eighteen

Hardly daring to breathe, Thea hurried through the shadows. So far no other monsters had appeared, but she couldn't help glancing over her shoulder at every little sound.

Elora moved quickly, darting from cover to cover, and Thea did her best to keep up. She could feel Roland's presence close behind her.

Elora stooped and examined the ground closely, then gestured to the undergrowth. As Thea approached, she saw the small, burrow-like hole that was the entrance to the Littles' tunnels.

As Elora disappeared into it, Thea glanced over her shoulder to make sure the others were following. When they were all in sight, she crouched down and followed Elora into the darkness.

Thea crawled through the narrow tunnel until she collided with Elora.

"It's blocked," Elora whispered.

Thea reached past her and felt the wall of stone and dirt that filled the passageway. If she hadn't known better, she would have thought that was the end of the tunnel. It didn't seem like a barricade that could be moved.

"What's happening?" Sylica's whisper echoed from beyond Roland.

"The tunnel is blocked," Thea whispered back.

"Why is it blocked?" Sylica protested. "They knew we were coming back."

"Kais would have left something," Elora replied firmly, "some way of knowing we've come."

In the near-darkness, Elora's hands moved back and forth across the barricade.

"Kais!" she whispered, "Kais, we're back! Let us in!"

Thea touched the cold, hard dirt surrounding them. "Do you think they can—"

"Wait ..." Elora leaned forward. "A talking pipe!"

She bent down with her face almost to the ground. "Kais!" she called, and this time her voice had a strange, hollow sound to it. "It's Elora. We're home."

Thea held her breath as Elora waited in silence. She almost thought she heard a distant thumping sound, but she couldn't be certain.

Leaning down again, Elora called with words that Thea couldn't understand. In the silence that followed, Thea heard a voice, distant and muffled.

"There's another way through," Elora whispered, turning to Thea. "They will open it for us."

Thea heard—or felt—a distant rumbling.

Roland leaned closer and whispered in Thea's ear. "What's the Dryad's name?"

"Arl."

"Arl told me they're going to cover our tracks. They will be back soon."

"Okay."

"And the Elf is?"

"Sylica. But she thinks she's a Little. And this is Elora. She's actually a Little."

The sound was closer now: a scrabbling, scraping sort of sound, almost directly above their heads. Thea covered her face as bits of sand and gravel started to fall. A sudden emptiness loomed above her head.

"Elora?" a voice hissed from above.

Thea looked up, but couldn't see anything in the darkness.

"Yes, Aya, it's me," Elora replied.

Something dropped from the darkness above Thea's head. A rope ladder. Elora started to climb.

"Arl's back," Roland whispered.

Gingerly, Thea stood up. Feeling around, she found that some kind of trap door had been opened above their heads. Whispering for the others to follow, she began to climb the ladder. It led to another tunnel, even narrower than the first. Pushing herself on her stomach, Thea eased her way through. Gradually it sloped down and grew larger until she emerged into the small space that had been the antechamber that guarded the original tunnel.

The light from a small lantern showed Elora having a hushed conversation with two Littles. She turned to Thea as she approached. "We will carry on. The guards will stay here to secure the entrance."

With a nod to the Littles, Elora continued down the passageway. Thea squeezed past the Littles and followed. Glancing back, she saw that Roland was following, hunched over to avoid the low ceiling.

A short time later, the sound of footsteps approached, and Kais appeared around a corner in a pool of green light. Setting his lantern on the ground, he embraced Elora.

Elora spoke to him in a hushed voice, glancing back at Thea and the others.

Lifting the lantern, Kais looked beyond Elora to

those who followed. "We will bring you in. We can talk once we're there."

Elora nodded silently and they followed Kais down the shadowy corridor. The lights on the walls were gone. When they reached the large wooden door, Kais knocked and spoke a few words.

Slowly, the door opened and the face of a Little peered through. After another hushed conversation, the door was opened the rest of the way, and one by one they filed into the room.

It was the same room they had left, but now much of the furniture had been piled by the door. Some of it had been disassembled and was burning in the fireplace. Two Littles were hunched over one of the few remaining tables, busily fletching arrows. A Little sat by the fire cradling a bloody arm. Another Little was lying down on a bench. Elora's grandmother was there, wrapping a long, well-used bandage around his head.

As the door was shut and barred behind them, Kais turned to Thea. "I am afraid we cannot give you the same hospitality as before, but you are still very welcome." His glance strayed to the injured Littles. Worry lingered in his eyes.

"We will do all we can to help," Thea assured him.

"I am sure you are tired," Kais replied. "The rooms you used before are available for you again." He said a few words to Elora, then went to join the injured ones by the fire. Elora dropped her pack by the wall and followed him.

Thea glanced at Roland. "That is Kais," she said in a low voice. "He and Elora are engaged."

Roland nodded.

Sylica scurried over to join Sami. Thea followed.

"Sylica, I don't know if they want help right now."

Sami glanced up and waved a dismissive hand that clearly said "leave her be, she's fine".

Thea turned to Roland. "This is Sami, Elora's grandmother."

Hearing her name, Sami looked up again. Glancing from Thea to Roland, she gave a big grin.

Suddenly self-conscious, Thea turned to Elora. "If you don't need us, I will take a few moments to speak with Roland."

Elora gave her a brief nod and continued speaking with Kais.

Without a word, Thea led Roland out of the great room and through the corridors to the room that she and Arl had stayed in before.

Shutting the door, she turned to face Roland. "Okay, what is going on? How are you here?"

Lantern light twinkled in Roland's eyes. "Short answer or long answer?"

"Roland," Thea protested, unable to tear her gaze away. There was something different in the way he talked and held himself. Maybe it was the light within, but there seemed to be a steadiness and a confidence that she didn't remember seeing before. She had never been so glad to see anyone.

"Why shouldn't I be here?" Roland grinned.

"I thought you needed to stay with the Eagle."

Roland glanced around the small room. "I lost my place on the Eagle."

Thea gasped. "Oh Roland, I'm so sorry. What happened?"

Roland shrugged. "I helped you get away."

Thea felt sick. "Roland, I—I don't—"

"It's alright," Roland smiled reassuringly. "I knew that might happen and I decided it was worth it. Anyways, I've been sailing with the Raven since then, and I like that a lot better."

"The Raven?" Thea stared. "But ... you're First House."

Roland shrugged. "The Raven lost her place in the league too, so it doesn't matter. We've been too busy for racing anyways."

"But—but that was your life."

"I'm working for the Chancellor now."

Thea stared. "You're working for my *uncle*? Does ... does he know that you're here?"

Roland nodded. "He's the one who sent me. Khariton used his magic to send me as far as his old place in Enzhelika, so I didn't have to walk as far as you did."

Thea's mind was spinning. "Khariton's what? And my uncle ... how did he ... what ..."

"He sent a letter for you." Roland pulled a folded envelope out of his belt pouch and handed it to Thea.

With shaking hands, Thea opened it. In her uncle's precise, even handwriting four words were written: You need Roland's help.

Thea stared at it. "I don't understand. He wanted you to come help me? How did he know I needed help? How did he know where to find me?"

"He didn't. It was Micai who told me where to find you."

Thea gasped. "Micai told you?"

"Sure did," Micai grinned, appearing beside her.

"Micai!" Thea gasped.

In an instant, Roland straightened and stood at attention. Micai gave him a nod of acknowledgement, then waved a greeting to Thea.

Thea looked from Roland to Micai, slow understanding growing in her mind. "Roland ... is Micai your General?"

"Yes." Roland said, still standing at attention. "Ready for orders."

"*What*?" Thea stared, mouth agape. Of course, she had asked Roland to learn from Khariton and start serving the Deity for himself, and if he did he'd have to have a General, but ... but ...

"You!" She turned on Micai. "You *knew* and you never told me?"

Micai grinned. "Never told you what?"

"Oh, maybe that Roland was checking in with you *every single day* and taking orders from you? Don't you think I might have liked to know that?"

Someone knocked on the door. It cracked open and Sami's wrinkled face appeared. "I brought you some cookies, dear, for you and your friend."

If Sami saw Micai standing there, she didn't seem surprised. With a friendly smile, she handed the plate to Thea and closed the door.

Micai's eyes lit up. "Cookies?"

Thea shoved the tray into Roland's hands and stood in front of Micai with eyes blazing. "You could have at least told me!"

"You didn't need to know yet." Micai reached past Thea to take one of the cookies.

"I *specifically* asked you how he was doing, and you *still* didn't tell me?"

"I recommend the cookies," Micai mumbled with their mouth full. They washed it down with a drink from their mug.

Thea glared. "Give me that." Grabbing the mug out of Micai's hand, Thea took a long drink.

Roland stared from Thea to Micai. "So ... you know each other?"

"My turn." Micai took the mug back from Thea.

Thea glared at Micai. "Yes, Micai travelled with me almost *every day* for the first part of my journey."

"Wait ..." Roland looked at Micai. "Is that the important job you kept leaving to do?"

Micai grinned. "Someone needed to keep her company."

"But—"

"You were busy," Micai shrugged.

"*My* turn." Thea grabbed the tankard back.

Bright light flooded the room as Allulien appeared by the door.

"Allulien!" Thea gasped, dropping the tankard, which somehow appeared back in Micai's hand.

Roland attempted to stand at attention, still holding the cookies.

Micai grinned and waved his tankard at Allulien. "Everything ready?"

Allulien's keen glance took in the entire room. "Almost."

"I am here." Raphea appeared, standing by the table. "Enkeli will not be coming."

"Seriously?" Micai protested. "Is Enkeli *ever* at a council of war?"

A what? Thea stared. Both Allulien and Raphea glimmered with ethereal light. Micai still had the common appearance that Thea was accustomed to seeing, but in the presence of the other Generals she again caught a glimpse of the majesty she had seen in the throne room. The tankard had disappeared. Silently, she stepped back towards the wall. The small room had become very crowded.

Allulien looked at her. "Welcome, Thea and Roland, to the council of war. It has been a long time since we've had others join us." They smiled. "I am glad that you are here."

There was something about Allulien's expression, the depth of joy and confidence, that was absolutely terrifying. Thea opened her mouth, then hoped that she didn't have to say anything.

Allulien's gaze left Thea's face. "Raphea, you may begin."

Thea glanced at Roland. He held the plate of cookies as if his life depended on it.

"It is time." Raphea spoke slowly. "The Littles have done well, holding back the advance of the darkness for longer than many thought possible. Now the risk has become too great and for their safety they must be evacuated. Has all been prepared?"

Micai nodded. "My pieces are in place." He gave Thea and Roland a wink.

"Good." Allulien turned to Thea. "Tomorrow you will lead the Littles out of their home and take them south to the river. Depart before first light. You will not check in tomorrow. You are receiving your orders now, and you will need to leave early if you are to make it to the river before dark. Once you cross the river the worst of the danger will be behind you and you will be safe to rest for the night."

Thea swallowed. "How far is it to the river?"

"It is possible to travel the distance in a workday's travel, but you will have young, old, and injured people in your care, so it will take much longer than that. You must do everything in your power to cross the river by the end of the day. Do you understand?"

Thea nodded.

"Roland." Micai spoke in a clipped, firm tone that Thea had not heard from them before.

Roland snapped to attention immediately.

"Your orders for tomorrow are to accompany Thea and protect her and those she is escorting. You are also absolved of your duty to check in tomorrow. Get out there and do the Ravens proud. Understood?"

Roland gave a firm nod. "Understood."

Raphea stepped forward and gave Thea a long, steady look. "Always remember, the safest place is the path of duty. There are many here who are afraid, and understandably so. They have suffered much, at the hands of evil as well as those who claim to be good. Without new hope they may not dare to undertake the journey, but if they remain here they will die. Their lives are entrusted to your care. You must and you will lead them out."

Thea felt responsibility sink like a weight in her stomach. How was she going to bring so many people through the Deorcian?

Micai gave her an encouraging smile. "There will be help, you just won't be able to see it. We can't risk drawing out the full forces of the Fallen One. That is something the resistance is not prepared to face."

Thea looked at Roland and saw firm resolution gleaming in his eyes. She took a long, unsteady breath. She had made a promise, a promise that would hold for as long as she lived. From the light in his spirit, she knew that it was a promise that Roland had also made.

At least two Elves would be faithful. She looked up at Allulien. "We will obey."

Allulien smiled and laid a hand on Thea's head. "The blessing of the Deity be upon you as you undertake this task."

Thea felt the warm glow rush through her. When she looked up, Allulien and Raphea were gone.

Micai grinned and took the plate from Roland's hands. "Thanks for the cookies!" Micai disappeared, and so did the cookies. Micai's voice drifted through the air. "I'll return the plate later!"

Thea and Roland stared at each other. There was something in his gaze that steadied her. Allulien's confidence in her was overwhelming. Roland's confidence gave her hope. The passion and excitement in his spirit almost took her breath away.

"Well?" A smile crept over Roland's face.

Thea shook her head, trying to wrap her mind around what had just happened. The imprint of the Generals' presence still overwhelmed her spirit sight. Slowly she let out the breath she had been holding. "I guess we have a job to do."

Roland nodded. "Let's go do it."

Thea smiled. Getting to serve the Deity alongside Roland was more than she had ever dreamed. Her own confidence rising, she stepped towards the door.

"Thea?"

Thea looked back. Something in Roland's expression made her pause. "Yes?"

Roland seemed to struggle with what he wanted to say. His eyes rested on the silver flower pinned to Thea's cloak. "You still have the brooch."

Thea smiled. "Of course I do."

That seemed to satisfy Roland. He smiled. "Let's go."

When they returned to the great room, they found the entire community of Littles gathered around Elora, talking in hushed, anxious voices. Ulfgar sat alone on a bench, staring forlornly at the splintered pieces of his broken keg. Arl paced silently along the far side of the room, frowning darkly. Sylica sat in the midst of the Littles, happily braiding a small child's hair.

As Thea approached, the Littles fell silent.

Elora looked at her with tired eyes. "My people are worried," she explained. "Every foraging party that goes out is ambushed and injured. Some do not return." Pain was etched in her eyes. "We can't stay here, Thea. We've lost too many people already."

"I know." Gently, Thea stretched her magic to cover the room. "I have come to tell you that it is time to leave." She watched the eyes of the Littles grow wide as they heard her speaking in their own language. "We will lead you out of here and bring you to a new home. A home that is safe, where there are no monsters and where no one wants to kill you."

Elora gave Thea a sharp glance, but didn't say anything.

An elderly Little scrunched up their wrinkled face. "Where is this place?"

"You will see," Thea assured them. "First you must get ready to leave."

"Go out in the Trees?" one of the Littles protested. "Everyone who goes out there gets hurt!"

"Or doesn't come back," another added.

"It isn't safe!"

"We don't know where we're going, how are we going to get there?"

"I will lead you there." Thea spoke above the hubbub. "You have people to protect you. We *will* make it through."

"But what if the dark things find us?"

"Will we have to fight?"

"What about the little Littles? And the hurt ones? They can't fight!"

"Listen!" Thea yelled, and slowly the noise subsided. "If you stay here you will not be able to hide forever. We need to leave. Soon. While we still have the chance."

Silence filled the room.

One of the Littles ventured, "How soon is soon?"

Thea glanced at Roland. "We must leave tomorrow, before first light. Any later, and it will be too late."

Elora's eyes grew wide and another clamour rose from the Littles.

"What?"

"That's so soon!"

"But it's already night!"

"We can't get ready that fast!"

Kais waved his hand for attention. "I know! I know that it's soon. I know you're scared, but Thea is right. The longer we wait, the more dangerous it will be. We will only take what we cannot live without. Everything else can be made again."

A timid-looking Little raised his hand. "How will the hurt people be able to come? Dana can't even walk."

Kais smiled at Elora. "We will make carriers and walking sticks. The little Littles can ride on our shoulders and we can hold the hands of our grandparents. We will all walk together towards our new life, and no one will be left behind."

Thea looked at all the Littles with their big,

frightened eyes. "The Deity—the Great Big Big—cares about you. You must believe that. We know how much you have suffered, and we are here to help you. We will do everything in our power to bring you through safely."

"Why should we trust you?" Zaki stood and faced Thea with blazing eyes. "You're a Big. Bigs don't care about us. You and you and you," he pointed from Thea to Roland to Ulfgar across the room, "I don't even know why you are here. But that one—" his eyes bored holes in Arl, "—that one will follow us. It will follow us and kill us, one by one. It is a goblin killer. I know."

A fearful hush fell across the room.

Slowly, Arl walked towards them. A strange look was in their eyes. "You're right. I am a goblin killer. I kill because I am a protector. But Thea and Elora have shown me that the Littles are not a threat, but are people who also need to be protected." Arl stared around the silent crowd. "If a single Little dies during our escape it will be my life for theirs." They looked at Zaki with gleaming eyes. "And your hand can hold the knife."

Zaki stared at Arl.

Slowly, Thea started to breathe again. She watched in amazement as Arl's spirit shone with a new kind of light. A small glimmer of it reflected in Zaki's.

"I accept your offer." Zaki's voice wavered and he looked at Elora.

She placed a hand on his shoulder. "And maybe you will choose not to strike."

Zaki frowned, but Elora turned to the rest of the Littles. "Kais and I are going with Thea. I cannot make you come, but I urge every one of you to join us. Going is our hope for survival."

"My people and I will come," Faris replied. His hardened face seemed softer than it had before. "We already lost our home, and we trust Thea to find us a new one."

Sami's face cracked in a toothless grin. "And the Great Big Big cares for us, as I've always said. Sing a song of praise and go pack your undies."

Smiles and chuckles spread throughout the crowd of Littles.

Elora put her arms around the old Little's shoulders. "I love you, Grandma."

"I love you too, dear," Sami crooned. "Your mother would be so proud."

Roland glanced around the dispersing Littles. "Those who consider themselves to be fighters, stay here. Everyone else pack and get what sleep you can." He gestured Thea, Elora, and Arl together to confer. "Hey Ulf!" he called across the room. "Get yourself over here! We need you!"

Kais stood beside Elora with his arm around her shoulders. Faris and a few other Littles also stayed behind.

"Right," Roland said as they gathered around, "who are our long-range fighters? Thea has Raybow. Elora, I saw you have a bow too."

"Most of our best fighters have been injured trying to get food," Faris said, "but there are still a few of us who are good with a sling."

"That's good," Roland nodded. "All the ranged fighters will be positioned around the main company. Any monster that tries to get in close will have a barrage to deal with. Ulfgar, you've got a good head on your shoulders. You take point and I'll back you up. We can switch if you ever need a break. Arl, you've got versatility. You can scout, but if the ranged fighters are pushed too hard you can pull back and lend them a hand." He glanced around the group. "Sylica, what's your fighting style?"

Elora gave a wry smile. "She swings a mean frying pan."

Roland thought about this for a moment. "Maybe you could provide some defence for the ranged fighters?"

"Frying pan's no good," Ulfgar grumbled. "Handle's too short and the balance is all wrong. You need something with a big long stick ..." Muttering to himself, he wandered away from the group.

"Maybe we can find you a better weapon," Roland smiled at Sylica and turned to Elora. "Do you have any sort of armoury here?"

"There's hunting knives." Elora glanced at Kais. "But they're too small to be much use to a Big."

"Those knives will be useful, though," Roland smiled. "Make sure every ranged fighter has a knife. Or two or three if there's enough for that. Kais, what about you?"

Kais shook his head. "I'm not a fighter."

"You'll be responsible for the injured and any others who have difficulty walking. We'll try to move as fast as we can, but without leaving anyone behind. If you're ever stuck, make sure you get help." He glanced around the group. "Is that everyone? Good. Get your weapons ready, then go pack and get some sleep. We'll send the word around when it's time to gather again."

As everyone dispersed, Elora stepped close beside Zaki.

"You will help Kais," she said in a low voice. As Zaki

opened his mouth to argue, Elora gave him a firm glare. "The last line of defence is no less important than the first. Kais will need all the help he can get."

Grumbling, Zaki turned away.

"Where's Ulf?" Roland asked Thea. "We have more prep to do."

A wooden crack echoed from across the room and Ulfgar returned with the leg from a table. "That's more like it," he muttered. "Now something for the end ..."

"Does anyone else here use magic?" Roland asked Thea.

"Not that I know of," Thea replied, but she glanced at Sylica. Sometimes she wasn't sure.

Sylica lay on the rug in front of the fire, happily humming a little song to herself. She seemed unfazed by all the excitement going on around her.

"It's too bad we don't have any of Enkeli's people with us," Roland mused. "That would really be helpful."

Ulfgar collected the metal band that had once held the wine barrel together and started hammering it with the blunt end of an axe head.

"We'll let everyone get about four measures of sleep." Roland paced with his hands behind his back. "We don't want anyone collapsing from exhaustion before we make it to the river. If we each take a turn sitting up while the others sleep we can make sure we don't miss our start time, and there will be someone up to answer any questions. Will we leave by the same tunnel we came in?" He glanced at Elora.

"That depends on which way we are going."

"South," Thea replied.

"South?" Elora frowned. "I don't know the land to the south. Why go that way?"

"That is the way the Deity has told us to go. If we make it beyond the river we will be safe, at least for now."

Elora gave Thea a long glance, then nodded. "Then we will go south. Our southmost tunnel is the one we came through. I will see if the barrier can be removed before we leave."

Roland nodded. "That would be good. We'll try to leave one measure before daylight, if we can."

"We will do our best," Elora replied. "If you will excuse me, I must help Kais make carriers for our wounded."

"Let us know if we can help," Thea called after her.

As Elora left, Sami came bustling into the room carrying an armload of bundles. The effects of Thea's magic had worn off and she could no longer understand the elderly Little's words, but Sylica hopped up immediately and went to help. Sami's burden turned out to be bundles of bandages, herbs, and bottled salves. Soon she was instructing Sylica in how to mix poultices and prepare them in advance for travel.

Wrapping some cloth around his hands, Ulfgar reached into the fireplace and pulled out the metal lining. "Won't be needing that anyways," he muttered.

"We'll need signals," Roland said, "so we can let each other know about new threats or whether we need help. On the Raven we use bird calls and such. Arl, do you have any ideas?"

Arl gave Roland a sidelong glance and gave an eagle's cry, so loud and real that everyone in the room stopped and stared.

Roland laughed. "I don't know if I can do it that well!"

Leaving Roland to decide on the signals, Thea joined Sami and Sylica at the low table where they worked. As Sylica mixed, Sami spread the poultices on bandages and wrapped them tight, stacking them in baskets. She gestured to Thea that there were dried leaves that needed to be crushed to a powder. With a nod, Thea set to work.

"Thank you," Sami said, then looked very pleased with herself.

"Sami!" Thea smiled, "I didn't know you could speak Common."

"I am learning," Sami beamed. "Kais is ..." her face squinted in concentration, "... good teacher."

They were packing the last of the herbs and bandages in a basket, when Ulfgar dropped the table leg and what looked like a big metal plate onto the table with a clatter.

"Here," he said, handing the table leg to Sylica. It had been smoothed and rounded, and the end was wrapped in the metal band that had been pounded out into sharp spikes. "It's a mace. You hold here and hit things with that end. And this is a shield." He lifted it up, showing Sylica where the handle was and how to hold it. It was large, taller than Ulfgar, and curved gently at the sides to give additional protection. "See those spikes on the bottom?" Ulfgar continued, pointing them out. "You stick it into the ground if you need to hold your spot or shield someone who's been hurt. It's a half-assed job, but when we're through with this I'll make you a better one." His face fell and a look of pain crossed his eyes. "I mean, someone can make you a better one."

Sylica didn't seem to notice. She received Ulfgar's gifts with enthusiasm and immediately began dancing around the room, swinging the mace up and down.

Ulfgar trudged back to his bench and sat with his head in his hands.

"Thea," Roland rested a hand on her shoulder, "you should go and get some sleep."

Thea glanced at Ulfgar, then conceded. She was very tired. Slowly she walked back to her room and lay down on the small bed. The last traces of the Generals' presence filled the room with a warm, comforting glow. As soon as she closed her eyes, she was asleep.

Chapter Nineteen

A hand touched Thea's shoulder.

"Thea," Roland whispered. "It's time to wake up."

Slowly, Thea opened her eyes. Soft green lantern light filled the room.

Roland smiled. "We're gathering the Littles together now. Are you ready?"

Getting to her feet, Thea slung her bag across her shoulder and grabbed Raybow. "I'm ready."

In the great room, Littles hurried back and forth, piling baskets and bags against the walls. Small children blinked in the lantern light and clung to their blankets. Kais directed people this way and that, trying to keep some semblance of order. Sylica trotted around the room, handing out lanterns. Ulfgar lay on a bench in the corner, snoring.

"The barricade is being cleared as we speak," Roland explained, waving a greeting to Faris who was trying to help a Little with a bandaged leg up into a small wooden handcart. "Arl is out scouting."

"What's the plan?" Thea asked, sidling out of the way as another Little hurried through the door behind her.

"Ulf and I will head out first. If you come with us, you can guard the tunnel entrance while the rest of the Littles pass through. Elora is going to do a final check through the tunnels and leave last. Once she's out, the two of you can organize the ranged fighters into formation. A circle around the more vulnerable ones is probably the best you can do. Ulfgar, Arl and I will be clearing a way."

A group of Littles emerged from the entrance tunnel. They carried shovels and were caked with dirt. Waving to Elora, they signalled that the way was clear.

Elora shouted for attention and silence fell across the room. Littles set down their bundles and turned to look.

In a quiet voice, Elora spoke to the Littles in their own language. Some of them bowed their heads. Some looked solemnly around the room, tears gleaming in their eyes.

Thea didn't need to use her magic. She knew that they were saying goodbye to their home.

Kais spoke, and then Faris. Finally Elora turned to Thea. "We are ready to go now. Will you lead us?"

Thea nodded solemnly and looked across the crowd of Littles. They stared up at her with large, trusting eyes.

Oh Deity, she whispered in the privacy of her heart, *don't let me fail their trust!*

With a nod to Roland, she walked towards the door.

"On your feet, Ulf!" Roland called. "Time to go!"

With a grunt, Ulfgar pushed his helmet back off his eyes and struggled to his feet.

Taking the lantern that Elora offered her, Thea stepped through the door. Glancing over her shoulder, she saw Roland following close behind. Behind him she could hear Ulfgar's heavy steps as he hurried to keep up.

Finally they reached the place where the barricade had been. Piles of dirt lined the sides of the tunnel and completely filled the anteroom. Silently, Thea slipped by and continued down the tunnel. As it narrowed even more, she set down the lantern and crawled on her hands and knees.

She emerged from the tunnel into the darkness of night in the Deorcian. The smallest glimmer of blue-green light filtered down through the trees.

From the shadowy branches above her head, an owl watched her with blood-red eyes. Nodding to Arl, Thea took Raybow off her back and drew an arrow from her quiver.

Roland and Ulfgar emerged from the tunnel behind her. They conferred briefly in hushed voices, then Ulfgar turned and stumped away.

Thea's eyes met Roland's for a moment, then he was gone, disappearing into the shadows.

Positioning herself above the tunnel entrance, Thea watched as the Littles emerged, one by one. First came the sling fighters. Then Kais and the injured Littles, with bandaged heads and arms in slings. Faris pulled a small cart that Dana and the Little with the bandaged leg were sitting on. Sami followed with a large basket on her back, and then the rest of the Littles came. They carried bags and baskets. One pulled a rough, flat-bottomed sled. Children held their parents' hands, staring up at the large, dark trees with frightened eyes. Elderly Littles walked with the help of canes or walking sticks. Sylica walked with them, carrying her own large pack. A child hung off each of her arms.

Last of all, Elora appeared. Thea stepped down and met her by the tunnel entrance.

"Forty-eight Littles," Elora said in a low voice. "May the Great Big Big let us have just as many when we reach the river."

A shadow passed over Thea's head and Arl disappeared into the trees.

Gently, Thea touched Elora's bow, passing some of her magic into it. She nodded. "I believe that we will."

Elora gave her a half-smile, then glanced around the silent company of Littles.

"I'll lead," Thea whispered. "Keep Sylica and two of the slingers with you at the rear. We'll get the rest of the fighters to protect the sides."

"What about you?"

"I'll be following Roland and Ulfgar. I'll have help if I need it."

Thea slipped through the crowd of Littles, nodding to Kais and Faris as she passed. Elora's whispered instructions and the shuffle of footsteps echoed through the shadows as the Littles rearranged themselves.

Thea waited until Elora gestured that everyone was ready. Whispering a prayer, she turned and stepped through the trees. The Littles followed.

The eerie silence of the forest stretched around them, broken now by the muffled trudge of many small feet. Thea glanced back over her shoulder. The Littles huddled together as they walked. Along the flanks, the slingers eyed the forest with suspicious glares. Just visible through the trees, Thea could see Sylica, standing tall beyond the farthest Littles, her mace resting on her shoulder.

They seemed to be keeping up. Thea led them on.

Slowly, the blue-green glimmer of light turned to gold. Day had come.

Thea caught a glimpse of Roland through the trees. He crouched and slipped from shadow to shadow, glancing back at Thea and matching his pace to hers.

She could hear the soft tramp of the Littles' footsteps, the creak of the cart wheels, the hushed murmur of voices.

The forest was silent.

Every way that Thea looked, dark trees stretched as far as she could see through the gloom, now thin and tangled with brambles and underbrush, now thick as pillars, stretching tall overhead.

A small sound caught her ear, somehow different than the subdued clamour of the Littles behind her. She glanced around. The forest seemed unchanged.

There it was again! A rustling sound, unmistakable this time. As soon as it started, it stopped again. There was nothing to be seen.

Should she say something to Roland? She could just see him through the gloom ahead.

Something dark flicked by, just beyond her sight.

Roland glanced over his shoulder, his eyes darting around the forest. Had he seen it too?

Cautiously, Thea glanced back at the Littles. Through their milling throng she caught a glimpse of Elora, standing with every nerve as tight as her bowstring.

Quietly, Thea pulled an arrow from her quiver and nocked it.

Roland caught her gaze, glanced around the surrounding forest, and slipped into a deeper shadow.

Glancing from one side to the other, Thea pressed on, step after step.

Behind her, the Littles gave a gasp of alarm.

Thea turned and saw, beyond the Littles, the head of an enormous snake rising into the air. It towered above them, its tongue flickering like a flame of fire. From either side of its head a dark mist poured, stretching out like a hood. It bared its fangs and hissed.

Elora's bow sang. The arrow flashed with white light as it struck between the snake's eyes. With a gurgling hiss, the snake sank to the ground beyond Thea's sight.

With a snarl, wolves jumped out of the shadows on either side of the Littles. Screams and cries of fear tore through the silence. Slingstones whizzed through the air.

A wolf pounced and Thea shot, striking the wolf in the chest with a blaze of light. She caught glimpses of more wolves lurking in the shadows. Darkness seemed to flow from them, making the murky shadows even harder to see through.

With an eagle's cry, Arl swooped overhead, dove, and struck a wolf mid-pounce, sending it crashing to the forest floor.

A strange, smoky smell filled Thea's senses.

"Fire!" A cry rose up from the Littles. "Fire!"

Fire? Thea stared. A murky haze drifted up between the trees, coming from just beyond the Littles.

With a snarl, a wolf leapt at Thea. Stumbling back, she reached for an arrow.

Roland appeared from behind her. His knives gleamed as they cut through the air, plunging into the wolf with a flash of light. The wolf sank to the ground.

With a jerk, Roland pulled his knives out of the wolf's side and turned to face another wolf's charge.

The cries of the Littles grew louder.

Leaving the wolves to Roland, Thea pushed her way through the panicking Littles. As they parted before her, she saw Sylica beating down the smouldering moss with her shield. A haze of smoke filled the air.

"I think we're good," Sylica called as Thea hurried

towards her. She brought the flat of her shield down with a crash. It seemed that the worst of the blaze was already out.

"How did it start?" Thea asked.

Sylica pointed at a dark, unpleasant mass of blood and entrails that lay on the ground nearby. "That strange snakey thing." She pounded the ground again.

"How did that start a fire?"

"I don't know." Sylica swung her shield over her head. "Elora shot it, then fire started coming up all over the place!"

Thea hurried over to Elora. "What happened?"

"What, that?" Elora glanced at the remains of the giant snake. "When it died, its skin broke open. Everything the blood touched caught fire."

Thea ducked as a slingstone whizzed overhead. "What was it?"

"How am I supposed to know?" Elora demanded, shooting an arrow as a wolf leapt out from behind a tree.

"I don't know, you live here!"

"I've never seen one of those before!"

Thea stared at the snake's remains. A monster Elora had never seen before.

"You know what?" Elora shot another arrow, and another. "Call it a fire snake. That's what us Littles would call it, anyways."

Thea nodded. "Fire snake it is." She glanced across the seething mass of Littles. The wolves had drawn back. Thea could see them circling in the shadows, waiting to strike again.

They had to keep moving.

Pushing her way through the Littles, Thea returned

to the front of the group.

"Keep walking!" she called, gesturing the Littles forward. "Don't let the wolves stop you!"

Roland appeared beside her. "The fire's under control?"

"Sylica got it."

"Good. Let's go!"

Side by side, they pushed forward through the trees. Glancing over her shoulder, Thea saw that the Littles were following. Whenever a wolf approached, a barrage of slingstones drove it away again. Arl wheeled overhead.

Thea glanced at Roland and smiled. Through the trees, she caught a glimpse of Ulfgar, in hot pursuit of a retreating wolf. A flash of light lit up the trees whenever Elora let an arrow fly.

The further they went, the more cautious the wolves became. Thea could see them slinking in the shadows, but for the moment they seemed content to watch and bide their time.

Thea fell back to walk among the Littles. Kais greeted her with a smile.

"How is everyone doing?" Thea asked.

"They're doing alright," Kais replied. "The worst of the scare is over."

Thea watched as a wolf tried to approach the Littles and was met with a barrage of slingstones. "They're doing very well. Has anyone been hurt?"

"Not seriously. A few banged knuckles and scraped knees. Thankfully nothing's gotten close enough to hurt anyone yet."

Zaki was among the slingers, gripping a rock in each hand.

Kais gestured to the sled. "Get something to drink."

Pulled over the mossy ground by three Littles, the sled held an assortment of baskets and bundles, along with a crate full of waterskins.

Sylica was pulling the small cart, which now held three injured Littles and five children, all piled on top of each other and clinging to the sides as well as they could. One slender, curly-haired child was in possession of the much-coveted candy bag and was handing out candies to anyone who would take them. Thea accepted one gratefully.

Satisfied that the Littles were in good spirits, Thea returned to Roland and encouraged him to take a turn getting a drink.

A while later they passed a river, where they stopped to refill the waterskins and splash the cool water on their faces. It was becoming oppressively hot beneath the trees.

The wolves were still trailing them, but at a distance now. Thea didn't let the Littles stop for long; soon they pressed on again.

At Kais' instruction, the Littles passed food back and forth through their ranks, eating as they walked. Thea accepted the food that was handed to her with a grateful smile. The Littles looked tired, but they trudged resolutely on.

A little while later, light glimmered through the trees ahead. Was that the river? Quickening her step, Thea joined Roland and Ulfgar where they stood at the edge of the trees.

It wasn't the river. A large clearing stretched before them, beyond which the forest continued, as dark and dense as before.

The clearing was filled with athexes.

Thea stared. There were so many. She counted at least twenty, but there may have been more. They were crouched low to the ground, watching the surrounding forest as if waiting for something. The darkness seeping out of them gave the air a murky, shadowy haze, even in the brightness of the clearing.

Just then, the wolves that had been tailing the Littles began to bay and howl. The athexes straightened and looked directly towards them.

Ulfgar swore under his breath.

The athexes spread across the clearing, shoulder to shoulder. Fanged jaws snapping, they advanced towards their unseen victims, a seething wall of leathery skin, claws, and fangs.

In the distance, Thea could hear the snarling of wolves.

Arl landed beside Thea, shifting into human form as their feet touched the ground. "Which way—east or west?"

"No." Thea flinched beneath Arl's disapproving glare. "We're going straight to the river. No detours. Anyways, they know we're here. They'll just follow if we run."

"We cannot fight that many."

Thea glanced at Roland. "I think we have to try."

"Right then." Ulfgar shoved his helmet down firmly over his head. "Charge!"

Breaking out of the cover of the trees, Ulfgar ran straight towards the middle of the athexes.

"Ulfgar!" Thea yelled, but he just ran faster. Lowering his head, he ran straight into the largest athexe with a resounding *crash*. The athexe staggered and fell on its back.

Ulfgar stumbled, shook his head, then righted himself. With a roar, he charged another athexe, crashed into it head first, and sent it sprawling.

Thea and her companions watched Ulfgar, slack-jawed.

"We—we should help him!" Thea gasped.

Ulfgar staggered to his feet and charged another athexe. It scrambled to get out of his way.

With a yell of triumph, Ulfgar chased it down. The athexe swung a long, clawed arm and sent him sprawling.

Pushing past Thea, Roland ran. "Ulf! Get out of there!"

The athexe leapt on top of Ulfgar, pinning him to the ground. Another athexe leapt on top, and another.

Arl shot into the sky like a rocket. Passing Roland, Arl dove towards the writhing mass of athexes and disappeared.

Moments later, the athexes exploded outwards as a giant bear erupted in their midst, Ulfgar carried firmly in its mouth by the back of his chain mail shirt.

Ulfgar waved his axes, swearing profusely. "Let me down! I can take them! I can take them!"

Arl dropped him at Thea's feet in an undignified heap.

"To the air, Arl!" Roland yelled, approaching at a run. "Remember—we're working together!"

Grabbing Ulfgar by the shoulders, he heaved him to his feet. "Now, Ulf! Charge!"

Ulfgar didn't need any encouragement.

"We keep moving forward!" Roland yelled for everyone to hear. "We will make it to the river and nothing can stop us!"

Thea sent out her magic, touching every one of the weapons.

Ulfgar's axes shone with light as he closed in on the nearest monster.

"Now, Arl!" Roland yelled.

Just as Ulfgar was about to reach his target, Arl dropped with a scream. Startled, the athexe looked up and shielded its head, as Ulfgar's axes embedded in its abdomen. It crumpled to the ground.

Ulfgar roared in triumph and Arl's eagle cry rang through the sky.

"Arl!" Ulfgar yelled, pointing. "That one next!"

"Ready?" Roland called to the Littles. "Forward, march!"

With Thea and Roland at their head, the Littles advanced beyond the cover of the trees.

With a snarl, an athexe charged towards them.

Roland waved his arm. "Volley!"

Stones flew through the air, gleaming like bolts of light. The athexe staggered back.

Another athexe charged and was driven back. Slowly, the company of Littles advanced.

Athexes came from every direction now, advancing toward the Littles, driven back by a barrage of stones, only to advance again. Thea shot arrow after arrow, but the more athexes she killed, the more there seemed to be.

Still, the Littles held their own, moving slowly further and further into the field of battle.

Glancing at the trees, Thea could still see wolves pacing back and forth in the shadows, but they hadn't followed the Littles' advance. Good. The athexes were enough, charging the Littles again and again, only to be driven back at the last possible moment.

Through the chaos, Thea caught a glimpse of Roland, his knives flashing with light.

Elora's bow sang, and another athexe dropped to the ground.

Arl wheeled overhead and dove.

Wherever Ulfgar ran, athexes scrambled to get out of his way.

Thea bent over and rested her hands on her knees for a moment, trying to catch her breath. They were halfway across the clearing now. Her shoulder ached and her head was pounding.

"Candy break!" Sylica's cheerful voice broke through the chaos of noise.

Another athexe charged.

"I'm a little busy," Thea gasped, firing an arrow, and then another.

"That's okay," Sylica grinned. "Open up!"

"What—"

Thea felt a candy pressed into her mouth.

The athexe staggered and fell only steps away from her, the arrows embedded deep in its chest.

She glanced over her shoulder, but Sylica had already skipped off through the milling crowd of Littles.

Something was different. There were no slingstones in the air. The athexes had drawn back—

A shadow fell over Thea.

With a screech, a musharoc dove through the sky and crashed directly into Arl. Together they tumbled to the ground, a writhing mass of feathers and talons.

Musharocs filled the sky. Wheeling, they plunged towards the Littles, their stench filling the air.

Roland appeared beside Thea, staring at the giant, rotting birds as they dove from the sky. "What are *those*?"

With a roar, the athexes charged again.

Spinning away, Roland ran towards an incoming athexe, ducked a long sweeping attack and stabbed at its gut.

Behind Thea, someone screamed.

Spinning, she saw a musharoc flapping laboriously, rising slowly into the air with a dark, writhing figure clenched in its talons.

Thea grabbed for an arrow. Her quiver was empty.

"Roland!"

Roland ducked the swipe of the athexe's clawed arm and stared.

"Do something!"

Roland threw one of his knives. It struck the bird's wing and tumbled to the ground. The musharoc screeched, but kept hold of the Little.

Thea looked around wildly. Could she find any arrows?

Ulfgar appeared through the tumult and charged straight up to Roland. "Throw me!"

Roland grabbed Ulfgar by the shoulders and with a spinning heave, threw him towards the Little, just as another musharoc dove from the sky. Ulfgar collided into it mid-flight and clung to its neck, muscles bulging. The musharoc screamed and tried to shake itself free of its burden, but Ulfgar hung on.

Another musharoc dove from the sky. Ulfgar dropped himself onto it as it passed, landing on its back. He clung on with handfuls of feathers as the musharoc flapped its wings, trying to keep aloft beneath its sudden burden.

The musharoc carrying the Little circled higher.

Ulfgar jumped to another musharoc's back. Leaping, he managed to grab the talons of a higher bird. Pulling himself up, he reached over the screeching bird's neck and scrambled onto its back. Fixing his eyes on the airborne Little, he jumped, and grabbed the musharoc's tail.

The musharoc wheeled, out of control. Ulfgar grabbed the Little's leg and pulled.

With a screech, the musharoc released its burden and Ulfgar and the Little began to fall.

"Arl!" Thea screamed.

In an explosion of feathers and blood, Arl erupted from the melee and shot through the air, snatching Ulfgar and the Little in their talons the moment before they hit the ground.

With great, laborious flaps Arl kept them aloft long enough to ease their landing, then tumbled to the ground in a muddled heap.

Dodging through the chaos, Thea ran to help.

Ulfgar staggered to his feet. A wild light was in his eyes. "Ha! They couldn't get away with that one!" He waved to Thea. "Success!"

Arl glared at him.

"Thanks for the catch!" Giving Arl a friendly headbutt, Ulfgar grinned and charged off towards the nearest athexe.

Thea knelt beside the Little, who was just a child. Her clothes were torn and bloody and she stared at Thea with large, frightened eyes. Thea scooped her up in her arms. "Let's get you back to the others".

Dodging past a charging athexe, Roland hurried

towards her.

"Here." Thea lifted the child into his arms. "Take her to Kais."

Roland nodded and disappeared through the melee.

Arl still lay on the ground, breathing heavily. Thea crouched beside them. Slowly Arl unfurled one of their wings. It was mangled and bloody.

"Are you okay?" Thea gasped. "I mean, we should get you help—right away!"

Arl glared at her. Their face spasmed in pain as they shifted into the form of a large, fat squirrel, the front leg of which looked bloody and deformed.

In a flash, they scooted away and up the leg of an athexe, biting it on the neck. The athexe roared and swiped at its tiny assailant, but Arl scampered up its head, jumped, and with a screech of pain shifted back into the form of an eagle, diving like an arrow towards the nearest musharoc.

Arrows. She had to find more arrows.

Thea ducked past the raging athexe, barely avoiding its long, sweeping claws. Not every shot had landed a hit. Her spent arrows must be lying somewhere—but how could she find them?

There! A bit of fletching, poking out from that clump of grass. Thea pulled out the arrow, nocked it, and shot a diving musharoc. It screamed and tumbled from the sky. Thea dove out of the way, slipped, and landed on her side. The grass beneath her was slick with blood. It stained her hands and her clothes.

Shrieking musharocs dove overhead and athexes snarled. The darkness flowing from them clouded the sky. The cacophony of screams and cries flooded Thea's senses, like the vision Micai had showed her. The monsters fought with a relentless hatred, attacking, retreating, and attacking again. No matter how many were killed, there always seemed to be more.

"Allulien, how can we do this?" Thea whispered.

A curly-haired slinger ran past, her hair matted and caked with dirt and blood. She scrambled along the ground, groping for more rocks. A musharoc screamed overhead and plunged towards her, its talons tearing into her back. She screamed.

Arl dove from the sky. Crashing into the musharoc, they tumbled to the ground, biting and slashing with their claws.

With blood dripping down her back, the Little found a rock, and with a twist of her sling sent it skyward.

An athexe crashed to the ground behind Thea, two black arrows protruding from its shoulder. Scrambling on top of the shuddering figure, Thea grabbed the arrows and pulled them out. Elora's arrows were too short for Raybow, but Elora might be needing them. A musharoc shrieked and Thea jumped to the ground, rolled, and dove behind another athexe.

With a scream, the musharoc and the athexe collided. The athexe roared in pain.

Thea ran, catching a glimpse of Sylica through the chaos. With her shield planted firmly in the ground, she swung her mace with gusto at anything that came within her reach. Thea dove behind the shield.

"Hi Thea!" Sylica grinned.

Thea leaned back against the shield, breathing hard. Okay. She had to make it to Elora.

Nodding to Sylica, she ducked back out from the protection of the shield.

"Bye Thea!" Sylica called.

Where was Elora? Thea dodged through the chaos.

Someone screamed.

Thea wheeled to see an athexe rear onto its hind legs, clenching Faris in its teeth.

As Thea stared in shock, the athexe shook him like a dog shaking a stick. Blood splattered across the panicking Littles.

Thea ran, knife in hand. Reaching the athexe, she plunged her knife into its leg. The leg jerked away. Losing her grip on the knife, Thea staggered backwards. The athexe's tail snapped like a whip. Striking her side, it knocked her to the ground. Dark spots swirled in her vision.

Shaking her head, Thea struggled to her feet. There was blood in her mouth.

Where was her knife? There—still embedded in the leg. She ran to grab it, then threw herself out of the way as the athexe staggered towards her. Faris hung limp in its jaws.

Anger flooding her senses, Thea grasped a black arrow in each hand and struck the athexe in the flank with all the force in her body. The athexe roared in pain, and Faris fell to the ground.

Dodging past its claws, Thea scooped up Faris' blood-soaked body in her arms and ran.

The athexe screeched with rage.

Thea dodged through another athexe's legs and past a cluster of slingers to the tight core of Littles that still managed to hold together.

Thea found Kais crouched on the ground, wrapping another Little's arm in a bandage. He looked up and saw the limp figure in Thea's arms. Horror and grief spread across his face.

"Uncle Faris." Kais' mouth formed the words, but no sound came out.

"An athexe had him." Thea's voice faltered. She lowered her burden gently down to Kais' level.

"Is he dead?" Kais whispered.

"I don't know." Thea looked around for a place to lay him, but everywhere the ground was trampled and stained with blood or already held Littles, bandaged and bloody, huddled together in fear. The small cart had been abandoned. Gently, Thea lay Faris on it.

Kais leaned over him and laid a hand on his blood-stained forehead. "Uncle Faris," he whispered. He leaned over his mouth and listened. "He's still breathing!" Kais waved frantically at the Littles who were huddled nearby. "Sami! Someone get Sami!"

Thea stared wildly around the clustered Littles. She couldn't see Sami anywhere. The fight raged around them, closer than ever. Had something happened to her?

Thea pushed through the crowd. "Sami! Sami!"

Elora appeared beside her. "What's wrong? What happened?"

"Have you seen Sami?"

A look of terror crossed Elora's face. "No, I haven't." She stared across the tumult of battle. "Grandmother! Grandmother!"

Sylica's mace flashed with light as she swung it through the air. Thea caught a glimpse of someone huddled behind her shield. "Over there!"

Elora ran.

As the crowd of Littles scattered before her, Thea caught a clearer view of Sami, crouched behind Sylica's shield, wrapping someone's head in a bandage.

"Deity, thank you," Thea whispered as she ran to join her.

"Grandmother!" Elora knelt beside Sami. "Are you alright?"

Sami nodded a greeting and gestured for Elora to hold the bandage. As she did so, Sami cut the excess off with a knife and tucked the end into place.

"Thank you, dear." Sami wiped her bloodied hands on the stained handkerchief that had been tucked through her belt, then patted the bandaged Little on the shoulder, speaking in a comforting tone. The Little staggered to their feet and hurried away.

An athexe tumbled towards them, an axe embedded in its shoulder.

"Look out!" Thea cried as Elora and Sami threw themselves out of the way.

The athexe crashed into the shield and collapsed, crushing it beneath its motionless body.

"Hey! My shield!" Sylica protested, appearing beside them. Shoving her shoulder up against the athexe, she tried to push it off.

Muttering to herself, Elora pushed in beside Sylica and gave a firm shove.

"Sami," Thea helped the elderly Little to her feet, "come quickly. We need you."

Leading Sami by the hand, Thea hurried back to the cart where Kais hovered anxiously over Faris' still body.

Sami's face looked thin and drawn as she felt for a pulse and assessed Faris' wounds.

"Can you help him, Grandmother?" Kais whispered.

Chattering busily, Sami pulled another roll of bandages from deep in a pocket.

A musharoc dove towards them, screeching.

Thea ducked, shielding her head with her arms. When the stench had passed, she looked up to see Sami yelling and shaking her fist at the departing bird. A long trail of bandage flowed from its clenched talons.

Kais crawled wearily out from beneath the cart. "It just doesn't stop," he sighed, pain and exhaustion etched deeply on his gentle face. "I don't think we can hold on much longer." He glanced at Thea. "But thank you for trying."

"No!" Thea grabbed Kais' shoulders. "We are not giving up." A slingstone whizzed overhead and she ducked. "But we can't stay here. We have to keep moving!"

"Keep moving?" Kais stared. "We're hurt and trapped. How are we supposed to keep moving?"

"We have to! The monsters will win if we stay here. We have to get across the river!"

But how? Thea stared around the chaos of battle.

Ulfgar. He'd be able to break a way through. But where was he? She couldn't see him through the seething mass of monsters and Littles.

But she'd seen his axe, and he wouldn't be far from it.

Sure enough, as Thea ran back to the fallen athexe, she saw Ulfgar with both hands on the shaft of his axe, trying to tug it out of the athexe's shoulder.

"Ulfgar!" Thea yelled.

"Hrrmph?" Ulfgar grumbled. Muscles straining, he wrenched his axe free.

"We have to keep moving!" Thea waved her arm towards the south. "Get Arl and clear the way!"

Ulfgar gave a rakish grin and swung his axe over his shoulder. "Hey Arl!" he shouted up at the sky. "We've got a job to do!"

Thea ran back to Kais. "Kais! Get everyone up! Sylica? There you are. See if there's anyone who needs to be carried. Elora! We're moving out!"

"What?" Elora yelled from the far side of the cluster of Littles. Everywhere, Littles staggered to their feet. Parents clutched their children's hands, Sylica lifted two injured Littles up over her shoulders, Kais grabbed the handles of the cart.

"Ready ..." Thea yelled, staring to the south.

Axes waving in the air, Ulfgar charged. With a screech, Arl dove from the sky. The athexes wavered, then broke and ran.

"Go!" Thea yelled and charged after Ulfgar.

The Littles yelled. Thea could hear the stamp of their feet as they ran after her.

The stench of the musharocs broke over Thea like a wave. "Keep going!" she yelled over her shoulder. "Don't let them stop you!"

Sami crouched on the cart with Faris, wrapping strips of cloth tightly around his chest.

Light gleamed on Roland's knives.

Slowly, the Littles pushed their way forwards. Ulfgar charged again and again, driving the athexes out of their path. Arl wheeled and dove, pushing back any musharocs who tried to interfere.

Steadily, the forest grew closer. How much farther was it to the river? Thea prayed desperately that it wasn't much farther, or that the forest itself would provide some relief.

There—Ulfgar had made it to the closest trees!

Thea yelled in triumph and turned to wave the Littles on. Across their seething mass she caught a glimpse of

Elora, staring at the grasslands around them with a suspicious frown. Thea paused. What had she seen? Was that ... the smell of something burning?

Smoke poured out from the forest in front of them. Ulfgar staggered back and looked around in bewilderment.

Through the trees, Thea thought she caught a glimpse of something slithering out of sight.

The smoke poured thicker and darker. There were red flames now, blown higher by the hot, dry breeze.

Thea stared at the fire spreading from tree to tree. Now what? She glanced at Roland, but he seemed to be at a loss. They had to go south, but now that was impossible.

Arl landed beside Thea and shifted into Elf-form with a shudder of pain. Their body was streaked with blood. "The wind has caught the fire. We must turn back, before it reaches the grass."

"We can't turn back," Thea insisted.

"Do you *want* them to die?" Arl demanded, gesturing at the panicking Littles.

"The Deity told us to go to the river. If we cross the river we will be safe."

A strange look crossed Arl's face. Thea saw the light again, flickering in Arl's spirit.

Screams and cries erupted behind them.

Wheeling, Thea saw a fire snake emerge from the grass in the middle of the field. It reared its head high into the air, a tongue of fire flickering in its mouth.

"No!" Thea screamed. "Don't kill it!"

A barrage of slingstones flew through the air, pummelling the fire snake to the ground. An explosion of fire erupted from where it lay.

"Get water! Quick!" Thea ran through the Littles, but before she reached Elora, the fire was spreading like lightning across the field. Flames leapt into the sky, rushing towards the cowering Littles.

"We have to get out of here!" Elora yelled.

"I know! I know!" Thea stared around wildly. The fire in the trees had grown to fill the entire forest before them, and the fire tearing through the clearing cut them off from behind. Even if they could run, the fire would be faster.

As the flames roared closer, the Littles huddled close together, staring in mute fear. Sylica raised her battered shield. Elora clasped Kais' hand as they backed towards the burning trees.

The heat was becoming unbearable. The roar of flames filled Thea's ears. She caught sight of Roland. He stared at her with wide eyes.

Allulien, do something! Thea whispered. What could she do? Her magic was to affect people, not stop fires.

The flames had almost reached her now. She stepped back and bumped into the cart that held Faris' motionless body. There was nowhere else to go.

Sylica yelled.

In front of them, the forest exploded.

Thea ducked and covered her head, but to her amazement, nothing struck her. Instead, a rending gap had been torn in the forest. The trees were still burning, but the entire layer of topsoil, trees and all, had been peeled back on each side, leaving a dirt-lined passageway straight before them.

"Run!" Sylica yelled, scooping up a child in each arm. Everyone ran.

The cart jerked and leapt as Kais grabbed its handles

and pulled. Thea grabbed the back of the cart and pushed. Roland lifted a bloodied Little and swung him over his shoulders.

Walls of dirt stretched high on either side of the narrow path. Above the dirt, smoke billowed into the sky, tinted red with the flickering of flames. As Thea ran, the smoke sank down to fill the narrow causeway, stinging her eyes and clouding her sight. She could barely see Kais running ahead of her, muscles straining as he pulled the handles of the cart. Glancing over her shoulder, Thea caught glimpses of huddled figures, hurrying, stumbling, groping through the shadows.

Thea ran until her lungs felt like they would burst, but the corridor of dirt stretched on and on. The cart bumped and rattled as she and Kais propelled it over the uneven soil underfoot.

A sudden breath of wind swirled through the smoke. A few steps later the smoke cleared and Thea saw the river spread out below her like a shimmering ribbon.

The cart emerged from the dirt-lined canyon with a rumbling clatter. Past the last few scattered trees they ran, down the long, gentle slope, and stopped by the banks of the rushing river. The cart's wheels sank into the soft, loamy soil.

Thea let go of the cart and stared. The river was large. To cross it she'd have to swim at least as far as she had when she'd jumped from the Raven, but this water was quick flowing, surging past the banks with a steady, relentless strength.

She hadn't asked Allulien how they were supposed to cross the river.

Thea turned and watched the smoke billowing into the sky. The fire was coming.

A cluster of Littles emerged from the murky shadows, coughing and rubbing their eyes. Kais called to them and they hurried down the hill.

Another cluster of Littles appeared and stared at the river with wide, frightened eyes.

With shaking hands, Thea pulled the rope from her bag. Now what?

Roland ran into view, leaped down the slope, and grabbed the rope from Thea's hands, replacing it with the knife she had left behind when Faris was injured. He gave her a wink. "My job." Expertly, he untangled the rope, pulled a second rope from his own bag and knotted them together. He handed one end to Thea. "Hold this!" Grabbing the other end, he dove into the river. By the time he reached the far side, the current had swept him significantly downstream. He ran back along the bank, found a sturdy tree, and tied the rope to it.

Beside Thea, Sylica was busily organizing the Littles into groups, although what exactly determined the reasons for the groupings, Thea couldn't discern.

Thea looked around. Littles were still emerging from the smoke, limping and coughing. She turned to Kais. "Here. Take this." She shoved the end of the rope into his hands and ran back towards the dirt passageway.

The shadow and smoke made it nearly impossible to see. Feeling with her hands, Thea stumbled on, almost colliding with another cluster of Littles that limped forwards as quickly as they could, covering their faces in an attempt to shield themselves from the smoke.

"Come on!" Thea gestured for them to hurry. "You're almost there!"

Ulfgar emerged from the gloom, carrying Dana who

clung to him in terror.

Another Little stumbled by, and another.

Thea ran on. Where was Elora? There she was—running so fast she nearly collided with Thea.

"They're coming!" Elora gasped. "They're following us!"

Beyond her, Thea caught a glimpse of shadowy shapes, rushing down the corridor towards them.

Thea turned and ran.

"How much further?" Elora panted, keeping pace by Thea's elbow.

"Almost there," Thea gasped between breaths, "but we still have to cross the river."

Suddenly there was no one beside her. Spinning, Thea could just see Elora through the murky haze, her bow aimed into the darkness beyond.

"Keep going!" Elora called over her shoulder. "I'll buy us some time."

Heart pounding, Thea ran. A few steps later, she burst out into the daylight.

"Quick!" she called, gasping for breath.

Arl, wheeling overhead, caught her gaze and dove like an arrow towards the narrow passage.

With a roar, Ulfgar charged up the slope and disappeared into the darkness.

Thea tumbled down the slope to where the Littles were clustered along the riverbank. "Kais! Elora needs help!"

Kais looked up sharply, hands frozen halfway through helping an elderly Little down the riverbank.

Thea got close and spoke in a low voice. "The monsters are coming. Do you have anyone who can still fight?"

Kais nodded and looked around. He called a few of the Littles by name and quickly told them what was going on.

Four of the Littles ran back towards the forest, grabbing stones off the slope as they ran.

Roland had the rope line secure and was escorting a group of Littles across the river. The Littles clung to the rope, pulling themselves forward, while the current tugged at their limbs and clothing. On the far side of the river, Thea could see a large cluster of Littles, clinging to each other and staring back at them with wide eyes.

Thea helped Kais escort the next party of Littles down into the water. Shrieks and cries from the forest behind them mingled with the roar of the fire, drawing ever closer.

Roland was back, and the next party of Littles began their crossing. Sylica scrambled down into the water next.

"All on board who want a ride!" she called with a grin. Two of the children scrambled down after her and she lifted them up onto her shoulders. A mother reached down and handed her infant into Sylica's welcoming arms.

Tucking the baby into a fold in her clothes, Sylica wrapped one arm around it and grabbed the rope in the other. "Hold on tight!" she called to the children and started slogging through the water. As it got deeper the children shrieked in delight and clung to her. The water swirled past, making ripples and whirlpools behind Sylica's surging form.

"Can you help me?" Kais asked Thea. He wheeled the cart as close to the edge of the water as he could. "I don't think I can lift him."

Thea looked at Faris' still form and the blood-soaked cart. Lifting him at all could do more harm than good. "Do you think the cart will float?"

Kais cocked his head and gave the cart a long slow look. "We can try."

Cautiously, they pulled the cart down towards the water. It was heavier than it looked.

"Here. Let me help." Roland appeared beside Thea and tucked his shoulder beneath the cart's axle, helping guide it down to the water.

Gently, they set it on the river's shimmering surface. It stayed afloat.

Sami slid down the slope after them, chattering urgently. With a nimble leap, she pulled herself up onto the cart. Gently she lifted Faris' head and set it on her lap. With a nod to Kais, she gripped the side of the cart. Her small, wiry figure did not seem to affect its buoyancy at all.

Roland slipped around to the upstream side of the rope and gripped the handles of the cart. Slowly he eased himself out into the current.

Thea glanced around. That was everyone, besides the fighters up in the trees.

"I'll go get them," Thea said to Kais. "You can cross if you want."

Without waiting for a reply, Thea ran up the slope towards the trees.

"Elora! Ulfgar! Everyone's across! We can go!"

A tree exploded in flames. Thea ducked and ran, diving into the darkness of the dirt-lined corridor. There were the shadowy figures of the Littles, slowly retreating, slinging stone after stone. Elora shouted and waved them back, no longer shooting her bow.

"Where's Ulfgar?" Thea called.

Elora gestured into the smoky darkness beyond, where a cacophony of noise raged above the roar of the fire.

"Ulfgar! Arl!" Thea yelled. "Get out of there!"

An eagle's cry screamed above the chaos and Arl emerged from the darkness, Ulfgar clasped firmly in their talons, waving his axes and shouting with gusto.

As Arl swooped overhead, the line of Littles broke and ran. Thea followed, running back down the long slope to the river. Kais stood by the rope, waiting with an expression of fear etched on his face.

"Go! Go!" Thea gestured for the Littles to cross.

Arl sped the full length of the river, dropping Ulfgar in a heap on the other side.

The scream of a horse rose above the noise. Thea stared at the forest, flames reaching high above the trees.

"Cross the River!" Elora yelled, pushing the last of the Littles forward. "Now!"

Out from the flames, the figure of a horse emerged. It was jet black, and its shape shifted and moved as if it was made from darkness itself. Smoke flowed from its mane and tail. Its eyes were glowing coals.

Before Thea could gasp, a small figure jumped out from the trees and with a yell, threw a stone at it.

Kais had seen it too.

"Zaki!" Kais ran up the slope towards him.

Around the night mare, the trees burst into flames.

Tossing its head, the night mare kicked Zaki to the ground, then trampled him.

Zaki screamed in pain.

That instant, Kais was beside him. He lifted Zaki in

his arms as the night mare turned and charged towards him.

With a cry, Thea threw all the rest of her magic at it. Her magic to charm. *Don't hurt them. Don't hurt them.*

The night mare hesitated just a moment, then the magic disappeared in a flash. A tree exploded in flames and began to fall.

With a scream, Arl dove faster than an arrow.

The tree crashed to the ground, exploding in a shower of sparks and splintered wood.

With a roar, the darkness split apart and Arl emerged, a giant elk, leaping the charred remains of the tree in a single bound.

Kais and Zaki clung to Arl's back.

They pounded down the slope towards Thea, blood streaking down Arl's sides. With a burst of flame, the night mare thundered after them, shadow and smoke spreading behind it like a wake.

Skidding to a stop beside Thea, Arl dripped Kais and Zaki to the ground, wheeled, and with a scream of pain, shifted into cougar form, launching at the night mare's throat.

The night mare screamed as Arl's teeth sank into its neck.

Thea stared as the night mare reared and shook itself free. Arl's back hit the ground with a sickening thud.

"Go!" Arl yelled.

The night mare's hooves plunged through Arl's chest.

Eyes burning, Thea threw herself into the river and grabbed the rope. Elora, Kais, and Zaki were already halfway across.

"Hold on!" she yelled, and cut the rope.

The water engulfed her.

Clinging to the rope, she struggled back to the surface, lungs screaming for air. The current rushed past her as she took great gulps of air that felt like sobs. Pain racked her body, as if all the breath had been sucked from her lungs.

She couldn't unsee what her eyes had just seen.

As the river swept her along, she drew closer and closer to the farther bank, drawn irresistibly by the rope still secured on one side. Overhanging roots brushed against her and she clung to them. Shouts and calls rang out further upstream as people rushed to help Elora, Zaki, and Kais out of the water.

As Thea pulled herself onto shore, her eyes were irresistibly drawn to the far bank. The night mare screamed and paced the riverbank, its eyes blazing in red fury. Beyond it, athexes emerged from the billowing smoke. They approached the river, then stepped back, eyeing the water with fear and hatred.

Musharocs screeched overhead. Wheeling through the smoky haze, they spotted the Littles and plunged across the river towards them.

From the midst of the Littles, Roland shouted and raised his hand. A surge of magic swept across the river. The musharocs screamed and tumbled into the river with a splash. The current swept them away.

The magic hung like a haze across the river. Beyond it, Thea watched a translucent figure rise slowly from the ground. It lifted a knotted, ball-like shape from the ground and drifted past the monsters, who did not seem to notice it at all. Hovering, it crossed the water and floated past Thea to a low, rotting stump, protruding from the forest floor. The object it carried, Thea saw now, looked like a very large seed. Gently, the ghostly figure set the seed in the hollow cavity of the stump, then turned and looked at her.

The shadowy form had bright red eyes, and its spirit glowed with a warm radiance that pierced the shadows.

Tears filled Thea's eyes, but Arl smiled and held out their hand.

A breath of wind rustled in the branches overhead, and Arl was gone.

Thea knelt in the dirt and cried.

Chapter Twenty

Slowly, Thea wiped her face with the sleeve of her sodden tunic and got to her feet. Following the sound of voices, she walked along the bank of the river until she found the cluster of Littles that had gathered around Elora, Zaki, and Kais.

Zaki saw her and waved urgently.

"I told them!" Zaki yelled as Thea approached, "I told them that Arl is strong! Arl can fight all the monsters and win! They won't … they can't …"

He stared at her with large, pleading eyes.

Thea's heart ached as she knelt on the ground beside Zaki. "Arl is not coming back."

"No! It's not true!" Zaki hit the ground in blind fury, tears streaming down his face.

Thea's eyes met Elora's, and the pain that she saw there made the ache in Thea's chest throb worse than ever.

Kais put his arm around Elora and stretched his other hand out to Zaki. "Arl died to save us," he said in a quivering voice. "We would never have made it if Arl had not come."

"No! You don't understand!" Zaki shouted, pushing Kais away. "We all made it out, every one of us! Arl wasn't supposed to die!" His face crumpled and sobs shook his body.

Elora held him close, tears streaming down her face.

Roland was watching them. "I'll tell the others," he said in a quiet voice, then turned and walked away.

In Elora's arms, Zaki cried.

Kais wrapped his arms around them both. He glanced up at Thea and nodded. She didn't have to stay.

Slowly, Thea turned away and followed Roland back towards the rest of the Littles. Everyone sat in silence. Some of the Littles held each other or gently nursed their wounds. Others glanced fearfully back across the river where the fire continued to burn out of control.

Roland stood at the riverbank, watching the monsters that still paced the far bank.

Thea stepped beside him. "They won't come after us?"

Roland shook his head. "I used the last of my magic to banish the monsters that could cross the river. Nothing can reach us now, unless it comes from the forest on this side of the river."

"Allulien said this side of the river would be safe." Her eyes took in the Littles as they huddled together. The air was still warm, but many of them seemed to be shivering. "I'm glad we don't have to go any further today."

"Is it true?" Sylica asked, joining them by the river. "What Roland said. Did the night mare kill Arl?"

Thea nodded.

Sylica looked down at the ground. Her hands twisted the edge of her tunic. "My Uncle Bob died before. It's sad when people die." Her usually cheerful face twisted in an expression that Thea had never seen on it before. When she spoke again, there was a quiver in her voice. "The Great Big Big will take care of Arl."

Sami hobbled over to them and laid a hand on

Sylica's arm, her face carrying all the gentleness and compassion of someone who knew grief all too well.

"Arl ... saved us," Sami croaked. "We will not forget."

"Thank you," Thea whispered.

Sami nodded sagely and patted Sylica's arm. She held up a sodden lump of cloth. "Now, bandages."

Sylica smiled. "Of course I'll help you, Grandmother."

Together, Sylica and Sami walked back to the rest of the Littles.

Thea's eyes roamed across the group. Where was Ulfgar? He was nowhere to be seen.

Without saying anything to Roland, Thea wandered slowly around the small clearing. Silently, Littles comforted each other and cared for their injuries. Ulfgar wasn't there.

When she was certain that everyone was being cared for, Thea slipped away into the surrounding forest. Silently, she paced back and forth through the trees, but she couldn't see any sign of Ulfgar. He'd made it across the river, but where was he now? Had he gone further along the riverbank?

Thea wandered further and further away. Rounding a gnarled oak tree, she saw him.

Ulfgar sat on the ground, alone, his head bowed over the helmet he held in his unmoving hands.

Quietly, Thea went to stand beside him. He didn't acknowledge her presence.

"Ulfgar," Thea whispered.

Ulfgar didn't move.

Thea waited, tears stinging her eyes. They had been so close to making it out—all of them—but now Arl was gone. Ulfgar still did not move.

Thea sat down beside him. "Ulfgar?"

She waited.

Light glimmered at the edge of her sight. Micai stood in the shadows, watching them.

Silently getting to her feet, Thea hurried over to their side. The look in Micai's face told Thea that they knew what had happened. She glanced back at Ulfgar.

"Let me," Micai said softly. As Thea watched, Micai walked over to Ulfgar and sat down on the moss beside him.

After a few moments of silence, Micai's tankard appeared. Micai took a thoughtful swig, then held it out to Ulfgar.

Ulfgar glanced at it. Without expression, he took it from Micai's hand and took a long drink.

Startled, he lowered the tankard, stared at it, then took an even longer drink. He turned to Micai. "Where did you get this?"

Micai grinned. "You like it?"

Ulfgar took another swig, then stared at the tankard. "It's still full."

"Always is." Micai took the tankard and had a drink, then handed it back to Ulfgar.

They sat in silence for a long time. Ulfgar sipped the beer reflectively.

Micai gave him a sidelong glance. "Arl fought well. They earned their rest."

Ulfgar stared into the tankard's murky depths. "Yeah."

Micai shifted slightly. "What about you?"

Ulfgar looked at Micai for a moment, then shrugged. "I'll drink. That's what I do."

Micai nodded at the tankard in Ulfgar's hands. "I'll

hire your blade, for the price of that mug."

Darkness clouded Ulfgar's eyes and he shoved the tankard back into Micai's hands. "I'm not a blade for hire. Not anymore." He turned away and glared at the ground, as if his eyes could bore holes beneath his feet.

Micai looked at the tankard thoughtfully. "When you've lost so much, one more loss can be very hard to take."

Ulfgar didn't move.

Micai looked at him with an expression of deep, heart-wrenching compassion. "I know, Finni."

Ulfgar's eyes snapped to Micai's face. "You know?" he demanded, eyes burning. "You know what it's like to lose everything again and again, to never be able to say goodbye or to know when you—when you'll be—" his voice broke and he put his head into his calloused hands. Silent tears coursed down his face.

Micai rested a hand on Ulfgar's broad shoulders.

A sacred silence spread across the clearing as Micai sat and watched Ulfgar's heaving shoulders.

Thea hardly dared to breathe.

After a long time, Micai leaned closer and spoke in a low, gentle voice. "I know how long your road has been."

Ulfgar looked up into Micai's compassionate eyes. For a moment, something inside his spirit shifted.

Micai smiled. "I will give you the tankard for a promise."

Ulfgar looked at Micai with an almost eager glance.

"A promise that you won't give up hope."

A shadow crossed Ulfgar's face and he looked down.

"I—I'll think about it," he murmured after a long silence.

Micai nodded. "When you decide, let me know."

Micai stood and glanced at Thea with a smile. Walking past her, Micai stepped through the trees and disappeared.

When Thea looked back at Ulfgar, he was looking at her. Slowly he got to his feet. Thea walked over to join him.

"I'm sorry," she said, not really sure what she was apologizing for, but with the feeling that she had witnessed something deeply private and precious. Something she wasn't sure she was meant to see.

Ulfgar harrumphed and fidgeted with his helmet.

"Thank you for your help getting the Littles out of the Deorcian. I don't think we could have done it without you."

Ulfgar shrugged, looking at the ground.

"Will you stay with us?"

Ulfgar looked up. "I guess I will. For now."

Thea smiled.

As they began their walk back to camp, she gave Ulfgar a sidelong glance. "Finni?"

Ulfgar stared back at the place where Micai had been. "No one in this world knows me by that name." He glanced at Thea. "But somehow, they knew."

"If someone should know, Micai is a good one for that."

She watched the light flicker again, deep in Ulfgar's spirit.

He swayed slightly and looked up at Thea with a small frown on his face. "Maybe I should have a nap."

Thea nodded.

Quietly, they walked back to the company of Littles, where Ulfgar found a corner that was out of the way.

Unwrapping his sodden bedroll, he lay down and closed his eyes. Soon he was snoring.

Thea looked around the subdued crowd of Littles. Faris had been laid on the moss beneath a spreading tree. Sylica was attending to him.

"Will he make it, do you think?" Thea asked, joining Sylica.

Sylica nodded. "Sami says that his wounds have stopped bleeding and his heartbeat is steady. She thinks he will be alright."

"I'm glad." Thea watched Faris' haggard face. It seemed peaceful now.

"Sylica," Thea frowned thoughtfully. "What happened, when we were surrounded by the fire? You made a way through, but I thought you couldn't do any magic."

"What did I make?" Sylica blinked at her with genuine confusion.

Thea stared at Sylica. "The path through the burning trees. Don't you remember?"

"Oh that. That wasn't magic."

"Then what was it?"

"I don't know." Sylica frowned. "I just wanted there to be a path, and then there it was. That kind of thing happens sometimes, you know."

Thea stared at her strange friend. All magic came from the Deity, she knew that for sure, but she'd never met someone who could do magic that wasn't magic. She frowned. "Does it happen often?"

Sylica cocked her head. "Sometimes it does and sometimes it doesn't. I never really know what to expect." Her countenance brightened. "It makes it quite exciting, don't you think?"

Before Thea could respond, Sylica skipped off to join Sami, attending to the injuries of another Little.

All Thea could do was shake her head.

Thankfully it was a warm evening. No one seemed interested in lighting a fire, but some of the Littles strung up bits of rope and hung their wet things up to dry. Small packets of food were produced and shared. There wasn't much to go around.

Thea glanced at the sky, then realized she was watching for Arl to return from hunting. Grief rose again to overwhelm her. Arl would never soar overhead again, landing by her side to bring news of the road ahead. Arl was gone.

Tears stinging her eyes, Thea glanced around the makeshift camp. Everyone seemed to be doing alright. They wouldn't miss her for a little while.

Slowly, she made her way back to the old rotten stump and sat down in the shadows beneath a nearby tree. The ache in her chest hurt her in a way that a physical injury never had. She pictured Arl slinking through the shadows, shifting forms, and taking to the sky. Probably glaring at her for some reason or other. It seemed so impossible for her mind to grasp that she would never see them again. Death had only seemed like a strange curiosity before. Now it was a horrible reality.

She heard a footstep behind her.

"I checked the area, and everything is secure." Roland stepped lightly to Thea's side and crouched beside her. He glanced at her tear-stained face. "Sorry. Did you want to be alone?"

Thea looked up at Roland. "You can stay." There was something about him that reminded her of Micai.

Maybe it was the gentleness in his eyes.

Roland sat beside her and stared across the river at the bare, scorched trees of the Deorcian, still smouldering in the evening light.

"We made it," Roland said after a while.

A breath of wind stirred the branches above. Thea felt a sob well up in her chest. "I wish Arl didn't die."

Roland squeezed her hand. "I know."

Grief washed over Thea like a wave, carrying her in its painful embrace.

Slowly, through her tears, she became aware of the river flowing by, the light reflecting on its ripping surface, its sleepy murmur drifting through the air.

She took a long, trembling breath.

"You went through a lot together," Roland said in a quiet voice. "I didn't really get to know Arl, but I would have liked to. They were a good fighter, with a lot of passion."

Thea nodded. "When Arl decided to protect someone, they gave everything they had." Her voice broke as tears rose to choke her. "Arl was willing to die for them, and ... and then did."

Roland looked thoughtful. "It's strange to think that I've known someone who actually died."

"It was strange to Arl that Elves don't die." Thea stared at the rippling surface of the river as it drifted past. "Dryads die, eventually, and so do humans, and Littles. But our people don't die. Not usually, anyways. I don't know how they do it, all those people who know that they will die someday. But then I remember that I am fighting in the war now. Elves died in the war. Maybe I will die someday too."

Roland looked at her with a strange expression. "It's

better to die doing the right thing, I think, than to live because you didn't do it."

Thea nodded. "I know." She had given her life to the Deity, whether to live or die, and nothing would change that.

The tide of grief ebbed, leaving a strange feeling of calm in its wake. Thea leaned her head on Roland's shoulder. His presence was familiar and comforting.

Slowly the light faded into the blue-green shadow of night. Roland put his hand on Thea's. "You should sleep."

Thea nodded. She was tired. Slowly she got to her feet and walked back to the campsite. There was an open space available beneath a large oak tree. She wrapped herself in her cloak and lay down.

Through the spreading branches above, she watched the great blue-green planet continue its journey across the sky. Micai's planet.

Thea fell asleep.

She awoke when Allumen emerged from Micai's eclipse, flooding the shadowy forest with light. All around her, Littles were waking and starting their day. Slipping away, Thea found a quiet place for her check in.

Kneeling, she waited to hear what Allulien wanted her to do. Even though the day had just begun, the air was warm and muggy. She could hear the murmur of the Littles drifting through the trees.

Time stretched on, and no word from Allulien came. Thea waited longer. Surely Allulien would speak to her today. She had to find the Littles a home, and she didn't know where to go. What would she do if Allulien said nothing at all?

"Please," she whispered, "please tell me what to do. The Littles need a home, but I don't know where to go!"

Bowing her head, she waited in silence.

You know where you are going.

The voice grew like an imprint on her heart. She knew where she was going? No she didn't! She had no idea where she was going!

Well, she knew where she *was* going, but that was before she met the Littles and promised to help them. Surely she had to help them first, *before* going to Gedwyld.

"Thea?"

Thea looked up to see Elora watching her from a cautious distance.

"Sorry to bother you, but everyone is wondering where you are. I think you should talk to them."

Slowly, Thea got to her feet. She didn't know what she was going to say, but she would talk to them anyway.

As Thea returned, silence fell across the crowd of Littles. They stared at her with large eyes.

Feeling the presence of magic within herself again, Thea stretched it across the company of Littles, touching their ears with understanding.

One of the Littles that Thea recognized as Hana rose to her feet. "We have followed you, and you led us out of the Trees as you said. Now you have promised us a new home. Is it here in these trees?"

"No." Thea glanced at Roland. "These trees will not be safe forever. They are safe for now, but only for us to pass through. We will have to go farther to reach your new home."

"Then are we going across the sea? We heard that

Sylica knows of a home across the sea."

"No." Thea took a deep breath. "We are going to run *to* the people of Raphtova, not away from them. We are going to Gedwyld."

Elora's eyes widened and an outcry of dismay rose among the Littles.

"Gedwyld?"

"That's a Big city!"

"We can't go there, they'll kill us!"

"The Bigs hate us!"

"Not all Bigs hate you!" Thea yelled above the chaos.

Silence fell as everyone stared.

"I'm a Big," Thea pointed at herself. "Roland is a Big. Ulfgar and Sylica are Bigs. Arl was a Big and Arl *died* to save you. You cannot say that all Bigs hate you, because it's not true."

A low murmur rose among the Littles.

"You need to trust me." Thea spoke in a low, urgent voice. "Follow me to Gedwyld. I promise you, you will find a home there."

Slowly, Elora stepped forward. "I know the Bigs have hurt us, but now we have seen that not all Bigs are bad. There are the Bigs like the dark things, but these Bigs are not big like that. They are between the Bigs and the Littles. They are Middles, and they are people, just like us. Maybe we can find a home, in peace with the Middles."

Kais stood up. "We will go to the city of the Middles. Won't we, Zaki?"

Zaki nodded. His eyes were still red from crying.

Sami waved her cane in the air. "The Great Big Big saved us. We won't turn back now!"

The rest of the Littles looked at each other nervously,

but Thea could see tentative nods of agreement.

Roland stepped beside Thea and spoke in her ear. "Gedwyld is a human city?"

Thea nodded.

"You think they will accept the Littles?"

"They'd better," Thea said in a low voice, "because that's where we are going."

Roland watched her for a moment, then his eyes twinkled.

Grumbling, Ulfgar got to his feet. "So are we going or not?"

Several days later, the Littles came within sight of the large stone walls of Gedwyld. The journey had been uneventful, for the most part. They had to travel slowly, because of the number of injured, but through hunting and foraging along the way they had more than enough to provide for everyone's needs.

As they followed the river east, the land gradually rose, or perhaps it was that the river sank, because now it flowed through the bottom of a deep gorge. The company followed along the top of its high banks. Yesterday, Thea had heard the crying of gulls.

Now they stopped and stared at the imposing sight. The city of Gedwyld rose before them, built into the sides of the cliff that rose on either side of the gorge. On the north side of the river, a large castle predominated the skyline. Below it, stone houses filled the slopes of the hill all the way down to the perimeter wall. On the south side of the river, several large manor houses crowned the hill, and were surrounded by more buildings, all hemmed in by a continuation of the protective wall. Across the gorge, two massive stone bridges spanned from one side to the other. Around the city walls, farms and fields stretched out to the north and west and south. East beyond the city, the blue sea glimmered.

"Now what?" Elora asked in a low voice, stepping beside Thea. The Littles murmured among themselves, glancing at the imposing city of stone with worried expressions.

Stepping forward, Thea cast her magic over the group. As everyone turned to look at her, she gave them an encouraging smile. "We are almost there. Now it is very important that you listen to what I say. Something I have learned about humans is that if you act like you belong, they seem to believe you. We are going to walk into Gedwyld, and we are going to walk as if we belong there. There will be no weapons drawn. No hiding or sneaking. If any talking needs to be done, I will do it, and we will trust them to accept us. The Great Big Big made all the peoples of Raphtova to live and work together. It is time for us to start doing that."

Thea glanced at Roland. He gave her a wink.

"Okay." Thea took a deep breath and turned towards the city. "Follow me."

She felt the assurance deep within herself that this was right. She would not stand by and let the peoples of Raphtova be separated anymore. But still, images of fearful, angry faces rose in her mind. Humans with swords and torches, ready to drive the goblins from their land. Was it possible for things to be different? If it was possible, she had to try.

Passing fields and barns, Thea led the Littles on the broad dirt road that led towards a gate in the city wall. The humans working in the fields stopped and stared, but none of them seemed to say anything.

Finally the gate loomed large before them. It was open. Thea stood tall and walked through the gate.

Within the city, cobbled streets led in every direction. Large stone buildings loomed overhead, dark with age and the dirt of many circles. A pack of crox rooted through a heap of garbage, tucked away in an alley.

Setting her face towards the upper reaches of the city, Thea pressed on. As they went, she saw more and more people turning to stare at the Littles as they passed. Hushed whispers rose from the growing crowds.

"Why are there so many children?"

"They can't be children—that one has wrinkles."

"But why are they so short?"

"Are they goblins?"

"No! What are you talking about? Everyone knows that goblins are horrible, ugly creatures."

Understanding rose inside Thea with a wave of excitement. None of these people had actually seen a goblin before! They knew about goblins, of course, and had maybe seen one sneaking through the shadows, but fear had painted a very different reality than the one that walked before them now.

The excitement in the crowd was growing. Thea could hear them calling to each other: "Come! Come look at the little humans!"

A tall woman in long white robes walked down the street towards them. Her long brown hair was curled away from her face and drawn back into a bun tucked behind her head. Her robes swished as she walked.

Approaching Thea, she bowed. "Welcome to

Gedwyld, Thea of the Elves. Raphea told me of your coming."

Thea gasped in delight. It had never occurred to her that there might be people who served the Deity in Gedwyld—but then, this was the place where she was told to find Davis. Why wouldn't the Deity's people be ready to receive the Littles and give them a home?

The woman smiled. "My name is Acwellan. I am foremost of the healers of this city." She glanced at the ogling crowd. "I did not know if I would have to intervene, but it seems that you have done my work for me."

Thea gestured Elora and Kais forward. "Acwellan, this is Elora and Kais, leaders among the community of Littles. They are here in search of a new home for their people."

Acwellan nodded. "I will take you to the Lord of this city. He is the one who can give you permission to settle here. I don't think you will have any trouble with him, though," she added, her eyes glinting with mischief. "One has a lot of influence when one is the principal healer in a community."

Thea glanced at Sami who had hobbled up to join them and laughed. "Isn't that right, Sami?"

Acwellan turned to Sami with a smile. "Are you a healer? I heard there would be one among your company. We are always in need of good healers."

One of the young Littles had toddled over to the crowd. Thea watched as a woman set down her basket and lifted the child in her arms.

"Oh Octric!" the woman gasped. "Just look at her! Isn't she the cutest thing!"

The young man she had spoken to was staring at the

cart as it rattled up the road.

"Excuse me," he called, approaching the Little that pulled the cart.

The Little stopped and stared up at him.

The man knelt down to the Little's height. "Can you tell me about this cart? I've never seen wheels made like this before."

The Little looked around in confusion and Kais hurried over to translate. On the other side of the cart, Sylica waved excitedly to the growing crowds.

Thea watched understanding grow in Elora's eyes.

"They're not killing us," she whispered, staring at the humans who were now clustering around the Littles, chattering excitedly. "They're not yelling or driving us away."

"I won't say they're perfect." Acwellan gave a wry grin. "They have their moments. Trust me. But they're decent people, when you get to know them."

Slowly, they made their way up the cobbled streets. As they went, people peered out of their windows. Stall vendors called their wares as the Littles stared at carts filled with fruit and pastries. Crox scampered along the rooftops, swooping down to claim the crumbs the children threw out for them. Banners waved overhead in the breeze.

Thea glanced at Elora and smiled.

"Welcome home."

Epilogue

Thea and Roland sat on the city wall overlooking the sea. Several days had passed since they arrived in Gedwyld, but they had been very busy. First there was the meeting with the Lord of the city, then the seemingly endless process of finding temporary homes for the Littles.

The humans had welcomed them into their city like long-lost children. Thea watched with fascination the way that the humans seemed to have an innate desire to baby anything that was small. This led to the bewildered, but grateful, Littles being showered with gifts and care, and soon they had more than enough to compensate for all they had lost in their flight from the Deorcian.

The Littles, for their part, had been shocked by the state of the houses in the city, without running water, sewers, or central heating. Soon they were fixing up the homes where they were staying, to the interest and fascination of their hosts. As the news of their work spread throughout the city, more and more people wanted "pipes" in their houses too, and they paid the Littles well for their work.

Some of the Littles had even started to build their own houses, preferring to live in something low to the ground, rather than the tall buildings of the humans. Sami was busily employed in the House of Healing, and the injured Littles were on the mend.

Sylica spent her days wandering the city, and soon she knew at least half of the population by name. Music and laughter seemed to follow wherever she went, as well as crowds of children, eager to receive the handfuls of candy that Sylica shared with indiscriminate enthusiasm.

To Ulfgar's dismay, he was treated as one of the beloved Little people, despite his insistence that he was simply a vertically-challenged tall person. He took to following Sylica around the city in her adventures, since wherever she went she drew all the attention, and he could fade into the background.

Elora and Kais announced that their wedding would be held as soon as all their people had been settled into permanent homes. There was much excitement in the city over this anticipated event, and many of the citizens of Gedwyld had taken it upon themselves to decorate the city with banners and garlands, and the great hall in the castle had been offered for the event.

Thea smiled and stared out across the glittering sea.

An eagle feather drifted down on the breeze. Thea caught it and held it gently in her hand. Tears stung her eyes. Arl would be very glad that the Littles had found a home.

Overhead, Allumen flickered through the rings of Micai. The wind off the sea blew stronger. Thea pulled her cloak tight.

Roland touched the spot on the cloak where the image of a raven had been stitched in its fabric. He smiled. "Svetka said she'd given you an oilskin. I'm glad. It's like a piece of the Raven has been with you all this time."

Thea looked down at the cloak thoughtfully. "You've been doing a lot on the Raven?"

Roland nodded. "At your uncle's orders. He's started up a messenger service, so that's what I'm doing for the most part. Delivering letters. When something needs to go beyond Larsya, I take the Raven."

Thea thought for a moment. "I still don't understand. If you got in trouble for helping me, why did my uncle send you to help me now?"

"That's because your uncle is serving under Enkeli now."

Thea stared. "My uncle is *what*?"

Roland's eyes twinkled. "I think Khariton had something to do with that."

"But—" Thea stammered, "—but he never—"

"Well he's serving the Deity now, and he's in the thick of things, from what I hear. That's what the messenger service is really about: a way to connect the people who are faithful to the Deity, right across Raphtova."

"So that's what you're doing now."

"And I help train the new recruits when they get to be too much for Khariton," he added with a private smile.

"New recruits," Thea echoed in a faint voice.

"Khariton is doing his best to get them in shape before it's time for the Elves to join the war again."

Thea stared. "You think the Elves will join the war again?"

Roland shrugged. "That's what we're hoping for, but it's all very underground right now. No one knows about what we're doing, except for the resistance." He stared off into the distance. "I'll have to go back there soon. I only have a short leave of absence."

Thea's spirit fell. Of course, Roland had only been sent to help her save the Littles, and they had been saved. But she had hoped that, maybe, he would be able to stay.

"Speaking of letters," Roland reached into his bag, "I have another one from your uncle. He wanted me to leave this one until things had settled down." He pulled out an envelope and grinned. "I'd say that things have settled down now."

Thea took the letter and opened it.

Dear Thea,

I trust that you are well and have seen success in the tasks set for you by the Deity. If you find that those tasks are now completed, I would urge you to return to Lyudmyla. Your departure caused quite a stir, as I am sure you are aware, and because of the high status of your parents many of the royal council had "opinions" on the subject. However, I believe that if you return quietly I can arrange a private audience with the Queen and procure her approval for your residence outside of the traditional lands of the Elves.

Your role within the service of the Deity could be of great assistance in conjunction with the Messenger Service, and I am eager to hear in person about your adventures.

Sincerely,
Uncle Mykyta

Thea looked up. Roland was watching her intently.

"Do you think you'll come?" he asked after a long silence.

Thea held the letter out to him. "Do you want to read it?"

Roland shook his head. "Mykyta told me what it was going to say, more or less. He really does think that it would be good for you to come back, Thea, even if it's just for a while. Besides, you did promise you'd come back someday." He glanced down at the brooch that was still pinned to her cloak.

Thea sighed. "I know. I will come back someday, but I don't think I can yet. I was supposed to find Davis, but as far as anyone can tell me he hasn't been here in ages. I need to keep looking for him."

"Well, technically—" Micai appeared, sitting beside Thea.

Jumping, Roland stood at attention.

Thea laughed and shook her head. "Micai, I never know when you'll turn up!"

"It's fun that way, isn't it?" Micai took a sip of beer. "What was I saying? Oh right. Allulien never told you to find Davis, you know. You were supposed to go to Gedwyld, where Davis was going. You filled in the rest yourself."

"But—" Thea gasped, "—but I was supposed to learn—"

"And you did learn. Very well." Micai nodded. "You learned from Arl. You learned from the Littles and you learned from the humans. Maybe you learned a bit from me too." Micai winked. "Want a drink?"

Thea accepted the mug. "But … I hoped that Davis was going to teach me about what I'm supposed to do next."

"What do *you* think the Deity wants you to do next?"

Thea stared down at the city full of humans and

Littles, learning for the first time that they were not as different as they always thought. "I think ..." she said slowly, "that the Deity wants me to live among the people of Raphtova. I think that I am supposed to show them that we can live together and learn from each other and care for each other. And I think ..." her eyes widened as thoughts grew and took shape in her mind, "I want to live in that old building that I found. It was made by Elves. Elves used to live in it, so why can't I? It's a big house. Maybe some other Elves will come and live there too. The Littles can come and visit us whenever they want, and the humans too, and ... and we don't have to be separated anymore."

Micai grinned. "I think that's a great idea. You can talk to the Lord of Gedwyld about it. It's about a measure's travel north of here and being held under the city's authority, I believe. Oh Roland, you can sit down. It's fine."

As Roland cautiously sat, Thea frowned. "Do you think they'll let me have the building?"

"I don't know why they wouldn't. It's empty, after all. I'm pretty sure they think it's haunted."

"Haunted?" Thea was taken aback. "Why would they think that?"

"Oh, I'm sure you'll find out at some point." Micai's eyes twinkled.

"Micai!" Thea protested.

Micai grinned. "Sometimes things need to come as they come. Besides, it's not like I know everything. I have my orders to follow too."

Micai turned to Roland. "Speaking of orders, Mykyta has agreed to extend your leave by a cycle or two. Thea will need someone to help her settle into her new place."

Thea gasped in delight. "You'll come, Roland?"

Roland grinned. "Of course I will!"

Micai looked from Thea to Roland with a twinkle in their eyes.

Thea beamed. "And if it's only a measure away we can come back whenever we want to see everyone!"

"I'd suggest asking Ulfgar to join you," Micai added with a nod. "I have a feeling he'd be glad for something to do."

"That's a great idea!" Thea cried. "Let's go ask him now!" She jumped up, waving for Roland to follow her.

Laughing, they raced down into the city, jumping and tumbling down the cobbled streets beneath the blue-green light of Micai.

TOVA

a tabletop roleplaying game
designed by Jesse and Leane Winger

◇ Create characters in any of the five races of Raphtova
◇ Serve under a General and wield magic
◇ Explore Arvera and beyond
◇ Lead your friends on an epic quest against evil
◇ Encounter the heroes of Raphtova
◇ Expansion races and more coming soon
◇ Free digital download

WWW.RAPHTOVA.COM

Digital Downloads - Raphtova Wiki - Updates and News

Spark

High on the wall of Gedwyld, Micai watched Thea and Roland disappear down the ancient, crooked streets. A fond smile lingered on their face.

"I'm really proud of those two," Micai said, as if to someone standing nearby. "They've come a long way."

"And they still have a long way to go." Allulien materialized beside Micai and nodded a greeting.

"Yes, that's true." Micai took a drink and offered the mug to Allulien.

Raphea appeared beside Allulien and took the mug. After an experimental sniff, they took a sip and frowned. "That is not medicinal." With a sidelong glance, they returned the mug to Micai.

Micai shrugged and took another drink.

Looking down into the city, Raphea sighed. "I feel for Roland."

"Oh, he'll hang in there," Micai grinned. "That's what he does."

"And Thea?" Raphea asked.

Allulien nodded. "She is the spark that was needed. You were right, Enkeli."

Enkeli smiled.

Spark

Leane Winger is a multidisciplinary creator and recovering perfectionist who always dreamed about going on an epic quest—as long as there would be plenty of snacks. Author of the mountaineering adventure novel, The Door, Leane is thrilled to be diving into the world of fantasy with The Reawakening Trilogy, the first of many stories to be set in Raphtova—a world co-created with her sword-wielding husband Jesse. Together they live in Mackenzie, BC with their growing crew of littles who keep pestering their mom for "the next chapter of the story".

Learn more about Leane's books and other projects at:

www.leanewinger.com